Stanley West was born in Saint Paul and grew up during the Great Depression and the World War II years. He graduated from Central High School in 1950 and attended Macalester College and the University of Minnesota, earning a degree in history and geology in 1955. He moved from the Midwest to Montana in 1964 where he raised a large family and he has lived there ever since. His novel *Amos: To Ride A Dead Horse* was produced as a CBS Movie of the Week starring Kirk Douglas, Elizabeth Montgomery and Dorothy McGuire and was nominated for four Emmys.

Also By Stanley G. West

Amos
Until They Bring the Streetcars Back
Finding Laura Buggs
Growing An Inch
Blind Your Ponies

Finding Laura Buggs

"A story that reaffirms the miracle and wonder of life, and ultimately its preciousness . . . a terrific, uplifting read, written with great insight and compassion."
—Harvey Mackay, New York Times best-selling author of *How To Swim With the Sharks*

Until They Bring the Streetcars Back

"It's great storytelling. Reminded me of *The Last Picture Show*. A wonderful way of life was dying, and nobody could stop it."
—Steve Thayer, author of *Weatherman* and *Silent Snow*

"Stanley West, an extraordinary novelist and storyteller who writes with searing beauty and truth, has written a lyrical and moving novel . . . a story that pierces to the core of life . . . compelling reading for people of all times and places . . ."
—Richard Wheeler, Golden Spur Award author of some thirty novels

"West has again captured an often untold yet important part of the human story... encouraging for all who may feel it's too late to make a change . . ."
–Brad Walton, The Brad Walton Show, WCCO Radio

"One of the most gripping books I read all year."
–Marjorie Smith, *Bozeman Daily Chronicle*

Praise for Other Novels by Stanley G. West

Blind Your Ponies

"Stanley West writes novels that transform the world. In this tender story of love and courage and grit, he gives each reader a vision and a dream. This is the best reading you will find."
–Richard Wheeler, award wining author of *The Fields of Eden*

"Stanley Gordon West, one of my favorite authors, has done it again. *Blind Your Ponies* is the kind of novel that takes years to write . . . but well worth the wait. A wonderfully haunting book . . . where every character has a ghost, and every ghost has a great story to tell."
–Steve Thayer, author of *The Weatherman* and *Silent Snow*

Amos: To Ride A Dead Horse

"West's first novel is powerful and moving . . . a celebration of the human spirit . . . a heart-stopper, a strong, unblinking deeply human tale." *–Publishers Weekly*

"West has penned an unusual, well-written novel . . . The book features some marvelous descriptive passages that will be remembered long after the last page has been turned. The skillful plotting and the warm human relationships make it exciting, first-rate reading."
–Judy Schuster, *Minneapolis Star Tribune*

"I have just finished Amos—an extraordinary book. I read it straight through–literally unable to put it down . . . it is a celebration of the capacity of the human spirit for compassion and sacrifice and courage . . ." –Millicent Fenwick

Growing an Inch

"This third volume in St. Paul trilogy is a charm—"
–Mary Ann Grossmann, *St. Paul Pioneer Press*

"A young boy takes you on an emotional journey as he faces life at its most unbearable and its most sublime. Just when you think everything is fine, he gets slugged in the guts. A feel good story you can't put down. "
—Bill Neff, PhD, Professor of Film and Video, Montana State University

Sweet Shattered Dreams

Stanley Gordon West

Lexington-Marshall Publishing
Shakopee, Minnesota

Published in the United States by Lexington-Marshall Publishing
P.O. Box 388, Shakopee, Minnesota 55379.

"Carefree Highway" by Gordon Lightfoot ©1974 renewed 2002 Moose Music.
Used by permission.

"If You Could Read My Mind" by Gordon Lightfoot ©1969 renewed 1997
Early Morning Music. Used by permission.

ISBN 978-0-9656247-2-5
ISBN 0-9656247-2-2

Book design by Richard Krogstad
Book production by Peregrine Graphics Services
Printed in the United States by McNaughton & Gunn, Inc.

5 7 9 10 8 6

First Edition: August 2005
Second Printing: February 2006
Third Printing: February 2009
Fourth Printing: January 2012
Fifth Printing: March 2013

for David Erling West

for Jean Marmion West

"... each of us must live with
a full measure of loneliness that is inescapable,
and we must not destroy ourselves
with our passion to escape this aloneness."
—JIM HARRISON IN HIS NOVEL *DALVA*

"If you could read my mind, love,
what a tale my thoughts could tell."
—GORDON LIGHTFOOT

Sweet Shattered Dreams

Chapter 1

IF HE'D NEVER LISTENED to Rita Costello, he wouldn't be running for his life.

He'd been driving for hours. Fast. Staring into the desert darkness his eyes felt like they were full of sand. He couldn't keep them open. He pulled off the highway into a primitive rest stop and as his headlights raked the area he could see there were no other vehicles. The convertible was so crammed with his personal belongings there was no room to sprawl. He rolled up in a blanket on the desert floor a few paces from the Cadillac. He had to sleep a few hours and then keep running north before the sun winked in another day.

He had outrun the assassin, temporarily. But as he fled, he couldn't outrun the dream, the nightmare, the haunting. It always came to him uninvited, in vivid detail, as if it had happened yesterday, not a dream, really, but the unbearable memory he'd tried for years to erase and failed.

He was a young boy living on a Minnesota farm with his father and mother. His father, in a hurry to get the plowing done before the freeze-up, urged the faded green tractor north. At the end of the row he lifted the three-point plow out of the soil and swung the Oliver to turn. A glaze of frost covered the ground along the ditch that bordered the field, and the tractor slid as it turned, skidded sideways down the incline, caught for a second, and overturned. In the instant his father was given to leap from its merciless embrace, he failed.

Unconsciously noting the chug, chug, chug of the laboring diesel engine from different parts of the farm, Sonny and his mother heard it suddenly go still. With the exhaust pipe driven into the earth, the fall afternoon turned deathly silent. When that distant thudding pulse of the farm stopped, they looked north. The tractor and driver had vanished. With terror in their throats they ran, Sonny from the pond where he was breaking little skins of ice, his mother flying from the yard. He never got over how swiftly she ran, there before him, having to go almost twice as far.

They found the tractor upside down, four wheels pointing skyward, his father pinned beneath it like an insect on a cork board. His legs stuck out one side, his head and shoulders out the other. With his left arm free he furiously swept it back and forth over the ground as if trying to swim out from under the massive machine, as if making a one-winged snow angel in the dirt. Speechless, his father's eyes begged for help.

On hands and knees his mother dug furiously under her husband's body to relieve the crushing weight. She didn't cry or speak, only animallike grunts while she clawed at the hard clay earth. Sonny set his shoulder against the massive machine and drove with his legs. It didn't budge. He looked down into his father's bursting face and remembered overhearing his recent comment to his mother that *The boy had to start pulling his own weight around here.*

With bulging eyes his father pleaded soundlessly, blood frothing from his mouth, his arm furiously sweeping across the ground. Sonny fell to his knees, and with his face only inches from his father's, he tried to dig beside his mother. He could smell his father's sweat and tobacco. He covered his father's gapping mouth with his own and blew as hard as he could, again and again, but the air only bubbled out his father's nose, unable to force its way down his windpipe to his crushed lungs. Sonny could taste alcohol with the tobacco and blood. "One snort for the cold" his dad would always say.

Knowing time was running out, Sonny sprang to his feet and slammed his body against the traitorous Oliver again and again, but he could not tip its tonnage off his breathless father. When his dad desperately needed him, he hated himself for being so weak, so useless. He cried and howled and strained against the iron brute, but under gravity's indifferent jurisdiction the tractor ignored him while diesel fuel gurgled gently out onto the ground with his father's life. His father's arm stopped, the angel's wing clearly cut in the soil, his eyes wide open, unblinking.

His mother continued tearing at the soil with shredded hands, her tears falling on the lifeless body and neither of them did him any good. Neighbors finally stopped her when Sonny was unable to, her hands like dirty raw meat. Sonny had been unable, after all, to pull his own weight.

The nine-year-old farm boy wondered where his father had gone. The old Oliver 90 snuffed his life out as though it had puffed him up its stack. The exhaust pipe would sometimes puff out a perfect smoke ring, maybe two or three in a row. Had Willard Hollister been only a smoke ring? When Sonny undressed late that night to go to bed, he saw that he was covered with bruises, black and blue and orange and red, as if he'd been beaten with a baseball bat. His shoulder hurt and he had a hard time getting his shirt off. Three days later, with little complaining, they discovered with X-ray that his left shoulder was broken.

When the haunted dream swooped down on him, he was always slamming his body against the massive tractor, over and over, shouting and howling, but the Oliver 90 never moved and his father always died.

Chapter 2

HE WAS SAVED from the nightmare by a tug on his boot.

At first he thought it was part of the dream, but the yank on his leg told him this was no dream. He fought his way out of a groggy sleep and found himself lying face down on the ground. Though he didn't remember where in the hell he was, someone *was* pulling off his boot. He rolled over and pushed up on his elbows.

"Well I'll be a cat's ass," a shadowy figure said, about to pull off the other boot. "I *know* you! You're Sonny-gone-to-hell-Hollister."

Sonny grunted into a sitting position and squinted at the early morning light. With the back of his hand he wiped sand from his lips and struggled to come out of his stupor. The grubby character, with a greasy backpack beside him, came into focus as he pulled off Sonny's other alligator boot. The guy looked as though someone had dug him up in a landfill.

"Hey! what are you doing with my boots?"

"I'm borrowin 'em." He snarled with the manner of a wolf.

Gruff and road-worn, the drifter had what appeared to be a pearl-handled switchblade lodged in his belt. Long, thin blade. Fear pooled in Sonny's stomach. The vintage convertible stood only twenty tantalizing feet away, but he knew he couldn't make a dash for it the way he once could have.

"I was about to get a new pair anyway," Sonny said lightly

The hostility slackened a bit in the man's expression and he yanked off a frazzled tennis shoe. A red bandanna held his dark stringy hair out of his gaunt face. Sonny realized he was in no condition to resist.

Play it cool. Stay alive.

Overnight the world had turned savage—he'd learned only hours ago Costello had put out a contract on him. He found it unbelievable, inconceivable, on *him*. But he knew if Tony Costello whispered your name you were a dead man walking, in your grave. Sonny had shuddered at some of the gruesome stories he'd heard from time to time about people who ended up dead. In sheer panic he'd fled until he could drive no further.

"Son of a bitch, Sonny Hollister." The man pulled a boot over a filthy sock. "Look at that, like we was twins. Let's have that belt."

Sonny unlatched the large silver buckle and pulled the belt from his jeans. When he handed the thief his belt, he glanced into his stony eyes, glowering out of a surly, unshaven face. This man would slit his throat as casually as spit.

Don't rile him.

"I should've recognized that old Caddy," he said, squatting on his haunches, "especially them plates. What the hell you doing in the middle of the desert?"

"I'm—"

"Now your watch and that fancy ring," he said and peered down the highway.

Sonny handed him his watch and struggled with the ring, attempted to distract him with talk.

"It's a fake, sold the real Rollex a few years back."

With some pain, Sonny twisted the ring and forced it along his chubby finger, fearing he'd lose the finger if he failed. It popped free and he handed it over. The thief slipped it on his right ring finger, where Sonny had worn it.

"Look at that, a girl's best friend."

He held the diamond ring up in the sunless sky and admired it on his grimy hand, the last token of Sonny's wealth and glory.

"I'll be damned, Sonny Hollister, must be my lucky day. Let's see what's in them pockets."

Sonny pulled out a nail clipper, several coins, a soiled hanky, car keys, and his dog-eared wallet.

"I don't have much money."

"I don't feel sorry for you." He snatched the wallet and keys. "Glory be, there's a time you coulda bought the state of Nevada."

He dug through the wallet, fingering the few bills.

"No credit cards?"

"Credit ran out long time ago."

While the man scrutinized the wallet's contents, Sonny wondered if he could get one quick punch to his head. He gave it up as a very dicey play.

"Could I keep the photo, it means a lot to me."

"Hell no; might need it to convince some hot lady that I'm Sonny Hollister. People always told me I looked like you, until you turned into a Jimmy Dean pork sausage."

Sonny despised himself for not being man enough to rip this maggot's throat out, giving up the tattered snapshot of his wife and boy he still couldn't bear to look at.

"Are you taking my car?"

"Sure as hell. I let some lamebrain give me a ride half-way up this game trail."

"Please don't take the car, listen, please, I'm in a lot of trouble, they're out to kill me. Take the other stuff, I don't care, but leave—"

"My heart bleeds for ya." He stood. "Now the jacket and I'll be on my way."

"My *jacket?*"

"Hey, you're always singing 'Carefree Highway.' I'll just make it a little more carefree for ya." He laughed.

With difficulty Sonny pulled off the worn flight jacket while he sat on the ground, leaving him in his light western shirt. The man slipped the jacket over his threadbare Levi.

"Damn, it's too big. It'd fit the bloomin' Goodyear blimp."

He stooped and grabbed his old shoes.

"Aren't you leaving me any shoes?"

"I don't want you travelin' far. Hell, the way you look no one'd give you a lift."

He picked up his backpack and turned for the car. Then he stopped and whirled in his tracks as though he'd changed his mind. No witnesses? Sonny held his breath. The thief came back and knelt an arm's-length away. He opened his backpack and rummaged through it. Sonny clenched his right fist, hidden beside his leg. The predator pulled a ratty little notebook from the pack and a ballpoint pen.

"How about an autograph?"

"What?" Sonny exhaled, trembling slightly.

"An autograph, maybe I can sell it."

"Oh . . . yeah . . . sure. . . ."

Sonny accepted the ballpoint and the soiled notebook.

"Write it to my good friend, Roy."

Sonny dashed it out and handed it to him. He examined it and regarded Sonny with a pensive expression.

"You know which of your songs I like best? 'Wichita Lineman.'"
He gazed out across the desert. "I had a woman in Wichita once.
Damn good woman. Shoulda stuck with her. Shoulda."

He paused. Then he stuffed the notebook and pen in his pack,
sprang to his feet, and hurried to the car.

"I'll freeze!" Sonny shouted.

After tossing in his shoes and backpack, Roy looked over the
ragged top of the '65 Fleetwood. "Sonny Hollister, I'll be a three-
legged rooster, sure my lucky day. Nice meeting you, Sonny."

When he slid into the jaded Cadillac, Sonny heaved his body up
and stood in his stocking feet, a little off balance.

"Leave my guitar!"

The engine started. Sonny picked up a stone and hurled it at the
car. It bounced off the trunk. With sand spitting from the back
wheels, the Caddy squealed onto the blacktop and roared down the
highway like a traitor, carting off the residue of his life. The well-
known license plate reflected the early morning light: CR FR HWY.

"I screwed-up my autograph, you mangy vulture!" he shouted at
the fading dot on the distant highway. "I hope you burn in the fires
of hell!"

The words faded softly into the desert as the sun came over the
endless horizon low in the southeast. It couldn't be much over thirty
degrees. Sonny sighed and glanced around at the dreary rest stop.
Two crude picnic tables, a weatherbeaten outhouse, a water spigot
and a trash can. Damn! No other sign of human habitation in any
direction. A cow would die of hunger walking between blades of
grass in this godforsaken country. But strangely, the isolation clothed
him with an intangible sense of momentary safety.

A car humming out of the distance broke the silence and he hobbled toward the roadway, waving his arms, shouting, but the driver
in a gray station wagon only glanced at him as he hurtled by. Then
it hit him! He couldn't be flagging down a ride, couldn't even be
seen! The next car could carry the assassin. He winced back to the
outhouse and stood behind it, with one eye on the road. A red pickup went by going south. His feet felt frozen.

Sonny's heart started the drumbeat of panic in his chest; he had
to get on the road, get out of the country, disappear where they'd
never find him. He gazed down the bleak and empty highway and a
chill rattled through his bones, a sudden fear gripped him. A black

suburban with shaded windows sailed north. He'd have to wait until dark and then walk, ducking into the ditch whenever headlights appeared. He settled to the ground behind the outhouse and he couldn't help but wonder how the journey of that skinny farm boy would end. Caught out in the desert in his stocking feet, without a nickel to his name, he was running for his life.

And then a semi came from the south.

Chapter 3

OUT OF THE SUN'S low winter arc, an eighteen-wheeler geared down and crawled off the highway with its air brakes spitting. A cow bellowed, then another, and the load of cattle stomped their hooves, seeking their balance with the stopping. The diesel engine idled and a short bandy-legged man in a cowboy hat appeared around the back of the trailer, whacking the tires with a hammer.

Sonny pried himself off the ground and hobbled stocking-foot toward the driver, who beelined for the sun-bleached outhouse. Sonny tiptoed around the scattered cactus and called.

"Could you give me a lift? I got robbed last night!"

The man glanced at Sonny's getup and hurried to evade him.

"Sorry, don't give rides," he said from the side of his mouth. He gripped the ballpeen hammer while hotfooting it for the latrine. "Insurance don't allow it."

"Please," Sonny said as he approached, "I'm Sonny—"

The words caught in his throat.

"Can't, sorry."

When the driver ducked into the crude wooden shanty, Sonny stopped short and it started sinking into his logy brain pan. Damn it, he didn't dare identify himself to anybody. Who could he trust? He picked up a rock and hurled it at the big rig, its stacks gently popping. He missed. The cattle continued to shift and mill, calling mournfully out of their crowded captivity.

It hit him like a thunderbolt. A crazy thunderbolt.

He scrambled to the back of the trailer and saw that the door slid up on a track. He raised it several feet and glanced back at the outhouse while he pulled himself up onto the back bumper and squatted under the door. The young steers stampeded away from him, climbed one another's backs, wedged themselves into a terrified heap. When he slid the door shut, he was standing in fresh cow manure in his stocking feet.

Like a refugee he leaned into the corner of the trailer, clung to the metal frame, and tried to stay upright above the cesspool. The cattle closest to him shoved and bucked and worked their way back into the headlong frenzy. Through the narrow vented sides he watched the bantam operator come cautiously from the outhouse, scanning the desert for any sign of the shoeless hitchhiker. The cowboy hat bobbed along the left side of the trailer and Sonny heard the cab door slam.

With a lurch, the stock carrier started forward, the stacks belched black smoke, and the cattle danced and slid back toward him. With each shift of the gears, all of them fought for their balance on the slimy urine- and dung-covered floorboards. After several were pushed against him and frantically plowed back into the crush, one Hereford stood next to him tamely. Used to people; someone's 4-H calf?

The big diesel hit its stride and numbing air flushed through the trailer. He shivered violently. The bleak winter sun, streaming through the ventilation holes, dappled the backs of the Herefords but offered no warmth. The cattle snorted wisps of steam and peered at the passing landscape on their journey to the slaughterhouse. Figuring they had a lot in common, Sonny reached out and stroked the tame steer. It accepted the human touch calmly and Sonny scratched its head.

"Good boy, good boy."

With his arm around its neck, he leaned heavily against its body. Unperturbed, it bore his weight and partially sheltered him from the wind, sharing its body warmth.

God almighty, how had he come to this? He was born on an obscure Minnesota farm. When his father was killed he moved into the village of Boyd with his mother, who raised him until he left home before finishing high school. He hitchhiked into the world with the clothes on his back, eleven dollars and forty-three cents and his guitar. Yet when he was at the height of his power, millions knew his voice and sang his songs and came out of the landscapes to cheer at his concerts. Then it all came unraveled.

Now, forty-three years and a lifetime later, he found himself in the dark and devastating void of utter abandonment. He was lost. He'd been given a life and he'd squandered it. When his wife and boy were killed, he fled to the false promise of alcohol and food and drugs, tumbling from the spotlight, embarrassing his fans, gambling with extravagance, often losing in six figures, exhausted physically, financially and emotionally. And finally, he was fleeing for what was left of him, across the Nevada desert, as barren and desolate as his life. Standing in the swaying cattle truck, clinging desperately to the docile steer, he was weak, his manure-soaked feet were numb with the cold, and he feared he would slowly sink into the cattle shit and freeze to death.

While he hung onto the steer, Sonny awoke with a start. The truck was slowing, the cattle shifted and stomped as the rig crawled to a stop. He looked for a ranch house, a building, any sign of civilization, ready to flee that dung hill. He heard voices shouting.

"Jumpin' Jesus, what happened?"

"Car hit a tanker."

Sonny strained to see ahead through the narrow ventilation slots, but all he could make out was empty land. The cattle churned and a frigid wind blew some of the words away before he could catch them.

". . . hell of a fire. . . ."

". . . Sonny Hollister! . . . n-o-o-o-o!"

". . . trucker jumped clear . . ."

The exhaust pipes popped a rhythmic rumble and the cattle complained.

". . . eighteen thousand gallons . . . burned to a crisp. . . ."

". . . made out the plate . . . back bumper blew clear. . . ."

". . . Sonny Hollister . . . son of a bitch. . . ."

". . . melted everything in sight. . . ."

Sonny shouted, "No, hey, I'm back here!"

He pounded on the metal wall; the cattle bawled.

". . . better take her through. . . ."

He tried to stick his arm through the ventilation slot but it was too narrow. The wind whistled. Sonny fumbled with the door but as he lifted his feet slid out from under him.

"Take it slow, shoulder's soft."

The eighteen-wheeler crawled ahead and the driver shouted.

"Can't believe he's dead, poor bastard."

Sonny opened his mouth to shout again but caught the words before his vocal chords translated them into sound. The stacks crackled and the truck rolled along the shoulder, listing to the right.

Momentarily stunned, Sonny gawked at the grisly scene. The charred wreckage of the tanker and what was once his car were flanked by a highway patrolman, a patrol car with lights flashing, a large wrecker, and a handful of onlookers and their vehicles. The twisted metal frames were hardly recognizable, a testimony to the heat generated in the consuming inferno. Portions of the blacktop had boiled and buckled and the blackened ruins looked like ground zero for an errant missile from the nearby firing range. Somewhere in that settled ash were the remains of the drifter, Roy, on his lucky day.

"I didn't mean it, Roy," Sonny said.

The highway patrolman and the curious travelers gazed at the wreckage as the diesel belched and lurched forward. The cattle slid and skated into one another as the truck gained momentum.

He hung on to the domesticated steer for dear life, shivering and gulping for air. The cattle truck came up to speed and a strange feeling overtook him.

They thought Sonny Hollister was dead.

Would some clue in the ashes prove them wrong; would Costello believe Sonny was dead and call off the hit man? Was Roy some kind of angel who swooped out of the dawn to save him? The cold desert air stung his face and he was overcome with an eerie sense of surprise.

Chapter 4

THE TRUCK PLOWED NORTH while the sun faded behind them. The driver was highballing it, making up time. Wide awake, Sonny clung to the gregarious steer that had adopted him while wild thoughts collided in his head. Would they really believe it was him in the ashes? Would Costello buy it? What could he do? No car, no money, no shoes.

When he was about thirteen, he inadvertently discovered that his mother's boyfriend, a traveling salesman, was married. For the first time she spoke to him as she would to a grownup, explaining that lucky people were given two lives: the first to learn with, the second to use what they'd learned. Maybe Roy was wrong, maybe this was *Sonny's* lucky day, the beginning of his second life.

Who'd be sifting through the ashes other than public servants doing monotonous routines? It was a sad comment that no one's life would be affected by his death, no one would miss him, except his mother, though he'd neglected her badly in past years. He left behind no wife, no children, no close friends; no life insurance, no benefactors, no one stood to gain anything by his death, only Costello and his outfit had lost—his six figure gambling debt, but he knew it wasn't the debt that put him on a hit list; it was her, Costello's wife, and what she *told him* in that moment of emotional relapse.

The sharp wind numbed his face and he felt exhilarated. An hour ago he was a dead man and now it seemed he'd been given a reprieve.

"What do you think, amigo?" he said, leaning against the steer and stroking its neck, "are we in the clear?"

The Hereford regarded him mutely from its friendly watery eyes. While he clung to the animal over the cold endless miles, the outrageous idea took root in his head and a strange happiness covered him like a warm blanket.

There was only one person he could trust, Corkey Sullivan, the fledgling agent who cocked an ear at a young drifter with a guitar and recognized potential no one else could hear, the loner who stuck with Sonny through a year of misfiring until Sonny caught on and turned Corkey into a millionaire. Sonny had driven their relationship into the ground in the last ten years, borrowed and never paid back, called on Corkey at all hours to bail him out of one jam after another, until Corkey quit taking his calls.

The driver geared down and Sonny peered ahead the best he could. In the descending dusk he detected lights, lots of lights, and his stomach knotted. The cattle shifted, the truck slowed on the outskirts of a town where small crescents of drifted snow dappled the desert floor. Sonny steadied himself against the steer and it saddened him that the benevolent animal that had kept him alive was on a hit list too. The truck turned off the highway and pulled alongside another eighteen-wheeler, a flatbed stacked with lumber. The air brakes spat and as they stopped the steers found their footing. He held his breath when the trucker slammed the cab door and came back around the trailer. Thump! thump! he whacked on the large tires, back up the right side. After several minutes, Sonny cautiously lifted the rattling metal door and crouched out onto the back bumper, allowing the door to slide closed behind him.

In the murky dusk, he took stock of his surroundings. The large truck stop sat on the outskirts of a town, its CONOCO logo shining brightly over a patch of desert. The truck idled in a row of semis whose engines knocked and purred while other trucks stood at attention on the far side of the red and white building. Diesel fumes burned in his throat. He climbed down and slipped around on the driver's side, shielded from view by the Boise-Cascade truck. LEROY RIGGS, TWIN FALLS, IDAHO was lettered on the cattle truck door and Sonny made a mental note.

When he tried the door it opened, an interior light came on, and he quickly inventoried the cab. A pair of overshoes designed for cowboy boots, a Levi jacket, a MACK TRUCK cap, and sunglasses. He could see no money as he attempted to get into the jacket. Damn, too small. A lariat hung behind the seat. Then he spotted a red sweatshirt with I LOVE LAS VEGAS emblazoned across the chest. He grabbed it and slid out of the cab, latching the door quietly while a car transport rumbled in to the pumps to take on fuel.

He pulled off his vile socks and with some difficulty forced his bare feet into the undersized overshoes. He buckled them and squeezed into the sweatshirt. With the MACK TRUCK cap and the sunglasses—which he slid into his pocket—he figured he'd blend in nicely with the characters who'd inhabit a desert watering hole. He headed for the empty ground behind the truck stop when a steer bellowed. He kept walking. A steer moaned. He stopped in his tracks. "All right! All right! I hear you!"

In the pinching overshoes he wobbled back to the cab and grabbed the lariat. With a grunt he hoisted himself up onto the back bumper and scrambled through the door. Another semi grumbled in beside them on the right. A tanker. He looped the lariat around the steer's neck and waited. When the tanker driver came past the back of his rig and headed for supper, Sonny lifted the door, slid down from the bumper, and pulled on the rope.

"C'mon, boy, c'mon." The steer struggled to dig in its hooves and hold its ground, stiff-legged. "C'mon, damnit!"

Sonny wrapped the rope around his waist and leaned back with his two-hundred-and-twenty pounds. The frightened Hereford couldn't get a foothold on the slimy floorboards. Suddenly, it bounded out the door and lit on the ground with the grace of a moose.

"Good steer, good steer."

Sonny pulled the door down and, like a tinhorn rustler, led the brown and white critter off into the accumulating desert night. When he was out of the radius of the CONOCO lights, he tied the steer to an old car body.

"Now be quiet, boy. I'll be back."

Sonny headed for the truck stop, but at the edge of the darkness he hesitated. He relieved himself. Then he squatted on his haunches and waited. Whew! He smelled like a stockyard.

Excitement pumped through him, his breath came short, he shivered with the cold, inhaled the crisp night air, and realized that for the first time in years he was looking forward to something. In a few minutes Leroy Riggs came out and crunched across the gravel to his truck. No time for a leisurely dinner; had to get the stock to water and feed, the poor devils. Sonny held his breath. Would the trucker notice anything missing? The twin chrome pipes belched, little amber lights blinked on, the headlights flared, and the truck crawled across the gravel and back onto the highway, the rhythmic sound of its shifting gears fading into the darkness. Sonny stood.

"So long, Leroy."

It was as if his former life were sailing off and he had jumped ship. He stood with a grunt, slipped on the sunglasses, and walked into the truck stop like a woman in high heels.

He skulked past the half-filled restaurant and lounge, but through a glass partition, he noticed that every eye was riveted on a large TV, a report on the death of Sonny Hollister. He hesitated. Though he couldn't hear the words, goose bumps rose on his back and legs. People were pausing with a forkful halfway to their mouth, gaping at shots of the charred scene and shaking their heads. Then the solemn-faced anchorman appeared and the scene cut to President Carter stepping off a helicopter. Sonny pulled the visor of the cap down over the sunglasses and slunk off in search of the rest room, thirsty and hungry and without a cent.

In the empty men's room he took a long drink and washed his face and hands. The odor of manure rose from his feet and jeans and he gazed in the mirror. God! The sweatshirt high-lighted the weight that had silently accumulated with his despair. The two-day's growth on his face helped, but he had to do something about his renowned bronze-colored hair. With the manner of a starving bear pawing through garbage he dug into the large wastebasket, and almost to the bottom, found a discarded razor. Carefully he cut away his long locks, anything that hung below the cap. He nicked his ear in his hurry and flushed the shorn hair down one of the toilets.

A driver came in and went into a stall.

"Colder than a grave digger's ass out there," he said.

Sonny nodded and regarded himself in the polished steel mirror. Looking like a dog that had been caught under a lawn mower, he trimmed the edges the best he could and then gave it up. If Corkey wouldn't help, he was a goner.

A bay of phones stood across the hall from a grocery section and gift shop, and a washed-out middle-aged woman was pleading into one of them, ". . . please, Mel. . . ."

He called collect, an unlisted number he'd never forget. Reach Corkey wherever he was, on a plane, in a car, the moon.

"Who shall I say is calling, sir?" a female operator asked.

"Squeaky Sullivan." It was a nickname Sonny had given him which referred not only to his voice but also to his purse strings.

The phone rang. Sonny's mouth went dry; his hands sweat.

"Yeah," Corkey's harsh, no-nonsense voice blustered on line.

"I have a call from Squeaky Sullivan. Will you accept the charges?"

"Squeaky Sullivan! Who is this?"

"Will you accept the charges?" the operator repeated.

"Yeah, yeah."

"Go ahead," she said.

"Who the hell is this and how did you get this number?"

"Corkey," Sonny said, "it's *me.*

Chapter 5

"WHO IS THIS?" Corkey said.

"Are you alone? Don't let on who you're talking to."

"How the hell am I going to do that when I don't know who the hell I'm talking to—"

"It's me, Sonny."

"W-h-a-t . . . listen, if this is some sick prank I don't—"

"Cork, Cork, it's me, *Sonny*. If you're with someone, get rid of them, I have to talk to you."

An awkward interlude on the line—he could feel the wheels turning in Corkey's head, hear his erratic breathing. Then Corkey found himself.

"O-h, y-e-a-h, I *know*, terrible tragedy, just awful, I can't believe it, hold on for a minute."

He could hear Corkey's voice away from the receiver.

"Sid, could you wait in the other room for a minute. I got an old friend here I want to talk to."

Sonny heard a voice in the background, a pause, then a door shut. Corkey came on the line with the intensity of a hurricane.

"You're *alive!*"

"Yeah, I'm alive. I was—"

"You're *alive!*"

"Corkey—"

"What the hell's going on? Everyone says you're dead, the papers, TV, I hear there's a contract on you one minute and the next thing I hear you're Kentucky fried and I figure they put a bomb in your car and—"

"I know, I know, but I wasn't—"

"I couldn't believe they'd do that, not to you. They don't like the publicity, know what I mean."

"I couldn't believe it either, but I know things—"

"My phone's melting all over my desk, everyone's going crazy. Sid's here, he thinks there's money to be made."

"Corkey, Corkey, shut up and let me—"

"Where the hell are you? I can't believe you're not dead."

"I'm alive, but you're the *only one* who can know, the *only one* I can trust."

A pot-bellied trucker in worn Levis and boots eyed Sonny before he slid into the phone stall beside him. Sonny huddled closer to the phone and lowered his voice.

"I need your help, Cork."

"I told you a long time ago, I'm not getting involved in any more of your screw ups."

"This wasn't my idea."

The trucker tapped him on the shoulder. Sonny turned slightly, keeping his head down.

"Hey, mac, you got a quarter?"

"No . . . no change."

"Hell!" He slammed down the receiver and walked away.

"What," Corkey said.

"Nothing, nothing, a guy wanted a quarter."

"What are you going to do, go to Mongolia?"

"A while back you bought a little ranch in Montana, a place no one knew about, to get away . . . you still got it?"

"Ah, yeah . . . I turned it over to a realtor last summer, never used it, but it hasn't sold."

"So you still have it?"

"Yeah, I jacked the price up pretty good, but I don't—"

"It's the only place I can think of, Cork."

"Oh, Jeez, I don't think that would be a good idea."

"Just for a while, lay low, figure this out?"

"I promised myself: no more bailing you out. Why don't you just let people know you're alive?"

"And give Costello's hit man another shot at me?"

Corkey cleared his throat.

"What's wrong with your voice?" Sonny said, fearing he was losing his only hope, "you got a cold?"

"Nothing, just a little hoarse."

Sonny smiled. His hard-assed ex-manager had been crying.

"Will you help me, Cork?"

"I should've known you weren't dead," Corkey said with a sliver of vexation that stabbed Sonny. "Who was in your car?"

"Roy Rogers . . . on his lucky day, plowed into a tanker."

"What the hell are you talking about, what are you using?"

"A drifter, stole everything I had, the skunk, even my boots, which reminds me, I need money. Will you wire me some?"

"We made our deal three years ago and not another dime."

"Corkey, I'm stranded, I don't have a nickel, I swear to God you'll get every cent."

"I've heard that song before."

"It's funny you should mention song—"

"Don't try that guilt horseshit on me, damnit, it won't—"

"Cork, I'm cold and hungry, and if they find me they're going to kill me. I've got nowhere else to turn. No one else I can trust."

"Where on earth are you?" Corkey's voice softened.

"I don't know, just a minute."

Sonny set down the phone and stepped across to the convenience shop. A young female cashier regarded him from a face where large brown eyes overshadowed a bout with acne.

"What town is this?" he asked, hoping she couldn't smell him.

"Winnemucca," she said as though it even surprised her.

"Is there a Western Union in town?"

"At the bus depot, right off Main Street."

"How far is that from here?"

"About a mile. Be open until nine-thirty when the late bus comes through."

"Thanks." Sonny crossed back to the phone.

"Corkey, I'm in Winnemucca."

"Winnemucca! Holy cats, you're already *in* Mongolia."

"There's a Western Union here. Wire the money to Tom Sommers, remember that movie?"

"Yeah, yeah, Tom Sommers."

"And be sure to tell them I lost my I.D."

"We have to come up with a question and answer. What'll it be this time?"

"Oh . . . yeah," Sonny said, thinking. "How about Who was on the horse? Roy Rogers."

"Who was on the horse?" Corkey said, "Roy Rogers."

"Yeah, and hurry, please, I'm starving."

"How much you want?"

"Send me five hundred, I don't have any clothes, and I have a steer to take care of."

"A what?"

"A steer, it saved my life."

"Are we talking about a blasted cow? Please tell me we're not talking about a real live cow?"

"Listen, Corkey, I'll explain later, please wire the money."

"Okay, okay, it'll be there within the hour."

"Can I hole up at your ranch?"

"Wait a minute here, wait a minute, this isn't some penny ante game here, I need some time to think about this."

"I haven't got any time."

A long silence. Sonny could feel the anger and resentment zinging over the line and he admitted it was well deserved. There was no response. The line hummed.

"Please, Cork, you're my only chance."

Sonny held his breath. He glanced at an older couple coming out of the gift shop and turned his face to the floor. Finally Corkey exhaled slowly into the receiver.

"Jeez, I hate this, I hate this," Corkey said.

"Please. . . ."

"Okay, okay, but just till you figure this thing out. I'm talking temporary here, *very temporary*"

"Thanks, Cork, thanks a million. I can make it to Montana by late tomorrow. I'll need you to fly up there and get me in the house and all."

"Oh, Jeez, what are we getting into here. I can't go flying off to Montana, know what I mean. What if they're watching me?"

"They think I'm dead, remember. Just an hour or two and you can hop right back. I can't do this without you."

Sonny waited—a lull on the line. Then a resigned sigh.

"Okay, okay, meet you tomorrow night at the bus depot in Belgrade, that's right outside Bozeman, try to be there by ten o'clock, that last flight comes in around then."

"Great, thanks, oh, and Cork, just one more thing. Bring a stethoscope."

"A stethoscope! You still some kind of a nut about your heart?"

"I just like to keep tabs on it."

"I got an easier way. If your heart quit beating you wouldn't be talking to me on the phone."

"Please, I need it."

"Okay, okay, I'll bring one."

"And remember, don't trust anyone. My only chance is they keep thinking I'm dead."

"You think I'm some kind of moron; I'm sticking my ass in the ringer with yours, ya know, don't forget *that!*"

"Thanks, Cork, I'll owe you."

"Yeah, yeah, I must be gettin' senile. See you tomorrow night, and Sonny. . . ."

"Yeah?"

Corkey's voice cracked. "I'm glad you're not dead."

"So am I, Cork. You were always reading the damn obituaries. Tomorrow, when you read mine, try to look sad."

"Holy cats, this isn't going to be easy."

"I want to let my mother know, she'll be hurting."

"That's not a good idea, that's a very dangerous proposition, I don't want to get—"

"Okay, okay, I'll see you up the highway, and thanks, Cork."

Sonny hung up. He had to hike a mile into town in his pointy rubber overshoes, dressed like a clown, and stinking like a feedlot. On his way past the brown-eyed cashier he paused. She was bending, slipping post cards into a revolving rack, looking like she'd been vacuum packed in her jeans.

"Do you sell shoes here, ma'am, boots, anything?"

"No," she said brightly, glancing at his tapered overshoes. "Sorry." She giggled.

He pushed through the glass door, out into the night, and removed the sunglasses. A fugitive from his own life, he headed for town through the darkness, driven by the instinct to survive that he'd anesthetized for more than a decade.

Chapter 6

Sonny trudged toward the lights of Winnemucca and couldn't remember when he last walked a mile but he didn't dare hitch. The wind chill savaged the warmth from his body and he cradled his arms around his chest in self-defense. Though the traffic was sparse, he stayed as far off the highway as possible, out of the headlights. Yard lights outlined several hardscrabble places scattered on the edge of town as if they weren't welcome in Winnemucca proper.

Every outfit staking out the desert had at least one barking dog, and they tracked Sonny's passing as one gave up the howling and the next picked it up. Muted light from melancholy windows became quickly shrouded by the desert's nocturnal pall. A wave of loneliness swooped out of the darkness and hit him without warning. He held course. His body ached from the cold and from the way his feet hurt, he knew he was working on more than one blister.

Finally he crossed an invisible boundary where houses, sidewalks, and an occasional street light, materialized, and by degrees the town outcropped from sand and cactus until all at once he found himself downtown, what there was of it. When he shoved on the sunglasses and limped into the bus stop, the Coca-Cola clock said six fourteen. The small cafe sported cheesy metal tables, glittery formica counters with chrome and vinyl stools, and a handful of homegrown people having supper. A rancid, over-cooked aroma hung in the air like old fly paper.

An unoccupied ticket booth squatted at the far end with a few grimy benches for waiting passengers. He shuffled over and leaned on the sill of the grated window, hoping his cap and sunglasses would do the job.

"You need something?" a man with a small black mustache and slicked-back hair called from behind the lunch counter.

"Yeah."

Sonny tipped his head behind the bill of the cap. The skinny, middle-aged man didn't respond, refilling the coffee cups of two old women who looked as though they had taken up permanent residence on swivel stools at the counter. The guy had a pencil sticking behind one ear, a long, soiled apron, and the color of one who'd soaked too long in margarine. He wiped his hands on a towel and scooted into the booth and regarded Sonny.

"What'll it be?"

"I have some money to pick up, Western Union."

The man whipped out a form and laid it on the small sill.

"Fill this out."

He was gone, fleeing through the kitchen door as if something were burning. Sonny examined the form and hesitated. He didn't want any paper trail and he'd forgotten the red tape involved. The man brought food to a booth where an overweight couple sat across from each other like strangers.

"You got something I can write with?" Sonny said.

The narrow-faced man pulled the pencil from behind his ear, passed it off to Sonny like a baton on a relay team, and swooped toward the kitchen. Sonny filled out the left side of the form with an uncharacteristic print, noticing that the agent would have to fill out a physical description of him: eye color, height, hair color. He bent his knees slightly and caught a snippy-looking woman at a table scrutinizing his apparel with obvious disapproval. It was another three or four minutes before the harried fry cook returned to the wooden cage. He examined Sonny's printing thoroughly.

"Has it come in?" Sonny asked.

The man stroked his black mustache and looked up with suspicion in his small dark eyes.

"Who was on the horse?" he asked.

"Roy Rogers."

"You Tom Sommers?"

"Yeah, that's me."

"Got any identification?" he asked, twitching his pointed nose like a nervous rat.

"No, that's why I needed the money wired, got robbed, wallet, credit cards, I.D., everything."

"Robbed, you say?"

"Yeah, robbed, did the money come in?"

"Wanna call the cops?" He raised one thin eyebrow.

"No, no . . . it happened a long way from here, please, I just want my five-hundred dollars . . . and a bus ticket to Salt Lake."

A man at a table called, "Floyd!"

He was gone like a shadow.

Two college-age girls came in and lined up behind Sonny.

Doggone it, why didn't the guy get some help?

"I thought he was cute, really sexy, until he got fat" the shorter, stocky girl said.

"I never liked him much," the taller girl said, "but my mother is really shook up. You'd think someone in the family died."

Floyd appeared behind the wire-mesh window.

"Yer money came in, but we have a two-hundred dollar limit," he said, slightly out of breath.

"What! Okay, okay, that'll have to do."

"Wanna cash the check?"

"Yes."

Sonny struggled to keep a rein on his temper.

Leave no impression, nothing to remember.

The agent took the pencil from him and jotted in the other side of the form. Sonny watched closely as he filled in the date: January 5, 1978, then the check number, amount, approaching the line that required a physical description. When he reached the line, Sonny beat him to the punch.

"Brown eyes, five foot ten, blond."

The gaunt-looking cook glanced at Sonny's hidden face for a moment. Then he scribbled in the information.

"Damn Loretta," he said, "she's been a fan of his since day one. You'd think the president died or something, leaves me with the evening rush. . . ."

He slipped a check and a ballpoint onto the sill.

"Endorse it."

In an unnatural hand he signed *Tom Sommers*. When the agent took the check and opened a cash drawer, Sonny expected moths to take wing. Floyd sniveled his mustache and counted out ten twenty-dollar bills as if he were giving away his inheritance.

"I'll need a ticket to Salt Lake."

The girls shuffled and muttered behind him. From another drawer the Greyhound agent pulled out a ticket, stamped it more than once, and said, "That'll be eighteen seventy-five."

Sonny gave him a twenty, took the ticket, and accepted the change.

"Should pull in here around nine-thirty," the man said and before the girls could move up to the window, he zipped into the kitchen.

Sonny was starving but no one had to tell him to get the hell out of there before Loretta showed up. At the door, a large red-eyed woman, wearing an apron over her western dress and bearing a terrible sorrow in her tear-streaked face, blustered in and bumped into him without noticing.

"Oh, Floyd, I'm sorry . . . but it was so sad, s-o-o sad. He's gone, Floyd, he's *gone*."

"So's our business if you don't get your ass in gear."

Sonny ducked out into the night. He had three hours. Would buxom, silver-haired Loretta be off by then, pack her sorrow home with her? He had a lot to do.

There wasn't a store open in town; only the bars and a bowling alley. The bowling alley! In minutes he was back on the street in a size eleven worn-out pair of green and red bowling shoes and a pair of mismatched socks. Five bucks. And four Milky Ways. God, the socks and shoes felt good.

When he could've holed up in the corner of some warm, poorly-lit saloon, he headed back out of town into the cannibalistic wind. He gobbled the candy bars, baffled at Loretta's grief. His fans pulled stakes years ago. Were there others out there crying over him tonight? And more puzzling than that, why had Roy Rogers come along and given Sonny another chance?

Chapter 7

By THE TIME Sonny reached the outskirts of Winnemucca the cold had reached his bones. The town's lights glowed against the low-flung clouds and gave the world an eerie cast. He pulled the MACK TRUCK cap tight and leaned into the wind. Thoughts of turning around and giving it up plagued every step.

The first several places lacked animal pens but then he spotted a stack of hay and a corral. He turned in the gravel lane toward a double-wide with the kind of luminescent yard light the power companies push. The windows were lit from stem to stern and a newer pickup sat next to the homemade porch. A large wolflike dog appeared from under the porch and growled menacingly. Sonny froze. He crouched slowly and picked up a rock and the dog slunk around behind the pickup and barked. With one eye on the dog, he made his way to the porch and knocked on the aluminum door, clutching the stone in his right hand.

The door opened on a chain and a woman with long dark hair and wearing a white terry cloth robe peered out. He could partially see a television behind her and on it he was singing "By The Time I Get To Phoenix" from years out of his past.

"Hello, ma'am, sorry to—"

"What is it?"

"I had some trouble with—"

"I can't talk now, I'm sorry."

Her mascara traced a dark smear down both cheeks.

"I just need—"

"Please, I can't talk." She glanced over her shoulder at the television. "Oh, god, I can't miss this . . . I'm sorry."

She disappeared for a moment, the door still cracked against the chain. She came back and held two dollars out to him.

"Here, please, I can't talk."

"No, I don't—"

She dropped the money and closed the door. The bills twirled down to the wooden porch and he heard a deadbolt snap into place. He caught his breath and swallowed, wondering if he was still all there. He picked up the two dollars and with an eye out for the dog, he hurried down the shadowed drive, clutching the rock as if he were clutching his sanity.

At the highway he turned into the wind. The lyrics from the song he overheard in the trailer came to him on their own and he sang softly out of a dry throat, his voice grainy, changing, a fact that had contributed more than a little to his inventory of panic over the past years. No girl to leave a note for any more, no one, no one except himself. He tipped his head down out of the headlights as a car came at him and swished by on its way into Winnemucca.

No one but himself. All at once a cog slipped on some great gear-wheel somewhere deep within him, somewhere in his soul, and he saw clearly that he had quit, given up on himself, given up on his life, in a numbing fog of self-pity and regret. Immediately he saw with a light as bright and unmistakable as the sun that life was precious; he was alive, with a second chance, and every day was a gift, his next breath a gift.

Almost back to the truck stop, with his teeth chattering and the notion to give it up accelerating, he spotted a shanty back from the highway. From a low-watt light bulb by the door he could make out a pole corral, an animal shed, and a small stack of hay. With the rock in his hand he called ahead into the shadowed yard.

"Hello, there! Hello! Anybody home?"

No one responded. Buttery light leaked from the weather-battered house; one wall protected by tar paper and strips of lath. The flat roof sprouted a crooked stove pipe that spewed wood smoke and a broken-down horse languished in the corral. He made it to the step and knocked. Fright stood with him in the bowling shoes and he wondered what would confront him from behind the ornate wood door that had obviously been salvaged from some fancy house. When he was about to knock again, the door opened slowly on squeaking hinges and a small gray-haired man stood there with an old dog at his side. The dog woofed once as if doing its duty.

"That's enough, Borgo," the short, stooped man said, his face hidden in a cloud of gray whiskers.

"Hello. Sorry to bother you, but—"

"Come in, come in," he said with a deep soft voice. "You must be freezing."

The man backed into a snug lived-in kitchen, and Sonny flipped the stone aside and followed. Warm and cozy, an aroma of pipe tobacco and old man hung in the air. He cleared off a kitchen stool for Sonny.

"Sit down, sit down."

Music, an opera, winged from another room. The neatly-cluttered kitchen stored stacks of magazines and newspapers and books; knickknacks, house plants, and souvenirs filled sagging shelves and hung from the low ceiling as though the man had never thrown anything away. Sonny sat on the stool and suddenly remembered. The sunglasses! Couldn't put them on now, but he sensed that it didn't matter and he relaxed.

The funny-looking dog came to him. Impersonating a basset, it appeared as though a lovesick walrus had mated with a bloodhound. Drooping ears, eyes, and jowls shaped a face so homely it seemed familiar. Propped a few inches off the ground by short flipperlike legs, its hind quarters were slightly twisted and it walked with a limp.

"Are you hungry? I'll bet you haven't eaten," the old man said.

"That's all right. I broke down in my truck out a ways and I've got to find a place—"

"Let me fix you something, can't do much when you're hungry."

In a worn plaid shirt, black wool pants, and tattered slippers, the man opened the iron door of his wood cook stove and tossed in several precisely cut pieces of split log. Sonny noticed his hands, knotted and gnarled as an old oak.

"I have to find a place for a steer . . . just for a few days."

"A steer?"

"Yeah, it's my daughter's 4-H steer."

"How nice; you have a daughter."

He took a solitary can of Spam from a shelf and busied himself opening it.

"Yes. She was brokenhearted when it was sold, she'd become so attached to it. I figured I'd buy it back and she could keep it until she got tired of it, but they'd already shipped it and I had to chase it down."

"You're a very kind man."

"I need a place to board it until I can come for it. I'll pay you . . . five dollars a day."

"That would be much too much. You can keep it here as long as you need. Old Abe will appreciate some company."

"Really? That's great, that's just great." Sonny stood. "You saved my bacon."

"I thought you said it was a steer."

The man glanced at him with a smile in his eyes.

Sonny laughed. "Oh, yeah, guess you saved my hamburger. I better go get him, I'm a little short on time."

"You fetch the critter and I'll fix you some supper. Have to have some food in all this cold."

"Thanks, thanks a lot."

Excited with his good fortune, Sonny hurried for the truck stop, only a few hundred yards up the highway. He'd lucked out. The man had probably never given any notice to the likes of Sonny Hollister. He felt a new strength in his legs and he was overcome with a strange and unexpected happiness.

Chapter 8

AFTER SEARCHING in the darkness for a short time, Sonny found the animal where he'd tied him, his rump turned into the wind.

"Good boy, Toro, good boy, we'll get some hay and water."

The steer led like a well-broke horse and Sonny stayed as far from the highway as fence lines allowed. Would Leroy Riggs figure he'd miscounted when he came up one head and several hundred pounds short? With the steer in tow, Sonny knocked again on the shanty door.

"He's a nice-looking animal," the old man said from the doorway. The dog woofed. "You can put him in with Abe. There's water in there. Throw some hay over the fence."

In the corral, Sonny removed the lariat and vigorously rubbed the Hereford's back.

"No one's going to slit *your* throat, I promise you that."

He latched the gate and tossed a portion of an opened bale into the feed box. With a shiver of satisfaction, he headed for the house.

The old man had a place set for him at the wooden table. Spam and beans steamed from a metal plate, coffee from a metal mug, and Sonny couldn't remember food that looked so inviting. He wolfed it while his gentle provider sat and visited. A warm drowsiness flooded over him and a sense of safety embraced him while the opera, blustering from the other room, became the soundtrack for that dreamlike scene.

"I don't want to keep you from your TV," Sonny said.

The hound held his muzzle skyward and crooned softly while an unflagging baritone warbled an emotional tremolo.

"Don't have a TV, it's radio, *Turandot*, do you like it?"

"Yeah," he said with a mouthful of beans.

No TV, perfect.

"Borgo likes to sing along. This is one of his favorites. Go ahead, sing, Borgo."

The dog howled like a lost coyote.

"You live here alone?"

"With Borgo and Abe. He was my grandson's horse."

"Where's your grandson?"

"He got permanently detained in Viet Nam. Couldn't bring myself to sell the horse."

Sonny attempted to duck the man's sadness, shoveling beans and savoring the hot coffee. He handed the mooching-eyed dog a chunk of Spam and the hound took it gently and gulped it down, wagging his tail and licking his lips with a huge slurping tongue.

"Oh, Borgo, what do you say?" the man said.

The dog woofed quietly.

"How'd he get crippled up?"

"He lifted his leg on the tire of a truck."

Sonny looked up from his plate, waiting. The man regarded him from smoky gray eyes that appeared to have weathered many storms.

"The truck happened to be moving," he said flatly and Sonny detected a slight smile under the fleecy, well-groomed beard.

"I lost my wife eleven years, three months. . . ." The man paused and calculated. ". . . and two days ago."

"I'm sorry, it must get lonely."

Sonny knew about losing a wife you loved but he had to guard against revealing anything about his history. He cleaned his plate with a piece of white bread, the only piece on the table. He inventoried the shelves: few cans of food, coffee, sugar, a potato, two apples, flour, a pittance. The dog cocked his head to the opera again as though he knew Sonny's plate was clean.

"I talk to her every day," the man said.

"Who?"

"My wife, Margaret."

"Oh, yeah. . . ."

Sonny thought a moment and then dared one question.

"If you had your life to live over, what would you do?"

The old man sat silently for a moment. Then he sighed as though he'd found an answer and regarded Sonny.

"I'd say I'm sorry more often."

Sonny identified with his unnamed regret and nodded.

"I'd better get going; have to catch a bus."

"How about your truck?"

"Oh . . . it's shot; threw a rod, I'll sell it for junk."

Sonny stood and dug in his pocket for his wad of bills. He peeled off three twenties and laid them on the table.

"This will hold you for a while."

"Oh . . . no, that's much too much."

"Take it just in case, hay money. What's your phone number?"

"I don't have a phone. Not much use for one, just salesmen and such, but I'm always here, unless Borgo and I have walked to town for groceries."

"What's your name?"

"Ned, Ned Shores."

"Well, Ned, I'm Tom, and I sure want to thank you. I was really up a creek. I'll be back for the steer, but if anything should happen and I don't make it back, that steer is yours."

Ned shuffled into the other room and came out with a large tan winter coat.

"Put this on, you can't be out in the cold like that."

"I can't take your coat."

"My grandson's, much too big for me."

Sonny pulled on the insulated canvas coat and it fit snugly.

"Thanks, Ned, I was freezing. Your grandson was a big boy."

"He was a good boy; always took care of me."

Sonny zipped up the coat and turned up the wide collar.

"What's your mailing address?"

"Not much to it. Box 225, Winnemucca."

"I'll be in touch." He shook the old man's hand.

"You know," Ned said with a glint in his eye, "when I first saw you I figured you'd been in a bowling tournament in Las Vegas."

Sonny laughed. "That's close, Ned. That about sums up my life." He opened the door.

"Your daughter will be happy."

"My daughter? Oh, yeah . . . I can't wait to tell her. Good-bye, I'll keep you in mind."

Ned stood in the doorway with Borgo and waved with the opera playing behind them. When he closed the door, Sonny walked to the corral and found the steer feasting on the grass hay with the bare-boned black.

"I'll be back."

He hurried out to the highway, protected from the cold by a warm winter coat a grandson would never need again. With the wind at his back he turned for town, for Montana, for an outside chance to stay alive.

Chapter 9

FOR SONNY THE JOURNEY to Montana became a flight from the past, a letting go of all that had been, a crossing into a new land. The single-minded Greyhound sliced east across the stark landscapes of Nevada, sailed over the bleached and barren flats of Utah, and turned north, into the jaws of winter, up through Idaho, all night, all day.

He slept much of the trip as though he were drugged, vaguely recalling a large Indian woman in the seat next to him, then a college boy in a BYU jacket, a young woman who nursed a baby and smelled of sour milk. He found it hard to distinguish between dreams and reality, grubby rest rooms, the bitter cold at stops, packaged food and canned soda, a sit-down meal too risky. The further he went the more he felt disconnected and utterly alone in the known universe.

He huddled in corners and imitated sleep on layovers, afraid recognition would stop short his newborn hope. Salt Lake, Idaho Falls, Butte; the large collar on the winter coat did more to hide his profile than anything, and he hoped that his cattle-truck aromas had been cleansed by the bitter cold in Salt Lake where he stood outside most of the time to avoid people. He thought he caught a few snatches of conversation that included his name but the newspaper dispenser outside the bus depot in Butte broadcast a large picture from his glory years with a bold headline SONNY HOLLISTER DEAD! In the bleak afternoon sun, with his breath turning to frost, he thought he'd been hurled into some strange odyssey from which he would eventually awaken, a journey into uncharted wastelands.

Twenty-one hours and a lifetime from Winnemucca, he stepped from the bus into the darkness of a gripping Montana winter, the only passenger getting off in the one-horse town of Belgrade. The driver lost no time hitting the road, leaving Sonny standing in crystallizing diesel fumes. A few cars and pickups slipped and spun their way along the dimly-lit main drag as if frantic to reach the warmth of home before being overcome by the arctic cold.

A small cowboy cafe made do as the bus stop where only a handful of hardy locals escaped the cold long enough to eat supper. It was almost seven; where could he hole up until ten? Even with Ned's grandson's coat, the predatory wind chill would eat him alive in that time. The few stores along the street were deserted and darkened against the treacherous night, but the Hub Bar, in the middle of the block, invited him with a few shivering lights. He walked past and could see nothing through the small glass-block windows; on a night like this there couldn't be more than a handful of barflies. He was freezing. He turned around and pulled the sunglasses from his coat pocket. Hell, one beer wouldn't hurt.

The heater on the Hertz Skylark began to throw warm air by the time Corkey Sullivan drove the short distance from the airport. He hated driving on icy and snow-packed roads, never got the hang of it. The bus stop stood where the Hertz girl said it would, the Greyhound logo hanging below the sun-bleached cafe sign, but the place was shut down tight with only a faint night light casting shadows inside. The town appeared evacuated.

Corkey parked in front of the cafe, left the lights on, and revved the engine to heat up the four door. He waited. Occasionally a solitary vehicle defied nature and ground metal parts against the brutal cold, but not one pedestrian showed his face. He began to have that feeling—that he was making an ass of himself one more time when he'd promised himself there would be no one-more-times, and this time it was downright dangerous. He decided to drive around the block, look for something open. Sonny couldn't wait outside in this sub-zero hell. Why would anyone in his right mind live here?

In the middle of the block he spotted the Hub Bar, lethargic but still breathing. He pulled to the curb and eyed the seedy-looking establishment. Nothing but pickups out front, and just four of those. Only hard drinkers would brave a night like this, or maybe the natives got used to nature's prank of retribution. His second thoughts grew as he visualized Sonny inside, thoroughly soused and boasting that he was alive when everyone thought he was dead. The impulse to get the hell out of there was gaining momentum. He had managed to isolate himself from Sonny's plunge into the sewer, to salvage his own reputation and successfully distance himself from his one-time protege's disgrace. Now he was putting himself in the line of fire and it scared the hell out of him.

Well, that's it, I tried to help and he didn't show.

Corkey pulled the shift lever into drive; back to the airport. Someone knocked on the passenger window. Corkey squinted into the frigid night and saw a fat clown in a MACK TRUCK cap and sunglasses. He unlocked the door and Sonny dropped into the passenger seat with a blast of cold air.

"You *came!*" Sonny said, "Son of a gun, *you came.*"

"Judas Priest, you *are* alive!"

"Just barely. I'm freezing my balls off."

Sonny pulled off the fogged-over sunglasses and Corkey grabbed him by the arm as if to see if he was dreaming. They looked at each other for a moment and then they laughed out loud and grasped hands like two old sailors who had shipped together a long time ago.

"I can't believe it, you came!"

"Jeez, you smell like a stockyard."

"It's been a long trip."

"The whole time I was flying it got more and more unreal. I kept telling myself he's dead, who you going to meet? He's dead, and I kept checking out the other passengers to see if anyone was tailing me and after a while they all looked like Costello's torpedoes."

"Hot damn, I never thought you'd show, I never thought you'd show. Thanks, Cork, thanks for coming. I had no idea where your ranch is, trying to figure where I'd sleep tonight, been waiting in a laundromat."

"I figured you'd be in there." Corkey nodded at the tavern.

"Just about was, but I walked on by. I gotta get it right this time, Cork, I gotta. No excuses. It's my last chance."

They swung onto the trackless ranch road, the trunk filled with food stuffs. Corkey was thankful they'd made it to the local grocery store before it closed, wanted to get this over with and get the hell back to the Hotel California. He'd filled two shopping carts while Sonny huddled in the idling Buick with the heater blasting. On the drive north of town, with wild animation, Sonny related his bizarre adventures of the past two days.

The small ranch house sat off the county road about fifty yards and Sonny, who drove once they got out of town, had to bust through the small drift left by the snowplow. Five or six inches on the level covered the barnyard where Corkey swung his clubfoot out of the Skylark and slogged through the unmarked snow to the back porch. He had to fiddle with the key and jiggle the frozen handle to persuade the door to give in but when he snapped on the kitchen light, he found the house warm, the little propane furnace faithfully doing its job. With two armloads of grocery sacks, Sonny stumbled in behind him.

"I could eat a chicken farm."

They hauled in the rest of the groceries and the two suitcases full of clothes Corkey brought. He feared the clothes were too small now that he'd seen up close the large proportions Sonny had attained. While Sonny ate enough for three, took a long shower, and put on clean clothes, Corkey stashed the food in cupboards and worked at putting the kitchen in order, fortifying himself to play hard ball. Sonny blustered into the kitchen wiping his butchered hair with a towel.

"This is a nice little place you have here, real nice. I didn't know if it'd have running water."

"Holy cats, what happened to your hair?"

"Chopped it off with a razor blade."

"You look like a bushman."

Sonny hung the towel on the back of a chair and settled in it. "I'm going to shave it all off. From this day forward I'm going bald."

"Wish you could give it to me." Corkey stood at the sink and ran his fingers through his graying black hair. He combed what was left of it over his bald dome and he knew it looked like hell, but he'd be damned if he'd wear a toupee. It angered him that he still wasted time worrying about how he looked. He was a little man with big ears and a club foot; why couldn't he come to terms with that, why couldn't he accept his life without a woman to love? He rinsed out a dishrag and began wiping up the table.

"How'd you find out about the contract?" Corkey said.

"Guy named Ellis, an old fan, works for them sometimes. I threw everything in the car and took off."

"I never thought it would come to that," Corkey said. "They don't like the publicity of doing a celebrity."

"No problem, make it look accidental, just the way it happened. Maybe some guy is getting paid for the hit right now."

"And maybe," Corkey said, "he put a time bomb in your car that got you a long way from Las Vegas. And maybe it went off right next to the poor bastard driving the tanker. Who knows? Maybe the hit man earned his money."

Corkey rinsed out the dishrag and started on the counters.

"Word is their patience with your IOUs ran out and your name and sweet disposition were no longer enough to protect you."

"It *wasn't* the money. It was Rita, Costello's wife."

"His *wife!*" Corkey stopped and looked Sonny in the eye. "You foolin' around with his wife? You gone completely nuts?"

"No, no foolin' around, it was what Rita *told me.*"

"You must be outta your skull, you must—"

"She spotted me in Ceasar's, wanted to talk, asked if I'd come up to their suite and play a few of her favorite songs. Jeez, I didn't know what to do. She's a powerful lady, she could get me some important gigs on big stages. She said Tony would be there. So, what the hell, I got my guitar and took their private elevator to the top."

"Tell me you didn't, please tell me you didn't."

"As it turned out, Tony wasn't there and I only sang one song before she moved next to me on a sofa and wanted to talk. Cork, she was a slot machine that had been played all night and was ready to pay. She said Tony had loved her at first, but no longer, that she was just a trophy wife. I asked her why she didn't leave. She said she couldn't, ever, that she knew too much, she was a prisoner. She was desperately lonely, Cork, and I didn't know what to say."

"You didn't touch her?" Corkey said.

"No, I'm not stupid. She's still a stunning woman, but I'm not stupid. She didn't want to make love, she needed someone to talk to and I'll never guess why me. She was near crying and she started telling me things and before I knew it I was in trouble. She told me about all the skimming they do, much more than anyone knows, millions that no taxes are ever paid on. I wanted to get the heck out of there. I tried.

"She held onto my arm. She was desperate, I was afraid she was going to start some big scene. She told me that Tony had killed a dozen or more people who got in his way. She asked if I remembered how Jaco Burns got shot in the head, murdered along with his chauffeur, that Tony had told her he had it done. I stood up, picked up my guitar and tried to leave. She hung onto me, a lonely, frantic woman who needed someone to unload on, who needed to be loved. I told her she shouldn't be telling me those things and I had to go."

"And that was it?" Corkey said.

"Yeah. She pleaded with me to stay a little longer but I made it to the elevator. I felt so sorry for her. Ellis called me the next day, told me there was a contract on me. As I hightailed it across the desert I figured Costello had a tape recorder or video camera and he knew what I knew. Somehow he found out what she told me. And *that's* why Costello wants me dead."

"Judas Priest, if he knows I talked to you he'll want *me* dead too," Corkey said and continued furiously polishing counter tops. "When Costello names your name, buy a tombstone."

Sonny tipped back in the wooden chair.

"He thinks I'm dead, Cork, how could you talk to me?"

Corkey felt knots in his stomach, sweat on his brow.

"Okay, okay, have you figured out what you're going to do now?" Corkey asked.

"Yeah, kind of."

Corkey turned and stood with his hands on his hips.

"Tell me."

"Well, I'll hole up here until I can change my appearance—"

"How you gonna do that?"

"Change my body, it's the only way, lose fifty pounds, get in shape—"

"You're talking crazy, you can't—"

"I'll *do* it, damn it, I'll let this blow over until I can go out in the world and have a life and everyone will've forgotten all about me."

Corkey hung the dishrag over the faucet and pulled a broom out of a small closet.

"How long you figure that'll take?"

"Not too long; maybe until summer. I'll work like hell at it."

"What are you going to live on?"

Corkey worked around the table, poking the broom under Sonny's chair. Sonny slid his chair out of the way.

"When it's safe, I'll get a job. You'll have to stake me for a while, but I'll pay back every cent, I swear, every cent, starting with the two hundred you wired me. I want to keep track of what this food cost, and the clothes."

"I don't know if I can do this," Corkey said without looking at him. "If someone recognizes you, your life won't be worth a nickel and if they know I helped you, mine'll be worth less.

"No one's going to know, ever, but if I got found out, I'd swear you never knew anything about it."

"Sure, sure, with you hiding out at *my* ranch they'd know I was in it up to my eyeballs. And what about the booze and drugs?"

"I'm going to quit, I swear. I have a chance to start over, Cork, and I'm going to do it right."

Corkey took a dustpan from the closet and stooped to collect his sweepings.

"Think you can?"

Sonny paused and looked him in the eye.

"I've got to."

Corkey stood with the dustpan in hand and gathered his forces. He swallowed hard.

"I don't think you can pull it off, and I can't stick my neck out like this, know what I mean. I could end up dead or worse. I can let you have some money—"

Sonny sprang to his feet, tipping over the ladder-back chair.

"Don't try to buy me off, Sullivan, goddamnit! You owe me! You traded in my ass on your lousy deals, you sold me out and you know it!" Corkey dumped the dustpan in the wastebasket and stuck it back on the closet shelf, turning his back on Sonny. "I've never said it before, but you turned me into an egg-sucking puppet, a mannequin, and all you cared about was the money."

Sonny slammed both hands down on the table and leaned toward Corkey, livid. Corkey put the broom in place and turned to face him. Sonny shouted.

"Will you listen to me and give up being a neat freak for once in your life! I made you millions, and now you won't risk a thing to give me another chance. You're a stinkin' vulture! Now that my bones are picked clean, you don't want anything to do with me!"

"You never complained, you—"

"Yes I did! yes I did, and you just blew me off."

"You're a grownup, you didn't have—"

"We have to fulfill the contract," Sonny said and stood erect, pumping a finger in the air. "We have to fulfill the contract, that's the bullshit you fed me, over and over, contracts you got me to sign by telling me half truths. You were worse than the stinking drugs, you were worse than the alcohol."

Sonny turned and smacked a cupboard door. Corkey caught his breath, weighing what had been said, the unacknowledged abscess between them. He knew Sonny had never brought it up in the past because he was always sucking up to him to get something, but it was true, he hadn't given much consideration to what it was doing to Sonny and his talent, locking him into contracts making air-head movies and appearing in LA and Vegas, doing the same old thing, monkey on a chain.

"I gave my life to you," Sonny said and turned to look at him. "Now, by God, I want it back"

Corkey couldn't meet his gaze. He pulled out a chair and settled in it, suddenly feeling overcome with weariness.

"Damn it, kid, I'd really like to help, but—"

"Don't call me kid. Whenever you did I knew you were screwing me."

"All right, all right, *Sonny,* but it's just too dangerous, too hairy, it's crazy."

"You always worry too much."

"And you never worried enough," Corkey said.

Sonny leaned back against the counter and spoke softly.

"I thought it was crazy, too, I still think it's crazy, but what else can I do? Give up, give in to them? The longer I've had to think about it, the more it seems right, like it was meant to be, like it wasn't my idea at all."

Corkey glanced into his eyes. "Whose in hell was it?"

"I don't know, but what if that *had* been me in the car, what would my life have amounted to? This is the only trip I have, one more time around, and I'm through pissing it away."

"Swear on your mother's life you'll quit using, coke, alcohol, everything." Corkey pointed a finger at him.

"I swear, Corkey, I swear, on my mother's life."

"If you break your oath, I'll walk out the door and sell this place right out from under you. You got that?"

"Yeah."

Corkey fought it. That worthless beggar Guilt was looking for a handout, and something told him to make amends, to make things right. He always prided himself for staying away from feelings, those unreliable, betrayers; they always cost you.

"All right," Corkey said, "all right, but only for a while, and only so long as you live up to your end of the deal. You screw up and I'm disappearing."

Sonny's face shadowed with surprise.

"You *mean* it?" Then, slowly, his face lit up with that generous winsome smile. He started bouncing around the room. "Jeez, thanks, Cork, thanks. You won't be sorry, I promise, you won't be sorry."

"I already am," Corkey said with fear knotting in his stomach. "What happens next?"

"You'll have to get back here off and on for a while, just for a while, until I can go into town without being recognized."

"Wait a minute, wait a minute! Tell me I won't have to be coming out here, tell me, please, that I can stay in LA."

"It won't be long, just a few times, just a few."

"The phone isn't hooked up," Corkey said.

"I've got no one to call."

"But I could call you—see how you're doin."

"I'll make it," Sonny said. "Best if there are no phone calls to trace."

"You're going to need I.D."

"I thought of that. Can you do it?"

"Yeah," Corkey said. "It'll cost, but I know a guy could set up God with new I.D."

"I have two favors to ask."

Sonny took a ballpoint from the counter and a notepad. He picked up the chair and sat up to the table, jotting something on the pad. He slid it over to Corkey.

Ned Shores, Box 225, Winnemucca, Nevada—$100
Leroy Riggs, Twin Falls, Idaho—$600

"What the hell is this?"

"Debts. I want to pay them just like I'll pay you. When you get to California, please send them cash. Send a note to Ned telling him it's for hay. Send an anonymous note telling Leroy it's for a few things borrowed from his truck with many thanks. When the weather breaks, I have a steer to ship up here from Winnemucca."

"You really pulled a cow outta that truck?"

"Toro . . . kept me alive while I was freezing my ass off and sloshing around in the manure in my stocking feet."

"Holy cats, what're you going to do with a steer?"

"You always wanted to start a cattle ranch, didn't you?"

"This thing gets nuttier by the minute."

Corkey stood.

"Got to get some sleep. I can get out of here on an 8:20 flight in the morning, hope the clothes fit."

"Did you bring the stethoscope?"

"Yeah, yeah, in the suitcase."

Corkey went to one of the two bedrooms, leaving Sonny sitting in the kitchen listening to his heart through the stethoscope. But Corkey didn't feel pure or clean for his surprising commitment in the face of danger. Somewhere inside his promoter's skull, above the sound of his knocking knees, there were little chimes tinkling, a sound he always heard when he was onto a good thing.

Chapter 10

IN AN AVIS SEDAN Corkey cautiously negotiated the snow-clogged road from the airport, cursing and nearly sliding into the ditch on more than one occasion, scaring him spitless. The funeral had turned him introspective on the flight and he'd admitted he'd gone far beyond all youthful wide-eyed dreams of success. With his hand in the barrel like everyone else, he'd come up with the biggest prize at the party: a green country kid with a natural charisma and uncommon voice who would unwittingly fashion a captivating style of folk songs in a way no one had ever attempted or thought possible. Simple dumb luck.

But having come up with the prize apple in the barrel, Corkey shrewdly packaged it, promoted it, and made it a household word, a national commodity. Rather than an agent testing his wings, he'd become a matchmaker, and the country fell in love with Sonny. Corkey had engraved the name and image of Sonny Hollister on the face of America, imprinted his voice on its memory, and seduced it to dance to Sonny's beat. Even with Sonny's incredible talent, Corkey knew it could've been lost in the underbrush and side roads of the vast entertainment world.

Then it all fell apart, slipped away. The media never understood, never got it right. It wasn't the mushrooming popularity and wealth that ambushed the unsuspecting star, as the news hounds claimed. It was that terrible Christmas day eleven years ago. Sonny had a show in Dallas and he wanted Julia and Tommy to be with him. The weather was bad and the pilot of their Lear jet didn't want to risk it. Julia called, didn't want to fly, bad feeling. Sonny insisted, said they could out fly the storm. They *had to be there* for the big surprise. When they didn't arrive in time, Sonny went out and performed, but he kept asking if they'd arrived yet.

He'd written a new song, "Julia", and he sang it for the first time, hoping she'd show up in time to hear it. As the show was winding down, Corkey got word; Sonny's private Lear jet had gone down five hundred miles short, killing all aboard. Corkey couldn't tell Sonny as he watched him singing his final songs. He'd never forget how Sonny rushed off the stage while his fans howled for an encore and looked into Corkey's face with fear in his eyes. *They're dead* was all Corkey could say.

Decorated with scraps of Christmas wrappings and body parts the plane was scattered across a Tennessee hillside, and though Sonny drove himself for most of a year, fooling his fans, the media, and himself with his bravery, doing two albums and two movies, losing the wife he worshiped and a four-year-old son he adored had been a mortal wound. Unknown even to himself, he was hemorrhaging internally. Half the women in the country wanted to comfort him and for a year or more he held out. Then one day, as though the scaffolding fell away and the foundation cracked, he gave in, sought comfort in their beds, drank too much, ate too much, worked less and less, gave and gambled away his fortune, until he was broken and lost. His fans looked the other way out of shame and pity, as if they couldn't bear to watch him slide into the sewer.

Now Corkey was sixty-four years old and that was all over, and it was difficult to understand what brought him down this winter road, risking the reputation and respect he had gleaned on that mercurial journey, and maybe his life, when he could be anywhere in the world he wished. He had his suspicions. Suspicions lurked also about the satisfaction of his life. Molly slid across his memory—an unguarded thought he quickly sent packing. He reached for the headlight knob and pulled it on.

When he turned into the barnyard a foreboding hatched under his belt. All tracks around the white single-story ranch house were drifted over, giving the illusion it was uninhabited. He slid to a stop behind the weather-scarred dwelling and instinctively knew that he never should've left Sonny alone for so long with his history of depression-out-of-the-blue and suicidal behavior. He'd promised to be back in a week. It was nearly two.

The darkness came easily, no glimmer from the hideout broke the gray dusk settling silently on the valley, and his foreboding hatched into a lump of dread. He grabbed several grocery sacks and plowed his way through the clean crusted snow. To keep from dropping the food he leaned against the door and banged loudly, but when there was no response from within, he couldn't tell if it was the wind that drove a chill into his bones or what he feared he'd find inside. He'd come from burying Sonny Hollister in a Minnesota graveyard with great media coverage and solemnity and he sensed how preposterous it was, then, to expect to find him alive in this isolated Montana ranch house. Even more preposterous, afraid he'd find him dead.

When he came up with the key and struggled into the kitchen, he elbowed on the light and found he was not in the kitchen at all. It was a slum. Things were scattered, left open, spoiling, half-eaten, littering floor and table and stove, the sink heaped with dirty dishes and garbage. Caught red-handed in the saltines, a mouse Geronimoed from the table, splattered on all fours on the floor, and smacked into an empty Seagram bottle. Ignoring the bandit escaping under the refrigerator with salt on his whiskers, Corkey's eyes stopped at the drained whiskey bottle, evidence that Sonny had left the house against all promises and erupting sincere regrets in Corkey's mind that he'd ever agreed to take part in this dementia.

"Sonny! Hey, Sonny!"

He set the grocery sacks on top of the clutter, knocking some of it to the floor, and followed the hollow sound of his voice into the living room. There was no life. The slum sprawled up and over the room until it seemed nothing was where it belonged. Magazines, clothing, empty beer cans, a partially eaten bowl of chili growing mold, a once bitten sandwich turning hard. The TV glowed silently in the uninhabited room, a meteorologist explaining the weather without audience or voice. Alarm spread through Corkey's nervous system, prompted him to shout louder than necessary in the small house.

"Sonny, you here?"

He stepped over the debris and switched on the light in Sonny's bedroom, strewn like a padded cell in a madhouse, bedding and clothing heaped in clumps on the floor, the mattress drooping over the edge of the bed, unoccupied except for a tipped beer can that had stained the sheets like a bed-wetter. It appeared to be a room where someone had committed suicide by throwing himself at the walls, but there was no body. And what would he do with the body if he found him dead? Dump him in the Nevada desert to balance things out? Holy mother of God! Why had he ever let himself get mixed up in this mess?

He decided to search the bars in town as a last futile gesture to salvage Sonny's outside chance, when he heard a muffled sound, fragile, a lost child's murmur. He held his breath and tried to figure where it came from, hurrying to the hovel between the bed and the wall and peeling off the layers of blankets, pillows and clothing, unearthing a grave. There he found the cadaverous body in a fetal position where Sonny had crawled into the tomb and pulled the earth in over himself, his clothing unchanged for days, his face covered with whiskers, his head with stubble, a stethoscope hanging from his ears. Sonny awoke and looked out at him from a haunted face.

"Where have you been?" he said softly.

So overwhelmed to find him alive, Corkey knelt and kissed his prickly head. Sonny came out of his stupor and sat up in the grave of dirty laundry.

"Are you all right?" Corkey said.

"Yeah . . . yeah, but you said you'd be back in a week. The damn funeral was five days ago, or was it six?"

"It's been seven, and you're right, I should've been back sooner. We've got to hook up the phone."

"What day is this?"

With suffering visible in his bloated face, Sonny stood unsteadily and stumbled over the mattress. A sock hung off one foot.

"It's Thursday. Every time I thought of coming up here I was scared outta my wits. You don't know what it's like dealing with all those people, pretending you're dead and wondering what in hell they'd do to me if they found out."

"You're scared!" Sonny said as he shuffled into the living room. "What do you think it's like hiding up here and seeing everyone on TV making a media circus out of your death and you're glad because you think Costello and his goons will believe it and you can live but then you realize you can never be yourself again and you'll always be in hiding and afraid someone will blow your cover."

He turned and looked at Corkey. "I didn't know it would be like this, Cork, nothing like this."

Chapter 11

SONNY FLOPPED INTO the upholstered chair facing the television set.

"The TV quit on me, no sound. Ever watch a stinking TV with no sound for a week?"

"Have you gone outside?"

"Only in the dark, walk back in the fields, I have to get outta the house."

Sonny adjusted the ear pieces of the stethoscope and held the diaphragm to his chest.

"Where did the whiskey come from?"

Sonny held up his hand, listening. Corkey waited. Satisfied that his heart was beating normally, he pulled the instrument from his ears.

"What did you say?"

"Where did the whiskey come from?"

"Your good Samaritan neighbor. She stopped to see if there was anything I needed in town." He laughed.

"Did she *see* you?"

"No. I asked her to just leave the bottle on the porch, that I'd be gone for a few hours. I slipped some money through the door, told her I just got out of the shower."

With a grunt Sonny lifted himself out of the sagging chair and shuffled into the kitchen. He inspected the groceries with growing interest.

"Anyone else come by?"

"She came back one other time. I just let her knock and sat quiet, like I was dead."

"Judas Priest! Sally's a well-meaning neighbor. I stopped and told her an old friend would be staying awhile. They're the only ones close enough to pay any attention. Holy cats, you better run the Flexamatic over your head. You look more like a barrel cactus than a bald man."

"It doesn't make any difference when you're in solitary confinement."

Sonny found a package of bacon.

"That's the kind of half-ass thinking that'll blow a hole in your kite. You have to live as though you're still in the public eye, ready to perform your new act in a second's notice without your bloody entourage pampering you for hours ahead of time."

"They disappeared a long time ago."

"I know. I waved at them with you, remember?"

Corkey slid food into the refrigerator.

"As I remember it," Sonny said, "you may not've been on the same train, but you caught the next one out of the station."

Corkey opened his mouth as if to defend himself but deferred to slogging through the snow for another load of foodstuffs. Sonny regretted his sarcasm. He turned on a burner under an iron skillet and opened the bacon. Corkey hung around longer than most would have, and he had to admit he was damn glad that the little man had the guts to risk sticking by him now. The panic in his chest had subsided measurably since Corkey's arrival.

When the alcohol ran out, Sonny tried to sleep around the clock, often waking with no idea in what part of the day or night he found himself. He attempted to exercise, situps and pushups, running in place, but exhaustion and his body's mass defeated him quickly each time. As much as he wanted to, he feared he couldn't immediately survive without his booze and drugs, but he knew they led him back into the nightmare and he had to find the iron to disown them, somehow, somewhere.

Corkey banged and Sonny opened to a gust of frigid air along with another load of supplies. Sonny took the sacks from him, shoved them onto the overburdened oak table, and went back to frying bacon.

"I saw tracks going into the barn the other day. Going or coming."

"You mean human tracks?"

"I couldn't tell, they were drifted over some. Might be some animal looking for shelter."

"Well, you keep your ass in the house, out of sight. It could be some photographer from the *Inquirer* or worse."

"Why are they making such a stinking big deal outta this? I'd already buried myself. The funeral was over years ago."

"I think you're going to make some money. In fact. . . ." He stomped his good foot, dislodging the clinging snow. ". . . you'll be the first celebrity to ever personally benefit from the nonsense generated by his death." He laughed and began unloading groceries. "At least I think you're the first. Who knows, maybe Dean or Monroe is hiding out somewhere."

"Nonsense is right. Haven't people got anything better to do? Jeez, not one of 'em would've given me the time of day a month ago."

He turned the bacon with a fork. Corkey cleared one of the ladder-back chairs and gently eased his body down. His three-piece suit sagged on him like yesterday's lettuce.

"I talked with Travis. He wants to put out two albums with some of your golden hits. Figures if they have them on the street by spring they'll sell—"

"Sell? They haven't sold diddley squat for years."

"No, now listen. A lot of people want in on the action. Universal wants to revive some of your movies, try them on TV, run them around the circuit and see what happens. The thinking is it will be big and quick; dish it up to them before the tears dry up. Albums, posters, movies, you know the menu. If you're marketable through summer, you'll have something to live on for a long time."

"You mean *you* will," Sonny said.

Three years ago he traded away the final assets of his career when Corkey refused to loan him one more nickel. To get twenty thousand dollars out of his manager, Sonny insisted on signing over all his rights to royalties and residuals—which were bringing in zilch at the time—in the event of his death. He knew Corkey didn't think he'd live a whole lot longer the way he was abusing himself. Now that he was officially dead, all future profits went to Corkey.

"But I know you're not dead so it's still your money, and anyway, it'll take a little time to tell how much people want to remember you."

"I threw up on my life and they couldn't stand the stench. They'll be gone by Monday morning."

Sonny stood at the stove and ate strips of the half-cooked bacon out of the pan.

"Maybe yes, maybe no, but I got a hunch. I want a beer."

"It's gone," Sonny said, adding bacon to the pan as fast as he ate it.

"Gone! Do you know how many six-packs we had in there?"

"You sit up here alone for two stinking weeks and let's see what you go through, knowing there isn't a person in the whole human race you can talk to, who knows you're alive!"

"All right, all right." Corkey held up his hands in a gesture of surrender.

"You know, I was doing fairly well," Sonny said, forking bacon onto a plate, "until I watched the coverage of the funeral, listened to everyone tell how much they missed me—Sinatra, Ann Margaret, Baez. Then, when they showed you, and you told them how much you'd miss me, the stinking sound quit, shoot, it just quit, the TV gagged on your bullshit."

"Well, it was hard. I kept thinking of our charcoaled drifter lying in that elegant coffin and seeing more hoopla made over him in his death than was ever made over him when he was alive. Thousands of people walking by that silk-lined box and the whole time I'm feeling lousy, knowing they're crying over a homeless thief named Roy."

"Don't tell me about it, don't make it any worse."

He glanced over the table at Corkey.

"I feel bad, Cork, really bad."

"Well, what did you expect?"

"Not *this*, nothing like *this!*"

Sonny turned off the burner and he felt a weight in his chest, staggered and dumbfounded by the public's response to his death.

"Did you think anything like this would happen?" Sonny said.

"I never thought about it, but you were big . . . as big as it gets. A ton of people loved you and your music. They said all kinds of things about you that were never true, a few that were, and your hometown will probably prosper from your memory."

"That'll be some good out of it. They never had much."

Sonny set the plate on the table and pulled up a chair.

"You want to know something funny?" Corkey said and looked him in the eye—something he rarely did.

"I could use something funny."

"When I saw all those people crying, holy cats! I did too." Corkey tried to laugh. "It was like . . . like you were really gone and I started feeling sad. Son of a gun, I had to keep telling myself that you were still alive. A lot of those people were really hurting and that made me feel like a dirty bastard—"

"Made *you* feel like a dirty bastard! How do you think it made *me* feel when—"

"I broke out in a cold sweat," Corkey shouted. "I started thinking about what they'd do if they knew you weren't dead. You better make damn sure no one ever recognizes you. If all those fans who're crying their eyes out because you're dead found out you were still alive, they'd kill you . . . and me, if Costello didn't get us first."

"I didn't ask them to come, I didn't want them there!"

He felt the weight slide down into his gut. He only had one chance, he had to change his body. He pushed the plate of bacon toward Corkey.

"You want the rest of this?"

Corkey shook his head.

"You want to hear something funny?" Sonny said. "After the funeral I was so scared and lonesome I was ready to hike into town and find a cop—tell him I was alive. You wanna know what stopped me? The whiskey."

"You promised me—"

"I know, I know, just cut me a little slack. I've been exercising, I have, I've been trying, but I've got to have weights, a weight machine, dumbbells, a barbell set, the best money can buy. Will there be enough money for that?"

Corkey regarded him skeptically.

"Yeah, plenty . . . but will you ever use them?"

"Damn right I will. I'll use them or die trying."

"Hey, you want 'em, you got 'em. I'll have 'em on the truck the day I hit LA."

"I've been sleeping a lot, but I dream . . . can't stop dreaming, crazy stuff, nightmares." Sonny glanced at Corkey and then picked at a fingernail. "I dreamed about my dad."

"How old were you when he was killed?"

"I don't know . . . nine, ten I guess."

Sonny pushed away from the table and went to the window in the unlit living room. He knew exactly how old he was. Nine. He drew back the curtains and gazed through the leafless lilacs out across the land. The darkened sky seemed to rest on the mountains. In all the years of media coverage, no one had pried beyond the simple fact that his father had been killed in a farm accident. Neither he nor his mother had ever told anyone the truth about that day and he had buried it for years.

Corkey came into the darkened room and found Sonny standing motionless in front of the window.

"I brought you a present."

Sonny turned. Corkey handed him a small box and stumbled over the litter to snap on a light.

"You'll have to adjust them the best you can for now."

Sonny lifted the horn-rimmed glasses from the box, examined them momentarily, then slid them on.

"How do they look?"

"Let's see."

Corkey walked around him, studying the effect, evaluating the face that had turned against itself, eyes that once held a sparkle gone lackluster. The bows of the plain-glass hornrims pinched his head. Sonny had lost his attractiveness. Corkey searched for the shy young man who once lived in that carcass and was shocked at the comparison in his mind.

"Well, shoot, how do I look?"

"They'll help, a little, change your profile."

Corkey stepped back and tried to hide his skepticism.

"Yeah, yeah, when your beard grows full you'll make a good-looking Frank Anderson, but you'll have to lose a washtub of weight if we're going to get away with this."

"Frank Anderson?"

"That's your new name, Frank-O. Want me to christen you or something?"

"You got the I.D.?"

"Birth certificate, social security number, you even have a past history with the IRS. You know how many Frank Anderson's there are in LA alone? Four hundred and seventy-two. How's that for anonymity?"

"Frank Anderson," Sonny said. "Yeah, I can be Frank Anderson."

"Frank *G.* Anderson."

"What in hell is the 'G' for?"

"Ghost, gum drops, how the hell should I know. You ever think of cleaning up this place?"

Corkey gathered an armload of trash and returned to the kitchen while Sonny stepped into the bathroom to check the glasses in the mirror. Corkey was twisting shut a bulging plastic garbage bag when Sonny appeared with the glasses in place.

"I'm sure as hell glad you're back, Cork."

Corkey wasn't glad. He was more frightened than he'd like to admit. Unmitigated regrets and second thoughts quarreled in his head, pounded on the door of his sanity. Though he made it clear he'd walk out if Sonny didn't live up to his promise, he realized that at this point in the game he was up to his eyeballs in the outhouse no matter what Sonny did.

Sonny paced into the living room and back, finally settling in the stuffed chair. The television reflected silent images and he stared blankly, wondering if he was capable of surviving this. It frightened him somewhere in his dark and hidden core, and the future loomed out at him with a bleak and lonesome face.

Corkey continued working for several minutes and then edged into the doorway in a dirty apron.

"Did I tell you they were tearing up the sod with their bare hands in front of your house in Boyd, breaking off branches from the shrubs, trees, anything they could carry away. Judas Priest, they had to hire watchmen or they'd have peeled that little house down to the last nail."

"They're crazy," Sonny said, visualizing the house.

Without further comment, Corkey went back to humanizing the cabin and Sonny lay back in the chair and shut his eyes. Why in God's good name didn't those people come running when his mother tore at the sod alone? Did she blame herself for not digging fast enough, for not saving his father? She never said. He could see her kneeling there, clawing at the hard black soil with bloody hands.

Chapter 12

SONNY FUMBLED out of bed, soaked in sweat. In the dark he tugged at the rope tied around his waist.

"I'm here!" he shouted, jarring himself awake.

He dreamed he was dead; his fans peered at his rigid form in the casket, and he wanted to tell them he was alive, but no matter how he moved his tongue and mouth, he couldn't make a sound.

"You all right?" Corkey called from the adjacent bedroom, back on his third brief visit.

"I keep seeing the funeral and some moron keeps playing the tape over and over. I have a weird feeling that I'm not real anymore and I want to tell someone that I'm alive."

"Good, you just did, now for God's sake let's get some sleep around here."

Sonny crawled back into the damp bed.

"You ever think about dying, Cork?"

"Nope."

"Then why are you always reading obituaries?"

"Just a hobby, you can learn a lot from obits."

Sonny lay wide-eyed and found himself curled up with a new bed partner, absolute terror, and he couldn't kick her out of bed. Breathing was difficult and he sensed he was caught in something so vast that he couldn't imagine the outcome, nor could he ever control the consequences. Fumbling for his stethoscope, he fearfully checked his heartbeat. When the blubber made it difficult to find his pulse he'd panic, thinking his heart had stopped. For the past several years he was never without a stethoscope. Now, through layers of flesh, he located the faithful ka-thump, ka-thump, ka-thump and, with some relief and an oppressive fatigue, he lay back in his haunted bedding.

One night when Corkey was gone, he found himself out in the snow, freezing in his underwear. It unstrung him so greatly that he began tying a rope around his waist when he went to sleep, the other end secured to the bed frame. Like tying up his nightmare so it couldn't lead him over the edge. More and more he thought that if he had any integrity left he'd kill himself and save Corkey any further catastrophe. But he couldn't find the backbone to face that final isolation willingly.

He dreaded the news media that broadcast his story with a nostalgic voice and great melodrama, used weeping women as the national symbol of grief. But the most agonizing of it all, the most enraging, was a quote from Mr. Anthony Costello, noted Las Vegas czar, who stated how much he loved Sonny and it gave him great sadness to know that Sonny would *never sing again*. Overcome with a paralyzing depression, Sonny couldn't escape the haunting even in his sleep; the haunting that his life as he knew it was over, the haunting that he'd never sing again. He was keeping his promise about quitting drugs simply because the terror of being discovered prevented him from going out and getting them.

Like a husband who planned to sneak out on his wife, Corkey packed his bag while Sonny played solitaire in front of the new TV set. Sonny ignored him, manipulating the grimy deck in spite of the drama unfolding on *As The World Turns*. Corkey was beside himself over Sonny's preoccupation with death and he didn't know what to do without professional help. The phone had been connected and he could call, see how Sonny was doing on a daily basis, though he didn't trust phones—someone else was always listening.

At Sonny's insistence, Corkey had contracted a local cattle hauler to pick up the steer in Winnemucca. The trucker had dropped off the Hereford a week ago when Corkey was at the ranch. The only fencing adequate to hold the docile animal was a pen in the barn. Corkey ordered several tons of hay delivered and was glad Sonny had some after-dark chores to do, lifting bales and hauling buckets of water for the steer. Enthused with the task at first, Sonny quickly seemed to lose interest in the Hereford along with everything else.

"Don't forget to send Ned Shores some money," Sonny said.

"I won't, five hundred."

Corkey carried his bag to the door and stepped back to the living room.

"I'm going."

"Go."

Sonny stared into the television and ignored him.

"I'll call when I can, remember the signal. Don't use names on the phone, I'll be back a week from Tuesday."

"Keep me in mind," Sonny said without looking up.

"It's about time you got off your fat ass and started shaping up, or are you going to screw it up this time, too?"

Corkey slammed the door, having learned long ago not to pamper Sonny's moods. But he knew Sonny's insolence merely reflected his terrible fear that his only contact with the human race was going off and leaving him again.

Sonny continued playing solitaire as if the words missed their mark, but when the sound of the car faded, he hurled the cards against the wall, threw a shoe at the new Panasonic and roared as though someone were ripping out his intestines. Then silently, as if he were shot, he slid onto the floor and curled up on the rug like a dog. Was he going to grab onto this second chance or die like Roy, nameless, without purpose, in stark obscurity? He pulled part of the rug over his back and fell asleep and his newly forged nightmare found him there.

He was watching the funeral on TV again, hearing those first reactions to his death, and his mother was there, watching with him and applauding and patting him on the back with a mother's pride. She kept saying Isn't it wonderful, isn't it wonderful.

> "He had the kind of gift that comes along once in a life-time . . . when he sang it was as though he were writing the lyrics spontaneously from his heart . . . he changed our music forever . . . he told stories with his songs and people listened because it was their story . . . the world has lost a special man who touched our hearts . . . things will never be the same with Sonny gone."

Their words confused him. Were they all being hypocritical in the shadow of the undertaker? Had they truly felt like this through those last terrible years when they avoided him, ignored him, and ridiculed him? Now their praise embarrassed him and in his dream he tried to turn off the TV despite his mother's protests, but the knob turned freely in his hand and it kept repeating the tribute like a permanent rerun.

He jolted awake and sat up on the floor in a sweat. It came to him in an instant—he would kill himself by running! If he ran hard enough and long enough, he was certain his heart would give out. He hefted his body upright, pulled on a jacket, and flung himself outdoors.

Across the barnyard he ran into the north field. Most of the snow had melted in a mid-winter thaw and the weather was mild. Like a crippled man trying to get out of a burning house, he ran without direction, staggered and fell onto the hard winter ground, struggled to his feet and gasped for air. He drove himself until he thought he'd suffocate. He felt faint; a fist of pain clutched his side. He ran and fell and got up again.

Time blurred; the landscape went out of focus; his mind whirled. He found himself on his hands and knees, throwing up into the dry brown grass. It stunk. Hearing Costello's words like a drum beat, *Never sing again! never sing again!* he got up and ran. When he couldn't run, he walked; when he couldn't walk, he stood; when he couldn't stand, he propped himself on all fours and retched until he was sure his liver and spleen would come hurtling out of his mouth.

His heart refused to stop, and when it was dark, he stumbled up the steps into the house, collapsed onto the sofa, and found himself there near dawn. He drank gallons of water and ate whatever he could lay his hands on: peanut butter with a spoon, bananas, saltine crackers and chicken soup. He ramrodded himself out the door and fled into the fields, temporarily insane.

For six days and nights he drove himself, slogged through darkness, snow squalls, and bitter wind chills. Sometimes he found himself sprawled on the frozen ground coughing up blood, his feet blistered, his knees wincing with pain. Faint with exhaustion, he slept at all hours, ran at three in the morning, and convulsed with the dry heaves at dawn. He felt like a tenpin in an all-night bowling alley.

A heavy knock at the door brought him upright on the sofa. He shook his head and looked at the clock. One twenty-two. It was light out, must be afternoon. He dragged himself off the sofa and crept to the kitchen window. When he peered through the curtains he found a man in brown coveralls opening the back door of a large white truck with UNITED VAN LINES across its side.

The weights! He'd forgotten. Someone knocked again. Must be two of them. He pulled a cap down over his face and went to the door, showing as little of himself as possible. He signed the delivery receipt and told him to put the stuff in the barn. When the two sweating truckers were done unloading the wooden crates, Sonny couldn't wait for them to drive out.

In the far corner of the sun-bleached barn there was a room with concrete floor and solid plank walls, painted white years ago when, Sonny guessed, it was used for washing milking equipment and storing milk. Three small windows close to the ceiling filtered light into the room along the barn's concrete and stone west wall, too high to see in from the outside. Clouded with cobwebs, insect dribble, and fine ancient dust, he'd leave them in their natural state so that from the outside they'd blend with the whole. It took him until dark but he stripped the old tables and junk from the room until it was completely empty, swept clean.

With the room prepared, he began tearing open crates, made uncounted trips hauling the ponderous equipment to the milk room, and assembled it. After hours of pouring over instructions, fitting pieces together, and tightening bolts and nuts, the machine stood starkly like an instrument of torture from the Middle Ages, brandishing chrome bars and handles, vinyl covered pads and benches, and tiers of iron weights attached to steel cables. A bench with a barbell in its uplifted arms, stacks of free weights, and an assortment of dumbbells, squatted quietly on the old concrete floor, threw a challenge in the face of his unproven resolve, sneered from their heavy black faces that in the end they would win.

Exhausted from the work and hauling, he had one more chore before going to bed. In a quiet frenzy, he neglected to eat, refused to allow anything to distract him. He had to camouflage the weight room so that no one would ever suspect it was there. He dragged bales of hay from the stack just outside the barn and piled them against the two walls of the milk room, several layers thick until they pyramided to the first-floor ceiling.

When he finished, anyone coming into the barn would think there were several tons of hay in that corner without suspecting it was a hollow stack. Directly in front of the door, two bales high, he positioned one bale that would slide free lengthwise. He supported the bales above this concealed entrance with spanning boards so that when the bale was removed, none of the other bales would move, the boards recessed just enough to be undetectable. When he crawled through this passageway and replaced the bale, not even the creatures who prowled the old building would know he was there. He had finished. He shouted at Toro in celebration.

"We're going to make it, buddy, both of us!"

He dragged himself to the house and discovered it was two-thirty in the morning. He stunk. Stripped of his filthy clothes he stood under a hot shower, his knees and hands bruised and scabbed, his body sore, his legs and blistered feet ached; swollen ankles and strained muscles cried for attention.

The hot water forgave him and gladdened his heart. He caught himself humming. Not only had he not died, but he no longer wanted to. Somehow, during those murderous days, hope had insinuated itself into his unsuspecting heart and taken root. He looked forward to tomorrow, not as a day to die, but as a day he could begin the grueling task of reshaping his body. He sang the words in a whisper.

"Pickin' up the pieces of my sweet shattered dream,
I wonder how the old folks are tonight."

He'd call his mother in the morning.

Chapter 13

ELIZABETH KNEW SONNY could never understand why she returned to Minnesota in her later years after enjoying living in Nashville and Santa Monica; but it was really quite simple. This was the dwelling place of her best memories—the farm, Sonny growing up, the man she loved most, friendly ghosts, if not always happy. Her roots were here and she found a few old friends dwelling in the bright and clean retirement home in Clarkfield only a few miles from Boyd, the little village where she raised Sonny. He had taken good care of her when he became famous and he'd seen to it she was paid up here if she lived to be a hundred and twenty.

She had suffered for him through those bad years, understood, as only a mother can, how badly he was wounded that terrible Christmas Day. He never talked about them, but she knew the news people and all those trashy *Inquirers* and such just made up most of those nasty things so they'd have something to print. Land sakes, her boy couldn't have done all those ridiculous things. She couldn't believe he was gone, either, even though she'd seen them put him in the ground right next to Willard. She never dreamed that he'd go on before her and she wished she could talk to him one more time. The funeral was hard on her and she kept thinking that maybe she'd let him down somehow, maybe she could have helped more when he kind of went crazy.

"Betsy, you have a phone call," Alice, her favorite attendant, told her as they met in the wide carpeted corridor. She stopped, for a moment confused, and then Alice gently turned her around and started her back toward her apartment. The corridor was very long and sometimes she didn't know just where she was at.

"Oh, thank you, I'll just go see about it."

Betsy found the wreath with pine cones that marked her door, but sometimes her apartment seemed to be on the wrong side of the hallway. She settled at her small table and picked up the phone in her shaking hand.

"Yes, hello."

"Hi, Mom, it's me, Sonny."

"Oh . . . you must be mistaken, Sonny's dead."

"No, Mom, it's me, I'm not dead. I wanted to call you sooner but I couldn't."

"Sonny, can this really be *you?"*

"Yes, Mom, I know it's hard to understand, but it wasn't me in that car, it was someone else. I can't tell anyone I'm alive, so you mustn't tell anyone, but I had to let you know, I knew how bad you'd be feeling."

"Oh, Sonny, are you really alive, am I dreaming, am I talking to a ghost?"

"No, Mom, it's really me. I'll come and see you when I can, but right now I have to stay in hiding. I'll explain it all to you later, but I'm alive, Mom, and I'm taking good care of myself, no more drinking or drugs or any of that bad stuff."

"Oh, how can I know it's you? How can I know?"

Sonny thought for a moment. "Mom, think of something only Sonny would know, something about us, back in Boyd."

Elizabeth thought for a moment. What no one else would know, what no one else would know. She had it!

"When Fred gave you the guitar, what had he put inside it?"

"A 1935 sliver dollar," Sonny said, "the year I was born, for good luck."

"Oh, Sonny, it *is* you, it *is* you, but who did they put in your grave?"

"A stranger, it was an accident, I know it's confusing."

"I can't believe it; I just can't believe it."

"I know, I'm sorry I couldn't call sooner. How are you?"

"Oh, I'm so happy. It's a miracle, you're alive. Oh, thank God, thank God, now you can sing again."

"No, I won't be able to sing anymore, Mom, but I'll call again, soon. I better not talk long right now and, Mom, you can't tell anyone you talked to me, okay?"

"I'm so happy."

"Mom, do you understand, you *can't tell anyone,* it's our secret, I can get into a lot of trouble if anyone finds out I'm really alive. Do you understand?"

"Yes, I understand. Oh, thank God you're alive."

When Sonny hung up, Betsy sat at her table for several minutes and her head seemed to buzz and she wondered if she were dreaming. She *was* taking that new medication. But she'd know her boy's voice anywhere, it was really *him*.

She hurried out of her apartment with happiness and wonder spilling out of her like bubble bath and she almost bumped into Alice who had an armload of bedding.

"Did you get your call?" Alice asked.

"Oh, yes, it was Sonny."

"Sonny, your boy?"

"Yes, my precious boy, he's still alive."

Alice frowned. "Are you sure it was Sonny?"

"Oh, yes, it was Sonny all right."

"Someone may have been pulling a joke on you."

"Oh, gracious no, you don't think I know my boy's voice?"

Alice leaned against her slightly and spoke softly out of the side of her mouth.

"Maybe you shouldn't tell anyone you talked to him."

"That's what *he* said, that I shouldn't tell anyone."

Mr. Applebee, the administrator, came briskly down the corridor looking very busy in his navy suit and tie. He always seemed to be very busy with important things.

"And how are we this morning, Betsy?" he said, half pausing but keeping his legs moving as though he were treading water.

"I'm very happy. I just talked to Sonny on the phone."

Applebee glanced at Alice and then smiled into Betsy's face.

"Why that's wonderful, Betsy, simply wonderful, so glad to hear it," he said as he scooted away.

Someone was pounding on the door! Sonny flipped aside the blanket and sat up on the sofa, momentarily uncertain where he was. Like an arthritic old man he stumbled to the kitchen door and opened it, realizing too late that it was forbidden.

"Hello," a small boy said. "Would it be all right if I got a swallow nest out of your barn?"

Still in a daze, Sonny looked down into the kid's eager face. A patched Levi jacket overmatched his wispy frame.

"Are you a doctor?" the boy asked with an edge on his voice. His large chocolate eyes fixed on the stethoscope hanging around Sonny's neck and he lost his smile.

"Ah . . . no, I'm no doctor."

"What's that thing for?" He pointed.

"I'm like a hibernating bear, and once in awhile I use it to see if I'm still alive." Sonny smiled.

"Would it be all right?" The boy's face lit up again, his blond hair adrift. "I won't hurt nuthing."

"How old are you?"

"Nine. I've played around these old buildings a lot, but Mom says I have to ask now that someone's living here."

"Well, sure, it's fine, nothing in there you can hurt."

"Gee, thanks, mister."

He bounded down the steps and raced for the ramshackle barn, some of its shingles blown away by wind and time. With the sun assaulting the remaining snow drifts and much of the ground bare, Sonny was swept off his feet by the brash spring day and its messengers. He sucked in the sweet mountain air and watched the boy disappear into the faded red barn.

A swallow nest. Dang, there was a time when such treasure would've been the most important thing in his life. Reluctantly he shut the door and peered from the window for any sign of the boy. He felt drawn to join the adventure but worried that the bald head and glasses weren't enough. He paused, fighting the temptation. The nine-year-old kid had probably never heard of Sonny Hollister. With his jacket in hand he piled out the door.

"Hey, where are you?" Sonny shouted into the cool atmosphere of the barn.

"I'm up here." The shrill voice echoed from above. "I didn't know you had cattle."

Sonny followed up the wooden ladder, each rung dished from uncounted steps out of the past to feed stock.

"That's Toro, more of a pet than beef."

"Why did you name him Toro?"

"So he'd feel like a bull." Sonny laughed.

The large empty loft was covered with a layer of musty hay, and high above him, standing in the wide loft doorway, the boy reached toward several swallow nests that were cemented to the side of the barn under the eaves.

"Hang loose," Sonny shouted, squinting up at the spindly boy in his precarious perch. He hadn't considered that the boy might get hurt when he gave permission.

"I don't think I can get one. They just fall apart."

One of the nests crumbled when he tried to slide it away from the wall, and his disappointment showered down on Sonny with the fine dusty soil. He climbed to the boy, clinging with survival instincts to nailed steps that creaked under his weight, but the nests were too delicately constructed to disturb, and neither of them could salvage one intact.

"How do they make these?" Sonny said as he inched his way to the loft floor.

"They fly to a muddy spot and get a bite of mud. Then they fly to the barn and spit it out, making one little piece of the nest. They're awfully smart." The boy jumped into the moldy hay. "I guess I'll have to get some other nest."

"What do you want it for?"

"My Sunday school teacher."

"Well, we're not whupped yet."

They returned to ground level and the boy went to the stall and reached through the planks. The Hereford came to him easily and the boy rubbed it's head.

"He's friendly. Can I play with him when I come over?"

"Sure, Toro likes attention, but I don't know how you can play much with a steer. C'mon."

Sonny led the way out of the barn, and the two of them sifted through the discarded junk in the dilapidated buggy shed and the log-walled tool shed. Amid tattered old horse gear and wornout tools, they came up with a rusted hand saw. Then, to the utter amazement of the boy, Sonny cut a board from the barn with a flawless mud nest intact. The boy cradled the treasure out to the yard where they squatted and examined it in the sunlight.

"Gosh, this is super, it's perfect," the boy said.

Inside the outer mud shell they found a lining of soft down and feathers to comfort and shelter tiny chicks.

"They're down in South America now, but they'll be coming back soon," the boy said with an innate enthusiasm, "they always come back."

"You know a lot about them, don't you."

"You should hear my sister. She knows everything about birds and all that kind of stuff."

"Where do you live?"

"Just down the road." He nodded west. "In the trailer."

"Is Sally your mother?"

"Yeah, you know my mom?"

"Not really, just talked to her once a few months ago."

"What's your name?"

"Son . . . ah, Frank . . . Frank Anderson. What's yours?"

"Jesse." The boy picked up the board and nest as if to leave. "Thanks a lot for helping me."

"Anytime." Sonny got lumpishly to his feet and searched his mind for ways to detain the boy. "What else do you do around here?"

"Oh, look for snakes and frogs, when it warms up. Catch bats in the barn and sometimes pigeons, but my sister makes me let them go. Stuff like that. Sometimes I pretend I'm getting away from Vietcong guerrillas. I find stuff. I found a baby skunk last summer, but it was sick. We had to kill it. My mom said it was putting it to sleep, but we *killed* it."

"You always play alone?"

"Mostly."

"Me too. Want a partner?"

"You want to play?" The boy looked dismayed.

"Yeah, I want to."

"What do you want to do?"

"Hey, that's your department. You call it."

Jesse scanned the neglected barnyard as if sorting out the possibilities of what he might do with a chubby adult who wanted to play. They marked off boundaries and picked a goal and Sonny found himself hiding under the old work bench in the tool shed amid the dirt and junk, holding his breath with genuine fear that the seeking boy would find him, lost in an unsuspected happiness.

His sore and aching body reminded him of his morning's purging in the milk room, a strict routine he followed every morning since the weights arrived. The one to two hours in which he committed voluntary manslaughter each day helped ward off the stark isolation and despair of his newly emerging life. He couldn't get enough water, and to get through the day, when he wasn't in the milk room or running, he used the readily available drug of sleep.

Intense with choosing just the right moment to make his break, he was lost for a time in this kid's game. He listened for a crunching leaf, struggled to free himself from under the grimy workbench, and dashed for the designated post of the tumble-down corral. Jesse spotted him and outran him to the goal.

"One, two, three on Frank!" he shouted happily.

Sonny puffed for breath, bent over with his hands on his knees, "it" for the next round. If Sonny couldn't snatch the boy in close quarters he had no chance of running him down in the open. Once Sonny crawled under an old pile of tree limbs and Jesse couldn't find him.

"Come on out, Frank," he shouted from a distance. "You're just afraid of being caught!"

Sonny lay on the warming earth and listened to the boy describe his entire life with utter simplicity. He'd always been afraid to let people see who he really was, always chosen to hide. The boy was right; he was afraid of being caught. But by whom?

"Ollie, ollie, oxen free!" Jesse shouted from another point in the barnyard.

Sonny remembered that phrase from the playgrounds of his childhood. It meant everyone could come home free. It had a wonderful sound to it, and just then, he wished it was God shouting those words. He peeked through the tangled branches but couldn't locate the boy.

"Come on, Frank, that's half the fun," Jesse called.

With a silent grunt Sonny crept out from under the limbs and crawled to the corner of the tool shed. The boy spotted him and they raced for the goal. Jesse beat him by a lash, and they both dropped in the dry straw and manure of the long uninhabited pen.

"You said I could come in free," he said, puffing for air.

"I had my fingers crossed," Jesse said, his large eyes laughing.

"Why you little. . . ."

Sonny tipped him over backwards, and they lay sprawled for a minute.

"You're right," Sonny said. "Getting caught isn't as bad as you think it will be."

Jesse sat up and regarded him.

"Don't you like yourself, Frank?"

"Like myself? Oh . . . I don't know. Why?"

"'Cause there was a guy on TV that said fat people don't like themselves."

Sonny was tongue-tied. With no malice or ridicule the boy said out loud what was perfectly clear to all but the blind.

"I'll have to think about that," Sonny said.

Jesse sprang to his feet. "I gotta go."

Sonny sat up and watched him retrieve the nest.

"My teacher will love it. She wanted us to bring something about life starting over again." The boy hurried across the yard. "Happy Easter, Frank!"

"Easter! When's Easter?" Sonny hollered after him.

"Tomorrow."

Gone behind the barn, Jesse had flown away like the swallows. Sonny stood and moved to a place where he could spot the boy through the cottonwoods, already a small solitary figure to the west, halfway across the pasture, and he thought Jesse ought to take *him* to his class.

He savored the exhilarating experience of being seen by someone, interacting with another human being, and he turned for the house. In the kitchen he opened the refrigerator and searched for something to satisfy his robust thirst, passing up a frosty can of beer for the orange juice which he swilled from the bottle. He licked his lips and a shiver of hope touched him. The swallows would return after the frozen months of winter, and Jesse would come back another day. Tomorrow was Easter. He looked into the empty barnyard. Had God called ollie, ollie, oxen free? And if He had, did He also have his fingers crossed?

Chapter 14

WHEN CORKEY RETURNED a day later than he'd promised, he expected Sonny's disappointment to spill all over him. He'd called the day before but gotten no answer and though it was a lovely day near the end of March and signs of spring were evident, he was tired, angry that he had to apologize for coming back tardy like some school kid when he'd been working diligently not only on his own behalf but on Sonny's as well.

He opened the trunk of the rented Plymouth and heard the clank of metal from the tool shed. When he walked to the open door, he found Sonny, smudged with a rusty grime, throwing scrap iron into a pile. The shed was stripped, the dirt floor—which had been littered with old machinery parts and years of accumulated junk—was swept clean and the small windows scrubbed from decades of fly specks, spider webs, and layered film. Dust hung thick in the air as Sonny threw a brick into the pile and noticed Corkey with surprise.

"You back already?"

"Holy cats, I don't believe it." Corkey retreated to avoid the fallout. "You staying out of sight?"

"Who could find me in this?" Sonny wiped his hands on his filthy jeans. "I can get outside by working in the buildings."

Across the yard, Jesse came out of the barn, leading Toro with a makeshift halter.

"Jeez! who's the kid?"

"He's Sally's boy."

"You let him *see* you?"

"Yeah. We're buddies. We found out it's easier to take Toro to the water than haul water to him."

Jesse turned on the yard hydrant and the steer drank from a bucket.

"I don't think it's a smart move," Corkey said, scrutinizing the boy, "he could be big trouble, could blow your cover."

"He's nine years old."

"I don't care how old he is, this could be disastrous."

Sonny helped him haul his gear to the house. Corkey dropped his suitcase inside the door and regarded Sonny with suspicion.

"Would you kindly tell me what in the hell is going on."

The kitchen was immaculate: floor scrubbed, counters spotless, the oak-grained table gleamed.

"You've never carried a dirty dish to the sink in your life."

"O-o-o-oh, wait a minute, wait a minute, when I was a kid I did, used to wash dishes with my mom." Sonny scrubbed his hands in the beaming old porcelain sink. "We used to get into water fights."

Corkey checked out the living room and stepped back into the kitchen.

"You've had a woman in here!"

"Once I got started I couldn't quit. It felt good, like I was putting something in order."

Corkey settled at the table. "How are you doing, still exercising?"

"Every day, and running. I don't know why, but I feel a lot better. What's going on out there; it's been outta-your-skull quiet here."

"It's been quiet out there, too. It's petering out."

"Good! At least I won't have them on my back anymore. Oh . . . I saw an Indian guy the other morning, out behind the barn."

"Did he see *you?*"

"No, I saw him from the window. It was barely light."

"I wonder what he was doing out here? We can't go gettin' careless, know what I mean. I don't like that kid seeing you."

"You wouldn't be happy if you didn't have something to worry about. Look at this." Sonny pulled on the waist of his jeans and showed a slack two or three inches.

"You keep remembering about your mom. I spent most of Saturday with a guy who is going to write a book about your life. A history man by the name of Roger Least. Never heard of him myself, but he's supposed to have written some important books."

Sonny pulled out a kitchen chair and sat at the table.

"Why in hell would a history man want to write a book about *my* life?"

"Because you were history. Jeez! when I got done listening to that fella I couldn't believe how much history I'd been wallowing in."

Corkey lifted his attache case onto the table.

"He's offering me a percentage if I give him everything I know about our years together, and he wants it straight, no bullshit. But the guy doesn't know what he's asking. If I tell it like it was, you'll be madder than a Tennessee hornet, and he don't realize you're still around to kick my ass."

Corkey opened his black leather case and rummaged through it. Sonny reflected on those lightning years when their lives flowed together like a thunderstorm, pondered how superficial it always was between them, the product and the huckster, functioning successfully in the commercial pursuit of profit, cool, impersonal, compatible strangers—and sometimes not so compatible.

"The truth, that'll be different," Sonny said. "Why ask me about my life? It went on without me."

"Your old albums are selling," Corkey said. "That'll be some cash coming in."

"Is he going to want to know about when I was a boy?"

"Yeah, sure, everything you can remember."

Sonny remembered Natalie Jones, the first girl he ever loved. She married Zeke Zwingley, a tall angular farm boy who went into body work.

They made supper, spaghetti with meat balls, and Sonny's enthusiasm rose with his plans for the ranch. He gave Corkey a shopping list, mostly tools. The last item was a pickup.

"You've sure snapped out of it," Corkey said. "What happened?"

"I don't know, I can't figure it. One morning it was hell just to get out of bed, the next morning I couldn't wait."

The following day Corkey returned from Bozeman before noon, the car laden with hardware and a wheelbarrow sticking out of the trunk. They stashed it in the shed, and Sonny began playing with the Homelite chain saw on some of the overgrown limbs around the yard. When it was dark, they drove into Bozeman to get the '65 Dodge pickup Corkey bought. Sonny hunkered down in the Plymouth and drove it back to the ranch, following Corkey in the truck.

On the radio Sonny Hollister was singing "If You Could Read My Mind." When it finished, the disk jockey cut in.

"Sonny, we wish you'd stayed around, partner."

He said it in a familiar manner that intimated they were close friends. What a liar.

When he shut the car door and lingered in the moonlit barnyard, an owl called from the grove behind the sheds. He listened. *Whoo-who-o, who-o-o, whoo-whoo, who-o-o.* Tears blurred the moonlight. Like the owl, he had become only a sound in the darkness, a voice over the airwaves in the night.

"What are you doing out there?" Corkey called from the door.

"I'll be in later."

On remnants of the old corral he climbed onto the low-pitched buggy shed roof. He found his balance and looked up at the nearly full moon.

Whoo-whoo, who-o-o, whoo-hoo, who-o-o, the owl called.

"I'm here!" he shouted with his arms spread, gazing into the velvet sky. "I'm here! I'm Sonny Hollister and I'm still here!"

The back door banged open and Corkey stood on the porch.

"Judas Priest!"

Chapter 15

DAILY, SONNY HAD TO convince himself that his life depended on it, recognizing he'd lost any innate self-discipline in recent years. Awaken to the dream-shattering alarm, wrench a groggy body out of the comforting bed, refuse to allow the flesh to outwit the will into staying a few minutes longer. Pull on some clothing, cold water on his face, orange juice, out across the field, jog awhile and then push himself into a run. When his body pleaded to stop, he fought a running battle on the field of his internal civil war.

"Move! *I can't.* You can, a little farther. *Can't breathe.* Okay, walk. *I'm going to quit!* You can't. *Why not?* You know why. *I don't know.* Not good enough. *Because the swallows are coming back!*"

April had come on the shirttails of the early spring, warm and clear, leaving no trace of snow on the valley floor. Sonny drove the pickup around the ranch, smitten with the Gallatin Valley as though seeing it for the first time; bold, generous, expansive, a broad plain surrounded by such lofty mountains they wore a cape of ice and snow year around. He liked the way the mountains made him feel, their bearing so regal and everlasting. It appeared as though one could ride up into that massive rock and disappear forever like Moses. And he found gratification in the work he was doing, purging the ranch of years of neglect as if purging his life. He filled the pickup bed over and over and dumped the rubbish in a small gravel pit on the east end of the hayfield where it could be buried.

Several crows winged over him while he emptied the pickup bed. They settled in the cottonwoods along the fence line and laughed at him. He stood watching them and they carried him back to that fateful day. He couldn't erase his father's pleading face, forget his mother's hands caked with bloodied mud, the neighbor's tractor lifting the Oliver off his father.

When the hearse carried his father's body from the barnyard, several crows sat in the grove above the chicken coop, laughing. Sonny ran to the house and grabbed the .410 over-under. He took a hasty shot, but the crows swooped through the trees and escaped unscathed out the far side of the grove. He knew he should've used the ten gauge, but his father let him shoot it once, and it knocked him on his backside. Even at that his shoulder hurt with the .410.

When he walked to the house with the shotgun, his mother didn't say a word though he was forbidden to touch it without his father's permission. With that simple gesture he'd become the man of the family, his childhood ended. From that day on, he had always associated crows with his dad's death, and they were always showing up when it was the farthest thing from his mind.

Few recollections of the funeral remained, but he remembered wondering, after seeing the deep hole in the ground, how Jesus would ever get his dad out of there? A tall Scandinavian farmer who had a place two miles west of theirs stopped Sonny and his mother as they walked from the grave, assuring them that no man, no five men, could have moved that tractor an inch, and if they had, it wouldn't have helped; that the Oliver crushed his father the moment it turned on him. His mother thanked the unassuming farmer, and Sonny never knew if what he said was true or if that genial stuttering man was doing what he could to lift a crippling weight off a young boy's heart.

They lost the farm and moved into the sleepy village of Boyd, into the small wood-frame house where his life would be shaped and his journey launched into the fateful orbit he would travel.

While tossing junk in the pickup, he spied Jessie crossing the pasture west of the barn and he waved, invigorated at the coming of his first and only friend in this Frank-Anderson second life.

"Hello!"

"Hi, Frank. Did you get a new truck?"

"Yeah, a clunker, I'm cleaning up the place so we don't kill ourselves when we play hide and seek. You want to help?"

"Can I?" the boy asked with enthusiasm.

"Well, only if you'll drive the truck."

Jesse looked into Sonny's eyes as if trying to figure if he was serious. Then he came clean.

"I don't know how to drive yet."

The brightness in his face faded with his admission, and Sonny couldn't bear to see that light go out.

"You do now, amigo. Climb up in there."

The kid got behind the wheel with his jaw set, sighting through the steering wheel. Sonny shouted instructions and Jesse catapulted the truck out toward the open pasture, a bucking bronc out of the shoot. Sonny grabbed the wheel a few times to avoid tearing out a fence or wrapping a bumper around a tree trunk, and during the time the boy took to make a clear distinction between the brake and the accelerator, Sonny held one hand on the roof and one on the door handle. The harrowing ride mellowed some as Jesse got the knack of it and started to get cocky, but the difficult stick shift on the '65 Dodge kept him from arrogance, and while he was trying to shove one howling gear in line with another, Sonny laughed and hollered encouragement. Like a consumers' advocate testing truck springs and shock absorbers, the boy bounced Sonny from one end of the property to the other.

"Didn't your dad ever let you drive?"

"He doesn't live with us anymore, they're divorced."

Across the pasture they lurched and leaped in a joyful celebration of one more boy discovering the mystery of the clutch. With the promise that Jesse could drive, Sonny convinced him they had to get some work done, and they filled the pickup with trash.

"Do you see your dad much," Sonny said.

"No . . . not really. He's mean to my mom."

Jesse pulled up alongside the pit and reined the truck to a bucking stop. Sonny noticed the boy's mood dampen and while they threw the rubbish out of the pickup, Sonny confided how he'd lost his dad when he was growing up. Jesse made no response. When they finished, he had the boy stop the truck behind the tool shed.

"I gotta go or I'll catch it. Thanks a heap for letting me drive the truck, but I don't think I'll tell Mom about it."

He said it with a grownup matter-of-factness belying his age, then darted through the cottonwoods and across the ditch, gone like one of the silent creatures of the land. The sun also was running off to the west, leaving him alone to face that godawful time that was so hard to get through.

The old shaving commercials used to warn about a five-o'clock shadow, but no one had ever warned him of the five-o'clock dread that gripped him late in the day and compressed his diaphragm, rendered him partially breathless. While he ate he wished Jesse could've stayed and held off the emptiness that crept into his life like darkness into the valley. Bone tired, he cleaned up the kitchen and reminded himself that it had been a good day, he'd be able to sleep if he could shut out the bleakness and the terror long enough to slip away. On the shifting ground under him, he was trying to hang on to something, to make a beginning, but he felt he was diminishing day by day and that he'd vanish altogether when his fans no longer kept him in mind.

With the volume on the television turned up, he drank more than one beer, getting rid of each empty can immediately as if to keep the evidence from himself. Into the bedroom, he sat on the edge of the bed and listened to the cadence of his heart through the stethoscope, ka-thump, ka-thump, ka-thump. With the rope tied securely around his waist, he went to bed with enough hope to set the alarm.

Chapter 16

WITH HIS NEWBORN enthusiasm, and counting on Corkey's compulsion to always be doing something, Sonny drew him into the labor of rebuilding the corral.

"I ought to use this damn foot to *pound* these in," Corkey said. Sweat dripped from his face in the bright April morning while he carved out a post hole with a shovel and bar in the hard-packed soil of the barnyard. "Or my head."

"Just think how healthy you're getting," Sonny said.

"Yeah, so healthy it'll kill me."

Sonny tamped in a treated post, a real workout for his arms and upper body, and he figured the only reason Corkey went along with this nonsense, completely out of his element, was his fear of defusing Sonny's zeal. Always excused from hard physical labor because of his deformity, Corkey was expressing surprise at himself and the satisfaction he found in this digging and hammering and constructing something out of nothing, things that always seemed foreign and mysterious.

Jesse called as he rode Toro out of the barn like a pony.

"Look, Frank, look!"

"Hey, that's great, amigo!"

With a halter fashioned out of baling twine, the boy turned the docile Hereford around the yard like a cutting horse.

"Mother Mary," Corkey said, rubbing his perspiring forehead with his leather glove. "I think that crazy steer enjoys the kid on his back."

The boy played on the Hereford, the men worked, and honey bees danced in the sunlight, but Sonny was shaken inside, barely hanging on. From scattered, isolated incidents to a mounting tide, the country was breaking out in an epidemic of nostalgia for him, and merchants clawed and pawed to cash in on the harvest while his sun was in the sky.

Crocus pushed through the sun-warmed soil in front of the buggy shed and burdock and thistle stuck their heads out of the molding straw and manure in the old corral. In the same manner, long dormant fans were sticking their heads past the molding straw and manure of Sonny's last years and buying anything that bore his name or image. Albums had sold out and were on back order by the tens of thousands, posters, T-shirts, and all manner of Sonnyabilia were being swallowed up at unprecedented rates. The immensity of it all struck him with strange despair at a time when he started to believe he could slip out of the public's consciousness and be forgotten.

After years of worrying over what he would live on for the rest of his life, the prospect of the cash's imminent disgorging became inconsequential, and a renewed terror gripped him, told him that this incredible public outpouring forever sealed the passageway of his return.

Using whatever courage he could muster to keep his daily routine, he'd run a little further each day and then barricade himself in the milk room. With a dogged determination he never realized he possessed, day by day he whittled away at the years of fat and neglect, at the muscles flabby and atrophied from disuse, and after twelve weeks in that self-imposed limbo, the fluid had drained from his bloated face and he found himself in pants and shirt that had miraculously outgrown him.

With the small maul, Sonny nailed a twenty-foot pole to a bright new post while Corkey held the other end. So engrossed in the task at hand, neither of them noticed the red Ford pickup come coasting across the barnyard, catching Sonny out in the open with no chance to duck away. With a small puff of dust the truck squeaked to a stop and a petite dark-haired woman in western blouse and jeans stepped out and lifted a box off the seat.

Sonny understood immediately that this becoming woman represented an alarming danger, not only to his very life in recognition– *My god, you're Sonny Hollister!"*—but the danger that once again he'd try to find healing with this woman in the terror of love.

"Hello, Corkey. How are you?"

Corkey paled. "Hello." He set the pole on the one below and smacked his leather gloves together like he didn't know what else to do.

"And I'm finally going to meet the mystery man."

She handed the cardboard box to Corkey and held out a hand to

Sonny. Without hesitation he dropped the maul, pulled off his leather glove, and took her hand.

"Hi, I'm Sally Ramsey." She smiled warmly.

"Hi, Frank Anderson, but not much mystery I'm afraid."

In the moment he held her small warm hand he forged an instinctive smile and attempted nonchalance. Though not beautiful, Sally came across warm and appealing, a woman who stirred that inner churning he'd all but forgotten, a rain squall across arid land.

"You look like you're working hard," she said.

"Corkey's wearing me out, has to be doing something every minute," Sonny said, measuring her reactions.

With head shaved, glasses in place, and his face camouflaged with beard, he felt naked in her eyes despite his sweat-smudged denim work shirt and jeans.

"I went by an hour ago and noticed you two working, thought you'd appreciate lunch. It's my day off."

"That's awfully good of you, Sally," Corkey said with an uncharacteristic pitch to his voice.

"There's nothing in there you need return, so don't fret."

"Can't you eat with us?" Sonny asked, discovering where Jesse got his large fawn eyes.

"No, thanks, I have things to do." She glanced back and forth between them. "Jesse sure enjoys himself over here, I hope he's not a nuisance, he can get into almost anything if—"

"Oh, no," Sonny said, "I like having him around."

Jesse came from around the barn, riding Toro.

"Look, Mom, look!" Jesse called as he spurred the Hereford out behind the buggy shed.

"Put him away, now, Jess," Sally shouted. "Come on home with me!"

She turned to Sonny. "I'd appreciate it if you'd hold him down a little." Sally's cheery countenance faltered for an instant. "He's been sick and shouldn't overdo."

"I'll watch him."

"Jesse thinks you're the best thing that ever happened around here. All we hear is Frank this and Frank that." She laughed. "Are you going to be here long?"

"Oh . . . I don't know, just helping Corkey get the place in shape while I take a little time off."

"One of these nights I'll have you two over for supper. Bye, Corkey, nice meeting you, Frank. The corral's beautiful."

They both threw good-byes as she walked to the pickup. Fit and trim, she'd reached middle age with a ripened femininity and he couldn't help notice the appealing way she moved. Jesse climbed in and they drove out. When the pickup pulled out onto the county gravel, Corkey came unhinged.

"Oh my God, this is a disaster; this is a catastrophe!" He held his head in his hands, walking in tight circles. "Judas Priest, what are we gonna do?" He pulled off his gloves and threw them on the ground. "You have to get outta here, we both do."

"Relax, I don't think she has a clue."

"A clue! She's probably racing for town right now, TV station, newspapers, radio. I knew something like this would happen, I knew it."

Sonny picked up the box and headed for the cottonwood tree.

"She didn't recognize me, now will you relax."

"Relax! relax! and you invite her to *stay for lunch!*"

"You said we have to act normal. If she hadn't recognized me by then she never will."

"You got to stay outta sight, another month or two, or we'll be dead men."

Sonny sat on the grass and leaned against the tree trunk, looking over the lunch. Part of him shared Corkey's alarm and he struggled to keep his balance.

"C'mon over here and have some lunch."

"I can't eat at a time like this, ya know what I mean."

Sonny took a gulp from a mason jar of cold lemonade and offered it to Corkey. He took a swig and settled on the grass near Sonny.

"I can't take much more of this," Corkey said, "you gotta stay in the house."

Sonny didn't respond but dug into the egg-salad sandwiches and they ate and rested in the April sun while Corkey's pessimism slowly lost steam.

"Hey, did you hear that lady from Montana?" Sonny said. "She thought the corral was beautiful."

Drained from Sally's inopportune visit, Corkey retreated to the house and took a nap. Sonny resumed working, but after an hour of scheming, he kept prodding Corkey to come out and help, wanting

his watchman to be worn out by nightfall. After much needling, he badgered Corkey back to work on the corral.

"When I wanted you to use your first name you wouldn't do it," Corkey said, "but I can't remember why."

"I knew 'Sonny' was small town, but I wanted the people back in Boyd to know it was me, the ones who looked down their noses at my mom and me."

"Your school-girl sweetheart?" Corkey puffed, leaning on his shovel.

"Yeah, her too, but more her tight-assed father. But you know, when you wanted me to drop my nickname, I never really believed I'd ever be famous, never."

Sonny worked with the drawknife as he talked, peeling the scaly bark off the lodgepole.

"The writer asks me the why of everything, and I'm finding out there's a lot I never knew about you."

They worked into late afternoon, always with an eye peeled on the county road, and when the sun slid behind the Tobacco Root range to the west, they put away the tools and stood back for a satisfying appraisal of the day's achievement.

"I think we need a horse, Cork. At least two."

"You want to shovel horse manure?"

"Toro's lonesome, the place needs more animals, a few horses. Why have the best corral in the valley and no horses to appreciate it?"

"If Sally recognized you, *we* won't be around long enough to appreciate it."

Everything went as Sonny anticipated: supper—of which he didn't eat much—Corkey drowsing on the sofa in front of the TV, then off to bed early, muttering his apologies. Sonny waited until he heard that quiet snore. Then he showered, shaved his head, and left one light on in the living room with the TV at low volume for background.

Out into the pitch black barnyard he stood for a minute, listening. The chill of the night brought a shudder to his bones. He knew it would be wiser to wait until Corkey returned to LA, but after meeting Sally and feeling sure he wasn't recognized, he didn't have the will to put it off one day longer.

He slipped into the pickup and started the engine.

Chapter 17

ON THE ROAD to Sally's trailer, memories lost for decades shot into Sonny's awareness like comets, sharp and clear—driving Marvin Goodhue's pickup out the dirt road west of town, his solo driving date, a mouth of cotton, sweating palms, stepping haltingly onto Natalie's porch and knocking, breathless. Somehow he survived her father's interrogation about every move he'd make that night and escaped to the pickup with Natalie in tow. And here he was again, creeping down a country road in a pickup, with no advantage, no credentials, that same shook-up boy from so long ago. What if Sally was gone? What if a boyfriend was there with her? With all the vulnerabilities and possible rejection, he felt as if he were going on his first date. Then it occurred to him, he was.

The faded blue trailer and its adjacent metal shed sat off the road in a gravelly field with no trees, shrubs or lawn to give any semblance of permanence. Beside Sally's rusty Ford there slumped a GMC pickup that caused him some alarm until he remembered Jesse referring to their old junker. With a deep breath, he stroked his beard and stepped out of the truck. A hem of the retreating day outlined the mountain's jagged silhouette to the west. He didn't need his stethoscope to know his heart was beating and when he climbed the three narrow steps and knocked on the aluminum door, he almost expected Natalie's father to open it.

In a moment Sally appeared, smiling warmly with surprise.

"Frank, hello."

"Hi."

"Come in, come in."

She backed away from the door; he stepped in and found himself in a small kitchen. To the right a paneled living room with worn carpet and modest furnishings, to the left a narrow corridor leading to other doors, all whistle clean.

"We destroyed the lunch you brought. I wanted to thank—"

"Oh, that was nothing, but please keep your voice down, Jesse just went to bed; if he hears you he'll be out here like a shot."

She backed into the Pullman kitchen and he followed, caught a scent of her perfume.

"Listen, I'm heading for town to get some food, just stopped to see if you'd want to go along."

"Oh . . . that's nice of you, but I should stay home tonight. Hannah isn't here and I don't like leaving Jesse. Besides, you don't have to—"

"Hey, I'm a helpless tourist looking for a good steak, a cold beer, and maybe a little dancing. I'll probably end up in some dive with terrible food, lousy music, and be no better off than eating Corkey's cooking."

"I really shouldn't. . . ."

"If you're involved with someone—"

"No, no, it isn't that, I just. . . ."

A car pulled into the yard, the trailer door flew open, and four college-age kids scrambled in, ignoring the two of them on their way to the living room, flopping in the available furniture and urging the TV to warm up quickly. Sally stepped around the cupboards.

"Hannah, you going to be home?"

"Yes, *Day Of The Dolphin* is coming on."

Sally looked back at Sonny. He cocked his head and smiled.

"There you go."

"Gosh . . . I really shouldn't." She bit her lip. "Will you give me time to change?"

"As much time as you want, within limits."

They laughed, and Sally stepped back into the living room.

"Hannah, this is Frank Anderson."

Feeling like Clark Kent, Sonny moved to the edge of the room, held his breath and adjusted his glasses. "Hi."

"Hello," the girl said, scrutinizing him.

"And this is Butch," Sally said, nodding at a chubby freckle-faced kid, "and Rock," pointing at a reticent young Indian man who avoided eye contact. Sonny didn't catch the other girl's name as he broke out in a sweat.

"We're going into the Beaumont for a while," Sally said, "okay?"

Hannah glared momentarily at Sonny, not with recognition, but seemingly as a threat to some part of her life. Then she frowned at her mother.

"You ought to stay home and watch this, Mom."

The girl had on a pair of bib overalls with a knit long underwear top tucked in.

While Sally changed, Sonny retreated into the kitchen, exhilarated that three more people had looked him straight in the face and taken him for some anonymous local without batting an eye. Awkwardly alone in the partially lit galley, he stepped aside when a commercial break brought Hannah to the refrigerator for a glass of milk. She turned on a bright fluorescent ceiling light and called back to her friends.

"You want anything?" They didn't.

"Are you going to school?" Sonny said, unable to explain the antagonism she wore as obviously as the overalls.

"As often as the money allows." She kept her back to him. "But *now* we'll probably have to move."

She turned with the disappointment in her voice filling her large eyes, her only likeness to Sally.

"Move?"

"Yeah."

She returned to her friends, and to his relief, Sally appeared. In a light blue pants suit with a white turtleneck sweater she looked alluring, but he didn't dare say so in the present company.

"I'm ready. We'll be at the Beaumont, Hannah, okay?"

The girl didn't answer.

The Beaumont Supper Club stood isolated in a field west of Belgrade on old U.S. 10, and a tenseness crowded into his stomach at the jumble of cars and pickups jammed into the dirt parking lot. A hostess led them to a table, weaving through the congested L-shaped dining room and he was sure that every eye focused on him. At the table he maneuvered into a chair with his back to most of the clientele.

A few couples danced to the live music that funneled out of amplifiers cranked up to a murderous level. Sally pulled her chair closer so they could attempt to converse, and after they had ordered, he relaxed somewhat in the anonymity of the poorly-lit, smoke-filled noise, pumped up at being with people again. It'd been a long time since he'd dined with a woman, that part of him shut down for years, and he caught himself observing the sensuous way she ate her steak and sipped the red wine. Into a second bottle of wine, Sally turned more talkative than her already effusive nature, uninhibited, even silly, and she held onto him when they danced like a woman about to drown. Once, when they were on the floor between songs, the lead singer spoke in a solemn manner.

"This one's for you, Sonny."

Startled, he jerked his head to look at the performer, but the man was gazing at the ceiling.

"Sonny," the singer continued, as if Sonny were hovering somewhere above the Beaumont, "we miss you, big fella."

The group started singing "Carefree Highway" and streamers shot down his legs, panic swarmed over him, and he attempted to sort out the whirlwind of emotions. The vocalist was killing the song, and Sonny wanted to yank the guitar out of his hands and show him how it was meant to sound. A hollowness thudded into his chest and he heard Costello's confidence in crocodile tears.

Sonny Hollister will never sing again!

Sally danced affectionately, slightly woozy, and she laughed at herself. At the table he embroidered a tale of how he'd been selling real estate in Florida for years, and she rambled all over her life and had more wine.

"Oh, this is marvelous," she said, "I don't drink two times a year and I haven't been out like this for ages."

"That's hard to believe. What's wrong with the men around here?"

"Oh, nothing . . . that's not it."

When they danced, her firm waist felt good in his hand and the scent of her hair invited him. The night club emptied, the musicians finished their last set, and those who remained could carry on a conversation without shouting.

"I had a good marriage, I really did," she said. "Gary ran a backhoe, just paid it off, and he was so happy, said it would be all gravy from then on. One spring morning he was digging a sewer line for a new house in Bozeman. When he finished he went down in the trench to find the sewer stub with a shovel like he always did."

Sonny drained the last of the wine into their empty glasses.

"At noon the carpenters noticed he wasn't around, thought he'd gone for lunch."

He noticed the curve of her lower lip.

"Around two the plumber showed up and asked the carpenters

where Gary was, that he couldn't lay the pipe because the front end of the trench had caved in. They all stood there as it dawned on them as simultaneous as a bomb, and then they ran to the ditch."

Sonny set his glass down.

I don't want to hear anymore.

"One side near the street had slumped over and filled the trench. They dug as fast as they could, found him at the bottom by the stub in a crouched position."

Good God, it was his haunted dream, an experience he faced every time he went to sleep. Her husband had been buried alive.

"Hannah was eleven and we'd decided we could afford another kid or two, we always wanted more, but we wanted to wait until we could take care of them. You know, after I got to Bozeman that afternoon and it all sunk in, I called our doctor. I wanted to know if he could save Gary's sperm, if that might still be alive in his dead body. The doctor said it was too late."

She broke down. He reached across and touched her hand.

"God, I wanted another of Gary's kids."

Laughing lightly, she dug a hanky out of her small white handbag and wiped her eyes and nose.

"You might say I didn't do so well the second time around, in too much of a hurry to find another Gary. Sometimes, when things got bad, I'd pray that Gary could come back and save me from Steve, my second husband, and I'd hate Gary for leaving me alone, for being so damn careless with his life." She stuffed the hanky back in her bag and looked at him. "You weren't careless with your life," she said, as if testifying against her lost husband.

"Lady, you don't know what careless is."

"I drank too much, I'm really not—"

"Hey, it's all right, it's all right."

"You want to go out and have a good time, and I'm blabbing away about my problems. I'm sorry, I haven't given you a chance to talk. Have you been married?

"Yes . . . once."

"What happened?"

"She left me.

"Oh, I'm sorry. Was it sudden?"

"Yeah . . . it was sudden." He gently rocked a water glass on the table, clinking the ice cubes. "Like lightning on a clear day."

"Did you love her?"

"Yes."

"I'm really sorry, that has to be devastating. I don't know if it's worse if they die or if they walk out on you . . . at least Gary never walked out on me." She neatened the tablecloth in front of her. "Any children?"

Instantly he could see Tommy running across the lawn on the farm to welcome him home, hear his shrill sweet voice. When Tommy reached him, Sonny would grab him up in his arms and swing him around in the air until they were both laughingly dizzy and they'd fall to the ground in a heap.

"No, no children."

"Have you tried again, found anyone?"

"I don't think I was cut out to be married. I tell a woman right up front: No marriage for me."

"Well, we'll get along fine. Hannah's twenty-one but Jesse's only nine. I'm not going to get serious with anyone until the kids are grown and gone. I don't dare after I botched so badly with Steve. Go out, have some fun, but no getting serious."

"Sounds good to me."

"That's what men say, but they don't listen, don't hear. After a couple dates they want to start getting serious. Are you listening? do you hear me?" Sally said and laughed.

"Loud and clear."

They weren't the last to leave, but the pickup looked abandoned on the outskirts of the nearly-empty parking lot. On the way home through the night chill, a partial moon illuminated the snow on the distant mountains and Sally turned quiet. When he stopped in the yard, she spoke as though her giddiness had been discarded.

"This was fun, Frank, I enjoyed it."

"We going to do this again?"

"Oh . . . I'd better not . . . not for a while, maybe in a few weeks."

He felt her loneliness, heard the sadness in her voice, and for a moment they were awkward, hesitant. She kissed him softly and opened her door.

"Thanks, Frank, don't get out."

Quickly she was out of the truck and up the steps into the mobile home.

The moon had run off like a fickle lover, leaving the valley in a star-pierced blackness. Sonny drove the mile to the ranch in a state of numb. Out in a crowd, eating, dancing, enjoying it all, not a soul in the place gave him a second look. It'd been over twenty years since that happened and it was completely novel to him. Even during his bad years, anywhere he went they spoke to him, the once-great Sonny Hollister, and they could tell their friends they'd talked to him. During those bitter days he shied away from public places more than in good times when he'd be mobbed if he stuck a toenail out of his hotel suite.

He fought to stay in the present, now, in this Montana mountain valley, in his Frank Anderson self, when forces within kept drawing him back to that Christmas in Dallas, to the farm outside Nashville, to lovely faces and voices too painful to allow into consciousness.

That evening he drove out with fear and trembling and returned with a small hope that he could eventually leave this captivity and live in the world again as a normal unnoticed human being. He shut the truck door softly and stood a moment. Then he crept up the steps and unlatched the door, cringing at its squeak, afraid a tired little man might be waiting for him inside.

Chapter 18

THE MOMENT SONNY opened the door he sensed Corkey was up. As though he never intended to sneak in, he banged the door shut, snapped on the ceiling light, and found the jailer entrenched in front of the television in his bathrobe.

"Please tell me you haven't been with Sally," Corkey said matter-of-factly. "Please, God, tell me you haven't been with Sally."

"We had dinner."

Sonny went to the refrigerator and grabbed a half-gallon of orange juice.

"At her place?"

Sonny gulped thirstily from the carton.

"We went to a local joint, good food."

He moved to the living room doorway, using the juice container like a prop in a movie. Corkey looked him over as if searching for evidence on his face or fly.

"If you're going to risk everything on your stupid little escapades you'll have to do it somewhere else, I won't stand for it." Corkey turned back to the TV.

"We just went out for—"

"But now it's *my* ass on the line, and if you can't get along for a few weeks without laying some woman, you're on your own."

"Just because you haven't touched a woman in a hundred years doesn't mean—"

"Look," Corkey said, regarding him with a frown, "this is your last hurrah, kid, and you jeopardize it to go banging the neighbor lady. Jeez, why couldn't you grow up for once?"

"It wasn't anything like that, I just needed some company, so did she."

Sonny shoved the juice carton back into the refrigerator and slammed the door.

"And you never touched her."

"That's right."

Sonny stepped halfway back into the living room.

"I don't believe you," Corkey said, his voice even.

"Well that's too stinking bad. You think that every time I go out with a woman I have to lay her."

"Well?"

"Well nothing!"

"You probably never had a woman for all I know, there are rumors about *you,* old man. You think I'm strange, how the hell about you? It's *normal* for a man to need a woman." Sonny stooped in an attempt to divert Corkey's eyes from the TV. "You're the one who's queer, never wanting to be with a woman. How the hell would you understand!"

Sonny stomped into the kitchen table, slammed himself down in a chair, and pulled off his boots.

"And I never touched her."

Sonny sat silently brooding while the television filled the house with inane dialogue and music. The space between them was littered with the broken glass of resentment and bitterness. He wrestled with accusations and memories and the long accumulated weight of unspoken feelings. When Sonny was about to chance walking through the front room to his bedroom, Corkey snapped off the TV and stood in the doorway, a sock covering his club foot. He leaned into the doorjamb and spoke with his eyes on the floor.

"I was managing a supper club in Dallas, The Silver Spur. Molly came to try out for a singing spot, no experience but a terrific voice. She was gorgeous, young, innocent, and gorgeous. I gave her the job ahead of several more experienced singers and helped her every chance I got."

Corkey pulled out a chair and sat beside the oak table. He gazed back into the living room.

"She was appreciative, thrilled with her big chance, we worked well together, her confidence and stage presence started to catch up to her voice and beauty. I was twenty-nine, and I'd already given up all hope of ever having the kind of woman I wanted. I dared to dream, only half alive when we were apart."

Corkey rubbed his cheek and glanced at Sonny.

"We moved in together, big stuff in those days. I was jealous of other men, but I never said a word, I knew I was eating at the banquet table and had to be satisfied. I wanted to get married, but she kept putting me off, ya know what I mean. I ate, drank, and breathed that girl, an obsession, a mental illness, I knew, but knowing was only a diagnosis, not a cure."

Corkey rubbed his eyes with his fists.

"I never believed I'd experience the raw, sensual pleasure she gave me, I'd see her and touch her. . . ."

His voice drained off to nothing. Sonny squirmed uneasily, wished he'd never opened this old wound. Corkey's voice returned.

". . . and even in the moment of purest heaven, catch myself not believing it was true. She was eighteen when she walked into the club, sweet and loving and thankful for everything I did. Then she wanted to take another offer, I quit my job, went with her, became a manager. She got a good spot singing every night in a downtown hotel."

"You don't have to do this—"

"You started it, now let me finish," Corkey said. "I kept after her to marry me, said she would, we made plans, and I hyped her along, always suspecting I was cutting my own throat."

Corkey ran his fingers through his thinning hair.

"One night she went out with some rich high roller, it was like someone hit me in the stomach with a baseball bat. She said she was sorry, I believed her. She was unsophisticated in a nice way, child-like, ya know what I mean, but it all went to hell. She'd been to see the varmint and she discovered her incredible power over men. They were always better looking than I was, hell, that wasn't hard, and they all had more money than I did."

"That doesn't matter with real love—"

"Grow up, of course it does," Corkey said, "money damn well matters. She got involved with an older guy who had money coming out of his pores. That's why I always hated to see you fooling around with young girls you really didn't give a damn about. I knew that somewhere there were guys like me who loved them."

Corkey glanced at him and Sonny averted his eyes.

"I tried to keep managing her, but it was tearing me to shreds. I'd sit up all night imagining what they were doing, how he was touching her, undressing her, teaching her, I'd go with them step by step in my mind until . . . God, I was going mad."

Corkey snapped his head from side to side, as if to shake the vision from his memory. He sucked air and exhaled.

"Don't do this, Cork, I didn't mean—"

"You asked for it." Corkey regarded him with eyes blazing. "Now shut up and take it!" He caught his breath. "I only lasted a few weeks managing her, being around her, knew I was close to the booby hatch. I left. The last I heard, some oil tycoon took her home and made a house pet out of her. Never heard anything about her since—what a waste."

He slowly shook his head.

"What a waste, she could've made it big. When I wasn't trying to stop the internal bleeding, I regretted losing her as a talent, thought she'd be my only brush with the big time."

He laughed softly, his voice trailing off. Sonny let the silence lie in the room undisturbed until it became unbearable.

"Why didn't you ever find someone else? Shoot, there are thousands of women who'd be real happy to travel with you."

"I'd invested too much in Molly, it tore something in me. I knew it'd always end up that way between a woman and this club-foot. During the worst pain I had a panicky urge to find another woman instantly, to save me from dying, but then I vowed I'd never let myself be hurt like that again and I'd be richer than all those bastards who came around enticing Molly with their god-damn money."

"Did it work?"

"Yeah, it worked. I have a background loneliness, but nothing like the slaughterhouse when Molly left."

Corkey stood up and stuck his fist against his stomach, twisting it as he spoke.

"I've never allowed anyone else to reach in here and grab hold of my guts. Yeah, I want a woman, I need a woman, so what! Now I put my chips somewhere else, a few romps in the sheets along the way maybe, a one-night-stand, but nothing personal. As it turns out, I'm not the kind of guy who gets that much out of a romp in the sack with a stranger, ya know what I mean."

He shuffled toward his bed looking weary, solitary.

"You're smarter than I am," Sonny said, "I never learn."

Corkey stopped just inside the living room and listened.

"I always think a woman has what I'm looking for. . . ."

Sonny unbuttoned the cuffs of his shirt.

"But after I get inside her as deeply as I can, I know I didn't find it, but I never learn, I never do, I see an attractive woman and I think she'll be the one."

Corkey turned and settled wearily on the arm of the sofa.

"My dad kept bees," Sonny said. "Do you know about bees, how the worker bee does a dance to tell the other bees where he found nectar? That's what a woman is like to me, her swaying belly and hips and thighs point out where I can find the sweet nectar that'll keep me alive. I was always so damn glad I was famous and wealthy, it made it so much easier. They came humming, offering their honeycomb, and I'd keep tasting. Now . . . I don't think there is a woman who can love me the way I want to be loved. That kind of love doesn't exist."

He stood and pulled his shirttails out of his jeans.

"Listen," Sonny said, "I'm sorry about what—"

Corkey stood and waved a hand.

"Forget . . . I'm just plenty scared they'll find us out and you'll be dead and I'll be remembered as a swindler, a goddamn circus con man, that's all, ya know what I mean. I think getting involved with Sally is stupid, it's way too soon for you to be running around in public."

"No one recognized me. I'm just trying not to go nuts, I want to be around people, I want to get a guitar."

"No! No guitar, you sing in the shower if you want, but no guitar. Judas Priest, you got some crazy notion that you *want* to be discovered, like some of those psycho killers?"

"No, no . . . I just want to sing."

"If you even *see* a guitar you pretend you think it's a shovel, for God's sake."

"Okay, okay, quit worrying."

Corkey searched his face intently for a moment and then turned for his bed.

"That's my job to do the worrying. You sure as hell don't do any. See you in the morning."

With the house darkened, Sonny sat quietly on the edge of his bed. A slight breeze ruffled the curtains. In all their time together, Corkey had never opened the rusted gate on the wall of his soul. In the morning that passage would probably be bolted and sealed more securely than before, Corkey would be his crusty self, and Sonny would never mention the brief hemorrhage that bloodied the ranch house kitchen at two in the morning.

With the rope secured around his waist, he hoped for sleep, knowing Corkey was dead right. He should stay the hell out of Sally's life. The vicious words he spewed at Corkey upset him and he wished he hadn't hurt his only friend. God, he admired him, sucking it up and going on in life without Molly, living with the pain and sorrow and never letting on. Where was Molly now? Was she happy? It was sad. All Corkey's money and all Corkey's fame couldn't bring Molly back again.

Before he drifted into sleep, his last thought surprised him. Corkey ought to be thankful that Molly loved him for a season. No one can expect more than that.

Chapter 19

AFTER RUNNING more than four miles, with a few lung-burning wind sprints along the way, Sonny assaulted the tonnage in the milk room as if it were a lifelong enemy. After more than two hours of lifting, he finished with the bench press. Sweat ran freely off his face and into his beard.

He lived in a continual state of apprehension with the onrushing tide of fans coming out of hibernation. Corkey played the hand in LA, Nashville, New York, reaping a harvest in what they both thought was fallow ground. Resting the barbell in the supports, he sat up, his sixth set.

With fanaticism he drove himself to change the last echo of his past and the visible signs of his tortuous work encouraged him. One more set and then a rewarding shower. He reduced the weight by ten pounds and lay back on the bench. If he put in a long day, the corral could be horse-tight by dark. He hefted the bar. *One* . . . it would be fun to look for a horse . . . *two* . . . Jesse had been over riding Toro Saturday, but he hadn't seen Sally, *three* . . . the fear he harbored about moving back into the mainstream of life seemed to peel away with his fat . . . *four* . . . straining, one more . . . *f-i-v-e*. Done!

In his sweat-drenched T-shirt and jeans he stood in front of the full-length mirror and flexed. He couldn't believe his eyes, the fat man was leaving. Emerging from pudgy flesh like bedrock, he could barely recognize the faint definition of muscles never before visible. He penciled in his progress on the chart he'd taped to the wall, meticulous in keeping track of the total poundage. In eight separate exercises, thirty-four sets, he'd lifted three thousand seven hundred and sixty pounds. Good, and he flung it in the face of his childhood demon—the Oliver 90 weighed six thousand two hundred and eighteen pounds.

When he stepped out of the shower he heard knocking on the door. While pulling on his jeans, he hopped to the kitchen window. An old army Jeep sat over by the barn, empty. He crept to the door and peered through the curtained window. When he could see no one on the porch, he opened the door slowly and spotted a short man in rubber boots and a large black cowboy hat searching the yard. The stranger, craggy, eroded, walked toward the barn with a gimpy stride.

"Hello! What do you need?" Sonny stepped out on the porch.

"Huh." The man turned, acknowledged him, and came toward the house. "Hezekiah Linesinger here. Need ta turn the water inta yer pasture if you'll allow."

He stopped short of the porch and squinted up at him. Sonny stepped down and held out his hand.

"I'm Frank Anderson, good to meet you."

The stumpy man took his hand and gave it one firm pump before releasing it. Tobacco stain creased the side of his mouth, and Sonny noticed teeth missing along with a finger on the man's right hand.

"They've opened up the water, all the brush and junk's plugging my culvert, tear out my ditch if I don't turn the water."

He spat a juicy wad into the greening grass and gave Sonny the impression that time was wasting. With his rolled-down hip boots he looked like the Ancient Mariner lost in a wide-brimmed western movie.

"That's fine, whatever you have to do. Let me get my boots and I'll help you."

Happy with the diversion, Sonny hurried into the house and grabbed his shirt and rubber boots. When he came out, the weathered man was over working at the ditch that ran along the far side of the barn. Dry since Sonny had been at the ranch, it was running bank full.

"I can lick her before dark."

The rancher had placed two boards in the wooden head gate, sending the water flooding out onto the west pasture and preventing it from flowing down the ditch toward his land. His left leg appeared to be stiff and when he hop-scotched for the Jeep he nodded at Toro in the pen.

"That the fatted calf?"

"No, nobody's eating *him*, he's running in the Kentucky Derby."

Linesinger threw a leg into the old Army vehicle and followed with his body.

"Need any help?" Sonny asked.

"Whal, it ain't yer trouble."

Sonny sensed the old man wanted help but wouldn't ask for it.

"What do I need?"

"Got a shovel?"

"I'll get it."

Sonny ran to the shed and returned with the long-handled shovel. The World War II relic started with a horrendous roar, and Sonny climbed in. Hezekiah popped the clutch and sprayed the tool shed with bits of gravel and they catapulted out behind the buildings, racing cross-country, along Sonny's running path but at ten times the speed.

Holy Jeez, no muffler, no springs, no driver!

The rancher never slowed for the humps and dips, and Sonny grabbed the top of the windshield as he bounced free of the seat.

"Yeehaaw, whooeee!" Sonny shouted, "I'd like to get you on the Santa Monica freeway at five in the afternoon."

Damn, you're from Florida, remember, Florida!

They galloped through an open gate at the edge of Corkey's property and when Linesinger locked the brakes, they skidded several yards and stopped within a few feet of the plugged culvert. Overflowing the ditch, water was carving a wider and wider gap in the bank.

Hezekiah pulled up his boots and went into the ditch, over the boot tops, waist deep. He began struggling with the tangled debris and Sonny followed him into the water.

"Aaaaah!" Sonny shouted, his breath sucked out of him by the cold shock. "Holy Toledo!"

"That'll put hair on yer eyeballs," Hezekiah said.

Sonny got his footing and yanked on a wedged willow branch. They worked side by side, tugging at the limbs and gobs of trash against the water's pressure, and Sonny couldn't help but think that Hezekiah was about the age his father would be.

With an instinctive urgency he began tearing at the wedged branches and rubbish, ripped out stubborn clumps and hurled them onto the bank, stumbled and fell and attacked the snarled hodgepodge with his bare hands, breathless, sweating, unrelenting.

"Whoa down there a mite," Hezekiah said, "yer goin' like yer sweetheart's buried in there or somethin'."

Sonny stopped for a moment, surprised at his sudden frenzy, caught his breath.

"Let's whip this mother!" Sonny shouted.

They both took hold of a large tree limb tangled with straw and weeds. Just short of double hernia it broke loose, sending the two of them crashing back into the water. The dam broke, water exploded through the culvert like a huge flushing toilet, and they floundered in the mud and water.

"Git yer ass out!" Hezekiah shouted.

Sonny clawed his way up the slippery bank as the water gushed away, pulling the remaining debris with it. The water level rapidly receded, no longer pouring through the washout it had eaten in the bank.

Hezekiah stood dripping and screeched with laughter. "Ye've been baptized in the Jordan, son." He slapped his leg and rocked back on his heels. "Only trouble is, I ain't the Baptist."

He spat into the flowing water and then lay on his back and lifted his boots at just the right angle and the water ran out and splashed on the ground. Sonny imitated the waterlogged rancher but didn't achieve the correct angle, re-soaking his underwear and back with the icy residue from inside his boots.

"Aaaahh, damn!" He jumped up.

The gimpy old man went to the Jeep, his boots squishing and squashing with every step, and retrieved his worn-round shovel. Sonny waddled for his shovel, and they began throwing dirt into the breech. Sonny warmed up quickly with the work.

He remembered his baptism, in front of the whole congregation when he was nine or ten. All the other kids had been baptized when they were babies, so it was a minor spectacle, kneeling in front of the baptismal font, his mother beside him, in a suit that was too small, the one he'd worn at his father's funeral. After his dad was killed, his mother saw to it he got baptized; she wasn't taking any chances, though he never understood how getting baptized could protect him from overturning tractors. Sure the other kids were giggling, he watched the preacher's shoes through the ceremony—they needed polishing. In the hot and humid church he thought of crawling over to the sacristy door and sneaking out the back when the cool water surprised him, running off his hair and down his face. It felt good in the oppressive heat and formality.

"Thomas Rudolph Hollister, I baptize thee in the name of the Father, and of the Son, and of the Holy Ghost. Amen."

Several people made a fuss over him after the service, and he wondered why. Happy to get out of that scratchy wool suit, he never wore it again.

He and the old rancher worked in the cadence of their labored breathing and grunts, and Sonny, who was amazed at how much ground the water had torn away, slung dirt in step with this curious neighbor. Even when he fell in the water, his weather-beaten hat—patched in several places like an inner tube—stuck on his head.

"Ya gonna farm this summer?" Hezekiah said.

"No, I don't think so."

"Good, then there'll be plenty of water. Pearson was al'ays cuttin' me short. First thing I thought when I hears he kicked the bucket was Now I'll git ma water back."

Linesinger worked at a steady rhythm, not fast, but enduring, pacing himself over the years. He impressed Sonny, appearing as tough and durable as rawhide, outlasting whatever this land had thrown at him through the years. Sonny couldn't keep pace with the older man, just when he thought he was getting in shape, and he attempted to slow Hezekiah down with conversation.

"How much land do you have?"

"About three-twenty."

"It looks better than ours."

"'Tis."

"What do you raise?"

Sonny caught his breath, sweating while his clothes were drying in the sun and air.

"Ya mean besides hell." He snickered. "Alfalfa . . . barley . . . a few cows. . . ."

He gave an answer with each pitch of his shovel, then stopped and leaned on the handle.

"Sweetest alfalfa in the valley, if the damn weather'd ever let a body git it in."

He took a plug out of his shirt pocket, slightly soggy from the dunking, bit off a chunk, maneuvered it around between his gum and cheek, and went back to throwing the sandy loam into the breech.

"They been sniffin' round yer place?" he asked.

"Who?" Sonny picked up the pace again.

"They's after this piece ah ground. Ain't getting it."

"Who wants it?"

"Damn developers, want to build houses all over this land. Ain't meant fer houses, never was. Meant fer alfalfa, barley, good timothy hay. Keep offerin' me more money, every time, more money. What would I do with it if I didn't have no land? Dumbasses."

Hezekiah picked up a rock and tossed it into the cut.

"That city feller still own yer place?"

"Yeah, friend of mine, Corkey Sullivan, it's his place."

"I hope ta hell he ain't gonna sell."

"No."

For the first time Sonny realized that he didn't want Corkey to sell the ranch either.

They shoveled dirt for almost half an hour without speaking, and Sonny was rapidly burning out. At last, Hezekiah stopped and spoke, the cut in the bank nearly repaired.

"You know the law?"

"What kind of law?" Sonny stopped and caught his breath.

"Last time that slicker was out he sez he can git my ground with the law, legal stuff."

"Have you paid your taxes?"

Sonny wiped his bald head with a sleeve.

"Believe so, al'ays did, my pappy al'ays did, ever since he come on this land. Al'ays been Linesinger land, al'ays will be."

"Do you have any family?"

"Nope. Jest me and Partner."

"Who's Partner?" Sonny asked, relieved to be resting.

"My dog . . . dad blame it! there I go agin. Was my dog, keep fergittin' he died." He leaned on his shovel, gazing out across the land. "'T's all the family I got."

By early afternoon they'd repaired the ditch.

"I'll give ya a lift back," Hezekiah said, setting his shovel in the Jeep.

"No, thanks . . . I'll walk."

"Whal, if you'd turn the water back when ya git there, I'd welcome it. My ground can use it." He climbed into the olive drab machine and cranked it over. "Come on, Partner!"

"You better check on your taxes," Sonny shouted, but the uproarious engine drowned out his voice. The battered vehicle sped away with the wide-brimmed black hat the only evidence it had a driver.

He walked back along the ditch in the pleasant sunshine, tired and thirsty and a shiver of peace coursed through him. Hezekiah Linesinger, son of a gun, probably didn't have two dimes in his pocket, yet most important to him, he had his land, was wedded to it, his lover and family and life. There was something about the land Sonny couldn't name, but he felt it in his bones, and it was a good feeling.

Chapter 20

SPRAWLED IN THE upholstered chair, Sonny was dozing while watching TV when a faint rapping at the back door startled him. He sat up and listened to the gusting wind. Could be a tree limb against the porch. It came again, tentative, almost apologetic. He checked his watch; ten twenty-four. Who on earth would be knocking at this time of night? In his stocking feet he shuffled into the kitchen without turning on the light and peered through the window in the door. Pitch dark. When he snapped on the outside light he found Sally standing on the porch in a bulky turquoise jacket and jeans. He unbolted the door and swung it open.

"Hey, is everything all right?"

"Hi, yeah, fine . . . I was just going by and. . . ."

"Come in, come in."

She moved into the kitchen and shook out her dark shoulder-length hair. He locked the door.

"How've you been?" he said as he sucked in his stomach and tucked in his shirt tails.

"Fine, good, I hope I'm not imposing—"

"No, no—"

"It's so late, I shouldn't have stopped, gosh, maybe I'd better—"

"I was going to call," he said, "but I thought—"

"I know, I know, I just dropped over to see how you and Corkey were getting on."

"Corkey's in L.A."

"Oh . . . well, how are you getting on?" She laughed lightly, standing stiffly by the door. "Jesse told me all about Saturday. That boy is really taking to you."

"Would you like to go somewhere, get a drink?"

"No . . . no, thanks . . . it's late."

"We could catch the late movie on the tube," he said.

Sonny moved a few steps toward the front room. She paused, indecision danced lightly in her eyes.

"Maybe I should go."

"C'mon." He nodded toward the living room.

She started to unzip her jacket and hesitated. Her large eyes fought off something interior. He nodded again.

"Okay," she said, "I can sure use the distraction."

She pulled off her jacket and hung it over a kitchen chair, revealing a pink sweater she filled alluringly. Like rehearsing actors they stepped into the living room and she slid beside him on the old sofa. Her perfume came gently and took prisoners while *Rio Lobo* was already up to speed.

"Have you seen this one?" Sonny asked.

"I don't think so but they're all alike: someone makes John Wayne mad and he gets revenge."

He appreciated the way the sagging sofa brought them together involuntarily, and he felt her warmth against his arm. When he stretched to turn up the volume he grabbed his back with one hand.

"Ooooh."

"You hurt yourself?"

"Hezekiah Linesinger almost killed me today, helped him fill in a wash-out in his ditch. Holy smoke can that little man work. You know him?"

"No, I don't. See him fly by now and then. Where does it hurt?"

Sally ran her hand across his back, searching for the soreness. She pressed hard, and he winced.

"How'd you like a good massage?"

"You know how?"

"I earned my living that way at a women's spa in Billings. Gave it up when we moved here, although I could have worked in Bozeman doing both men and women but Gary wouldn't hear of it. He used to love them after he spent the day on the backhoe." She stood. "Take your shirt off, you can watch the movie while I do you. Have any baby oil or lotion?"

"Some hand lotion by the kitchen sink, will that do?"

He stood and unbuttoned his shirt.

"That's fine. Get a sheet and blanket."

She went to the kitchen and when he returned with the bedding, she'd turned out every light in the house; only the glow from the TV accented the inviting scene. Barefooted, Sally was kneeling on the rug with the lotion in hand. She'd removed her sweater and wore a white tank-top that made his mouth go dry. She wore no bra. Glad he'd shed much of his fat in the past months, he was angry and embarrassed that some lard still clung stubbornly to his frame. He sucked in his gut and pulled off his shirt while she spread the bedding over the rug. A familiar excitement coursed through his veins as he knelt on the sheet.

"I should ask what you charge before you start, you may be too expensive for me."

"Haven't you ever had a professional massage?"

"No . . . don't think I have."

"Let's start where you're sore."

He lay on his stomach, facing the TV. She covered her hands with lotion and smoothed it over his back. Immediately he lost all interest in the problems John Wayne was up against somewhere around Rio Lobo as her fingers began a soothing rhythm on the large muscles of his back. He realized how much he missed the magic of Kim's touch, the Korean masseusé who used to travel with him wherever he went. A good massage was part of the first baggage tossed in the ditch on his downhill slide.

Sally was good, knowing how to use her fingers to unknot and comfort his aching muscles.

"Aaaah, that's great."

"How come you never had any kids?" she asked, working the back of his neck.

"I don't know . . . I guess I didn't think I'd be much of a father, working all the time and. . . ."

He tried to censor all information moving between his mind and his tongue without too much hesitation and slippage in between. He decided it best to tell half-truths, allowing for fewer errors than a whole new pack of lies.

"From what I hear from Jesse, kids would love you."

"Oh, that's different. I don't have to raise him; we're just buddies."

"Well, if your marriage didn't last it's probably best, though I don't know what I'd do without Hannah and Jesse."

She worked his shoulders, finding hungry places he didn't know he had.

"Oh, God . . . you're terrific."

But there was a problem. A traitor in the ranks had risen and Sonny was concerned about how deeply he'd become involved if he took advantage of her obvious vulnerability. She worked down to the small of his back.

"You'll have to let me return the favor," he said, turning that delicious prospect over in his imagination, fantasizing removing her tank top and rubbing lotion along her spine.

Suddenly the back door rattled in its jamb as though someone were attempting to knock it down. Sonny sprang up beside her.

"Sally! I know you're in there!" The voice was harsh, more like a growl. "Sally, you get out here, now, you hear me!"

"Oh God, what'll I do, what'll I do?" she said, frozen in place.

"Who in hell is that?"

"Steve, my ex."

"What's he want?" he asked, getting to his knees.

"He follows me around, acts like we're still married."

"Stay right here," Sonny whispered, "stay right here."

He pulled on his shirt. The banging and shouting continued. Damnit, what if this jerk had a gun? Sonny crept to the kitchen window and tried to see the bastard in the darkness. An axe handle they'd bought to replace the one he broke stood in the entry. He picked it up, snapped on the porch light, and swung open the door. With the oak handle in his fist, he expected to hear a muzzle blast any instant, sweat immediately running down his face and chest. In black leather jacket and crewcut, the man backed off the porch as though he couldn't stand the light.

"Who in the hell are you?" Sonny said.

Around six foot, the guy carried more than two hundred pounds in a square, solid build, despite a large gut, and Sonny knew instantly he didn't want anything to do with the man.

"You get Sally out here, now, or is she hustling to get her whoring clothes back on?"

His face was almost handsome if it weren't for a mean turn of his mouth. With wide-eyed rage he stared up at Sonny, his fists clenched at his side, weaponless, to Sonny's great relief.

"You get her out here, or I'm coming in and dragging her out."

Sonny stood in the doorway with his legs slightly spread, tapping the axe handle in his left hand. He felt an ancient rage gathering in his chest.

"Sally isn't here. She was nice enough to lend me her truck when mine broke down. Now I want to get some sleep, and you're trespassing. Do you mind?"

"What's wrong with your truck?"

"Battery's dead."

"Why would she let you use her truck if you weren't diddling her?"

"I don't know her that well, but I guess she's a good neighbor."

"Huh, a good neighbor lay."

Sonny ventured forward an inch or two on the porch, holding in his stomach and standing tall.

"Look it, fella, you're way off base, whoever you are, and I'm beginning to lose my patience. You don't want to be standing there when I do."

"Hey, I *know* she's in there."

He seemed to be losing his focus, maybe entertaining the thought that he could be making an ass of himself.

"Isn't any of my business, but I heard Sally was divorced."

"Don't believe in all that garbage, everyone running around getting divorced. She's my wife, and every time I go on the road she's in someone else's bed."

Ramsey wiped his mouth with the back of his hand and Sonny couldn't tell if he'd been drinking.

"You saying she isn't here?" He wasn't sure any more.

"She isn't here."

Sally's ex-husband balked in the glare of the naked porch light. Then he pointed and snarled.

"If I find out you're lying, I'll be back."

He spun around and quickly disappeared into the murky night beyond the light's arc.

Sonny stepped inside, slammed the deadbolt home, and turned out the porch light. The TV illuminated the living room in flickering shadows, but Sally was gone.

"Where are you?" he called in a whisper.

There was no answer. He checked the front door, afraid that she'd taken off for the trailer and that idiot would overtake her in his headlights.

"Sally," he called, turning on the light in the bedroom.

"Is he gone?"

Her words came muffled. He found her huddled on the closet floor, trembling until her teeth chattered. He lifted her to him and embraced her.

"Hey, it's okay, it's okay, he's gone, he doesn't think you're here."

He held her tightly and tried to calm the fear that shuddered through her body, inhaled the scent of her and tried to sort out his colliding emotions.

"What'll I do, what'll I do?"

"Shoot, why didn't I just tell him you were here, and it was none of his stinking business. You're a free woman, we don't have to sneak around like we're cheating on someone."

"No-o-o-o, don't ever do that—he'd *kill* me."

"Okay, okay," he said, frightened by the intensity of the terror that washed over her face

He led her into the living room, arm in arm, neither willing to break their embrace. She wrapped her arms around his waist and pulled him tightly against her, breathing rapidly. He kissed her, a fragile bird in a fierce mountain gale, trembling, kissing him deeply, inviting him, no, pleading with him, to enter her storm. She looked into his eyes with a prayer he recognized.

"I've had a vasectomy."

"Good." She nearly pulled the buttons off his shirt.

On the way to the floor they removed their clothing and in a frenzied heat they fed off each other, tasting, stroking, searching, as if they might find life in the other's body. In a burning bed of fear they made love, she more frantic than he, as though seeking safety in the wedding of their flesh. John Wayne was also fighting back fear with his gun.

When the storm blew itself out they lay in each others arms, their wet parts slowly uncoupling though they clung to each other as if they were falling.

"I haven't been honest with you, Frank, and now I've gotten you mixed up in it. I'm sorry."

"It's okay, you—"

"No, it was wrong not to forewarn you. My ex-husband is a trucker, and after the divorce I didn't see him for over five years, he never sent me a dime, never wrote or asked about Jesse, but a year ago he just showed up one day."

She snuggled her head on his chest.

"At first he was nice, visited with the kids, hung around for a few days and then went on the road. The next time he showed up he was angry, accused me of going out on him. I couldn't believe it; he hit me a couple of times. I was seeing two men from around here, nothing serious, more like friends. He beat the hell out of one of them, burned up the car of the other, although nothing could be proven."

Son of a gun! Sonny didn't want to hear any more.

"He spread the word that he'd better not catch anyone fooling around with his wife. I'm not his *wife!*" She banged her fist on the floor. "Now you know why I haven't been on a date for eight months. I should've told you, let you know what you were getting into, but I really needed to go out the other night, and now, to be with you."

"And that's why your daughter wasn't too excited about seeing a man around?"

"I told her if Steve bothered us anymore we'd move away."

Doggone it, he didn't want to get mixed up with some yahoo trucker. But she was so vulnerable, all her troops scattered, and it angered him that this tin-horn could threaten these decent people and screw up their lives. He remembered when he and his mother were caught out in the open.

"It's all right; I like you and Jesse, and I don't give a Monkey's mother about your ex-husband. If he doesn't like it, he knows where I live."

He heard himself playing a familiar role from one of his insufferable movies and he realized he'd have to back up these lines with his own ass.

All at once she sat up with a start, as though she'd forgotten where she was and what was happening to her.

"I've got to get home."

He sat up, wrapping his arms around her from behind, cuddling her nakedness. They stared into the TV screen, blaring a late-night advertisement at all the sleepless faces. Sonny Hollister was singing, the picture cutting from one scene to another, showing him in various performances at the height of his popularity, cascading Sonny with free-falling memories that he could neither sort out nor block.

A salesman's voice hammered the hard sell: a fabulous album or eight-track of golden hits, unavailable in any store, operators standing by at the toll free number. Don't pass up this once-in-a-lifetime offer. Sonny winced, thankful she couldn't see his face. The announcer raved about the gone-forever folk singer, and the folk singer had returned to save her as surely as if John Wayne had materialized out of the screen and taken her in his arms. His life had turned into a lousy fairy tale.

"Did you like his music?" she asked.

"Whose music?"

"Sonny Hollister's."

"Oh . . . it was okay."

"I must go, the kids." She fumbled with her clothing.

"I'll take you, bring the truck back here to make it look like I really borrowed it, in case he drives by again."

She went into the bathroom to straighten up. He pulled on his boots, slipped out the back door, and stood quietly until his eyes became accustomed to the darkness. In the moonless sky there were more stars than he'd ever seen. He listened, holding his breath to find any sound, the snap of a twig, a crunching leaf. Only the mournful hoot of an owl from far back in the fields. Sally stole out of the house, and they slid into the pickup like thieves. He had her lie down on the seat with her head in his lap.

Sonny slowly coaxed the Ford out through the yard, without lights, barely able to make out the tire tracks while he peered through the discolored windshield. When he turned onto the county road, he was able to distinguish the broader roadway more easily and decided to attempt the mile without the lights unless another car came on the scene. They rolled over the gravel at a hiking pace and the one mile in that menacing atmosphere stretched on like ten until, at last, he could recognize the unlit mobile home off in the field.

With caution he turned into her drive, hoping he wouldn't miss the narrow wooden planking crossing the ditch. The old GMC pickup lurked in the darkness as a witness that she was home. He swung a slow circle in the yard, heading the truck out, and turned off the ignition. The truck shuddered to a stop without brake lights to be seen. Sally leaned toward him and kissed him lightly on the mouth.

"Thanks. I'll talk to you tomorrow."

"Want me to stay here tonight?"

His stomach knotted.

"No, that would make things worse, take the truck, I'll lock myself in."

Shrouded by the night, her form glided the steps and vanished within the dark aluminum dwelling. No light came on.

The trip back took half as long though he drove no faster. Some relief flowed through his exhausted body, slackening his grip on the steering wheel and allowing a sudden drowsiness to settle in his eyes. God, it had been a long time since he'd been with a woman, and Sally was a warm, giving lover. Already he wanted her again.

Safely in the yard, he parked the pickup where Ramsey had seen it. Once inside with the deadbolt in place, he felt drained, almost faint. He pulled off his boots and lay down on the rumpled sheet where they had found each other so insatiably only minutes before, feeling safer there on their scented bedding.

Like thunderstorms his feelings and memories swirled, giving him the impression he was floating outside of time and place. His compassion for Sally mingled with former passions, and anger generated from Ramsey's threats mingled with the rage he'd stored along the way, adrenalin turned loose with nowhere to go. Damnit, there were no more hangers in the closet of his heart for other garments of woe.

Sally generously offered him intimate shelter in the lee of her embrace, life for a moment while they were sharing heart-beats. Somehow he didn't believe Ramsey, that she was leapfrogging from bed to bed, but he suspected rather that she was as lost as he, simply trying to stay alive to see what life was going to come up with next.

After he lost Julia and Tommy, who had centered his life for the first and only time, he knew people thought him stupid in the piercing light of fame. But he understood all along that he used the fast living to hold off something dark, that when he was making love with a woman he was alive, and safe, receiving some magical flow of life from her, a transfusion, a life-sustaining mercy. And he did love them, for what it was worth, the only way he knew. Maybe that was the reason he reached out to so many. When they'd give him their room key it wasn't just a piece of ass they were offering, it was a small piece of eternal life. And the media portrayed him like some kid let loose in a candy store. Hell, he knew what he was doing, knew he needed to end some greater separation, to be reunited with something in the universe everlasting, needed a woman to keep him alive, but he didn't have one. All he had was a candy jar full of room keys.

Chapter 21

WHEN SALLY CAME THROUGH the door, her ex-husband grabbed her from behind and held an iron hand over her mouth. With terror in her throat she watched Frank drive out of the yard. After Steve threw her onto the couch, he turned on the television in the darkened trailer.

"So, weren't with that bald-headed cowboy, huh."

With the back of his hand he slapped her across the face. Immediately blood ran warm in her mouth.

"Dead battery, huh?"

He punched her in the head, changing the sound of his voice in her ear while the TV's garble muted the sounds of violence.

"You know what husbands can do when their wives go whoring?"

When he unhooked his belt buckle and yanked the belt from his pants, she sprang up and tried for the door, but he caught her with his vice-like grip and dragged her back to the sofa. In the confusion and blur of the struggle, she saw Jesse slip out the door, knowing there was only one place he would go.

Sonny awoke in a sweat, dreaming the idiot trucker was banging on the door again. With his thoughts muddled, he sat upright on the living room floor and the banging intensified, but it was Jesse's voice he heard.

"Frank, Frank!"

He sprang to his feet and stumbled to the door. Jesse fell into his arms, barefooted and wearing only pajamas.

"What's the matter?" Sonny shouted.

He steadied the exhausted boy by the shoulders, and Jesse tried to speak, stuttering empty syllables, breathless.

"Is _he_ there?"

The boy gasped for air and nodded. Sonny pulled on his boots, grabbed the axe handle, picked up Jesse with one arm, and dashed for the pickup. The truck was all but out of control when he careened into Sally's yard and dynamited the brakes. With the axe handle in hand, he burst through the door.

Sally huddled on the sofa in a bathrobe, her face swollen and bruised, while Hannah ran water in the kitchen sink. Sonny glanced around the trailer.

"Is he gone?"

"Yes," Sally said, "a few minutes ago."

"Damn!"

Jesse hobbled in and flopped in a kitchen chair. Sonny laid the axe handle on the table and gently sat beside Sally on the sofa.

"God, I'm sorry, I came as fast as I could."

"I'll live," Sally said with a raspy voice.

Hannah came with a washcloth and attempted to remove the visible signs of brutality from Sally's face. He had to turn away; his chest heaved with rage.

"What're we going to do?" Sally said.

"Put that bastard in jail for openers!" Sonny said.

"I've heard that before," Hannah said.

She carried the bloodied washcloth to the kitchen.

"Jeez, I wish I'd gotten here in time. Let's see how brave he is when he's not beating up women!"

He stomped around the tiny living room and Sally limped over to Jesse, who slumped at the dinette table, pale and exhausted.

"You did good, hon, are you all right?"

"Yeah . . . my feet hurt."

"You done good, Jess," Sonny said.

Sally examined the bottoms of his feet.

"You cut them on the gravel, let's get something on them."

She led him down the hall and Sonny joined Hannah in the kitchen

"She'll never go to the police," Hannah said.

"Has he beaten her before?"

"You get one guess." She spit the words.

"Why won't she have him arrested?"

She turned for her room and spoke quietly over her shoulder.

"Someone better . . . before it's too late."

Sonny picked up the phone, opened the phone book on the kitchen counter, and flipped through the pages for sheriff. He found the number on the inside of the front cover and dialed, feeling the flame in his nostrils. On the second ring he slammed the phone in its cradle. Out of the storm it suddenly occurred to him that if he got involved with the law, the sheriff might want to know who *he* was, where he came from. He might have to testify in court if he brought the charges, there could be photographs, publicity in the papers.

Sally returned from bedding down Jesse and settled gingerly at the small formica table.

"I'm worried about him, he ran all the way to your place in just his pajamas."

"I'm worried about you," he said, leaning back against the kitchen counter. "He's young, that won't hurt him any."

She gave him a menacing glance. "He's not well."

"Why won't you jail that yellow skunk, put him away? God, woman, after this?"

He threw one hand in the air.

"I can't, you don't understand." She spoke through swollen lips. "But I know I have to get Hannah and Jesse out of here. Especially Hannah. I'm afraid what it's doing to her."

"How about you? You sure you're not hurt?" He gently felt her back and arms. "What did he do to you?"

Sally gazed at the floor.

"What did he do to you?" he whispered.

He squatted beside her and with his hands gently turned her face toward him. She averted her eyes.

"He raped you?" he whispered.

She nodded. Rage rose out of his chest, stuck in his throat, and he was unable to reply. He felt wounded, violated, as if that psycho trucker had invaded his personal ground and family.

When he saw to it that Sally got to bed as comfortably as possible with an ice bag and aspirin, he assured her he'd be there the rest of the night. With the axe handle lying across his chest, he stretched out on the couch in an attempt to sleep.

By God, he'd have Corkey get him a handgun when he returned from LA and then he'd squash that psycho like a cockroach.

Chapter 22

THE RAIN THAT had fallen steadily for days lifted gently and Corkey noticed the animated sky while driving from the airport. He hurried for the house through the dripping yard with good news in his satchel.

"Jeez, am I glad to see you." Sonny held the door wide.

"You don't know how right you are."

Corkey set his attache case on the table and shook off the wet bombs the cottonwoods had dropped.

"How are things on the range?"

"I want you to go into Bozeman and get me a handgun."

"Oh, that's nice. Who do you plan to shoot?"

Corkey hung his damp suit coat over the back of a chair and attempted to look unperturbed.

"Sally's ex-husband came pounding on the door like KGB, threatened me in the middle of the night, then went over and beat her half to death and raped her. I'm not going to let him do that again."

Sonny stood ready to fight, his fists and jaw clenched.

"Oh no-o-o, that's terrible, is she all right?"

"Yeah, I don't know, she's healing . . . but what does that do to a woman?"

"Is the guy in jail?"

"She won't call the police and I can't. If I beat the crap out of him, he could have me picked up and they might fingerprint me. That's why I need a gun."

"Tell me that you're not serious, tell me please that you're joking."

"I'm not joking, I'm dead serious!"

"That sounds like a good plan for keeping a low profile, blow a hole in a neighbor and make the national news. Why not just tattoo your name on your ass and run around naked?"

Corkey sat in a chair and opened the leather case.

"God help me!" Sonny shouted, "I don't know what to do!"

He dropped into a chair on the other side of the table.

"Sally's in a meat grinder, and she needs help. There's really nothing between us, believe it or not, but even if she was an ugly old wart, I wouldn't let that psycho come back and pound on her whenever he took a notion."

Corkey looked up from the attache case.

"Hey, Son, stay out of it. You can't get involved with Girl Scout cookies right now, ya know what I mean. Let it go. I know it's hard, but life's hard. You can't right the world. Just take a deep breath, take another salt tablet, and drive on by."

"I can't, I did that in my other life, I'm not doing it again."

"We adopting a new family here, to replace Julia and Tommy?"

"Maybe . . . maybe I am, but I want to count to someone, to mean something. This is my chance to get it right. When everyone thought I was dead I realized that there wasn't a stinking soul on earth who really cared."

"Just a million fans."

"But not one special woman, or a kid . . . only my mother, God bless her."

"Listen to me, my friend, you're not responsible for these people. They're just neighbors down the road."

"Cork, I've had a lot of time to think." Sonny looked him in the eye. "I've come to believe the only thing that matters at all in this life is people, how we treat each other."

"You gave plenty to your fans—"

"No, I took from them, I fed off their applause, they pumped up my ego. I didn't give myself, only worried about myself. I wasn't there for the people in my life, Julia, Tommy, my mother. Maybe I can be for these."

"I'd have to give my name to buy a gun, and then you're going out and shoot someone with it. I'm not putting my neck on the chopping block again, ever! Hang tough for a while, maybe it'll blow over."

"I can't *shoot* anyone, for cryin' out loud, but if I wave the thing at him, maybe he'll wet his pants and get the hell out of their lives."

Sonny stood and looked into the soggy barnyard, brightening steadily with the fleeing clouds.

"I heard your plane. Every time I hear that jet-roar in the valley I want to go back. No one would recognize me now."

He turned and held in his stomach.

"You notice? Lost three more pounds since you've seen me. I want to see what's going on, I'm going crazy."

"That would be as smart as shooting a hole in a neighbor."

Corkey took a bulging manila parcel from his case and slid it across the hardwood table.

"Open the package, it'll calm you down."

Sonny split the seam and released several bundles of used bills, neatly wrapped in paper bands.

"There's one hundred and sixty thousand there. Just seed money. RCA is running its Indiana plant on a twenty-four hour schedule to catch up with the demand. You know how many they can press in one day? You want to know? Two hundred and fifty thousand, and they can't keep up. It's crazy. If half the stuff they're putting out sells, you'll be a millionaire again, many times over."

Sonny regarded the neatly stacked currency.

"Have you taken out what I owe you?"

"Yeah, we're even-steven. You'll have to invest this somewhere, can't have bundles of cash stashed around here for the mice to eat."

"Pay off Costello; pay off my debt in Las Vegas."

"What?"

"Tell them it's from my earnings, a trust, my estate, tell him anything, but tell him I had instructed you to pay it off."

"That's a stupid idea, paying off a dead man's gambling debt. Remember, he wanted to *kill you*, he *tried* to kill you."

"I think it will be my joke. He's getting paid off by a guy he thinks he killed, but the guy is alive and paying off his debt. It's like I get the last laugh."

"We'll see, we'll see, but why throw good money away to those maggots? You can find something better to do with it."

"Some horses, good horses. We can breed them."

"Horses?"

"And a gun. What would be more natural for a rancher than to have a handgun? You weren't here with that psycho threatening you. I don't ever want to be here again without one."

"Let's hold off on the gun for a while. You know the trouble you have with guns. They tend to go off, ya know what I mean."

"I was using then, and drinking, I'm clean now, no more hotel ceilings or TV sets or limo floorboards."

"Don't forget bathroom mirrors."

Corkey closed the leather case and snapped the two latches.

"That was an accident, we were just having fun."

"Some fun. I remember what it cost me to keep it quiet. Gad, those were wild times."

Corkey laughed.

An engine shattered the serenity of the barnyard. Corkey stood and edged to the window.

"It's an old buzzard in a Jeep."

"Oh, that's just Hezekiah."

Sonny went to the door and Corkey followed. A ripe old geezer rode the beatup Jeep as though he'd come off the assembly line with it generations ago. Sonny went to greet the man and waved a hand for Corkey to join them. Sonny introduced them and explained to the man that this was Corkey's place. They shook hands and measured one another briefly. Corkey noticed a missing finger on the rancher's right hand.

"The water running all right?" Sonny said.

"Yep, good water." Hezekiah turned to the other side of the Jeep and let fly with tobacco juice. "You fellas gonna irrigate?"

"I don't know." Sonny looked at Corkey. "Are we?"

"Not unless you want to fool with it, we don't know a damn thing about it."

"Oughtta. Ground'll dry up on ya," the rancher said.

"Would you like a beer?" Sonny nodded toward the house.

"I brought them papers."

Hezekiah picked a dirty cardboard box from the back of the Jeep and handed it to Sonny. One look at the hodgepodge of disordered papers and Sonny handed it back.

"Do you pay your taxes with checks?" Sonny asked.

"Cash, then I know right where I's at."

"Where do you pay your taxes?"

"Bozeman, county courthouse."

Sonny checked his watch and slapped his hand on the blistered hood.

"Let's hit it right now." He dashed for the house.

"I don't think—" Corkey said to the slamming screen door.

He nodded at Hezekiah and ambled toward the house, meeting Sonny coming the other way with an unbuttoned shirt on his back and stuffing a wad of bills in his jeans. Sonny ran for the Jeep and avoided all eye contact.

"I don't think we should be going off right now," Corkey said. "I don't think—"

"C'mon, Partner!" the stumpy rancher called, hesitating a moment. Then he started the horrendously-loud rattletrap and drove out of the yard with a flurry.

The excitement of a trip to town gripped Sonny, a farm boy on Saturday night with hard cash in his pocket. Hezekiah jammed his boot against the gas pedal and set his leg like a post. Out onto the interstate, the old machine would only do a little over fifty, but with no top and a short windshield, it felt much faster on Sonny's bald head. Everything on the freeway passed them, and the eighteen-wheelers sprayed them with the puddles of rain still pooled in the passing lane. He felt free.

"Hog-assed truckers," Hezekiah said, "throwing slush in yer face till ya can't find the dad-blasted road."

A car with California plates slid past them, and something from deep down surfaced, a longing, a hunger—God, he had to stomp it out for now. Look at this valley, green and fresh after the rain, the peaceful life he could find here. He hadn't been this healthy since his boyhood and he knew if he didn't find contentment right here he'd go out of his mind. He glanced at Hezekiah and tried to figure out why in hell the little man's hat didn't blow off.

Bozeman, about twelve miles from the ranch, was a clean-looking western town nestled up against the mountains at the east end of the valley. Hezekiah weaved down North Seventh past a strip of motels, gas stations, and fast-food outlets, turning on Main and hanging a U-turn right in front of the court house. He pitched one last salvo of tobacco juice in the gutter before climbing the stairs into the large stone fortress.

The clerk in the treasurer's office studied them from her pinched face, a wren of a woman with tiny spectacles. After figuring out what it was this odd couple wanted, she hunted up the scruffy landowner's tax statements. When the shrewish woman reappeared out of the tomb-like atmosphere, her displeasure mellowed into a grand satisfaction.

"Mr. Linesinger, you are two and a half years delinquent."

She said it as if it were a personal triumph. Hezekiah searched for a place to spit but found nothing on the waxed wood floor, forcing him to talk with an excess of saliva in his mouth.

"How much it come ta?"

Without a word the skinny clerk went to an adding machine and began punching keys like a crabby spinster schoolmarm correcting her least-liked student's exam.

"It's bad if'n they can't fig're her in their heads."

Hezekiah searched the room more desperately for a spittoon as she minced back with the graded exam, tickled with the results.

"You owe four thousand, eight hundred and ninety-three dollars and twelve cents." She turned the adding machine tape so he could read it. "That includes the interest due. That pays you through 1978."

Hezekiah swallowed. Sonny dragged his gagging neighbor aside.

"You got the money?"

"Nope . . . I'll pay it with the alfalfa."

"I have some money, let's pay it while we're here."

Sonny disclosed the roll of bills he had in his pocket. Hezekiah swallowed again, then balked.

"Nope, I'll pay it with the alfalfa."

"Listen," he said, glancing around the room suspiciously. "They'll be after your land, it may be too late by the time you get your alfalfa money. You can pay me back, but you'll be doing me a favor, this money is hot."

"Hot ya say?" Hezekiah cocked an eye.

"Yeah."

The clerk watched them smugly, standing rigidly behind the solid oak counter that protected her from people, triumphantly confronting the old cowpoke and his bald-headed partner.

"The tax men don't know about it. I could really put one over on them if I paid *taxes* with it." Sonny laughed.

"Hot ya say?"

"Yeah."

"I can pay ya back?"

Hezekiah held a hand on Sonny's chest, holding him off until the leery rancher could make up his mind.

"Any time you like, but you never have to. It's money to blow. I can't spend it anywhere or they'll be on to me."

Sonny hoped that made some sense to Hezekiah because it sounded half-baked to him. He pulled out the wad of bills and they counted it out like a two-man huddle hiding their next play from their sand-lot opponents.

"Hot huh, hee hee."

They moved back to the snooty public servant who appeared confident this pair of no-accounts could never lift the millstone she had yoked around their necks. Hezekiah methodically peeled out five thousand dollars in full view of her widening eyeballs, giggling as he slowly counted.

"Been saving it in my cookie jar."

Hezekiah winked at her frozen face. She recounted the bills three times, stamped the appropriate pages in a large black-bound book, and handed him carbons without a word. Hezekiah held out his gnarled hand for the one hundred and six dollars and eighty-eight cents change, the woman's final defeat. He nodded a cheery goodbye, handed the money to Sonny, and they strutted from the court house in a cocky mood, laughing at their victory over higher powers.

"Let's walk around a bit, I haven't been in town for a while," Sonny said, and his bow-legged neighbor fell in step.

"Where can I find good horses?"

"Blakely's, over in Paradise Valley. Prob'ly good as any around these parts."

Sonny turned into Poor Richard's, a magazine and tobacco shop on Main Street where he picked up several magazines with his face on the cover, a Bozeman newspaper, and six plugs of Day's Work chewing tobacco, Hezekiah's brand. Sonny handed him the chews.

"What ya do that fer?"

"Still a little money to blow."

Back at the Jeep Sonny searched the classified ads under Firearms and started believing it was his day when he found a Rugar .44 magnum 7½ inch barrel listed for sale. They found the house after searching through the muffled and sometimes elegant neighborhoods of Bozeman.

"I don't think he ever shot it," the widow said, standing with Sonny inside her front door. "He *said* it'd be worth a lot of money some day." She made no attempt to disguise her skepticism. "*Said* it was a good investment; he was always saying that." Managing a thin smile, she spoke with an apologetic tone. "He paid one hundred and forty-nine for it new."

She held her hands nervously in front of her plain cotton dress while Sonny examined the weapon, shifting her weight from foot to foot in the silence.

"If you think that's too much—"

"Ma'am, I don't think you realize the value of this gun."

He surveyed the shabby furniture in the front room.

"I collect guns, and your husband was a very shrewd man. This serial number is a rare bugger, I'd be stealing it for anything under two thousand."

"Oh, my, oh, my, *two thousand*! my Lord, that would be *wonderful.*"

Her hands began to flutter in front of her waist, then flew up and held her head as if it would fall from her body. He counted twenty one-hundred-dollar bills into her shaking palms which she held as though receiving the sacrament.

"Oh my, Harold knew what he was doing after all, oh my."

She gathered herself enough to scurry and fetch two boxes of ammunition.

"God bless you, oh, God bless you," she said at the door.

"My thanks to you, ma'am. It's a collector's item for sure."

The Jeep strayed from lane to lane, galloping for the barn like a sway-backed dude horse that had been conserving its energy all day. Sonny became increasingly anxious over the two or three inches of play he estimated in the steering wheel, expecting to see it loose in Hezekiah's hands at any moment.

"Ya gonna shoot varmints with that pistol?"

"No, some mean bastard who beats up women."

"Thas what I mean. Got a rifle ya can use, 73 Winchester .45-70, was my pappy's."

He wrestled the erratic steering wheel as if bull-dogging a calf, the tip of his worn boot jammed against the accelerator, the brim of his hat flattened back against his head, and once in awhile, to Sonny's immediate terror, flattened across his eyes.

"Are you a con, Frank?"

"You won't tell anyone will you?" Sonny shouted back, his words blowing into the ditch with the discarded beverage cans and scurrying gophers.

"Heh, heh, thought so, fig'red it right from the start," Hezekiah shouted. "I'll never spill the beans. Bet yer deadly with that six-shooter."

Sonny hoped he would accept the money with less reluctance if he thought it was illegal, hoped the old rancher wouldn't feel indebted, knowing too well that it could ruin the easy friendship growing between them. He remembered other people he had bought, always aware of that sticky membrane of obligation between them that smothered any spontaneity and honesty. He always meant well, but they began playing a role: careful, patronizing, always smiling, never disagreeing.

"Who ya runnin' from, Frank?" Hezekiah surprised Sonny.

"Running from?"

"Yeah, I seen ya about killin' yourself runnin' across the fields. Couldn't see nuthin' ya was chasin'. Who ya runnin' from?"

"I don't know. I just do it to keep me in shape."

"Hell of a way ta stay in shape."

They were back on the gravel between Belgrade and the ranch, and Sonny guessed the grimy bandana around his old friend's furrowed neck hadn't been removed that year. When they pulled up in the yard, Sonny looked skyward as an acknowledgement of thanksgiving for touching ground safely again.

"How long have you had that much play in that wheel?"

"'Bout long as I had that much play in ma knees, heh, heh."

"You keep those receipts in a safe place now," Sonny shouted over the unmuffled engine, "they're your only proof that your taxes are paid."

Sonny stepped back.

"Let me know if ya need the Winchester."

He gunned out of the yard, leaving a small cloud of white smoke hanging in the still air. Corkey stepped out on the porch.

"I see you found a gun."

"Yeah, a .44 magnum. Let's see what it'll do."

Sonny laid the magazines on the steps with the boxes of ammunition and slid one shell into the cylinder.

"That can wait, it's time to eat."

Corkey slammed the screen door.

Sonny stepped away from the house, took aim at a knot on a gnarly cedar post thirty yards away, and squeezed the trigger. The

heavy handgun boomed and tried to leap out of his hands, the valley flinched with the concussion, and a small band of magpies
sprung from the fence line back along the ditch. The knot in the
cedar post stared back at him with disdain.

"Judas priest!" Corkey came through the door with a spatula in
hand. "It's time to eat."

Sonny picked up the magazines and ammunition and slunk into
the house like a chastised kid.

"You sign your name for that gun?" Corkey said.

"No way. I bought it secondhand, no name, no record."

He laid the pistol and ammunition on the counter.

"You never should've gone into Bozeman."

Corkey banged the iron skillet around on the stove top.

"Who on God's good earth would recognize me?"

"You promised you'd stay out of sight until fall, that was our deal,"
Corkey said, pointing with the spatula.

"I didn't know how hard it would be. Hell, I know you're afraid.
So am I, but look at me. You know how many sets I do every day?
You know how far I run? I lifted over two tons this morning. *You*
wouldn't recognize me if you didn't know it was me."

"Sit down."

With a frown, Corkey slid a hamburger and onions onto each
plate.

"Maybe I wouldn't, but accidents happen when you mingle with
people, things you can't foresee, ya know what I mean."

"Shoot, traveling around with Hezekiah no one would notice me.
He'd out-Walter-Brennen Walter Brennen. Cork, I'm just a bald-
headed nobody, hobnobbing with a crazy old man, and no one on
earth will ever notice."

"With a .44 pistola," Corkey said. "With a .44 pistola."

Chapter 23

THE SUN HADN'T shown its face in over a week, it rained night and day, and Sonny grew surly under the canopy of gloom. Through the dripping yard, he came from the barn where he vented his frustration by firing the powerful handgun, shooting against a stack of railroad ties at various targets. In the kitchen he picked a magazine from the cluttered formica counter and shook it at Corkey as though Corkey were responsible.

"Have you read this garbage?"

"Wouldn't waste my time. You certainly don't take that kind of thing seriously after all these years. Coffee?"

Corkey nodded at the coffee brewing on the stove, while rapidly manipulating a hand calculator. Sonny ignored the offer.

"This idiot doesn't know what the hell he's talking about. All he did was take a pile of bullshit from other articles, which were never true, and make a bigger pile of bullshit. People read it and believe it because it's in print."

He stormed around the kitchen, his rage coming to a boil with the coffee.

"People don't believe it, not most of them."

Corkey jotted figures on a note pad as he lightly tapped the calculator.

"They're changing me, Cork, and I can't do a stinking thing about it. When all this manure has been thoroughly spread, the person everyone will remember won't even be *me!*"

He kicked a ladder-back chair against the refrigerator.

"I want to go back . . . and tell them how it really was."

"There's only one way you can do that. Talk to me, tell me how it was before I knew you, after I knew you, how you felt, ya know what I mean. The author wants to write a book that will show a real human being under the fiction and fairy tale. I tell Least—he's a decent guy—that I'll have to look at my calendars and notes when I can't answer his questions. Hell, I don't have any notes."

That evening, after they'd eaten supper, they built a fire in the fireplace and settled in the living room. Sonny sat on the rug near the fire as though it were a magic carpet, transporting him great distances back into his childhood.

"I don't remember much about the sale, people were stomping all over the farm like they owned it, poking into everything without respect, hoping they'd pick up something of value for little or nothing. Shoot, we didn't have much of value."

Sonny sprawled on the rug, his head propped up on one arm and elbow. He stared into the fire.

"The auctioneer was a tall, friendly guy with big ears and a fancy felt hat and he sold a lot of stuff that I wanted to keep. People crowded around and he talked so fast I couldn't tell what he said or who bought anything until they carted it off. I recognized some of the people, but I hated all of them, thought they were cruel scavengers, joking and eating a big stinking lunch the church women served, while my dad lay cold under the frost."

Sonny stirred the fire with a bent poker, searching the ashes for the sounds, the feelings, the shafts of light in his memory. Corkey, camped in the stuffed chair, lit a cigarette and waited.

"I remember when they were selling the tractor that killed my dad. God, I hated that machine, called it the Beast. I told my mom I was going to burn it, and I think she understood, because she said that'd be fine and she'd help me, but we needed the money it'd bring in. So I planned to burn it after someone bought and paid for it. It stood there with a small round patch of sod still stuck on the hood, as if the Beast had taken my father's scalp."

Sonny got up and went into the unlit kitchen.

"Where you going?"

"I don't know, I thought I heard something."

He paused in the dark for a minute, gazing out the back window. Nothing. Wait! By the tool shed, a faint glow. Sonny squinted into the darkness. Someone was standing there smoking a cigarette.

"Come here," Sonny whispered.

Corkey crept into the kitchen and peered out the window beside him.

"Watch," Sonny said.

Nothing. Then the faint glow again.

"Who in the hell?" Corkey whispered.

"Sally's ex-husband."

Sonny reached over the counter and picked up the .44 magnum.

"Turn on the porch light," Corkey said.

"No, no, don't let him know we're on to him."

"What's he doing out there?"

"He burned up one of her boyfriend's cars," Sonny said.

"Holy cats, what are we going to do?"

They saw the glow again, soft in the dripping yard.

"I don't know," Sonny said. "I can burn one over his head for openers."

They stared into the darkness for more than five minutes. The glow was gone. But was the trucker?

"Maybe you can't do anything, but I can," Corkey said.

He snapped on the kitchen light, thumbed through the telephone book, and called the sheriff.

"We have a prowler, yeah, out around the buildings."

Twenty minutes later a sheriff's car pulled into the yard with lights twirling. It stopped halfway to the barn and raked the barnyard with a spot light. Two men got out and moved around the buildings with flashlights and then they knocked on the door. Corkey thanked them and said he'd call if he spotted the prowler again. Sonny stayed out of sight. When the deputies were gone, Corkey turned off the kitchen light and Sonny went back and settled on the rug near the fireplace. For a while they discussed the trucker and what he might do, and then Corkey prodded Sonny to get back to his story.

"You were telling me about the tractor."

"That damn tractor got sold last and I couldn't tell which of the farmers actually bought it. When it was over, the shoppers and buyers drifted away, hauled off our belongings like vultures with hunks of my father's life in their talons, all that was left of his life working in the sun and rain and riding the Beast into a north wind. When they'd all disappeared, I let the air out of one of its big tires until it was flatter than hell. Then I went in to eat with my mom for the last time in that house."

Sonny added a split log to the fire, sending an explosion of sparks up the chimney.

"We moved into the little house in Boyd. I knew things weren't good for my mom, and I tried to help. Hell, I thought I could take care of her. She'd always—"

"Did you have any insurance?"

"Not a dime that I know of. . . . Whenever I'd come home there'd be fresh turnovers, sugar cookies, cupcakes, glazed doughnuts. My friends used to tag along home with me; the house smelled like a bakery. She sold most of it. Then she started working at the grocery store. But she'd always be home for supper.

She had that iron triangle we had on the farm. It hung from a chain and she'd beat that thing with an iron bar and you could hear it all over the farm. When we moved into Boyd, people could set their watches by it, every afternoon at five thirty sharp. You could hear that crazy thing all over town. People would tell me, 'Supper time, Sonny' friends, grownups, people I hardly knew, all tellin' me my mom was calling me. Jeez, when I got in high school, one day I asked her to stop and she did. And by then I think half the town was on her schedule. Jeez, Corkey, the day she stopped I think everyone in town was late for supper." Sonny paused. "You know, Cork, sometimes I think I can still hear that thing off in the distance."

Sonny popped up and paced through the house: kitchen, living room, bedroom, living room, kitchen.

"Sit down, you're driving me nuts!"

"I *am* going nuts."

He perched lightly on the edge of the sofa.

"You're living in Boyd now," Corkey said.

"Yeah, well one night a man stops over and Mom entertains him. They acted like they already knew each other and I went to bed with my ass out of joint thinking I was my mother's only man. I thought—"

"How old were you?"

"Twelve, thirteen . . . the guy came around more and more and I couldn't help liking him, though I think I played hard to get for a while. He was plain looking, a little chubby, a traveling salesman, and he was real good to her. She seemed as happy as I could ever remember, she'd cook fancy meals when he was coming by, table-cloths and candles, and when I'd come home from school I could always tell. She'd be singing as she worked, humming, and she'd horse around with me, wrestle me to the floor and tickle me and kiss me all over the face. I acted like I hated it, but I think she knew I liked it. I was—"

Sonny got up and went to the front window. He pushed aside the curtain.

"What's the matter?" Corkey whispered.

"Look."

Corkey came out of the upholstered chair quietly and peered out the window beside Sonny. Only wet blackness. Then, over by the lilacs, the faint glow of a cigarette.

Chapter 24

LIKE FUGITIVES, they settled in kitchen chairs with the house dark but the outside porch light on. Fire-dancing shadows glided from the lodge pole fire in the living room like ghosts. They talked about calling the sheriff again but agreed it had no effect on the psycho truck driver. Sonny banked the fire and since neither figured he was ready for sleep, Corkey turned him back to his boyhood.

"Where was I?" Sonny asked.

"You're mother had a boyfriend."

"Oh, yeah, well . . . the man started staying overnight. I remember the first time. I went out early to deliver papers and his car was still parked in front of the house. I thought he had car trouble or something so I went back in to tell my mother, thinking he had to hitch a ride to his hotel in Monty. When I opened her door, there they were, curled up together real naturallike, what a shock. I think I was mad at first, but she looked so safe, so peaceful. I quietly shut the door and grew up about ten years."

Corkey reached over and opened the refrigerator. He took out a can of beer.

"Want one?"

Sonny shook his head.

"Well, word spread that the Ford didn't pull out until after breakfast, and that became regular, once or twice a month. Mom ignored the gossip, but after a while she lost her job at the store. Some of the kids started razzing me with traveling-salesman jokes, and the older guys would make insulting remarks. I didn't get it. He was a good, kind man, and he made her happy. It wasn't hurting anyone."

"What were you living on?"

Sonny took an orange from the counter and began to peel it.

"I don't know . . . she baked some and I think she did laundry and cleaned houses. I began feeling uncomfortable around people, but she'd walk up town and look everyone straight in the eye. About ten years ago she showed me a snapshot taken with the salesman when they were off somewhere together. They looked happy, like they were more important to each other than anything else in the world and spit in the eye of those who pointed fingers."

Sonny shoved a section of orange in his mouth and limped on sore legs through the fire-lit living room. He parted the curtain and peered out at the road.

"See anything?" Corkey called.

"No . . . black as hell."

He pulled the drape tight, laid another log on the fire, and shuffled back to the table.

"I remember I'd avoid people when I could, you know, kind of duck out of things. We stopped going to church around that time—"

"How about your friends?"

Corkey took a swig of beer.

"It was like the Hollisters had something contagious and parents were afraid their kids might catch it. One day I asked my mom if she was going to marry him. She held me by the shoulders, the way she used to when she wanted me to listen real good, and she looked me straight in the eye.

"She said, 'Don't you ever repeat this to a soul—promise me.' I nodded. 'I love him, Sonny, but he has a wife and family, we can never be married, do you understand?' She watched my face. I nodded, and I've never told a soul until right now."

Sonny pushed himself out of the chair and started for the front window.

"Will you sit down! You're giving me the heebie-jeebies."

Sonny parted the curtain and checked the night for some sign. Nothing. He ambled back to the kitchen.

"I wonder if he's still out there?" Sonny said.

"I told you to stay away from Sally."

"I'm going out there."

"That'd be stupid; you shoot him and the whole thing comes down on our heads. Sit down and talk."

Sonny slid into the wooden chair. Corkey tossed the empty beer can into the basket.

"You want the writer to know about your mother?"

"Yeah . . . I want people to know the way it really was. I'm not ashamed, she never was. I'm glad she had a few years of love and affection, she had damn little of anything else. But that good man with the bald-tired Ford stays unnamed. He's probably long dead now, but I'd never let anything hurt his family."

Corkey nodded and Sonny plunked an orange section into his mouth.

"He told my mother that he'd stay away if it would be better for us. She wouldn't hear of it but I know the guy felt terrible. He wanted us to move, but she wouldn't let the gossips run her off."

Corkey stood. "Let's go in by the fire."

They moved into the living room like burglars. Corkey flopped in the stuffed chair and Sonny stretched out on the sofa.

"Had enough of this?" Sonny said.

"No, keep it coming, everything you can remember."

"Okay. One day he brought me a guitar, I never knew why. I'd never said I wanted one, shoot, I'd never touched one, but I loved it. My mother got me a book of chords and strums, and I spent hours every day practicing and singing."

The new wood in the fireplace caught, tongues of fire licked around the logs and danced shadows across the room.

"I was shy, real shy, didn't take any girls out until I started up with Natalie Jones. Oh lord, Corkey, I've got to tell you about Fame and Fortune."

Something lost in the layered dust of his memory sparkled.

"Fame and fortune?" Corkey said.

"Natalie was a willowy girl with a terrific smile. In our sophomore year she blossomed two spherical, lyrical breasts that, even in her modest clothing, gave her figure a devastating effect, a wake-up call to my sleeping manhood."

"I would've never guessed your manhood was ever asleep, ya know what I mean."

"One day in class, Natalie had to read an essay titled *Fame and Fortune*. She wore a yellow Angora sweater, and I was bug-eyed. Darryl Appleseth poked me from behind and whispered, 'I know what Fame and Fortune is. Her right one is Fame and her left one is Fortune.' From that day on, whenever my mom asked me what I wanted in life, I'd tell her Fame and Fortune. She'd always laugh at my answer, completely in the dark."

"Ha, the laugh's on you." Corkey looked over at him. "Your fairy godmother didn't understand either; she gave you the real article."

"We began going out when we were juniors. I went with her for weeks before even holding her hand, the first kiss came after five dates because I counted and planned, not to seem too interested in that sort of thing. Jeez, Corkey, it was scary, just being that close to her. I was a completely uninitiated kid and she was turning me inside out. The first time I dared touch her breast over her sweater she stopped me. Hell, I liked her as much as I loved her, so I settled for necking, and with the gossip about my mother, I swore they'd never be able to say anything about me."

Corkey got up and stirred the fire with the poker. Then he sidled over to the window and pushed aside the curtain.

"Jeez! now you got me looking for the bogeyman."

He closed the curtain and plopped into the chair.

"Tell me about Natalie Jones."

"The summer before our senior year, Natalie fell in love with me and gave in. I'd borrow a pickup from one of the kids and we'd drive out to Walther's grove, an old abandoned farm site where the house had burned down but the thick windbreak made a perfect place to park."

With his hands under his head, Sonny closed his eyes as if he were sleeping. He remembered.

"And, and?" Corkey said.

"I got my first taste of paradise in Walther's grove. I'd inch off her sweater and bra and almost forget to breathe. Zeke Zwingley said she had the nicest twin cams he'd ever seen, and he was right. The first time I saw her bare white breasts I knew they were perfect, what they were meant to be from the beginning of time. When I'd lay my head against her sweet-smelling skin and she'd hold me, I felt like everything was the way it was supposed to be. We talked about getting married, and I was sure I knew all there was to know about loving someone."

"What ever happened between you two?"

"In the end I got rich and famous, and Zeke Zwingley got Fame and Fortune. And I don't want any of this in print, except that Natalie Jones was my first true love."

Corkey stood and stretched. Sonny spoke with his eyes closed.

"We went together for almost two years. One night after a basketball game we were walking to the cafe for sundaes. A car with some older guys came by and one of them yelled, 'Hey, Sonny, what's your mother doing tonight?' I was so stinking mad I wanted to kill him. I couldn't think of anything to say to Natalie. I can still remember walking the last block, sweating, embarrassed, vowing I'd show that bastard."

Sonny's voice clogged with anger. He sat up and swung his bare feet onto the floor.

"That summer I drove a truck for the grain elevator, and Natalie and I spent a lot of time together. Then, in the fall, my senior year, she told me her father wouldn't let her go with me anymore. I pleaded with her, asked her to meet me secretly, asked her to run away with me, but she wouldn't. She said she loved me and we'd have to wait and see if he changed his mind. I went bananas, she was my whole life."

"I know what you mean."

"I hung around town for a few weeks, started skipping school, and then said goodbye to Mom. She didn't want me to go, but she didn't try to stop me. I think she figured I'd get it out of my system and come home. I guess I thought I'd be back, too. In my half-assed thinking, I left to show Natalie how much I loved her and hoped she'd miss me and change her mind when I'd write her."

"Did you ever finish high school?"

"No, never did. I always lied about that. I took my guitar with me and not much else, knew I could sell it if I got hungry. I worked my way west and south as it got cold. I sang a few places for a meal and got the shock of my life. They clapped, I loved it, and I fell in love with singing, or maybe with applause. I worked on a construction crew, did some stockcar racing in Oklahoma and Texas, and I was driving truck and trying to sing nights when I got into that amateur contest in Dallas. I didn't have a clean shirt, borrowed one from a kid named Charlie Twip. I never forgot."

"I remember, you gave him a Continental."

"Yeah, that was him. We ran into him tending bar in Austin, he'd forgotten all about it. Jeez! remember the look on his face?"

Sonny heard something. "Listen . . . hear that?"

"No, damnit, now cut it out, you're giving me the willies."

"That's enough."

Sonny got off the sofa and stretched, his finger tips touching the ceiling. Corkey shut the fireplace screen and turned on the television while Sonny settled on his haunches in front of the fireplace.

"Tell the writer this. If that stinking tractor hadn't killed my dad, and if that traveling salesman hadn't given me a guitar, I'd have probably been a farmer and never sung a note except in church. And tell him I believe I would've been happy, especially with Natalie at my side."

"I know what you mean," Corkey said with sadness in his voice.

"I don't know, Cork, maybe I was meant to sing, maybe I'd have come to it one way or another. The town gossips should get some credit, and the guy who yelled out the car window, and Natalie's father. Who knows what finally sent me away. They can explain it in all the books they want, but life's a mystery. When you boil it all down, no one knows, no one understands. Look at us, a gimpy guy managing a dive in Texas who ends up a multi-millionaire and a washed-up singer who was killed last winter on the Nevada desert who's still alive. If anyone would've told us this back then, we'd have called him a raving lunatic and sent for the paddy wagon."

Sonny sauntered into the kitchen, rummaged through the cupboards for something he couldn't name, fighting off the growing impulse to fill the emptiness in his chest.

Corkey turned from the TV screen and watched the few remaining embers glow in the blackened hearth. He thought about the years when Sonny brought so many people joy and excitement with his incredible energy and talent. He'd seen thousands held like a drop of water in Sonny's hand, hanging on his next note, spellbound by his intensity and power. He was always surprised that after all the traveling and haggling and rehearsals, when Sonny stepped out into the lights, he could step into a totally different dimension, leave all else behind and transform the audience, lift them right out of their socks, a magician, a storyteller, and to say that he was gifted would always be understatement.

Corkey stepped to the window and parted the curtain, gazing into the black dripping countryside. If Sonny had been a farmer all his life, would there have been a void, something missing in the world? Nothing he ever did would be classified as profound or historic, but his song filled a need for thousands, lifted their burdens, gave them music for dancing, for singing, for living their lives. Corkey tried to see the stars. Did it make a difference that the Oliver quit chugging one fall afternoon, that a lonely traveling man gave a kid a guitar? The answer came to him in a million cheering faces.

Chapter 25

IN HIS SOAKED SWEATSHIRT, Sonny emerged from the shadows of the barn and stumbled across the barnyard. The imminent possibility of a showdown with Sally's brutal ex-husband raised the stakes, and he drove himself beyond what he thought possible. Whenever any reserve of energy seeped back into his body, he prodded himself to the milk room to drain it away in an impulsive blood-letting.

At some moment in that hidden chamber he had crossed a line, become obsessed with exercising, addicted to its rushing high and sweet afterglow, not to overlook the visual rewards. If he skipped a session, his body yearned for the milk room like amphetamine.

He contemplated this newly acquired virtue as he stood like stone under the hot shower, but before he could puff with any hint of arrogance, he recognized that much of his motivation was cold-blooded fear. He watched the horizon like a hawk and stayed out of sight more and more. Though he nurtured the impression that he had some control over his life, that impression was fleeting, and everything seemed to be spiraling faster toward some uncertain end.

He'd seen Sally once in the past week, briefly stopping by on his way to the lumber yard, and even though healed up, she was obviously uneasy with him there. Jesse came often to ride Toro and those two had formed an affectionate bond in which it appeared that the sociable steer understood everything the boy said to him.

He finished his shower and gathered his forces at the kitchen table, eating only what conformed to his new regard for healthy food. No sugar, caffeine, little salt, cut down on fat, and almost no alcohol, changing Corkey's shopping list if not Corkey's diet.

Early afternoon he found the stamina to hang the green metal gates on the corral. The sky was clear, the temperature climbed into the sixties, and a gentle breeze winged from the southwest. With a brace and bit he was drilling holes in the gate post when Jesse and Hannah came around the barn.

"Hi, Frank," Jesse called, "what are you doing?"

"Hello, Jesse. Hannah."

Hannah didn't respond. The two of them were like the hot and cold water faucets.

"Can we look for a curlew in your fields?" Jesse said.

"A what?"

"A Curlew, it's a bird, they have real long bills and a cool sound when they call. You want to come with us?"

"Frank has work to do, Jesse," she said, "we shouldn't bother him."

Hannah tugged at Jesse's sleeve. The boy ignored her.

"We'd look on Linesinger's land, but he's a grouch, won't let anyone on his place. I sneak on from the other end sometimes."

Sonny lined up the bit and began cranking out another hole.

"You better go without me this time, but you know you can do whatever you want around the place, you don't have to ask."

"Do you ever hunt, Frank?"

Jesse's large eyes narrowed.

"No, I don't. Why?"

"If I tell you something can you keep it secret?"

"Come on, Jess," Hannah said with impatience.

"Hannah saw a black-footed ferret back there." Jesse pointed north. "In Linesinger's pasture, they're extinct."

"They're not extinct yet, you ninny, or I couldn't have seen one. But they're close to it."

"Why? What's happening to them?" Sonny said.

"No more prairie dogs," Jess said. "That's what they eat."

"What happened to the prairie dogs?"

"We've killed them off," she said, "poisoned them, shot them. The black-footed ferret lived off the prairie dog colonies."

"Can't they eat something else?" Sonny asked, intrigued by these two.

"Oh, they do," she said, "rodents, mice, ground squirrels, but if a rancher had the chance, most would shoot one. If someone hears that there's one out here, they'll want to kill it."

Hannah's voice carried a resigned abhorrence.

"What for?"

Sonny hung the brace and bit over the corral rail.

"So they could brag that they shot the last black-footed ferret on the planet and no one at the bar could top them."

Hannah shrugged her shoulders and looked out across the land.

Her long dark hair in braids, she had Sally's large eyes and they held a sadness that seemed beyond her years. The lithesome body she tucked into bulky bib overalls gave the impression of an athlete.

"Well as long as it stays on this ranch no one's going to shoot it," Sonny said. "By the way, what in the Sam Hill is a black-footed ferret?"

Hannah broke into a smile, her face relaxed.

"It's very much like a marten or mink, but bigger and it has a mask around its eyes, like a raccoon. Come on, Jesse, we'd better go."

She tugged on his jacket and the boy finally relented. Sonny watched them amble across the hay field and had a sudden impulse to run after them, two inquisitive kids investigating the mystery of their world, noticing what might be gone forever by nightfall.

He turned back to the work at hand, and a plan formulated in his head while he measured and drilled. He heard something and turned to see Sally's rattletrap GMC pickup bounce through the barnyard and stop alongside the corral.

She came toward him with much of the strain gone from her handsome face, decked out in jeans and pink blouse with bow tie and ruffles. He dropped his tools and went to meet her.

"You're looking mighty fine today," he said.

"Thanks. You don't look so bad yourself."

Without a word they walked side by side into the barn like conspirators, out of sight to the world. He turned and took her hands in his.

"How are you doing?" he said.

She leaned into his chest and he embraced her.

"I'm doing okay, but I miss seeing you."

She hugged him with an unexpected intensity and pressed her face against his neck.

"I thought you'd want me to stay clear—"

"I know, I know, but I'm human, I need someone around."

Sonny nuzzled her hair.

"I thought you might not want to—"

She turned her head and kissed him and he met her warmth with a hunger that surprised him. After a moment, she pulled back and caught her breath.

"My goodness, you must be going through mid-life crisis or something." She laughed.

"Yeah, or post-life crisis."

"What on earth is that?"

"The crisis you experience after you die."

With his strength he held her close, and she paused a moment, as if sensing something pensive in his humor. She spoke softly in his ear.

"You do say the strangest things sometimes."

She stepped back.

"I have to get to work. I only stopped to say hello, nothing serious." She laughed. "Playmates?"

"Playmates," he said

They walked from the barn, neither with hay in their hair, and he avoided mentioning that Ramsey had been stalking the house.

When she drove away he scanned the immediate horizons for any sign of their night visitor. He wanted to finish the gates, be ready when Jesse and Hannah returned from the fields. But as the bit bore through the sweet-smelling spruce, he paused, glanced over his shoulder, a black-footed ferret, holding very still, sure he heard the padded foot of the hunter just above his burrow.

Chapter 26

THE GATES WERE ready to hang when Sonny noticed the two vagabonds coming from the field. He made the pretense of not noticing them until Jesse's shrill greeting broke across the warm spring day.

"Hi, Frank, can we help?"

Sonny turned to welcome them.

"Yeah, am I ever glad you asked, did you find a curlew?"

"No, but we saw a lot of neat stuff," Jesse said, "golden eagle, two of 'em, and a red-tailed hawk and a neat nest."

Sonny stepped over to Hannah who cradled a nest in one hand.

"What kind of bird made it, can you tell?"

"I think a western kingbird," Hannah said. "Look at the hair and string it used and the way it's all sewn together."

She glowed with an animated wonder and pointed out the fragile intricacies of the bird's brilliant craftsmanship.

"And who taught them?" she said.

"What can we do?" Jesse asked.

"Well I'm all set to hang these gates. If you two could hold them steady while I bolt them, it'd sure help."

Sonny lifted the gate onto wooden blocks, and the kids balanced it in place. With some grunting and lifting, the three of them manipulated the heavy gates until their hinges lined up with the predrilled holes and Sonny bolted them solidly to the posts. Unable to stand it any longer, he turned and looked directly into Hannah's eyes.

"How would you like a horse of your own?"

"What do you mean?"

"You know, four legs, hooves, a tail, and it makes great piles of horse manure."

She cocked her head and squinted at him.

"What do you mean 'of my own?'"

Jesse leaned in beside her, bug-eyed.

"Well, I'm going to have four horses in here, and there's only one of me. Corkey wouldn't get on a horse if he knew it was going straight to heaven so that means there'll be three poor orphans who won't have any owners."

Jesse's open innocence broke through first.

"Can I have one?"

"Both of you, your own horse, for keeps."

The Ramsey kids gaped at each other. Jesse leaped into the air, whooping with delight.

"When will they be here, when?" he shouted.

"Hey, you better consider the responsibilities before you go off half-cocked. You'll have to ride them every day, feed and water them, curry them, that's a lot of work."

"I don't know what to say," Hannah said. "I've wanted a horse since the day I was born. I can't—"

"Every kid should have at least one horse," Sonny said.

"But the expense, I mean, to feed them and—"

"Listen, we'll have grass coming up to our eyeballs before long and I'm getting these hay-burners so we'll be able to find the house."

Jesse would not be put off. "When are they coming, when, when?"

"As soon as we mend the pasture fence. The way it is, they'd be heading down the road three minutes after we turned them loose."

The gates were soon hung, and after loading the pickup with the needed tools and supplies, the three of them drove the pasture fence line, stopping to splice broken wire, re-staple wire hanging loose, and replace broken or rotten posts with metal ones. Sonny drove a staple into a gnarled cedar post while Hannah held the wire in place, anticipating his every move.

"You know a lot about the animals and birds around here," he said.

"I don't know much, no one does. We give them names and identify them, but we don't know how they think, what they know, what forces guide them; we don't listen to what they're telling us. We trap them, poison them, shoot them, or drive them away by destroying their homes, but we don't learn." She paused. "I suppose you think I'm kind of weird."

"No, I don't think that at all. I'm the dumb one for never noticing them. Did you see a black-eyed ferret?"

Jesse cackled. "Black-*footed* ferret."

"Yeah, black-footed ferret. Did you see one?"

Sonny laughed and whacked Jesse lightly on the head while they all walked to the next post.

"No, he's probably gone now, or dead," she said.

Her happy countenance darkened some as she glanced back toward the wooded creek bottom.

"There are lots of us black-footed ferrets around," Sonny said.

She didn't respond. Jesse brought a metal fence post from the truck.

"Can I name my horse, Frank?" the boy asked as if he feared the answer would be negative.

"It's your horse isn't it? What do you want to call him?"

"Wildfire," Jesse said without hesitation, as though he had been contemplating a horse all his life. "Do you know that song?"

"Yeah, I know it."

In his bad years, singing in saloons, he had sung it many times, a sad song about a woman lost in a blizzard, searching for a horse. Sonny turned to Hannah.

"You have any names on the front burner?"

"No, I want to see him first, or her."

Still overcome with it all, her joy and happiness poured from her large eyes and flowed over Sonny. All at once, pleasing her seemed very important to him.

After Sonny convinced them that the horses would arrive on schedule even if they didn't work all night, they returned to the barnyard in the late afternoon, but before Sonny could get out of the pickup, Jesse was running toward the barn, shouting.

"They're here, they're back, look, look!"

His excitement was as new-born and unsullied as Eden and they watched the boy turn wildly and greet the swallows with waving arms. The birds flew in and around the barn in a frenzy, already building nests as though their eggs were about to drop.

"There's Rudolph back from Argentina, and Bilbo from Brazil, and there, it's Chi Chi, all the way from Chile, and Gert . . ." he twirled under the swooping swallows, ". . . she's back from Bolivia. Hello, Turnip! Hi, Wink! Midge and Fluff and Pebble! You're all here. I knew you'd come back, I knew it!"

Sonny was taken with this display of a boy caught up in the flashing homecoming of these darting, diving, fragile birds that had come two continents to this barnyard in western Montana. They would disappear with daring speed into the depths of the old barn, then, after a moments absence, blast out of its high loft door as if they'd been shot from a gun, barrel rolls and loop-the-loops not uncommon.

"Does he really know them by *name?*" he said.

"I don't know if it's a boy's runaway imagination," Hannah said quietly. "He says the birds tell him where they spend their winter."

She watched Jesse dance and shout under the swallows.

"One time I asked him the name of a swallow that was in a nest by the broken window. He said it was Feather. I waited several weeks, and then one evening, when we were over, I watched until that swallow came from the nest and sat on the wire over there."

She nodded at the electric wire going to the ranch house.

"Jess was busy digging at something. I pointed out the bird and asked him who it was. With hardly a glance he said Feather. I don't know, he sees things I don't see."

Sonny walked over to Jesse and pointed to a swallow perched on a protruding iron frame above the loft door.

"Who's that?"

"That's Mud."

Sonny studied the bird. "That's amazing."

"No, that's Mud, Amazing flew out a minute ago."

They both watched Mud dart around the west side of the barn.

"Where does Mud spend the winter?"

"In Venezuela."

Something kept Sonny from breaking in on the boy's fantasy. He couldn't remember witnessing such an electrifying scene, and he felt at ease in accepting it openly. The sun was far to the western rim of the mountains; its rays slanted through the cottonwoods with a luminous gold, gave the wings of the birds a translucent aura, and held all of them, for a magical moment, transfixed in time. The valley seemed very still, with only the rustle of their mirthful return. The faithful pilgrims flashed above them and he was seized by a baffling vision that happiness was falling upon them all, from swallow wings, like stardust.

Sonny awoke with a start, shivering in the darkness, his body ice cold. He was standing beside the irrigation ditch north of the barn, stark naked. He'd neglected to tie the rope around his waist when he went to bed and he'd come out of the house in his sleep, across the barnyard and to this spot, completely unconscious of the chilling night air against his bare skin. He stood perfectly still to find his bearings, to be sure, in fact, that he was truly alive. His stethoscope hung from his neck.

The stars pierced the black sky in numbers he'd never imagined, a million shafts of light, needle thin, racing at him with the speed of light. He listened to the stillness of this desolate stellar vault but all he heard was an owl hooting eerily from across the field. Who-o-o, whoo-whoo-whoo, who-o-o. Then the resounding stillness ringing in his ear. He gazed into the expanse above him without moving, listening to the strain of the star's silent song.

All at once he was very cold. He took up his stethoscope and listened to his heartbeat, standing naked under the sparkling sky.

Ka-thump, ka-thump, ka-thump, ka-thump.

It was a direct signal from out there, someone speaking to him in the darkness, in his lostness, but he didn't know who. He spoke softly into the sky.

"Keep me in mind."

Chapter 27

WHATEVER THE RISKS, Sonny could put off singing no longer. With the bearing of a bootlegger he smuggled the guitar from the truck to the house, bought that afternoon in Bozeman as though he were procuring drugs. He played through the night until his voice was strained and his fingertips raw.

June came to the mountains with a reborn beauty; the earth teemed with life, and he accepted the gift with optimism, believed he had weathered his winter of despair and was moving into the promise of summer. Emerging in him like the new season was an elusive awareness that all of life was precious. He crossed to the barn and inhaled some sweet blossoming that hung in the air like hope. And above, the massive eternal mountains still glistened with snow.

He worked through his routine, moving up methodically in the amount of weight used for each exercise. Corkey's morning phone call informed him he was again a millionaire. Gleason had cautiously bought the merchandising rights for one year shortly after the funeral, but now the huckster realized what a gold mine Sonny's name had once more become, and he persuaded Corkey to sell him the merchandising rights for seven additional years. Without all the legal mumbo-jumbo, it would mean well over fifteen million in his pocket after taxes.

He began doing squats, keeping the sweat flowing. They had to hire a watchman for the little cemetery outside Boyd, where disciples were chipping off pieces of his granite tombstone. Unchecked, they would unearth the charred bones of Roy Rogers, the drifter who once had a girlfriend in Wichita. A certain shame and uncleanliness settled on him like barn dust, cashing in on his fans' affection, though he reminded himself he never dreamed that anyone would pay much attention to his death.

With the power of their collective mind in this one swelling plea—while they dug at the graveside of his life—he secretly hoped that there was some miraculous way they could uncover him and bring him back to life.

He staggered from the milk room with a body of lead. The horses would be delivered today; Hannah and Jesse would be here soon, it was all in front of him.

Under the steaming shower he tried to look at it honestly. When the ground under him gave way, when he finally lost it, he could hold off the horror no longer. When Julia and Tommy were snatched away, he realized that his wealth and fame couldn't protect any of them from death and pain. Fame and wealth were traitors that lie to you to make you feel safe. So he gave them away, or pissed them away. He no longer cared about his fans or anything else. Instead of working harder, he let himself go to ruin, as if to test them, to become a paunchy, miserable pothead, daring them to remain loyal, proving to himself that they never really loved him. And though he thought he'd succeeded during those pitiful years, he now realized that he'd been mistaken. They were coming on like gangbusters.

He slammed his fist against the metal shower stall and shuffled naked into the living room, dripping, searching the barnyard for Corkey's return from town. Then he knelt in front of the upholstered chair and put his head in his hands. He felt ludicrous, an unbeliever at the temple gate, yet he prayed, he didn't know to whom, asking fervently for a miracle, that somehow, in the quirks of fate and idiosyncrasies of life, there would be a way for him to go back to them and sing.

Not only was the day waiting for him, but so was the trailer-house gang. Jesse rode Toro using a hackamore while Hannah stuffed the feed bunk with hay and carried water by the pailful to the newly-acquired galvanized water tank. When he emerged from the house they shouted their greeting and blistered him for information. He fended them off and hooked up a hose to the hydrant in the yard, telling Hannah there was no need to work that hard.

"I'd carry it from our house if I had to," she said.

Both of them nagged with questions of size and color and shape and how soon they'd arrive. He bantered with them, more giddy in anticipation of giving than they were in anticipation of receiving.

Corkey distracted them briefly when he arrived from town with an abundance of grocery sacks and other goods from Sonny's ever-expanding shopping list. Corkey's only comment, "The manure factories arrive yet?" did little to alleviate the insufferable wait. Momentarily preoccupied with hauling the stores of food and goodies into the kitchen, the pickup and horse trailer caught them off guard when it came around the side of the house in its little puff of dust, materializing as from a dream.

"They're here!" Jesse shouted and leaped from the porch, followed closely by Hannah.

The trailer stopped alongside the corral and the two kids immediately became speechless. A middle-aged man got out of the cab and nodded at Sonny, who followed last on legs burned-out from his visit to the milk room.

"Howdy, Morris. We've got two rustlers here who're about to explode if you don't come up with some horse flesh real fast."

Jesse and Hannah were peering into the trailer on tiptoe like happy kids around the ice cream vendor with cash in their hands, but they couldn't see through the green tinted windows. The slim horseman moved methodically in his faded denim pants and jacket, bearing the distinct walk of a man who had spent a great deal of his life with a horse between his legs.

After opening the left rear door, he slid in beside a sorrel gelding, backing him unhurriedly. With its feet on solid ground, the horse relaxed, ears up, nostrils wide, eyes bright. The breeder passed the lead rope to Sonny, and he turned to the expectant kids, their faces glorious, gaping at the beauty and quality of this fine quarter horse.

"Here's Wildfire, Jess, you going to just stand there and look at him?"

In a trance before this magnificent animal, the skinny boy came to the horse slowly, as if savoring the moment, allowing the horse to appraise him. Then he stepped closer, rubbed the side of the sorrel's neck and threw his thin arms around him.

"Hello, Wildfire. Holy cow! thanks, Frank, he's awesome."

Sonny turned back to the trailer. A black mare with a white blaze on its forehead followed and Sonny passed the lead rope to Hannah, who bounced lightly in anticipation.

"Would you put the mare in the corral. She'll give us our foals."

The girl stood immovable for an instant, and then, collecting her wits, led the excited black into the pen, keeping an eye on the trailer for what might next emerge. From the right side backed a large buckskin gelding, snorting as it found the ground and whinnying loudly to the other horses, the ringleader.

"This critter's mine, if he doesn't wipe me out," Sonny said, slapping the horse lightly on the withers.

"He's good natured, well broke," Morris said. "He'll get used to you real quick."

The horseman disappeared into the long trailer while Sonny led his buckskin to the corral. Hannah stood frozen. Another horse nickered from within the bright red trailer and stomped its hooves as it backed out cautiously. The resplendent blanket on its hind quarters shimmered in the sunlight.

"O-o-o-h, an Appaloosa," she said, "how did you know?"

The light gray gelding made her squeal with its vivid markings: black and white spots on a light gray blanket, a four-year old with warm dark eyes and a fine head. The girl was beside herself.

"He's yours," Sonny said. "His papers are in your name."

She accepted the animal in a rapture, caressed him, allowed him to sniff her hand and face. Then she tied the end of the lead rope to the other side of the halter and pulled herself up onto his back. She rode him through the farmyard and Jesse rode Wildfire, walking him under the ever-flitting swallows. The men talked for a while and watched the kids lavish their affection on horses that may have already suspected they had fallen on good times.

When the trailer was gone, Hannah slid off the Appaloosa and ran to Sonny, flung her arms around his neck, embraced him with a fierce intensity that caught him completely unprepared. He took her by the waist and swung her around in a common celebration of the goodness of life. When he set her down, she kissed him in the thick of his bearded cheek and they laughed.

"Oh, thank you, Frank, thank you." Her expression turned pensive, and she spoke softly. "I've never had anything like this happen to me before. He's the most beautiful horse I've ever seen, and an Appaloosa, I've always wanted an Appaloosa."

His words caught in his throat and he attempted to disguise his welling emotion.

"Hey! You better catch that horse, or we'll be chasing him all the way to Three Forks."

The horse stood grazing contently on the lush grass in the yard and she remounted, trotting him around the house, the sheds, the barn. Not to be left out, Sonny joined them on the buckskin, Jesse already circling on his sorrel.

The six of them began a spontaneous celebration, riders and horses, set to music the animals seemed to feel, the blending of heart songs rising in the afternoon air like a sweet fragrance, and the barnyard, all at once, turned into fairy tale. Corkey witnessed the mystical carnival from the porch, standing immobilized as though even he could feel the rapture, the mirth these magnificent horses seemed to evoke—shining flanks with snorting nostrils, switching tails against dimpling muscles, a symphony of motion circling together like a radiant carousel, hypnotic, euphoric, striking giddy all who participated in its spell.

Overhead, not to be outdone, the playful swallows glided and swooped to the same silent refrain, adding their zooming grace to the dance. For the moment, each of the riders triumphed over their own personal darkness, the concord of their heartstrings merged with a much greater serenity than they could dream, lifted the barn-yard on delicate wings of happiness, a song sung once and always remembered by those who caught this golden moment like a rustling in the grass. Sonny surrendered to its purity, clung to its promise that it would one day remain forever.

The rhapsody was shattered by a three-hundred pound man who stepped out of his car and slammed the door.

THE FAT MAN appraised the circus atmosphere and then headed for Corkey on the porch, who felt the blood retreat from his face on seeing what belched forth from the gray sedan, knowing instinctively the man was first an agent of the CIA, and secondly, an executioner with his hand on the lever of the trapdoor and Corkey's head in the noose. As the ponderous intruder made his way through the sunlight, Corkey hoped he still had control of his vocal chords, knowing that he was witnessing an apocalyptic visitation.

"Hello. I'm Lou Pinnelli. I'm looking for Corkey Sullivan."

"You've found him." Corkey attempted to smile easily.

"Thought I recognized you from pictures. How are you?"

The man came up one step and offered a ham. Corkey stepped down and shook it, his own hand disappearing in the meat.

"What can I do for you?" Corkey asked, gritting his mental teeth.

The man watched the riders, who were taking their horses into the corral, and then turned back to Corkey. His face looked like a pie tin in which some creative baker had such an elaborate idea for pastry that he had not been able to scrunch it all in.

"Well, I do some free-lance work for the newspapers, and I've been working on a follow-up piece on Sonny Hollister. Of course it would be incomplete without your input, Mr. Sullivan. I just want to talk." The rotund inquisitor eased his frame onto a sagging step. "Have you a few minutes?"

"What can I tell you?" Corkey asked. "That story's been beat to death, ya know what I mean."

Sonny penned his horse and was walking straight for the onslaught, as though he knew that any hesitation on his part, any ducking out, would put him directly on the bull's-eye of this cannonball.

"Lou Pinnelli, this is Frank Anderson," Corkey said, avoiding Sonny's eyes.

"Don't get up," Sonny said, and Corkey could see Sonny bearing down with all his newborn strength in the handshake, squeezing the reporter's meaty hand hard as they went eye to eye, clenched like steel mill workers vieing for the same job.

"Good to meet you, Frank," he said with a deep resonant voice.

He reached into his pocket and flicked several sunflower seeds into his mouth, his loose jowls jerking rapidly like a chipmunk's as he sorted seeds and spit shells into the grass. He turned back to Corkey.

"I don't want the normal stuff, Mr. Sullivan. Enough of that to choke a horse. I look for cracks, seams in a fabric that look to be smooth and unbroken at first glance. I look for the unexpected, behind the front page veneer. I'm suspicious of everything."

He threw another bunch of sunflower seeds into his pie face.

"I don't follow you," Corkey said calmly.

Sonny acted as if he might saunter off.

"Well, for instance. You may think me crazy, but did you ever entertain the thought that Sonny Hollister didn't die in that car?"

Corkey felt his face tightening like drying plaster and it seemed the swallows were suspended in midair without flying.

"That someone else stole his car, drove it up the highway, crashed and burned?"

Pinnelli glanced from one to the other. Corkey retained his composure; Sonny looked off toward the kids and horses.

"No, I never thought of that possibility. He was seen by several people the night before in his car: the store where he bought beer, the gas station attendant. I never thought it could be anyone else," Corkey replied, presumably fascinated with this novel idea.

It seemed Corkey and Sonny both sensed, without looking at the other, that they would win or lose right here and now.

"Well, I look at it this way. Whenever someone is burned up that badly, there is a possibility that it wasn't the person everyone thought it was. You know Murphy's Law. Well this is Pinnelli's Law. When a body is totally destroyed, there is always the chance its the wrong body."

"That's an interesting theory." Corkey didn't back off.

"Well, most of my peers think I'm some kind of nut, and most of the time I am way off base, but I figure that one of these times, when everyone else is looking the other way, ol' Lou Pinnelli is going to set them on their ears."

Like a combine, he processed sunflower seeds, propelling the shells aside with his words.

"If you're right with your hunch," Corkey said, "where is Sonny, and why doesn't he tell everyone he's alive?" Corkey shrugged his shoulders, subtly giving the impression of a detached interest in this nonsense. "You've probably heard the rumor that there was a contract out on him."

"Yeah, yeah, but the accident was too subtle to pull off. It was a legitimate accident all right," Pinnelli said. "There are all kinds of other possibilities.

The kids carried on with the horses, and Jesse, bless his heart, called to Frank.

"Come on, Frank, come on!"

"Be there in a minute," he shouted, now with a reasonable out.

"There is another possibility." Corkey tensed inwardly. "Sonny got robbed and dumped out. But by the time he gets to a phone he hears he's been killed, burned up in his car. He stops and thinks. He's been a bum for years, hated the notoriety. Here's a ready-made chance to start over, a new private life with no one out to kill him. He holes up, finds some place to live unrecognized, maybe another country, Mexico. That's why I'm talking to you."

The bulky head turned on Sonny and paused, then swung back to Corkey, whose body was seeping sweat like an old engine leaking oil.

"I don't know. I think he would get in touch with me if he could. I was the only one he had in the end. I'm still his financial manager. He was flat broke and in debt when he died. He would have trouble hiding without money. He would have to put the touch on me for that."

Corkey held steady. The reporter could have found out all of that with a little investigating. *Don't lie to him!* If he caught them in a lie, he'd know he was on to something. Corkey continued calmly, giving no indication of the terror gripping him. He brushed a pesky fly from his forehead.

"That's exactly why I'm here," Pinnelli said. "If he is still alive you are the one he would come to. I even toyed with the idea that you might be hiding him up here in Montana."

Lou Pinnelli laughed from deep in his massive frame, but he watched Corkey's face intently.

"Ha," Corkey responded easily. "Interesting plan, but not for Sonny Hollister. He wouldn't last out here for three days, ya know what I mean. He'd need the city, people, action. He'd go insane with all this peace and quiet. And besides," Corkey grew bolder, "if it wasn't Sonny, who was it who fried in the car? No one has ever filed a 'missing person.'"

The newsman seemed disappointed, turning more aggressively to Sonny, who sat on the edge of the porch.

"You a native to these parts, Frank?"

The way he turned his head, without a visible neck, Corkey thought he resembled an owl. It was the goddamned great horned owl that Sonny was always talking about, stalking them, his eyes piercing, his talons poised. What slippery path was he leading them down?

"No. I found this country about seven years ago, try to get back as often as I can from Florida. I think I'll settle in this valley."

"You in the entertainment business, too?" The predator kept stalking.

"N-o-o-o." Sonny grinned. "Real estate, have some great lots in the Sarasota area if you're interested. I might do a little speculating around here."

The hunter didn't respond, and Corkey guessed his brain was working at maximum capacity, sifting through their every word and inflection for any glint of gold. He turned back to Corkey.

"Did Sonny own any land around here, or anywhere?"

"Not any more, as far as I know. Owned and sold several places around the country, but nothing left. He'd hocked his cars, trucks, plane, everything, lost it all gambling."

"I've got to help the kids for a minute. Why don't you stay and eat with us, Lou," Sonny said, all but causing Corkey to choke on his Adam's apple. "You could find out more about Hollister, and we could hear what it's like to be a big-time reporter."

"That's mighty good of you, but I've got some other things to do. Corkey, I just wanted you to kick around some of the possibilities. It's a strange world we live in, my friend. Maybe you'll think of something now that I've planted a seed. If Sonny *was* alive, where on God's earth would he be?"

The fat man took a card out of his wallet, handing it to Corkey, and in the same motion, chucked several sunflower seeds into his mouth. Corkey almost laughed with the suspense, wanting to answer that one for this munching bowling ball. He's standing right in front of you, moron!

"I'd sure as hell like to see him again," Corkey said. "I wish Pinnelli's Law was operating this one time, but I really don't think there's a ghost of a chance, ya know what I mean."

Corkey avoided any eye contact with Sonny, fearing that their faces would betray them, understanding there was fatal danger here. *Do nothing to ruffle the feathers of this great bird of prey.*

"If you do come up with anything," Corkey added, "please let me know. I can see how your story could sell a lot of papers."

"We don't operate that way, Mr. Sullivan." Pinnelli was miffed. "They wouldn't print one word unless I had absolute proof. I'm looking for the truth, not some cock-and-bull story."

The fastidious reporter was obviously puzzled and frustrated, like he felt he was close to something, could smell it, but could not nail it down. Corkey knew the bald head, the beard, and the glasses would never fool this man. It was what Sonny had accomplished with his body. Corkey was betting that the dramatic change in Sonny's body would stop Lou Pinnelli from getting the brass ring.

"I'll stop again before I leave the country." The huge man tipped his finger as if from the brim of a hat and settled into the car, the gray sedan leaning with his mass. He propelled sunflower seeds from his brawny yap, closed the door, and watched them for a moment through the open window. They stood rigid, trying to call up nonchalance and casualness without success, schoolboys with firecrackers in their pockets, being eyed by an angry principal whose wastepaper basket had just exploded, still undecided if he would search them. Then he drove off.

"What in hell were you doing!" Corkey shouted, "inviting him to stay? Judas Priest! I didn't know if I could answer one more lousy question without coming unglued."

Corkey wiped his face with his handkerchief and wilted onto the step.

"Hey, I was dying, but I figured he'd expect us to try to get rid of him if there was anything to his hunch. So I did the opposite. Did you see how disappointed he was?"

Corkey tried to breathe freely, but his chest was so taut he could manage only gulps of air.

"Do you think he knows?" Corkey said.

"No. I think the man is always scratching, hoping one day he'll hit something big. And this time he did. He hit it right on the stinkin' head, and he didn't know it. The poor boob finally made Pinnelli's Law pay off, and he's going to blow it. He looked right at the living, breathing Sonny Hollister and went home empty."

Sonny hooted, some of the tension released in the air. A magpie skipped across the barnyard, and Jesse hollered for Sonny to join them.

"I'm going in and lie down," Corkey said. "We'll know soon enough if he's onto us. Maybe he's calling the paper right now. I won't be able to watch the news tonight. Mother of God, when this blows over, I'm getting out of here. I'll leave this place to you, but I'm not going to hang around anymore. My heart can't take it. Tell me my heart is still beating, tell me I'll be alive tomorrow."

Corkey swung his deformed foot up the steps and vanished behind the screen door with the manner of one who'd just survived a train wreck. Sonny turned for the kids and horses, hoping he could recapture some of the joy they had shared before the great horned owl swooped into their tree. It was a short distance, but he ran.

Jesse was walking Wildfire around the barnyard, and Hannah was getting acquainted with her Appaloosa: turning him with the shifting of her weight, speaking to him, backing him.

"Boy, Wildfire would break in two if that fatso climbed on him," Jesse said.

"Jesse! Watch your mouth," Hannah said.

"Well he would," Jesse said.

"He was enormous," Hannah said. "Who is he?"

"Just a guy looking for some land to buy," Sonny said, climbing onto the corral and causing the mare to shy. "So what are we hanging around here for? We can't ride them like this."

The kids rode their horses into the corral and Sonny shut the gate.

"Saddles?" Jesse said with his eyes widening.

"Saddles and bits and bridles and saddle blankets and feed buckets and whatever else the salesman can talk us into."

They scrambled off the backs of their horses and unsnapped the lead ropes from the halters. Sonny slipped through the rails, smacked his hands together, and raced for the pickup.

"Last one in the pickup buys hamburgers."

Then he remembered, he had no money in his jeans. He burst

through the door, dug a roll of bills from his closet, and explained to Corkey on his way by. His rush was all for nothing and the two saddle tramps were waiting for him in the pickup.

"You have to buy the hamburgers, Frank." Jesse grinned.

In Bozeman they started with hamburgers, then invaded Quality Wholesale, a large farm and ranch store where they all but filled the pickup bed to the amazement of the store clerks and the new equestrian kids. They finished the job at the elevator feed store on North Rouse and then headed for the barn. Jesse was worn down and slept with his head against his sister's shoulder, which forced Hannah to lean against Sonny.

"Frank, the saddle is gorgeous, and the blanket, but it cost so much," she said. "You spent over *two thousand* dollars."

"Did you have fun?"

"Yes, it was fun, I felt like Cinderella, and I can't wait to get back, I want to ride all night."

He felt her large eyes regarding him.

"Why are you so good to us?"

"Because it ain't no fun having a horse all by yourself."

"Be serious."

"I am. I enjoy doing it, and I want to have a horse with all the trimmings. Have you ever seen how sad a horse looks when he's the only horse on a place, one saddle hanging in a shed, one halter, one bridle? I hate lonesome horses."

Sonny felt good, calm inside, despite the obese reporter now on the same horizon as Sally's ex. He glanced into the rearview mirror and caught the reflection of her fetching face while she jabbered about the horses, while her eyes danced to the song in her voice, and her happiness sloshed all over him.

"Do you love Mom?" Hannah said.

"Ah, no . . . I like her a lot . . . she's a nice woman. Why?"

"I thought maybe you were being good to us to please Mom."

The girl's mind hadn't been able to grasp this overwhelming generosity without some underlying reason. He always made the same mistake; you can't blow people away with gifts and gold without their trying to find some reasonable explanation, some unspoken obligation—that a great deal is required of those who accept great and extravagant gifts.

"No . . . nothing to do with Sally. I'm simply having fun."

There was considerable commotion for some time in the barn-yard after their return. Jesse gave in first, sitting on Wildfire in the corral and lying against his blond mane while Hannah busied herself with the horses and tack, taking charge of organizing and storing the feed and equipment.

When the kids rode off to show Sally they'd found the end of the rainbow, he stepped around behind the shed and past the old out-house, standing quietly and scanning the fields north to the foothills. Like a dream he'd forgotten, he recalled the feel of Hannah's supple waist in his hands, his thumbs grazing her rib cage, and he felt a shiver down his back.

Chapter 29

THROUGH GENTLE heat waves of summer, Sonny guided the battered International tractor along the windrows, towing the thumping baler behind. Nostalgia clung to him with hay dust. In its wake the old New Holland baler left a patchwork of bales, winter rations for the livestock. Aware that he had experienced this back in another world, he prodded his memory and cast about for the veiled figures lurking in the heat mirages of his mind. He attempted to call up their faces and voices across the hayfield, but they fled every time he drew near, reluctant ghosts. The tines swept the rows of blossoming alfalfa into the mouth of the insatiable baler like a river of time flowing past him. The refrain from last night's singing lingered in his head.

"Picking up the pieces of my sweet,
shattered dream,
I wonder how the old folks are tonight. . . ."

Butch had scrounged three fifty-five-gallon oil drums so Hannah could barrel race in the pasture and in the evening the three of them often rode in the foothills while there was still light, exploring, following game trails, and playing hide-and-seek on horseback. Hannah named her Appaloosa Gusty; he called the buckskin Keemosabie, and anyone observing from a distance would trace their silhouettes as three kids enjoying summer vacation on horseback.

Like a nocturnal animal Sonny had plotted a course through the star-lit pasture, cottonwood groves, and weedy ditches by which he could reach the trailer and bring Sally back to the house unnoticed. They'd seen each other a few times like that: once she gave him a thorough massage at the ranch, a godsend to his weary muscles; another time they watched television at the trailer, but he always had the concealed .44 handgun in a jacket he carried.

Hesitant and skittish about becoming involved, they needed the affection and comfort the other could give. Though he recognized he had a strong inner yearning for a woman, he felt his luck ran out with Julia, and after countless shattered hopes of finding the right woman amid a sea of breasts and thighs and sex-soaked sheets, he'd steeled his mind against ever falling in love again. It always asked too much; it always bore too much pain. Sally kept insisting she didn't want to get serious, but the night she massaged him with her firm, warm touch, they tumbled into lovemaking like two kids who had run away from home.

Sonny found a great satisfaction in the work, guiding the tractor, the bales, neat and uniform, strewn across the bright green field in geometrical patterns. At the far end of the field he spotted Sally's pickup as the baler methodically ate the windrow toward her. She sat in the truck with the door swung open and talked with Hezekiah and by the time Sonny reached the pickup, Hezekiah was back raking hay in the adjacent field. Sonny climbed off the tractor and hobbled stiff-legged to the pickup.

"Couldn't last the day without seeing me, huh?"

"Thought you'd like some lunch," she said. "Hezekiah turned me down flat, afraid the weather would turn on him if he stopped to eat. I didn't know he had a dog?"

"He doesn't, not anymore, he just forgets sometimes."

Expecting her usual blithe spirit, he sensed a turmoil in her frown. "He been bothering you again?"

"I just ran into him in town. He said he knows I've been running around and that he'll be out to see me soon, that a husband shouldn't let his wife go too long without servicing, just like a good truck." Her shoulders slumped. "I'm so scared, and so damn weary."

"Why won't you report him?"

"We're going to move. A friend wrote me about a good job opening in Denver, but God, I hate to move the kids now, with the horses and all. They're so happy and—"

"Doggone it, woman," he said, pounding a fist on the cab roof, "tell me why in hell's name you won't turn the bastard in!"

"All right, I'll tell you!" She scowled at him. "I did report him, the first time he hit me. They locked him up and fined him. When he got out he took me by the throat and lifted me off the floor against the wall and told me that if I ever turned him in again, he'd pay his fine and serve his time and then come back and kill me. I believe him, Frank, he has nothing to live for, he'd really kill me."

Sonny couldn't argue with that. He shut the pickup door and spoke through the open window.

"Listen, don't worry about it, I'll take care of it."

He slapped the metal door as if spurring on a horse and turned for the tractor.

"How about your lunch?" she called.

"Just set it out. I'll get it later."

When he reached the opposite corner of the hayfield, he shut down the machinery and ran to where Hezekiah was working.

"I'm going to town for an hour," Sonny shouted, "thought you'd want to take over the baling."

He found Steve Ramsey in The Hub, the second bar he searched, where only a handful of customers hid from the mid-day sun. With his stomach sucked in and his posture tall, he walked up to the booth where the trucker sat with two other men, smiled friendlylike, and zeroed in on Ramsey.

"I'd like to talk to you for a minute."

The bully studied him defiantly, as though making sure Sonny was the one he'd seen on the porch with the axe handle.

"What about?"

His two buddies eyeballed Sonny with hostile expressions.

"About a job I've got for you," Sonny said calmly. "Good money."

Sonny turned, walked to the front, and settled at an empty table. There was no reaction from the booth, and Sally's ex-husband continued jawing with his comrades. One of them laughed loudly.

"Need anything?" the young girl tending bar called.

"No . . . no thanks," Sonny said.

The three men slid out of the booth and ambled toward him. Ramsey stopped at Sonny's table and the other two continued out of the bar. He took a drag from a cigarette and glared at Sonny.

"You arm-wrestle?"

"Not lately."

"We got a bench back there. Usually go at it Saturday nights. Let's go a round."

"Why?" Sonny glanced at the trucker's arm and shoulder.

"You got something to say to me? That's where I listen."

He strutted to the back of the saloon and Sonny hesitated. Now what did he do for cryin' out loud? He was losing his rage.

Remember, this is the slime bag that raped Sally!

Sonny got up and followed him, calculating which muscles would come into play in arm wrestling. What the hell, he'd been working out for months. In a corner, behind the pool table, sat a green vinyl arm wrestling table with two seats and handles to grip. Ramsey eased himself onto one of the seats and banged his right elbow down on the worn padded deck.

Sonny stood across from him. "Listen, you've been—"

"Hey, hey, hey!" the teamster said, "we wrestle first, then we talk. Otherwise, I'm out of here, you savvy?"

Sonny wiped his right hand on his jeans and slid into the other seat. He took hold of the trucker's hard hand, and Ramsey glared at him with a ferocity that set off alarms in Sonny's skull. He braced himself. Then the trucker spoke in cast iron.

"Whenever you're ready, *cowboy.*"

Sonny clenched the trucker's fist and drove his forearm toward the padded tabletop. The man showed no emotion, very little strain, and he held off Sonny's best effort without going down more than a quarter of the arc to the table. There, trembling, they were stalemated. Ramsey never took his hardened eyes off Sonny's, never blinked. Sonny felt the sweat seeping from his face. Then, suddenly, the trucker let up for a split second, and with a lightning stroke, slammed Sonny's hand flat against the table. Very slowly, as though his face were molten rock, he smiled.

"Now, what's the job?" he said.

Sonny jerked his hand free.

"The job is to haul your ass out of Sally's life! If I—"

"Hey, you're the one—"

Sonny held up his hand and went with the first thing that came to mind.

"Just listen, you yellow skunk. I have terminal cancer and I'm a little crazy."

He leaned so close to Ramsey's face he could smell the trucker's sweat.

"I won't live much longer so it don't make a good damn difference to me. You ever *see* Sally again, you ever *talk* to her, you ever *drive down that road,* and I'll just walk up to you with my trusty .44 magnum and lift the top of your skull off, just like that." Sonny snapped his fingers. "That's simple enough for you to understand isn't it, moron?"

Sonny stood quickly, keeping his eyes zeroed on Ramsey's. The man strained behind a bulging face, and Sonny tightened his fists, expecting an immediate assault.

"By the way, you never could've beaten me if it wasn't for the chemotherapy; takes all my strength. Don't need much for my trigger finger though." He wiggled his index finger, smiled, and winked. "It's been real nice talking to you."

Ramsey sat motionless, his radiator threatening to boil over, and Sonny turned for the door. An inner voice warned him to duck. Then he noticed a deputy sheriff lingering at the bar, visiting with the young female bartender. Maybe he hadn't bluffed the bully as much as he thought.

He laughed aloud to himself as he drove for the ranch, so pumped up his hands shook holding the steering wheel.

"Did you see the look on that bastard's face?" he shouted into the wind. "I think he was wetting his pants. Hoooeeeee! Terminal cancer, hell, I'm already dead."

Angry at himself for letting that psycho whip him, he wanted to go right to the milk room to do penance, but when he reached the ranch, the exhilaration from the confrontation faded, and with it his confidence. Maybe it was a dumb play, but it might work. That coward had his way with Sally because there was no one his size to stand up to him. Would he be willing to fool around with her when he knows that some nut with a .44 magnum has an interest in it? It might be all that was needed to send that mother and his eighteen-wheeler down the road for good. But Sonny noticed a cruelty in Steve's eye, hints of an irrational mind, and he was well aware that he could've made things worse. Either way, he'd soon find out.

Sonny recognized a satisfaction he hadn't known before as he loaded fresh bales on the wagon as insurance against the distant winter, preparing for the seasons like the wild creatures he was coming to notice and appreciate. He recognized that there was something deep within him that knew this rhythm by heart. At forty-seven bales he felt a natural weariness that was an exhilarating high, and knowing he would have trouble keeping any more on the wagon, he drove carefully for the ranch. While he was backing the wagon into the barn, the fat man came around the building and hailed him.

"Hello, Frank, Corkey around?"

"Oh, Lou . . . no he's not." Sonny shut off the truck and stepped out. "He's back in the city. Every year he slips away when the hay is ready, afraid we'll put him to work. Anything I can do for you?"

Sonny walked along the corral, the reporter keeping abreast. Rubbing the nose of the affectionate mare, Sonny fortified himself against the alarm arising in his bones.

"Magnificent horses," the sleuth said, impressed with the occupants of the lodgepole corral.

"They better be. I paid enough for them. I only hope I can make this mare pay off with some first rate foals. Could you go for a beer?" Sonny asked, looking directly into Lou Pinnelli's portly face.

Jeez! First a showdown with the psycho truck driver, and now a shootout with the fat man.

"It would be appreciated."

They walked to the house and into the kitchen, Sonny almost encouraging the newspaper man to scrutinize the house for any clue, any shred of evidence that would confirm his fantastic hunch, the guitar religiously stashed under the bed. They each finished a beer and started another through a guise of small talk, Pinnelli never asking a direct question, skirting the issue, mundane things. They settled outside on the edge of the porch with the second can, and Sonny took the initiative.

"Do you really think Sonny Hollister is still alive?"

"You know, it's funny." The huge man sounded congenial, appeared relaxed. "I'm disappointed as hell after coming up here and poking around. I could feel this one in my bones. After talking to Corkey and playing out my hand, I came up with nothing. And you know, I still got that feeling. I've got to get on with some other things, but I'm not giving up on it."

Lou Pinnelli tipped his massive head back and drained the tiny can.

A '55 Chevy rolled into the yard without a muffler, and the horses and swallows remained edgy after the unnatural rumble had been silenced. Hannah and Butch flung their greetings and went for the tack shed. Lou Pinnelli watched them and asked,

"What did you think of him?"

"Who?" Sonny asked, realizing this cunning boxer may be trying to bring down Sonny's guard before throwing his best punch.

"Sonny Hollister."

"Not much. I never paid attention to popular music in those days. Still don't, much. I didn't even realize who Corkey was until after I had done some business with him."

"Do you think it was the slaughter of his wife and boy that destroyed Sonny?"

Pinnelli's eyes bore in on him. He was playing dirty.

"I didn't pay much attention to all that, saw a little on the news, so I don't have a clue."

Sonny looked him in the eye.

"Christ," Pinnelli said, "everyone in that plane was shredded into bits and pieces, they never saw anything like it. First people on the scene said that from among the Christmas wrappings and clothing farm dogs were feeding and carrying off body parts."

The slime bag was playing his trump card and Sonny wanted to rip his stinking throat out.

"Sounds gruesome," Sonny said softly and he gazed at Hannah and Butch as they saddled their horses. He nodded at the kids.

"There's a story for you. Her father drives a truck and beats the hell out of her mother, and the law can't protect her."

"No, no, no, I stay away from that crap. You never know who's who in those deals, who's wearing the white hat and who the black. Usually turns out they're trading around. I learned the hard way a long time ago. Some of those women expect to get worked over now and then, or they wouldn't stand for it. It makes them feel cleansed. Some say it gives them a sexual thrill."

"That's bullshit." Sonny bristled, struggling to keep his composure.

The corpulent man raised his bulk and stood on the ground.

"Maybe, but I'm after bigger game. Who in hell wants to read about another slob beating on his wife? I'm much obliged for the beer and hospitality. Maybe I'll look you up when I'm in Florida some time."

"I'll tell Corkey you were here."

Sonny was drained, but he remained sitting, thinking it best if he did not appear over solicitous. He ignored the probe about Florida, hoping the reporter would not ask for an address, though Corkey had provided him with one. Pinnelli didn't, driving away with a wave of his pork chop hand. Sonny sat still, breathing more easily and wondering how much of this he could endure. He hoped he wouldn't run into Lou Pinnelli again, but he'd like to see him when this life was over, just once, and tell him that his instincts were perfect, that Pinnelli's Law had him drinking a beer with the presumed-dead Sonny Hollister, and he had blown it. For Lou Pinnelli, that would be hell.

He showered and found something to eat and tried to swallow the heavy-heartedness he could not identify. Lou Pinnelli? No. The truck driver? No, that was not it. He could never be himself again and go back . . . he had found it.

Chapter 30

THE HARVEST of Linesinger alfalfa brought them together on an extravagant summer day, though Hezekiah hadn't asked for help. They crisscrossed the bale-strewn meadow time and again and gathered the bales into a bright green edifice. Hezekiah drove the homemade haybuck that gobbled up bales like a huge prehistoric grasshopper and dumped them atop the rising stack. Sonny and Hannah dragged and hefted the bales into place after being thoroughly instructed by Hezekiah on the vanishing art of stacking hay by hand. Jesse drove the Jeep in first gear, slowly pulling the hay wagon while Butch and Rock, Hannah's Indian friend, loaded bales on the wagon by hand. When the bed was covered, they'd dump their load near the stack for Hezekiah to hoist with the haybuck. Methodically the bales disappeared from the field and rose higher and higher in the many-layered stockpile.

When Sonny and Hannah finished stacking the immediate load of bales, they could rest until the haybuck disgorged another half-ton of alfalfa. Sonny welcomed the refreshing southwest breeze and the radiant white clouds that occasionally crossed the sun high above their bustling activity. Caught up in this day with an all-embracing tranquility, he left everything else behind. Without warning he flopped on the stack spread-eagle, his face to the sun, and sighed.

"Aaaah, just tell Hezekiah to bury me right here."

Hannah gulped from the water jug and he admired her from his prone position, this five foot six girl who probably weighed no more than a hundred and fifteen pounds yet grappled with sixty-five pound bales and lifted, jostled, and wedged them into place in the intricate pattern of the stack. With a red bandanna around her head for a sweat band, she was charming in a blue cotton work shirt, faded jeans, and a floppy pair of leather gloves they scrounged from Hezekiah's tool shed.

"How are you doing, tough guy?" Sonny said, shielding his eyes from the sun's glare with one hand.

"I'm beat."

Her face had tanned with the summer, only adding to a natural allure he was becoming more aware of every time he saw her.

"Where did you find Rock?"

"In Bozeman. His name is really Fallen Rock but he wants to be called Rock. He's a gentle person, but some people don't tolerate original Americans in Bozeman, the enlightened college town of the West. Sometimes they go after them for the sport of it."

An uncharacteristic bitterness laced her words, and he let it go, hearing the engine roaring across the field with the never-ending bales.

Hezekiah rumbled toward them, the haybuck's long wooden teeth stuffed with bales, and it jettisoned them on top of the stack with the hydraulic pump screeching. Blue smoke belched from the old Ford's stack, Hezekiah gunned off to sweep up another fourteen or fifteen bales, and the two of them tugged and dragged the bales into place.

"Have you ever read anything about whales?"

Hannah puffed as she spoke.

"Whales!" Sonny laughed, kicking a reluctant bale into a tight fit. "Why whales?"

"I love them, they're the most fascinating mammals on earth, and before we find out much about them, we're going to exterminate them."

"I don't know anything about them, except they're big."

He grunted over a green heavyweight and reflected on what this kind of work would have done to him if he hadn't been working out like a madman for over five months. Hannah went on about whales, and the stack grew under the metallic sun.

"If you'd like to read about them I have a book I think you'd like."

She was an evangelist for the whales and he wanted to share her enthusiasm.

"I have a thing for elephants," he said.

A wagonload arrived; Butch and Jesse and Rock unloaded it below the high stack, and Sonny caught sight of Sally's truck coming through the fields with food and beverage, more welcome than a beer truck at an open pit mine. He shouted his joy to her with the prospect of chow and rest, and he followed Hannah down the ladder, a widow-maker Hezekiah had constructed from scrap lumber.

When he reached the ground, Sally was talking to Jesse, who had been shoving bales off the wagon, and they were arguing. The boy got off the wagon and stood rigid, accepting her reprimand stoically. Jesse jerked his arm away from her and stomped off by himself, and she began spreading out the food on the tailgate like a chuck wagon cook, prodding the hands to help themselves to her offerings in her usual good-natured manner.

Fallen Rock hung back until Sally led him to the picnic, and they all ate ham sandwiches, potato salad, and drank cold lemonade in the shade of the monument they were collectively constructing. Small talk prevailed, with some tall stories of ninety-pound bales, Jesse's erratic driving, and Linesingers gathering hay over the decades amidst typhoons and earthquake.

Sonny drew Jesse into the conversation with some difficulty, but it was obvious the boy had lost his spirit. With the others seemingly oblivious to it, Sonny attempted to ignore the tension Sally brought to the hayfield. The crew sprawled in the shade and allowed the food and drink some time to rejuvenate them while Sally gathered dishes and packed away what was left. He drifted over to the pickup where she busied herself.

"I hope I haven't gotten Jess in trouble, he's worked like a man all morning."

"That's the trouble," she said without looking up. "I'm taking him home with me."

"Why? You can't do that to him, he's feeling awfully important right now."

He recalled how it was for a young boy on a farm.

"Please stay out of it, Frank, I'm taking him with me."

Her voice was calm but strained, and when she glanced at him, he could not decipher the storm there in her eyes.

"You should see him driving that old Jeep, he's ten feet tall. Let him stay, please, we need him."

He helped her slam the tailgate.

"I need him too."

She got into the truck, leaving the door open.

"I don't get it. Why don't you want him to stay?"

"Well there are just some things you aren't supposed to get, so please stay out of it."

"What the hell is wrong with you, lady?"

"Okay, okay," she sagged behind the wheel. "I'm going to break a promise to the person I love most in this world. Jesse likes you, he likes being with you, he tries to do what you do, and damn it, you just don't understand." She caught a sob. "And I can't take flack from any more directions, so Lord. . . ." She looked up at the roof of the cab. ". . . I'm going to tell him."

She gripped the steering wheel, stared blankly through the bug-pocked windshield, and delivered the blow with a soft, iron voice.

"He's dying, Frank, he's dying, and there isn't a thing anyone can do about it."

She covered her gaping mouth with both hands, as if she were trying to contain the horror and prevent it from pouring out all over the hayfield. He steadied himself against the pickup cab.

"Dying!"

His legs felt as if someone had lifted a four-hundred-pound bar-bell onto his shoulders.

"Oh God, Sally, I'm so sorry, so. . . ."

His throat filled, he couldn't think. She bit her lip and struggled to remain in control.

"What's wrong with him?"

"Bone cancer . . . his body is eating itself."

He sucked a breath. "Oh, God, oh dear God."

"The big words the doctors use are obscene, words they use to hide their helplessness. It's like fifty thousand boys walked across a desert barefooted and only Jesse stepped on a thorn."

"Would money help?"

"No . . . he's been to Mayo, Seattle, the Shriners in Texas, God, what they've put that boy through. He's been to the best but the 'best' isn't good enough. It's always the same. They don't know anything else to do."

Sonny regarded her in shock, recoiled from the blow with his own seething rage. How misled he was when he assumed he knew another person's life, remembering how he first assessed her: a curvy, happy-go-lucky lady who hadn't a care in the world, while all along she was living out a personal holocaust. He labored to ask the question he didn't want answered.

"How long?"

"In Texas they said maybe a year, that was seven months ago. You don't see him when he's bad, you don't see the long nights, the times he can't keep food down, my god, I never think I'll get through the next hour . . . and then it clears up, and he seems normal again. Only every time, I can see . . . he's a bit smaller, a bit weaker, a bit paler. When he feels well enough, I let him go, damnit! I don't want him to spend his last days in bed. I'm not stupid, I know what it means to him, but I don't want to lose him yet, either, is that so wrong?"

She turned and looked pleadingly into his blurring eyes.

"Is it so wrong to want him for as long as I can?"

He glanced over at the crew, sitting along the shaded side of the stack. Jesse was one of them, enjoying his part in harvesting the hay, pulling his own weight. Sonny draped his arms on the roof of the cab and hung his head between them. He spoke softly.

"And he knows?"

"Yes, he knows. I swear he's a saint, Frank. Hannah knows, but no one else and he wants to keep it that way. I broke my trust with him. Promise me, you must never let on that—"

"Never," he said, catching his breath. "Never. Let him stay, I'll have him sit up on the stack and keep a count of the bales, and I'll do it so he feels it's the most important job out there."

She pulled the door shut and handed him a package of Oreo cookies through the open window. Without a word she started the engine and drove off into the shimmering summer sea.

Though he approached the waiting crew with a light-hearted bearing, Sonny gathered himself for the toughest acting job of his life.

"Cookies," he said and tossed the Oreos to Butch.

"Is Mom leaving?" Jesse asked with surprise.

"Yep, had to get going. I told her how much we needed you, so she figured you ought to stay and help."

"A-l-l RIGHT!" Jesse said.

The boy held up his hands and Sonny slapped them sharply, and the crew scattered to their different tasks. Sonny attempted to sound matter-of-fact when he asked Jesse to work on the stack, and the boy was delighted to climb to the top, shouting down to Butch and Rock.

When Sonny overheard his father say *The boy has to start pulling his own weight around here,* it confused Sonny because he had wanted to help on the farm and offered many times. But his father usually said he was too young or it would be too hard for him or Sonny wouldn't do it well enough. His father's words were engraved into his being. He didn't want to do that to Jesse.

Relentlessly, Hezekiah steamed toward them with the haybuck creaking under its load. With muscle and sweat, Sonny and Hannah worked the rising stack while Jesse chattered continuously, but Sonny couldn't remember the conversation. At times the anguish nearly choked him and he gulped for breath, his mind muddled, his chest a heavy stone. That morning he'd worked with these people, struggled together against the harvest tonnage, laughed and joked in the charity of this July day. Who would suspect, with all of creation springing forth in the butterfly-air, that hell had stained it with its filthy joke? With his own loneliness so close to the surface, he felt like a dwarf next to this boy with a giant's heart. Jesse carried his own death around in his pocket with a fishhook and some baling twine and a rusty jackknife, and he bore it alone; he wanted no one to accommodate him with a sugarcoated pity, to poison his remaining days.

Sonny castigated himself for not reading the signs, for never suspecting. Doggone it, he'd run the boy pretty hard on occasion, but just when he was becoming most severe with himself, he understood that was exactly what the boy wanted: no kid gloves, living vigorously with every heartbeat, running freely with his final step. Rage filled his senses as he shoved and slammed the bales into another layer. He wanted to punch something in the face!

And he wanted to say something, to tell them how he felt, to warn them that these moments in the sun together were precious and fleeting. But he had no way to show them the windstorms in his heart. He thumped a heavy bale into place and regarded the crew in the field. In spite of this sun-drenched summer day, they each carried their own death in their pockets with fish hooks and rusty jackknives.

They finished the stack by mid-afternoon and everyone but Hezekiah cheered when those last few bales completed the thirteenth and final level because the ingenious but primitive haybuck would simply lift them no higher. In the Jeep, Hezekiah roared out to begin irrigating the lower end of the field, and the rest of them loaded a ton of hay onto the sagging Dodge pickup and headed for the ranch.

Sonny conjured up some form of retaliation as he drove, and at the barn, he put them to work stacking the bales while he went in and frantically scrambled on the phone. When he emerged from the house with a plan in mind, they were waiting for him. Butch had to be at work at the Conoco station in Belgrade, and Sonny gathered them to pay off the crew.

"Hezekiah wanted me to pay you by the day so the books are up to date."

He gave each of them fifty dollars, causing shocked surprise and a great deal of happiness.

"Wow, thanks," Butch said, "if I get some more time off I'll help again."

"Fifty dollars!" Jesse said, "I thought we were just doing it to help Hezekiah out, I never made so much money in my whole life, I wish I could stack hay every day."

Fallen Rock accepted the money with a passive gratitude and shoved the bill into his jeans. Butch got into his Chevy sedan and growled the engine like an animal.

"Hey, Frank, want to race some time?"

"Sure, I'll race you, but don't bet that money on your Chevy."

The freckle-faced young man laughed and rode out of the yard on his noise. Under the pretense of giving Rock a ride into Bozeman, they all piled into the pickup cab and were soon streaking down the interstate. They had several frosty mugs of root beer at the A&W, and then dropped off Rock near the high school.

"He looks like he could play basketball," Sonny said as they pulled away.

"He can, but the white kids hit on him so viciously that he gave it up," Hannah said.

"In Bozeman? Gosh, it looks like such a decent town."

"Yes, it looks like it, but under the picture postcard there's a malignancy."

Why did he keep forgetting about small towns?

With a mysterious air he drove a serpentine route over the many roads south of Bozeman, only slipping once with the phrase Your mother's going to kill me. That didn't help Jesse or Hannah who kept asking where they were going and acting as though they expected something good to happen. They pulled into an acre lot where a new home stood.

"I hope this is the place," Sonny said. "Wait here."

Sonny knocked on the door and when a man appeared, Sonny went into the house. When Sonny reappeared twenty minutes later, bundling a huge brown puppy in his arms, Jesse was asleep. Hannah had him up and awake instantly, and they beamed at the clumsy surprise Sonny held up to the window of the truck.

"This here poor puppy ain't got no boy," he said.

Then he knelt and set the squirming pup on the lawn. Jesse bounded from the pickup and raced around the front only to be pounced on by a warm ungainly lover with a huge wet tongue. Hannah got into the act, unable to resist this Teddy bear of a dog, but soon she stepped aside, and Sonny and Hannah witnessed the love feast on the grass. Mischievous, bearish, amorous, the heavy-footed behemoth butted and chewed and waylaid the boy at every opportunity. He knocked Jesse over and rolled him across the lawn, dug the boy's face out from under his arms to assail it with kisses, sporting so much excess skin the puppy resembled a kid wearing his mother's fur coat. Jesse laughed so hard he could hardly catch his breath and when this canine clown took hold of a pant leg and began dragging him back and forth across the yard like a rag doll, Sonny came to the rescue, fearing that the boy would die with delight. It was a match made in heaven—or wherever it is that dogs are yoked with boys in eternal bonds—and the three of them shanghaied the mutt and sallied forth against the darkness.

"What kind of dog is he?" she said.

"He's a Rhodesian ridgeback. The fellow told me they were bred to hunt lions, Jess. He's an African dog, and if they get too hungry, they eat boys."

The breeder informed Sonny they were known for their diligence in guarding and protecting children. Not this child. Against lions and thieves and swollen rivers, maybe, but the Rhodesian ridgeback could do nothing to protect Jesse from his own cannibalistic cells.

They rolled along the tourist-cluttered highway and the wind flushed through the cab, sucked hay dust from their faces and hair. The pup was already the size of a small Labrador and gaining, with a milk chocolate coat and large, friendly eyes. Jesse was ecstatic with his new companion; Sonny could see it, and it lifted the weight momentarily from his chest. The dog and boy fell asleep with the motion and hum of the truck, worn out from their romp on the lawn.

"You know, don't you," Hannah said without looking at him.

"Yes." He gripped the wheel tightly.

Now he was one of them.

They had to disturb the roustabouts when Sonny pulled into the parking lot of Lee & Dad's supermarket in Belgrade. He bought six fifty-pound bags of Puppy Chow, hoping it would lighten the impact of this gregarious beast on Sally, more than a little uncertain about her reaction to the unexpected pooch.

"What're you going to name him?" Sonny asked.

"I don't know," Jesse said, "will he get much bigger?"

"You ever seen an elephant?"

"Then the name's got to be big." Jesse was quiet for a moment. "How about Goodyear?"

"Why good year?" Sonny didn't connect.

"For the blimp." Jesse laughed.

The sun was nearing the western rim of the mountains when they arrived at the trailer, and the homecoming had a fairy tale resplendence. Time seemed to stand still for the moment, not counting it against these weary harvesters in the uplifting spell of the ragamuffin whelp. Outside the trailer, the young dog attacked Sally with its merciless affection and then turned to exploring the wide new world with Jesse's company. Sonny slung a fifty pound sack over his shoulder and glanced at Sally,

"Where would you like this?"

"Put most of it in the shed, if you can cram it in. Gosh, Frank, that ought to be enough for the rest of his life."

"Don't say anything until you've seen him eat. Three hundred pounds ought to get him through the first week."

He set the sack in the shed and turned back to face her.

"I should've checked with you first, but I just had to do something. I hope I didn't—"

"I know, I know, it's a wonderful idea."

"I always go off half-cocked, but I thought—"

"Frank, it's all right, really, Jesse's happy, that's all that matters."

When the dog food was unloaded, Sonny slipped back into the truck, only then recognizing his complete exhaustion. Sally came to the truck door, and they watched Jesse and the ridgeback engrossed in what might be lurking under the wood pile. Sonny felt a small leap of joy, knowing the dog had taken to the kid as if they were out of the same litter.

"Why didn't I think of that?" she said.

"He's had all his shots and his food is all paid for at the grocery store, anytime you want to pick up a bag just. . . ."

They searched each other's eyes for an instant, and then turned away. He wanted to take her in his arms and hold her until she forgot everything else—until they both did.

"We have to make the moments count," he said quietly.

He was about to lose it when Hannah saved him. She came barefooted from the trailer and handed him a paperback.

"Here's the book I was telling you about, read it whenever you get around to it, no hurry, are you going to stack tomorrow?"

"Yeah, I guess I'll help the old buzzard until he's done. But you don't—"

"I want to, I'll revive, see you tomorrow."

He turned the pickup and headed out onto the county road. Jesse and the puppy ran him down and he hit the brakes.

"Thanks, Frank, I love him," the boy said, winded from the run. "I'll always love him."

"That's great, Jess, you two stick together."

Sonny broke down and cried on the way home, desperately wished there was someone there waiting to wrap healing arms around his ransacked heart.

He dragged himself into the house and thought about getting stinking drunk, but it seemed cowardly, as though he'd be leaving Jesse to face it alone. He filled the tub with hot water and stripped his clothes from his body, leaving scattered hay seeds and alfalfa leaves on the bathroom floor. He rummaged through the house for something to read, anything to escape the present moment and then he remembered Hannah's book, still in the truck. He ran bareassed to the truck, snatched the book, and beat it back into the house.

Settled into the soothing water, he halfheartedly escaped into the book, but by the second chapter he couldn't put the true story down. A great Fin Whale was trapped in a cove on the southwest coast of Newfoundland, and one man was trying to save her from the natural perils and the local inhabitants who were using the ill-fated whale for target practice. He prepared and ate supper with one hand, unable to lay the book aside, *A Whale For the Killing* by Farley Mowat. It opened another world to him and he wanted to go see a whale before it was too late.

The author pointed out the species that would soon be extinct if drastic measures weren't taken and after they were gone, all that would remain would be pictures and bones in a museum.

A gentle breeze moved the curtains as he lay under a sheet, his body riddled with fatigue and longing for sleep. But his mind refused to lie down, reeled from the blow Sally delivered in the hayfield. Like a cabin in a sinking ship, the room was filling with a solitary despair, forcing out any trace of hope.

His thoughts raced from his own funeral, to the dying boy at play with his dog, to a huge Fin whale trapped in a cove on the southwest coast of Newfoundland, and he sensed they were all in this together, that we all walk the narrow precipice every day, acting as though we're skipping down a broad roadway because we've been taught to never look down into the abyss.

He fled from the sheets, pulling the guitar from under the bed. In the dark living room he settled on the floor and he played and sang late into the night.

Chapter 31

CORKEY CAME IN on the early morning flight and arrived at the ranch while Sonny was in the shower.

"Hey, good to see you," Sonny said, coming into the kitchen in only his Levis. "You had breakfast?"

"Once on land, once in the air, shot anyone lately?"

"No, but Pinnelli was here, looking for you."

Sonny filled him in on the fat man's visit. He always looked forward to Corkey's return and was grateful for his companionship because despite his new friends, Corkey was the only one in the world who knew he existed. With the others, he was an actor and his life a strange fiction.

Sonny hurried with a banana, toast and a glass of milk.

"You want to do a little haying?"

"Hell no. I came back to rest, not kill myself."

Corkey opened his attache case. Sonny ate and tried to swallow the magnitude of what Corkey matter-of-factly told him: trusts, Swiss accounts, real estate in Florida, deposits Frank Anderson could withdraw from in a dozen large banks, a CPA who would handle his taxes. Corkey pushed himself back from the table and looked him in the eye.

"I'm tired, dog tired." He allowed his hands to flop to his sides as he sat in a kitchen chair. "I'm running my ass off back and forth to L.A., New York, Nashville. I got nothing better to do? I'm not going to live forever, ya know what I mean."

"Then don't do it, quit."

Sonny gulped the glass of milk.

"That's easy for you to say, but I'm the one with his neck out on the line, everybody wanting a piece of me because my dead client is making money for anyone who farts his name. Every time I sign another contract I can see myself going to prison for fraud."

"All I meant was you can pull out now, make it look normal, retire. You said you have the money channeled. Tell them you're tired. Go to Florida like you want to."

"I have to finish with the author, a few other deals, then I will."

Corkey stroked his thinning hair and his face reflected the finger-prints of accruing stress. He pulled his shoe and sock off his right foot but left the sock over the shapeless bulk of his left. He opened a pack of cigarettes and unconsciously offered Sonny one.

"I quit, remember?"

"Good. I'm going to next year."

Corkey lit the cigarette and closed his eyes with the first drag.

Sonny stood and put his plate and glass in the sink. He tucked in his blue cotton work shirt.

"Well at least I don't worry about you anymore, ya know what I mean. When I first had to leave you last winter, I'd watch the news every night with my guts turned into knots, sure that I'd see you'd screwed it up out here."

"I won't screw it up, Cork. I can't." He picked his leather gloves off the table. "But I want to sing again, somehow, some where." He felt the weight in his chest.

"Swell, sing in the shower."

"Gotta go."

Sonny went out the screen door.

Sally and Jesse dropped off Hannah on their way to church, and Sally invited the two men for dinner. Corkey declined, saying he wasn't budging from the property for a day or two. When Sonny and Hannah arrived at the bright green field, Hezekiah had already built the bottom layer of a new stack.

"Where's the kid?" Hezekiah said.

"He went to church," Sonny said. "Any dew last night?"

Sonny pulled on his gloves and peered out at the waiting bales as if he were assessing the strength of an opponent.

"They's a little damp on the bottoms, but by the time we handle 'em, they'll be all right. Yer crew shrunk a bit." Hezekiah spit. "I see yer pretty little girl is still game."

He winked at Hannah and climbed on the haybuck.

"I'll see if I can keep you two from falling asleep."

From that moment on he assaulted them with tons of alfalfa that they struggled to pack into place. The sun brought its heat and Sonny's vigor drained away under its copper canopy making him regret he'd visited the milk room that morning. His shirt darkened with his leaking endurance.

"Did you like it?" Hannah said after he told her he read the entire book before sleeping.

"Yeah, but it was sad, I wanted to do something. How long have you been reading about whales?"

"A few years, I think I fell in love with them. I don't tell anyone, they'd think I'm weird." She grunted and jammed a bale in place. "Or they'd think I'm too idealistic. What's wrong with that? People act as though it's like having braces, like I'll outgrow it."

"Then don't outgrow it, dang it!"

The bales on the stack were in place and Hezekiah was at the far edge of the field. They could rest.

"Other girls have pictures of John Travolta and Sylvester Stallone in their rooms, I have humpbacks and blues and rights." She laughed easily, resting on a bale. Then her browning face turned sorrowful.

"There was a film on TV that showed the Japanese hunting a blue whale. After they'd hit it several times it sounded, but finally it had to surface, and they shot an exploding harpoon into it. The whale seemed to shudder as it watched these men attacking it, as if it was wondering why they were doing this. It made me so angry I ran out of the house and shouted. Then I cried." Hesitantly, she glanced into Sonny's face. "You think I'm strange?"

"I think you're terrific! Don't ever outgrow that anger, don't ever stop shouting."

Hezekiah arrived with his monotonous cargo and they began stacking again.

"Wait till you hear what Jesse named the ridgeback, I promised I wouldn't tell."

"Did he come up with a good one?"

"Yes. Sometimes I think that boy is far beyond me, It's scary." She let her arms hang limp and stood puffing.

"Had enough?" Sonny said.

"No, I'm okay. I was sure Rock would show up."

"Did he say he would?"

"No, he just has a way of showing up."

It was noon, and none too soon when they climbed from the stack and shouted to Hezekiah.

"We'll be back in awhile, lunch time."

"Yep. We're gaining on her."

He steamed off to scoop up another heap as if black rain clouds were lurking just over the horizon.

At the ranch, Hannah went to check out the horses while Sonny stopped at the house to see if Corkey had changed his mind about eating with them. Sonny found her at the water tank. He slid through the rails of the corral, grabbed the hose from the tank, and turned it on the unsuspecting girl. She screamed and grabbed for the hose, sending the horses cantering to the far end. The water shot into the air and rained back on them, its breathtaking cold shocking him into yelps and hoots, refreshing his hot sticky skin. He grabbed her by the arms and bent her backwards over the tank, threatening to dunk her, water dripping from his beard.

"No, no, please, my contacts!"

He glanced from her face to her soaked shirt, which clung to gorgeously sculpted breasts she'd somehow concealed until now under bulky, loose-fitting clothing. She was stunning. He pulled her upright and turned her loose, hoped she hadn't noticed anything in his eyes.

"I didn't know you wore contacts."

"I don't."

She slipped through the rails and ran.

"Why you dirty little. . . ."

He turned off the water and followed her to the truck.

On the way to the trailer Sonny only stole one glimpse at her skin-tight shirt, but it was enough, a vision recorded somewhere in his mind where all things indelible are filed. His mouth went dry and he felt as if he were riding with Natalie Jones on his way to Walther's grove, as though she had come back to him at last. He was a kid again and, unaware, Hannah sat next to him in the pickup, jabbering about the horses. All at once her many dimensions came swirling together in an arousing, breathtaking portrait of a captivating woman who would lower the voice of a eunuch.

He prolonged the trip as long as he could, but how slowly can you drive one mile? To his disappointment, Hannah scrambled into the mobile home, and he joined Jesse and the dog in the yard.

"He's learning to sit, Frank. Last night he slept with me, when he started moving around I took him out, not one accident."

The boy beamed from his thin face while Sonny knelt and allowed the overgrown pup a swipe at his ear.

"Guess what I named him?"

"Let's see . . . how about Spot?"

"Come on, Frank, you're not even trying."

The three of them sat on the ground while Sonny pretended he was deep in thought.

"How about Tiny?"

Jesse pushed him over and held him down and the ridgeback helped by slobbering his face with his ten-pound tongue. Sonny rolled over and sat up.

"Okay, okay, I give, I give!"

He held his hands high in the air in surrender and the dog looked skyward.

. "What did you name him?"

"Guardian."

It didn't strike a note of recognition immediately and Sonny smiled and started to comment on the boy's choice when the sledge hammer-blow caught him in the chest. He stammered and held his face in a smile while he tried to marshal his troops behind it.

"Hannah read the book about the whale to me the first time," Jesse said, "and then I read it myself. Do you think it's a good name?"

Jesse looked at him as though he'd just named his dog Rover.

"We said it had to be big."

Sally called from the trailer door, and Sonny, thankful for the respite, hurried up the steps while Jesse and Guardian dallied. In a yellow tank-top and her damp hair in a ponytail, Hannah made him gawk.

"Do you know what he named the dog?" he asked.

"Of course,"Hannah said.

"Does he realize—"

"He told me that when Guardian was left alone, like in the book, he wanted him to be my dog."

Her voice skipped a beat, a small portion of heartache spilled over and she went to the set table to pour milk. Jesse and the dog burst in the door and the boy sat and gulped his milk.

"Don't be a brat! Go wash your hands." Hannah chased him.

They sat at the table and ate and talked like any normal family, laughed and scolded and visited about nothing.

"Don't you dare feed that dog at this table."

"I saw George Hayes in church this morning."

"Please pass the gravy."

"Guardian ran into a fence post chasing a butterfly."

Everything seemed as normal as hell, and Sonny recognized that that was the hell of it. That every family around the kitchen table looks normal, as if there's nothing more important in their lives than these trivialities, ignoring what truly matters, and the moments pass, taken for granted, taken with ketchup and a second helping.

Sonny recognized that we've been taught never to break into this litany, never to disrupt this sacred ritual. No one lets on what is at the center of his soul, what is deeply important, no one interrupts this domestic tranquility, this memorized script, to speak of the heart of the matter. Jesse, more than anyone else at the table, knew that these were the only moments, that they were measured, significant, rich, and final, and yet he ducked it, avoided at all cost any hint of the truth, lest all this play-acting be thrown into chaos and his family be utterly swept away.

"More milk, Frank?" Sally lifted the carton.

"A little, thanks."

Like the rest, when he wanted to scream he followed in the dance.

"Jess, you and Guardian are taking a nap," Sally said.

She stood behind Sonny and used her experienced touch on his neck and shoulders, kneading his muscles, and though he wanted to moan with the pleasure, he remained stoic. All at once he felt extremely uncomfortable with Hannah observing Sally's affection toward him.

Jesse took a piece of cake and led his hairy sidekick to the bedroom.

"He sure goes easily with that dog around," Sally said.

She started down his back. Abruptly, Sonny stood up.

"Take off that shirt and come in on the sofa. I'll give you a proper back rub."

"We've got to get back," he said. "Hezekiah will have bales coming out of his ears by now. Thanks much for the chow."

He turned and shouted down the hallway.

"So long, Jess!"

Jesse hollered back and they were on their way, but not without the quandary that'd hatched at the table—his fresh awareness of

Hannah's tantalizing appeal coupled with his enjoyable response to Sally's sensuous touch. He'd experienced the loving affection of more than one woman at a time before, but this was a different kettle, and between the two of them, it confused the hell out of him. It didn't get any easier.

Chapter 32

THAT EVENING Corkey taught Jesse how to play gin rummy and the boy immediately started cleaning Corkey out of toothpicks.

"You've played before, you little hustler."

"I never have," Jesse said, enjoying beginner's luck.

"I don't believe you," Corkey said with a frown.

Sonny couldn't tell if Corkey was honestly getting beat or pulling a beautiful scam, but he hooted every time the boy turned a card over on the discard pile and said Gin. When he came through the door after taking Jesse home, Corkey was slumped in front of the TV. Sonny flopped in the sofa and watched the local news, weather and sports with him.

"You shouldn't let the kid have so much pop," Corkey said, "it ain't good for kids."

"I know."

How could he tell him it didn't matter, that Jesse's body would become a decayed cavity long before his teeth ever got around to it.

The newscaster gave scores and Corkey waited to see how the Dodgers came out. Then he looked over at Sonny.

"I always wanted to have a kid. Maybe it's best I never did. We put an end to this stump right here."

He slapped his left leg.

"Did you have brothers or sisters?" Sonny said.

"I never knew, but I probably do."

"I thought your parents died when you were real young."

"No, I've told that lie all my life. I was raised in an orphanage. When I was twelve, a buddy of mine and I sneaked into the orphanage office late one night. I found my records. My parents dumped me when I was a little over two. The only thing it said was *Boy's father couldn't accept crippled child.* I was so ashamed I told my friend that the record said my parents died in a fire. I've told that lie to anyone who asked the rest of my life."

Both of them stared into the animated screen. Sonny could come up with no response to this man he'd never known and his mind flew back to Hannah's book.

When the huge fin whale had become entrapped in a small cove on the coast of Newfoundland, its mate lingered in the adjacent bay. Separated as they were by a rock peninsula, the whales couldn't see one another, but they obviously communicated through the water by sound, for at exactly the moment the entrapped whale sounded, the free whale sounded also. At the same instant the captive whale rose to the surface, so the other rose.

The free whale stood guard the whole time its mate was trapped, and when the infections from the hundreds of bullets savagely shot into her by the men of Burgeo finally killed her, the whale in the bay was seen no more. The whale that stood guard, the whale that waited and watched and tried to save the other, they had given a name. Guardian.

After peeling off his damp sweat suit, Sonny stood naked in the bathroom, studying his profile in the mirror while drops of sweat still seeped from the morning's workout. Today they would record his face on official documents to be filed at the state capitol. A dead man was applying for a Montana driver's license. He shaved his brown dome and trimmed his beard. The dark smoky-brown frames he wore lately were totally out of character and they reminded him of a genuine egg-head professor.

"The horsemen are here," Corkey shouted from the kitchen.

Sonny rushed through a shower, pulled on clothes and boots, and hustled outside to join them.

"Hey, you banditos, what's going on?"

Jesse was busy graining the horses, and Hannah was saddling Gusty.

"You still planning on taking me in this afternoon?" he asked her.

"Yeah. Have you been studying?"

She lifted one of her horse's hooves and inspected it.

"I've looked it over, not much different from Florida, you going to take a run at the barrels?"

"Yeah, I want to cut another few seconds."

"Let's put the horses out after you're through."

"Okay, but the pasture's getting awfully dry," she said.

"You're right. I've been meaning to get over and talk to Hezekiah about irrigating. I'll go right now and get a shopping list from him. Whatever we need we'll pick up this afternoon in town."

"Can I help irrigate, Frank?" Jesse said, coming up to them on Toro's back.

"We'll all have to take a shot at it to keep the water spreading."

"I don't have any boots," the boy said.

"I'll get rubber boots for the whole crew. Wouldn't want anyone shirking his responsibility because he didn't have a pair of boots."

"You sure are rich."

"Jess!" Hannah turned to scold him. "That's rude."

"He's right, I am rich, I've got this sassy woman of a morning, those wild, high-living mountains, and you two."

He looked into Hannah's face. With an unblinking warmth she met his gaze and displayed a devastating smile that shot straight to his spine. Guardian bounded from the ditch and stopped between them, shaking his water-laden coat all over them, their shouts and leaps of evasion too late.

"And I've got a water buffalo for a friend."

Jesse applauded the dog while sitting astride the Hereford.

"How come you're still riding that cow?" Sonny asked.

"He wants to become a bull sitter," Hannah said and laughed.

"You're not supposed to cuss, Hannah."

"I didn't, I said bull *sit*-ter."

"I heard what you said."

Jesse prompted Toro into a tight turn.

"Riding a cow isn't the way you become a cowboy." Sonny said.

"I know, but now with Wildfire and the other horses, I don't want Toro to feel left out."

Hannah and Sonny exchanged a glance and he had to turn away.

He drove out of the yard determined to make the moments count for Jesse, for all of them, and it gave him a renewed sense of purpose, lightened his spirit in the fresh morning air. He turned east, down the gravel road for the fork that would take him north to Hezekiah's spread. The cab was warm; he rolled down the window. Up ahead several redwing blackbirds were chasing off a crow. Game little buggers, the crow ten times their size. Just like Jesse.

"Go get him."

With the dog-fight going on above the road, he leaned forward to catch a last glimpse of the gutsy little defenders dive-bombing the villain as he drove under them.

He never heard the shot!

The glass of the passenger window shattered with a sucking sound, a swish, a frozen instant. He slammed on the brakes and skidded down the gravel. There was a hole in the passenger window head high, and though it fractured into a thousand pieces it remained intact. He kept his head low and peered back up the road. His heart thumped; someone tried to kill him!

He was certain the shot came from his left, the north side of the road, where untilled land, scrub grass and sagebrush fanned into a bushy slough with scattered cottonwood and willow. He listened. Flies buzzed on the windshield, the land oppressively still. Primal instincts shouted to take off but his ignited rage held him.

He backed the truck along the road to where he locked the brakes and examined every blade of grass, every bush. Nothing moved. He berated himself for becoming careless, leaving his .44 handgun in the bedroom, wishing he could blast the countryside and see what might flush from cover.

A chill invaded his bones, anger and terror debated for control and left him immobilized, crouched in the cab. The blackbirds were settling back into the brush, having routed the predatory crow. If he hadn't been watching them, the bullet would've smashed into his brain pan and he'd be gone, no longer here in the quiet sunshine of this mountain valley.

Where would he be? Hurtling out past the galaxies at the speed of light? Collapsing inwardly into a microcosm of nothingness? Whatever, that passage still lay in his future thanks only to a crow and those brassy blackbirds, or was it to Hannah, who taught him to notice them?

He gripped the wheel and hung on, driving away slowly, his foot wobbling on the accelerator. In that moment he hadn't thought about his past life, or the muddle his present life had become. When he was close enough to smell the damp breath of death, it was Hannah he thought of.

Chapter 33

HEZEKIAH SAT on a pine block in the greasy log shed next to his barn where he sharpened the blades of a sickle bar with a steel file. The dirt floor was caked with ancient oil slicks, strewn with wire, old tires, and worn-out machinery parts; junk hung from every possible space. A musty aroma of rust and burlap tainted the air, and the old man looked as if he'd been fashioned from the helter-skelter inventory. He wore irrigating boots and his gnarled hands moved the file with precision, honing each triangular blade to a keen edge.

"Any varmint hunters around?" Sonny asked, standing at the entrance.

"Nope, don't let 'em on the land."

"Well some sonofabitch just breezed a slug through the cab of my truck, and I don't think it was an accident."

"Someone out ta git ya, Frank?"

Hezekiah kept his eye on the blade.

"Not unless the weasel I ran off has come back."

"Bushwhacker."

"What?" Sonny didn't catch the word.

"Bushwhacker. You buffaloed him, he's afraid of ya, shoot ya in the back."

Stopping his rhythmic stroke to look up at Sonny with a wily grin, he appeared to be savoring the prospect of a shootout.

"Ya gonna use the .44?"

"I don't know what to do." He attempted to conceal how unnerved the close call had left him. "I'm not used to having someone take a shot at me."

"Aw, ya's funning me, Frank." He squinted until his eyes were little beebees peering from slits and he spit into the dirt floor. "How many dudes ya powdered?"

"Will you keep an eye open for anyone with a rifle?"

"Al'ays do." He resumed stroking the blade.

"What the hell, maybe it *was* someone out shooting gophers. Those stinkin' bullets'll go a mile without anyone realizing it."

Sonny asked him what he needed to start irrigating, and the ancient mariner gave a lecture on the philosophy of nurturing the land before he mentioned one item. Finally, with a shopping list in mind, Sonny turned for the truck.

"I'll be over in the morning ta show ya how ta spread the water. It ain't jes' making mud puddles ya know."

Part way down the road, Sonny stopped and, with a rock, broke out what remained of the fragmentized side window. If it was Ramsey, he'd be high-tailing it out of the area for a while, figuring the law would be in on it.

"Hi, crow," Sonny yelled at the large bird drifting across the freeway on a summer zephyr.

He and Hannah rode the Dodge pickup for Bozeman.

"I thought you didn't like crows?" Hannah said.

"I changed my mind, I love 'em."

He had his counterfeit birth certificate and a roll of hundred dollar bills in his pocket along with Hezekiah's shopping list. Happiness touched him when he glanced at her beside him with the driver's manual open.

"Any motor vehicle must be equipped with signal lights when the distance from the center of the steering post to the rear limits of the body or load is more than: what?"

"What?" he said. "Where'd you get that ridiculous question?"

"Right here in the manual you were supposed to study."

"Give me that."

Sonny grabbed her around the shoulders and attempted to wrestle the booklet from her. They laughed and played and his heart ached. He wanted to wrap his arm around her waist and pull her beside him. He wanted to say Be my girl. But he didn't, and all the way to Bozeman she plagued him with obscure questions, until he feared he wouldn't even pass the written test. But he did, and the driving test as well. He wanted to tell the Highway Patrol Officer that there was no passenger window because Steve Ramsey was trying to kill him.

Hannah returned from shopping in time to witness the photograph. She made faces to get him to smile, but the joke was on her, on all of them. They were documenting the miracle without ever knowing it, an official photograph of Sonny Hollister dated July 17, 1978, when he'd been pronounced dead on January 5, 1978.

"Why are you laughing?" Hannah asked as they walked.

"Because I'm alive in spite of everything."

"What do you mean?"

"Nothing."

Out on the sidewalk he asked, "Didn't you buy anything?"

"No."

"That's no way to go shopping. Here, go and get eight or ten albums you like and some clothes you've wanted."

He handed her two hundred dollars.

"No, Frank, I can't do that."

She held the bills as if they were contaminated.

"Listen." He turned her by the shoulders and looked into her captivating eyes. "Make the moments count, please. That money doesn't mean a thing, not a damn thing, they're just scraps of paper. Please do this for me . . . for Jesse."

He took the bills and shoved them into her jeans.

"I'll meet you here in an hour."

And he did, the pickup bed cluttered with irrigating tarpaulins, rubber boots, shovels and other hardware. He swung the door open for her, and she climbed in, her arms laden with packages.

"Oh, Frank, I found so many good albums, and best of all, I found one of the whales. The songs of humpbacks and blues and rights recorded at sea. I can't wait to hear them."

Her bright enthusiasm stirred him.

"Did you get some clothes?"

"Yes, I got some jeans I wanted for a long time, and two shirts." She squealed with glee. "It was really fun, thank you."

She tried to hand him what change she had, but he refused.

"It isn't having money that's important, it's knowing how to use it, to refuse to allow it to run your life."

One more stop, the Western Bank of Bozeman, where he opened a checking account and ordered printed checks. The attractive young man named Greg who helped him noticed Hannah, and Hannah took note of him. It was at that moment that he knew he loved her.

On the trip home, he had a piece of paper in his wallet that certified he was a legal driver in the state of Montana. Soon he would have photo I.D.—a bearded and bespectacled Frank G. Anderson. The process of evaporation went on; printed checks with his name and address; Sonny Hollister had disappeared like smoke, and in his place would stand a bald, middle-aged rancher from the Gallatin Valley.

He passed a pickup from Kansas towing a beat-up aluminum trailer. Could it be Roy's old girlfriend from Wichita?

Hannah was going to be twenty-two in August, he was forty-three. Already he had more than he could handle, yet in place of the upheaval so long at the center of his life, there was a warm excitement, a calmness, an unlikely assurance. She was there beside him, and he loved her.

Sonny and Corkey stood in the barnyard as the sun flattened over the mountains. The swallows swished overhead in their usual evening frenzy.

"Good God, this is her trouble," Corkey said, "tell her about it. They'll move away and everyone'll be better off. Can't you see how harebrained this is? All that we've gone through to pull this off, and just when we can see the end of the tunnel, you get shot and maybe killed by some rummy truck driver who doesn't even know who he's shooting at, for cryin' out loud."

Corkey turned and threw his arms in the air.

"I don't want to tell her about it, she's got enough leaning on her right now."

"Look, it's *her* ex-husband, it's *her* problem, ya know what I mean. Tell her, have her get the sheriff in on it. No, better still, we'll pull out for Florida. We'll get the hell out of here before the roads turn to ice and you freeze your balls off if you stick your nose out the door."

"I don't want to leave right now. I'll take care of him."

"How, with that bloody cannon?"

"No, no, maybe I can buy him off. I've been thinking about it. I could offer him a bundle to move permanently to the coast or somewhere. He doesn't give a damn about Sally."

Sonny's voice carried some optimism.

"And how do you plan to get close enough to make him an offer? While he's shooting at you? The man's a psycho."

"I'll find him, I'll leave a message for him."

"Well you better find him before he finds you, or I'll have to bury you again, and this time I won't cry."

Chapter 34

UNABLE TO SLEEP, Sonny ran the boundaries of the property after first light. The world seemed at peace at this time of the morning, but he carried the loaded handgun in a nylon backpack just the same. He ran a different route each morning and always followed a fence line, the ditch, or a grove of trees for cover.

He'd been out dancing with Sally the night before, over south of Livingston, where no one would know her. She was happy because she'd heard that Steve was driving a new route, that he wouldn't be coming through Montana any longer, and Sonny didn't have the heart to tell her that the lunatic was still making visits to the neighborhood. When he drove past the ranch on the way home she voiced her disappointment.

"Aren't we stopping for a while?"

"No, it's kinda late."

"Is anything wrong?"

"No, I've just got a lot of stuff on my mind."

He pulled into the yard beside the trailer and left the engine running. She reached over and turned off the ignition.

"We've already agreed we're not getting serious or anything, so relax. We can at least make each other feel good."

He almost laughed. That had been his line for years. After a few minutes of nonsensical conversation that, like popcorn in a drive-in movie, began piling up on the cab floor, she carried her disappointment into the trailer. He drove home through the cutting despair and sadness. None of their needs were being met. He wanted to get it right, but he didn't always know what was. Sally needed him, and he sure as hell needed her warmth and affection. Why not? With Hannah it was the same painful road he'd been down with Natalie Jones, loving someone he could never have. Why not share his hurting and lostness with a woman who wanted him?

He broke a sweat. In the northwest corner of the ranch you can see across Hezekiah's pasture to the creek bottom and woods. When he reached the boundary and headed east, he caught a glimpse of something moving. He dropped to his hands and knees behind the weedy fence line. Some one was sneaking his way. Cold sweat immediately broke out over his face. He slipped off the backpack to reach his pistol and took the heavy weapon in his hand. Ramsey would find a new batting order this time. Peering over a clump of thistle he spotted two figures sneaking up the brushy fence line toward him, strangely familiar silhouettes. Hannah and Jesse?

At five o'clock in the morning?

While he remained crouching he slipped the .44 into his pack and swung it onto his back, his curiosity soaring as to what these two were up to. They glanced repeatedly over their shoulders as if they expected someone to come after them, Hannah with a shovel, Jesse with a flour sack, and they both wore leather work gloves. When they reached friendly territory, they came through the fence, no longer in a skulking posture, but when he stood, they stopped in their tracks and their mouths opened like kids who had seen a ghost.

"Good morning. You two are up early."

He walked over to where they were frozen to the ground.

"Are you going to tell on us?" Jesse said.

"First I'd have to know what to tell."

"We were picking up poisoned oats that Hezekiah put out around gopher holes," Hannah said, regaining her composure.

"What for?"

"The oats are laced with strychnine," she said.

"You don't think you can save every wild creature in the valley from this kind of thing?"

"It isn't just the gophers, it's the predators that feed on the poisoned gophers—hawks, fox, eagles, the strychnine kills them, too. Even Guardian could die if he found a poisoned gopher."

"Shoot, I never thought of that."

"We picked up as much of the poisoned grain as we could," she said, "but we never get it all."

"Are you going to tell Hezekiah?" Jesse said.

"Of course not. Why the shovel?"

"To bury the dead gophers," she said, "before any predator can find them. Some won't touch them if they're dead, but what if they come along when the gopher has eaten the poison but is still moving? We found five dead gophers this morning."

"When did Hezekiah put the poison out?"

"Jesse saw him yesterday afternoon," she said. "He's put it out a lot this summer. Even if he kills dozens of gophers in one baiting he might also kill a fox or hawk, creatures that would eat hundreds of gophers year after year."

Hannah turned to leave.

"We have to get back before Mom wakes up. She'd kill us if she knew what we're doing."

"Will you help us?" Jesse asked.

Sonny put his hand on Jesse's shoulder. "How?"

"We want to switch clean oats for Hezekiah's poisoned oats," she said. "You can't tell the difference."

"If you could get him away from his place long enough," Jesse explained with a dead seriousness, "I could do it."

"Why you little. . . ." Sonny laughed. "So while Hezekiah is out throwing oats down their holes and thinking he's getting rid of the gophers, he'll actually be fattening them up."

"Exactly," she said. "We know if we just steal his bag of laced oats he'll go buy more."

"He's coming over today, to show me how to irrigate. I'll keep him tied up for an hour or more one way or another, but you be careful with that poison."

"He knows," she said.

Moved by their tough compassion and dedication, Sonny watched them scurry for the trailer. How many kids would get out of bed at four in the morning? He felt happy and lucky that he'd crossed paths with these two. Against depressing odds, they'd preserved the life of a single hawk or fox that day, though they'd never know for sure. They were keepers of the green.

In the afternoon Hezekiah came over and demonstrated the art of irrigating. Hannah had to get to work at the bank, so it was up to Jess to find where Hezekiah kept the poisoned oats and switch the clean for the laced. Sonny asked a great many questions and learned something in spite of himself while they strung poles through the tarps, and the old rancher showed him how to set them across a ditch, damning the water and causing it to overflow onto the pasture. It looked simple enough, but Sonny soon learned that it was a clever skill not to miss parts of the uneven ground and to completely cover the area in question.

"Ya can make water run uphill if ya's good at it."

Sonny kept one eye north, watching for Jesse, while he felt a real satisfaction seeing the water run onto the parched ground, soaking it, nourishing it, and bringing the grass back to life.

"You have much trouble with gophers?" Sonny said.

"Yep. Damn varmints always digging holes."

"How do you get rid of them?"

"Poison."

"Isn't there a better way than that?"

"Nope. Poison 'em deader'n a doornail."

"What about fox and hawks and owls?"

"Ain't many a them dad-blasted critters around anymore, don't know what happened to 'em all."

Hezekiah spat and dug a small "V" in the ditch to run the water where he wanted it.

Go, Jesse, go.

Sonny imagined the kid searching Hezekiah's barn and shed for the strychnine-laced oats and all at once he realized the greater fear that drove Hannah. The black-footed ferret! Of course, they feed on gophers, and Hezekiah, in his indiscriminate use of poison, could be ending the species. In his heart of hearts Sonny pulled for the boy, and for Hannah, and for all those who fought against the dark currents.

Sonny worried about Jesse when Hezekiah peeled out in the Jeep for home, but moments later, the boy came down the ditch line with his flour sack full of poisoned oats and an invincible smile dancing in his large bright eyes. Sonny took the poison oats from him and insisted he take a good soapy shower in the house. He had to laugh. For the rest of the summer, whenever Hezekiah had a mind to poison gopher holes, he'd be doing nothing more than serving up hors d'oeuvres.

Sonny kept himself continually occupied and trusted that tomorrow he'd feel less pain, that tomorrow he'd accept the impossibility of him and Hannah and the utter dislocation of his life with greater calm and understanding. He was shingling the house with the tutelage and help of Barnaby, a local carpenter, and he planned to shingle the tool shed and buggy shed on his own. He'd turned the buggy shed into a tack room, built saddle racks, wooden pegs for bridles and halters and other gear, and put in several mouse-proof barrels for the feed and grain. The old shed had become a sanctuary for horse gear and horse lovers alike.

With all the other, and the irrigating, he found himself tired every night and able to sleep, though not without the stethoscope and the safety rope tied snugly. The kids were in and out with the horses, and he rode with them in the evening, never without the concealed handgun in the saddlebag. He decided he'd never let Hannah know that he loved her, that he longed for her the way swallow wings long for the sky.

Sonny and Hannah were returning from a ride in the foothills while the afterglow hung suspended in the sky long after the sun slid behind the mountains. She led him a way they'd never come before, up the creek into Hezekiah's land. They had to get off the horses and lead them over the barbed wire where it stretched low into the creek, cluttered with brush and weeds. They remounted and walked the horses up the shallow stream, ducking under the overhanging brush and weaving through willows until they climbed out of the creek and onto a small peninsula of dry ground that penetrated the lower scrubland.

Suddenly Hannah stopped the Appaloosa, leaped from the saddle, and knelt on the ground.

"Oooh no-o-o-o, oh God, no-o-o-o."

Sonny rode up and slid from his horse. A black-footed ferret had clawed at the earth as it writhed on its side, leaving a record of its agonized death over a broad area on the dry ground. Hannah ran her hand gently over the sleek animal's brownish pelt. Its mouth was open, its tongue outstretched in a grotesque expression of death.

"Strychnine," she said.

They found four young ferrets similarly dead near the mouth of a burrow that was subtly hidden under a large slab rock. She sat down among them, her face ashen, her breathing labored. Unable to think of anything to say, he mutely held the horses' reins.

"It's the female, we didn't get the poison in time."

"You did what you could."

"We can't tell Jesse."

He squatted on his haunches beside her.

"No, there's no need to."

She picked up one of the young and held it in her hands.

"I know he put out the strychnine so a cow won't break a leg in a gopher hole, but for that we wipe the black-footed ferret off the face of the earth? Is a cow more important than a ferret?"

"I don't know, Hannah. I'm the last one to ask."

They buried the female and four young ferrets deep, so that no predator would continue the chain-reaction of death. With their hands they dug the hole right in the burrow, packing it and stomping it tightly with their boots, covering it with rocks.

"I only hope the male didn't get into it," she said. "He may still be around here somewhere."

With that slim hope, they rode away. The twilight had dissipated, leaving a clear, moonless canopy of darkness while the stars gradually took up their appointed positions. The horses went quietly for the barnyard and Hannah carried her sorrow silently within her. He found his breath coming short, a panic in his chest, as he viewed the great emptiness above. He was a black-footed ferret.

Chapter 35

WITH THEIR DRIVERS, the pickup and Chevy seemed to lean forward like ponies at the gate, engines revving, while Butch and Sonny taunted each other. Sonny saw to it that Jesse was buckled in. He had bought a motorcycle helmet to add to the boy's fun, and though it was somewhat too large, Jesse strapped it on with a touch of drama.

"You ever in a crash, Frank?" Jesse said.

"Once."

"Did you get hurt bad?"

"I got killed." Sonny laughed.

Jesse laughed at the joke he'd never understand.

They aimed the '55 Chevy and the '65 Dodge pickup like rockets about to go off. Jesse shouted Go! and the tires shot gravel like starving bulldogs digging bones. With their rear wheels going sixty miles an hour while they inched forward at about five, the Chevy caught first and hurtled away from the stuttering pickup. Eating dust, Sonny found second gear and flattened the gas pedal against the floorboard.

He glanced at the astonished boy, who clung to the seat wide-eyed and open-mouthed. Sonny let out a hoot, Jesse blurted a mixture of terror and joy, and for that brief moment, they were flying together on the magic carpet of speed. The pickup fish-tailed from side to side above its spinning rear wheels in a futile attempt to catch the dust-spewing Chevy.

"Hang on!" Sonny shouted.

He tried to bring the truck back but overcompensated, hurtling down into the barrow pit, through the rusted pasture fence and across the open field, bouncing both of them off the ceiling more than once.

"Eeeee-yaaaa!" Sonny yelled, turning the truck slowly back toward the road.

"Man, Frank, that was COOL!"

"Don't ever let your mom find out!"

"I promise, she'd skin *me*."

"You mean she'd skin me," Sonny said.

Butch was waiting beside his car on the road, withholding his gloating until he was sure they were okay. Sonny stopped in the pasture alongside the fence.

"Too light?" Butch called.

"Yeah, next time I'll put some weight in the bed."

"Any time you think you're ready."

Butch swaggered and the freckles danced on his face. Jesse peered out from the oversized helmet.

"Can I go with you next time, Frank?"

"If your mother doesn't get wind of it."

"We're going to *whip* you, Butch!" Jesse shouted.

Awake early, Sonny came from the house. The morning had a hazy frown, blinking promises of the sun somewhere behind the Bridger Mountains. In his running shoes and sweats, he strode across the barnyard, watching the swallows' flying circus in the air above him. About to launch out into a jog, he glanced over at the corral to find Toro sprawled on the ground, still asleep.

"Time to get up, you lazy beggar!"

He began jogging. Funny. He'd never seen the steer flopped on the ground during the night, only in the warm sunlight. He turned and jogged back to the corral.

"Toro! Get up, buddy."

Sonny opened the gate and approached the grounded Hereford.

"Oh, no-o-o, oh dear God, oh dear God, no-o-o."

The pool of blood had soaked the manure and straw under the steer's neck, his throat neatly cut. Sonny knelt beside the animal and stroked it's head.

"Oh, God, I'm sorry, boy, I'm sorry."

He broke down and sobbed. He'd neglected to warn the friendly animal that there were evil men, failed with his promise to protect Toro from the cutthroat. With his sweatshirt sleeve he wiped his teared face and stood. With his fists clenched, he searched the countryside for any sign of human or vehicle.

"You sick son of a bitch! Let's find out how big you are when you're not hitting on helpless women and animals!"

Hannah came around the side of the barn and startled him. She walked to the corral.

"Who're you yelling at?"

He tried to block her view by filling her line of vision to the steer.

"You're here early," he said.

He wiped his eyes and came to the rail where she'd stopped.

"I want to ride before work. What's wrong with Toro, is he sleeping?"

"Yeah, lazy, can I help you with the tack."

She hesitated, and then she bent and stepped through the corral poles.

"Don't come in here!"

He took her by the arm, but she pulled away and walked to the slaughtered steer.

"Oh, Frank, oh, n-o-o-o." She slumped to the ground. "Oh, Toro, poor, poor Toro, oh, God, who did this to him, who would do this to him?"

She cried and stroked the Hereford's back. Sonny didn't answer.

"Steve? Did Steve do this?"

She looked up at him with tears washing her face. He nodded.

"Why . . . why? Toro never did anything to hurt him."

"He's trying to get to me." He knelt beside her.

He wanted to take her in his arms. She looked into his eyes.

"Didn't he know this was Jesse's pet, is he trying to hurt Jesse?"

"No, he probably didn't know, it's me he's after."

She stood quickly.

"Oh, oh God, we've got to hide him, Jesse's not far behind me, we can't let him see this."

Sonny stood and took hold of one of Toro's rear legs.

"Grab a leg," he said.

Hannah took the other rear leg. They pulled. Nothing happened.

"We've got to get him as far as the stack," he said. "C'mon."

They tightened their hold and heaved their bodies backward. Begrudgingly the heavy carcass began to move across the corral, the pall bearers grunting and panting with their heels chopping into the loose dirt and straw.

Pull your own weight, damnit!

His legs churned in short, quick, powerful thrusts, out the corral gate and toward the stack. He strained with everything he could call up from his body and mind, his legs became pistons, his breath a steam engine.

"Don't stop! Don't stop!" he shouted.

With her face bulging, Hannah stayed with him, dragging the slaughtered steer twenty feet further to the stack of bales. They both knelt, breathless. Sweat covered his face.

Hannah caught her breath. "Gosh you're strong."

"Couldn't have done it without you."

They covered him with loose hay and piled bales around the body. Hannah kicked dirt and straw over the puddle of blood and wiped out the drag marks to the stack only moments before Jesse arrived with Guardian.

"Hi, Frank, where's Toro?"

"C'mere," Sonny said.

He walked over by the main ditch under the cottonwoods where he sat on the ground and Jesse settled beside him. Sonny looked into his questioning face.

"Toro died, Jess. I'm really sorry, I know what good buddies you two were."

"Died?"

"Yeah, last night, he just went to sleep, I don't think he felt any pain or anything."

The boy looked into Sonny's face for understanding, struggling to hold back tears.

"Was he sick? Why'd he die?"

"I don't know, no one knows, animals just die, like people."

Hannah came and sat beside her brother and he began to cry.

"Toro died," Jesse said, choking on the sobs, "but it didn't hurt him or anything."

"I know," she said. She put her arm around him.

"Animals die," Jesse said, "just like people."

The boy glanced around the barnyard as if he didn't believe Toro was gone.

"Where is he?"

Sonny glanced at Hannah. "We buried him . . . so nothing would eat on him. We need you to make a marker for his grave."

Jesse wiped his eyes with his shirt sleeve.

"Okay . . . I'll make one." He looked at Sonny. "I never got to say good-bye."

"I know, Jess, neither did I, but Toro knows you loved him."

Jesse cried. Hannah hugged her little brother and Sonny wrapped his arms around the two of them but hatred overrode his grief. He began thinking no longer as the hunted but as the hunter.

When Jesse went home, Sonny got Hezekiah's tractor, and with the front-end loader, they buried Toro out in the gravel pit. When evidence of the gruesome death was covered over, they showed Jesse the grave. He picked wild flowers and made a wooden marker, printing on a board with a black marking pen.

TORO WAS A GOOD STEER
AND MY GOOD FRIEND
1976–1978

Several nights later, Hannah came over to share the album of the whales, the strange, haunting song of these mammals of the sea. She sat silently on the sofa, her knees pulled up to her chin, drifting far away, somewhere at sea. He sat across from her and traced her face and form from the corner of his eye while this primordial refrain accompanied his primitive yearning. When the record ended, Sonny spoke first.

"I've never heard anything like it."

"I wonder what they're saying," she said. "Wouldn't you love to know?"

Her eyes flashed with a wild curiosity, a hunger to know.

"I would," he said. "Maybe some day."

She read from the record jacket, how the humpback whales sing a different song each year, that all the humpbacks in a herd sing the same song and then change to a different song the following year, that there is no other animal known to change songs each year. Hannah laid the album cover aside.

"It's like they're keeping chapters of their history."

Her scent and presence remained in the room when he stood in the door and watched her go away. At that aching moment, he sensed that he'd never have her love anymore than he'd ever understand what the whales were trying to tell him. This young woman had slipped behind every safeguard he'd carefully constructed around his heart, awakened in him, not only this undeniable passion for her, but an awareness of the mystery of it all. And he knew he'd love her for as long as he was a part of that mystery.

IRRIGATING HAD its rewards: the slow monotony of land and water, the detail he noticed under foot, the multitudes of living things he ran across with his hands and face close to the soil. The water soaked the arid land and he was alone with his thoughts, perplexed over how to deal with the sadistic trucker and his vicious and brutal insanity. It was as if Costello's contract had somehow been passed to the trucker like a baton. The handgun lay on the Dodge seat and he calculated the distance to the pickup. It angered him, always looking over his shoulder, but when he thought of leaving, Hannah came softly to all of his senses and said Stay.

With the tarps in place, he drove the pickup to the hole he'd torn in the fence and began splicing wires. He shied when a car rippled by on the gravel, catching him off guard. About the time he calmed his jitters over that, Guardian announced Jesse's coming with his lavish greeting and almost knocked Sonny flat. Though the boy hadn't been around much of late, he appeared out of the sunlight while Sonny scuffled with the ridgeback.

"Is that where we went through?" Jesse asked.

"This is the place. Some navigator you turned out to be. I thought I'd better fix it so we can let the horses back on the grass."

"Are you irrigating?"

"Yep, third ditch down."

"Can I do it?"

"All right, but check the bottom of the section. If it isn't running over into the next ditch, don't change it yet."

Jesse whistled and the big dog came dashing across the pasture, his tongue flopping to the side. Together they ran, Jesse's hair and the dog's ears bouncing in rhythm with the song they wrote as they splashed through sunlight and water. Sonny could see them in slow motion; a poem, the lyrics of life in the act of being created. Captured by their spell, he stood entranced until they were far across the field. Then he pulled on his gloves and returned to the fence.

When he had the barbed wire spliced and the broken post replaced, he threw his tools into the pickup and peered across the land. Jess should've been done long ago but he couldn't see him and figured he and the dog were playing in the trees beyond. Then he saw Guardian, wagging his tail and barking with purpose. The wind came from behind Sonny, and only when it momentarily paused did he actually hear the dog. He squinted across the bright land and began walking toward the excited ridgeback, but he couldn't see Jesse. Guardian continued his frantic uproar, probably after a gopher or . . . it was Jesse, on the ground!

Sonny broke out sprinting, racing across the neglected pasture with terror in his throat. He'd done this before—running across a field to someone he loved, terrified that he would be too late! When he hit the wet part of the field the shallow water exploded under his boots like gun shots, and Guardian welcomed him with wagging tail and wild howling.

The boy had collapsed, a fragile bird shot out of the sky by some malevolent unseen hunter. Sonny gathered him in his arms and headed for the truck, frightened by the weightlessness of the boy.

"Hang in there, partner."

"Home, take me home," Jesse whispered.

Sonny slid him onto the seat, shut the door, and cradled him in his right arm as he drove through the fence, up onto the road toward the trailer.

"How are you doing?"

"I'm all right," the boy said weakly. "You broke the fence again."

"I'm practicing for our next race." Sonny held the boy firmly. "Does it get bad?"

"Sometimes. Mom gives me a pill."

"You've got a lot of moxie, Jess."

"What's moxie?"

"Guts, courage, balls."

With the boy in his arms, he met Sally's uncertain face at the door and carried Jesse to his bed. She gave him his medication and sat with him while Sonny drifted back to the living room. Several minutes later Sally joined him at the far end of the trailer.

"He wasn't doing much, he'd just gone to change a tarp."

Sonny shrugged. Sally's face held storms and squalls of confusion. "He can't work anymore! Nothing!"

"I'm sorry."

"It isn't you, Frank, he won't stay in the house. If he has an ounce of strength he wants to spend it, every drop. I let him go. Will I regret that some day? Maybe if I kept him in bed he'd last longer, but these are his *only* days, am I wrong?"

She looked at him, pleading for some sort of consolation, some absolution.

"I think you're right. You should have seen them today, Jess and the dog, God they were beautiful. It was as if he were saying, If I'm going to die, where better than in a greening pasture with the summer sun and my dog. Come and get me whoever you are!" Sonny choked for a moment. "He didn't have to run to the tarp, but he did."

"When he's gone I know I'll blame myself," she said. "I'll wish I'd kept him in bed for the weeks or months it might have extended his life."

"I don't think so, I think you'll be glad you gave him this."

"Oh God, I've got to call the doctor. I'll let you know if he gets worse."

On the way to the house, Sonny changed the tarp in the field, driving through the hole he'd retorn in the fence. He found Jesse's cap drifting slowly in one of the ditches.

"Jesse is real sick," Sonny said, finding Corkey in the kitchen working his hand calculator over a small pile of papers.

"Bad?" Corkey looked up from his figures.

"Yeah . . . it's going to kill him."

"No-o-o-o-o." Corkey pushed his calculator aside. "How awful, how cruel, how beyond understanding."

Sonny dug a Pepsi out of the refrigerator.

"You never will beat that kid at gin rummy."

Sonny fronted with a cool hardness, trying desperately to hold it together.

"When?"

"Soon, I think, no one knows. Sally said she'd call if he turned for the worse, keep him in mind."

Sonny sat at the table with Corkey.

"That's what my mother would always say when she'd pray, Keep me in mind. It's the last thing she says when I say good-bye on the phone."

Sonny collapsed the empty can in his fist and leaned back against the sink.

"Hell, I let her down, too."

"You haven't seen her much in these last years have you?"

"She lived in the house I got her in Beverly Hills, you know, and she loved the climate, and her garden, and living near all the famous people. I think she was happy, as happy as she could be, until I started making the news with the scandal sheets. I didn't go see her much then. I knew she'd see it in my face, in my body. Jeez, you know how I ballooned. She'd call me all the time and ask how I was, and we'd play the game. I told her I was much better, clean, straight, and she said that was good to hear. She knew I was lying and I knew she knew."

Sonny looked out into the barnyard.

"She was so damn proud of me, coming out of the plowed fields of Minnesota and making something of myself. And then I tore it all away from her, stabbed her with every byline, and everyone could say that they had been right, knew we Hollisters were no good all along. She really surprised the daylights out of me when she wanted to move back there. Doggone it, I guess it was home to her, no matter what."

Sonny threw the crushed can at the wastebasket and missed.

Silent for several minutes, Corkey stared at his neat columns and sums. Then he turned and regarded Sonny.

"You know, I'm proud as hell of you, the way you've come back these months. I wish you could go show her how you are now."

"I will one of these days, if she doesn't die first."

Sonny went out and walked to the corral as the sun blared colors in the western sky. He mingled with the horses; they nuzzled him, and he felt a certain contentment and safety among them. He hung onto the Appaloosa and began to cry. It felt good, the release, the letting go. He didn't understand why he was weeping, but he did nothing to hold it back. Was it for Jesse, the sunlit child he carried in his arms with his life draining into the pasture? It was more than that, but he couldn't name the sorrow engulfing him. The gelding's back was wet with his tears and it stood very still, as though sensing this human need for its warmth and comfort.

He held his breath, listening, and far to the North, it was as though he could faintly hear his mother banging on that iron supper gong, calling him to come home.

Chapter 37

THE HOSPITAL RECEPTIONIST pointed the way, and Sonny didn't wait for the elevator. He took the stairs two at a time to the third floor, pushed through the large metal doors into a corridor, and quickly surveyed each room as he passed. When he found them— Sally standing at the window, Hannah dozing in a chair—he hesitated for a moment. Tucked in the high hospital bed like a Teddy bear, Jesse seemed much smaller, almost unreal. Sonny took a deep breath and went in.

"Hello, how's he doing?"

"Oh, hi." Sally took his hand. "He wanted to see you, Frank, I hope you didn't mind my calling."

Hannah didn't stir.

"I wish you'd called sooner. When did you bring him in?"

"Last night, the doctor thought we should, there was nothing you could do."

"Is he going to be . . . ?"

"The doctor doesn't know, they're doing what they can. He's had blood, he may bounce back and be fine for a while, or. . . ."

"Hi, Frank," Jesse said quietly, opening his eyes without moving, a fragile bird as white as the linen on the bed.

Sonny went to the side of the bed and sat in a plastic chair, his head at eye level with Jesse.

"How are you doing, partner?"

"I'm okay. I'm glad you came."

"They couldn't keep me out of here."

"I told Mom you'd come." Jesse closed his eyes, faintly breathing the words.

"Why don't you rest now, I'll come and see you when you're a little stronger."

"Wait." Jesse looked at him, his eyes alert now. "If I don't come home—"

"You're coming home, don't even talk that way."

He rubbed the boy's head lightly and tried to escape the rending truth of the moment, withering in the gaze of Jesse's soft eyes, but the boy wouldn't be put off.

"One of these days I won't come home. Hannah promised to take care of Guardian. Do you think you could give Wildfire to another boy?"

"I'd like to keep him," Sonny said, choking on his words.

"I'd like that, I know you'd love him."

Jesse had used up what strength he could muster and closed his eyes. Sonny stood cautiously and backed toward Sally at the foot of the bed, but when he took his eyes from Jesse, he found the trucker standing by the doorway, regarding him with an uncompromising stare.

Sonny clenched his fists and returned Ramsey's icy gaze, sensed the meanness under the clean shaven face and dress clothes. The two men didn't give an inch, never blinked until Sally stepped between them. His rage now far outweighed his fear and Sonny ached to break the scum's back, throw him from the third-story window.

"Frank, this is Steve." Neither extended a hand.

"We've met," Sonny said.

Steve finally unglued his eye from Sonny. "How's Jess?" He had a baseball mitt in his hands. Sally accepted it for Jesse, and they both turned and searched the clean sheets for any sign of life. Sally visited with him as though he were an interested neighbor rather than the brute who violated her and slit Toro's throat, not to mention the bullet that breezed past Sonny's head.

Hannah awoke. She stood abruptly at seeing Steve and slipped out of the room without a word. Sonny was trapped, not knowing what to do, what to say. Like a jackass he stood there, watching the trucker's face from the corner of his eye. The man seemed wounded, bleeding internally for his small stricken son. The paradox confused Sonny, this contradiction in human nature. Is it possible that this grieving man, crumbling now at the foot of his dying son's bed, could blow out Sonny's brains like so much suet? The baseball mitt was a symbol of Steve Ramsey's impotence, his common helplessness, but Sonny knew he had to trust his instincts and ignore this scene where two estranged parents, brutally at war with one another, met on the neutral ground of their son's affliction.

He slipped around behind them and found Hannah at the end of the corridor, gazing out the window at the traffic below. He came up behind her quietly.

"How are you doing?"

"I'm okay. How do you like the visitors around here?"

"How did he know you were here?"

She turned around and sat on the large sill.

"He called Mom last night, right when we were going to bring Jesse in. He was in Bozeman, just for the night he said, wanted her to come in and have dinner, sweet-talked her, but she refused. Then he got nasty, started threatening. She didn't want to tell him, but we were in a hurry. He accused her of lying. When we arrived at the hospital with Jess, he was waiting. When he saw Jess he went to pieces. I can't stomach him."

"He looked pretty shook-up in there just now."

He wanted to put his arms around her and hold her.

"Jesse is Steve's only child as far as we know, he'd never say much about his life before he met Mom. He's my step-father, so I can handle it when I hate him, but I feel sorry for Jess. He knows Steve is his father, and he sees how he treats Mom, and I know he can't figure out how he's supposed to feel about his own father. I lost my dad in a digging accident, but as hard as that was, I think it's much easier than having a father like him."

She had fire in her eyes, and standing there in the hall with her gave him a sense of well-being. He knew how hard it was to hang on to fathers.

Up the corridor the trucker came out of the room. He paused and regarded the two of them, tracing a faint smile across his scarred mouth.

"How's the arm?"

"Better than your aim," Sonny said.

Ramsey turned and walked toward the elevator.

"What's that supposed to mean?" Hannah asked.

"He's baiting me."

"Filthy bastard," she said.

Ramsey stepped into the elevator and the doors glided shut. Hannah and Sonny sauntered to the room.

"I can't keep him away," Sally said. "Jesse's his child, too. I think he's really hurting. He's such a lonely man, I don't think he really has one close friend, trying to get by in a world he thinks is all against him. I think I hate him. I know it's wrong, but I think Jesse hates him too. Isn't that a terrible thing for a little boy, to hate his father."

Her lips trembled.

"Well I hate him," Hannah said, slumping in a chair.

"Listen, why don't you two go out and get some fresh air and some food. I'll stay with him," Sonny said.

Reluctantly, and with Hannah's persuasion, Sally agreed, assuring him they wouldn't be gone long. He nudged them to the door.

"Don't hurry. He'll probably sleep for a while."

When they had gone, Sonny watched Jesse sleep as if the boy were in a coma, and it gave him time to sort out his feelings. Across the hall someone was plinking on a guitar, town noises drifted through the partially open window: a car's horn, children shouting, a barking dog, life was flowing by. In the bed it seemed almost stopped.

Jesse woke, asked for water, and Sonny helped him with the bent straw in the glass.

"Is Wildfire all right?"

"Smart and sassy, prancing around the pasture looking for you this morning. I told him you'd be back in a few days, and to be thankful he could get some rest for a change."

He wished it were true, but Jess didn't ride much any more.

"He's a good horse," Jesse said.

The boy looked out the window, as though his mind were hurrying back to the ranch and his life there. Only the treetops and the sky were visible from the bed and the idea came to Sonny out of the sky. It involved some risk, but to hell with it.

"I'll be right back, don't go away," Sonny said with a smile.

He went into the hall, knowing full well that the boy might fly away while he was gone. A young man in a room down the hall had the guitar, and after Sonny talked with him for a minute, he returned with the instrument and sat beside Jesse.

"I've been learning to play one of these things," he told him, "and I've learned a song for you. I'll only sing it if you promise not to laugh."

"I promise."

"No cursing, no throwing garbage, no raspberries," he went on as he tuned the guitar. "I'm no Michael Murphy you know."

"Wildfire?" Jesse said.

"Yep, I'll try."

The boy slid slightly closer to the edge of the bed. Sonny began with a simple strum, playing and singing softly, the sad song about a horse lost in a snow storm. Jesse mouthed the words and gazed at Sonny with an irrepressible glow. Sonny's voice faltered. He remembered other times, in front of thousands, when he become so personally touched by lyrics he'd start to lose it. He found ways to fight off the emotion and go on then, and he did now, finishing the song.

"That was great, Frank!"

Jesse's eyes were animated with such zest it gave Sonny a feeling of hope.

"I wish you'd sing like that for lots of people."

"Why?"

"'Cause they're sick and scared . . . and it makes them feel better."

Sonny swallowed and fought for his voice. "When you get home I'll teach you. Then you can sing 'Wildfire.'"

"Honest?"

"Honest."

Someone clapped softly, startled him, and he glanced back to find Hannah and Sally standing in the doorway. Like an awkward child, he'd been caught with his hand in the jelly beans. His mind raced. Had he sounded too much like his former self? His voice had changed considerably over the past ten years, now more rusted and weathered. Sally came to the foot of the bed, obviously delighted and encouraged by Jesse's enthusiasm.

"You're full of surprises, Frank Anderson, that was beautiful, I don't know what we'd do without you."

Hannah remained in the doorway and regarded him with a benign expression. He stood.

"Listen, amigo, I need you to keep that ranch running, so don't think you can get away with lying around on your butt for long, okay?"

"Okay, Frank."

The boy was observably stronger, with color coming back into his face. Sonny slipped to the door, and Sally followed him into the corridor.

"Thanks so much for coming," she said.

"Call anytime, day or night. I'll keep him in mind."

He returned the guitar on his way down the hall and hurried out of the building. In the pickup he sang softly as he drove for the ranch.

Chapter 38

Jesse recovered and came home. With Guardian he was visiting some of their old haunts in a restrained fashion, brushing the horses, drifting around the barnyard, sitting on Wildfire but not riding him out of the corral. Sonny was extremely protective and gentle with him, though he tried to conceal his concern with humor. For all of them, the days of August were probationary, fragile, illusory.

With Sonny, the metamorphosis was almost complete, and physically he seemed to be going in the opposite direction from Jesse. His body was firm, hard, fit, dark brown from the waist up, and his bald head looked like a chocolate egg after he helped Hezekiah bale and stack his second cutting of alfalfa. Jesse, on the other hand, seemed a shadow of himself, a frail spirit among them, yet a lively spirit, full of happiness and inquisitiveness and wonder over the world around him. They had become close, a strange brace of journeymen stirring the dust of the same galaxy.

Hannah was gone much of the time, working in Bozeman and dating several young men who had recently discovered her. Sonny knew it was as it should be, but couldn't allow himself a moment to imagine a young stud with his arms around her and worse. He based his hope on Hannah's assessment of the local boys as she expressed it one evening at the corral.

"The boys around here are all the same. All they want to do is drink beer, chew snooze, drive around town, and make out in a pickup. Not one of them ever opened a good book or noticed a meadowlark."

When the coast was clear, meaning Sally was at work, they had raced again. Jesse wore his crash helmet, Butch blew his engine halfway to the finish line, and Jesse claimed the victory. Butch left the '55 Chevy in the barnyard where they towed it, and before he decided what to do with it, weighing the cost of a new engine against his available funds, Sonny had it hauled to Bozeman, fitted with a new engine, and back in the yard. Butch was ecstatic when he came to haul it away, and Sonny told him the ranch had insurance that covered such things.

"Hold the string tighter, hear that buzz? The string has to be tight against the fret."

The two of them sat on the porch steps and Sonny attempted to manipulate Jesse's thin fingers. The boy strummed across the guitar strings, pressing the fingers of his left hand as hard as he could.

"How's that?" Jesse said.

"That's good, hear the difference. Now learn it so you can play it without looking. That's a D chord."

"I know C and G and now D."

A sheriff's car pulled into the yard and stopped. An officer scampered to where they sat, and Sonny thought Ramsey had finally done it.

"Are you Frank Anderson?" the lawman asked.

"Yeah."

"Would you help us out? Your neighbor says you're the only one he'll talk to."

The young officer sounded more like he was asking a favor than flaunting authority.

"Hezekiah?"

"A Mr. Linesinger. He's holed up in his house and won't let anyone near him. We don't want anyone hurt over a piece of land."

"You keep practicing until your mom picks you up," Sonny told Jesse and he hurried to the patrol car. The deputy gunned down the gravel and turned north at the fork.

"What happened?" Sonny said.

"As far as we can tell, some surveyor came out this morning and started surveying a piece of land. Seems that Linesinger is past due on a mortgage and the bank is foreclosing. Linesinger ran him off, turned the guy's pickup over with a tractor, and ran over his surveying equipment. The surveyor got hold of the banker, and he called us into it. When we got out here, Linesinger was holed up in his house. He fired a warning shot to keep us back."

They pulled into Hezekiah's barnyard where two other patrol cars and several civilian vehicles were parked helter-skelter. A group of men congregated behind the woodshed, and two officers crouched behind the hood of one patrol car with their pistols drawn. Sonny walked to the group by the woodshed.

"What in hell is going on here?"

"Who are you?" an executive-type in suit, tie, and white Stetson demanded.

"I'm Mr. Linesinger's personal advisor."

Sonny looked as though he'd been raised in the valley with his worn Levis and boots, his brown face and full beard—he'd switched to wire rimmed glasses recently—and his faded blue cotton shirt.

"Well, if that's the case, you'd better advise Linesinger to put down the gun and come out. We won't be as hard on him if he does."

The middle-aged man with distinguished-looking gray in his dark hair inhaled from a filtered cigarillo, holding it precisely with delicate fingers.

"What's a surveyor doing on this property?"

"Mr. Linesinger was notified thirty days ago that he'd defaulted on a trust indenture with our bank. But, as his personal advisor, you know that."

The man glanced at his cohorts and smirked.

"The collateral for the loan, as you also must know, was a ten-acre tract along the creek over there. We put a notice in the paper as required by law and have received no response from Mr. Linesinger or his personal advisor. Mr. Gleason here, with Homeland Realty," he nodded at a younger, jock-type man, "got our permission to divide the tract into several house sites. The man we hired was viciously attacked by Linesinger, his pickup destroyed, his equipment ruined! That puts your client in a whole bunch of trouble. He may lose this whole place now."

The banker was almost salivating as he painted an irreversible situation. Sonny kept a firm grip on his anger, speaking evenly, politely.

"Do you have a copy of the notice, any of the legal documents with you?"

The banker snapped his fingers. The man behind him opened an attache case and handed him several papers. The man Sonny presumed was the sheriff stood by silently and listened.

"Here's a copy of the trust indenture. This is the official notice which was mailed to Mr. Linesinger in July. He never replied."

Sonny took the documents and examined them for several minutes, not sure what he was looking for. Then he struck gold.

"You say this requires a thirty-day notice?"

"Yes."

"And Mr. Linesinger can pay the loan off in that time?"

The three men glanced at one another; the banker smiled.

"That's correct, the whole ten thousand plus five interest payments."

The banker's confidence that the old rancher could never raise the money surfaced on his face and celebrated there.

Sonny smiled at the well-dressed man. "What's your name?"

"Brooks, Henry Brooks, Gallatin Federal Trust," he said with a slight swagger.

"Well, Mr. Brooks, this notice is dated July twenty-first."

"That's right." The financier's eyes darted to the realtor.

"Today is August nineteenth. Now I'm no human calculator, but that doesn't come out to thirty in my head."

Sonny began to drop the pleasant demeanor and redecorate in a kick-ass attitude.

"Only a technicality. The twentieth, tomorrow, falls on Saturday. We figured it wouldn't hurt to start the survey today, before the weekend, since on Saturday it would be our land."

"*Our* land? I thought the bank was selling the land to Mr. Gleason here?" Sonny nodded at the realtor.

"Well, I meant . . . his land."

Brooks coughed and flipped his cigarillo into the dirt.

"Gentlemen, I'm afraid you've got this all screwed up. Sheriff, I'll go in and try to convince Mr. Linesinger not to press charges for trespassing on all of these people, if they forget about the pickup and surveying equipment. Otherwise, we may have some folks going to jail. I'm sure, when the truck is turned upright, you'll find it isn't destroyed, maybe a little caved in."

Sonny grinned, anticipating his coming joy.

"What in the hell are you talking about," Brooks said, "that land is no longer his, and—"

"Hold on there, Henry," Sonny said. "That land is his until midnight Saturday. I always advise him to pay a loan on the final day it's due, make the money work full time. He's instructed me to pay off the loan this afternoon in full, with cash. I do believe your bank is open this afternoon. That means, Henry, that your misinformed surveyor and your dumbass realtor, and you, you sneaky, slimy snake, are trespassing on this land right now! And you've illegally brought the law onto Mr. Linesinger's land to harass him in his own home, threaten him with violence, and cause him great mental anguish. Now, Henry, I think you better get your dumbass back to your little bank and try to think up better ways to screw little old men out of their land!"

Sonny stepped toward the banker, eyeballing him with great hostility, muscles taut. With his boat springing a leak, Henry Brooks looked at the sheriff, but the sheriff wasn't about to start baling. The three men turned and stomped off to their late-model cars. The banker kicked at the realtor and the real estate man scurried behind his car door and slammed it.

"I told you not to let that surveyor on here before the thing was closed, God damn it!"

Sonny approached the low-slung ranch house.

"Hey, Hezekiah, it's Frank, let me in!"

"Ya got yer .44?" the old settler asked as he unbarred the front door and opened it cautiously. He'd barricaded the front windows with furniture and catalogs and bedding, ready to make his last stand.

"What are you doing?" Sonny said, shoving his way through the debris, vacillating between the hilarity and the sadness.

"Me an' Partner is holding the land."

The gnarly old rancher was ready, fallen back in time when you could protect your home from invaders with a gun or a bluff. Sonny didn't try to explain that he couldn't hold his land like this anymore, that they take it with paperwork and computers now. A man out of his time, born seventy years too late, there seemed no place for him in the modern West as a Boeing 727 roared its departure across the valley. He was one of the remaining black-footed ferrets. Sonny put his hand on Hezekiah's shoulder.

"They're gone, they can't take any of it."

"Ya put the run on 'em, Frank, they must know who ya is."

The bowlegged homesteader stepped outside and squinted over the land.

"Too damn dry. Only rains when a body's trying ta hay."

"Let's go down and turn the pickup back on its wheels so they can drive it away."

The two of them walked down the dirt road having outgunned the outlaws who came to steal the homestead.

Sonny paid off the loan. With a fancy lawyer and Hezekiah's under-standing, he set up the two ranches so that when Hezekiah died, they'd become one ranch. It would be called The Linesinger Ranch. Hezekiah would be paid in advance for the land and would never have to worry about taxes or payments again. The developers were held at bay for as far as Hezekiah could see into the future. The look on his furrowed face made Sonny's heart dance.

Chapter 39

SONNY WAS NAILING cedar shakes on the tack shed when Sally drove in. The roof on the house and tool shed were finished, and with a few more courses he'd be to the ridge on the shed.

"Hello up there, you ever coming down?"

She stood directly below him in a pink low-cut blouse, shielding her eyes from the sun.

"You look awfully good from up here."

He stood, stretching aching muscles, staring down at her with no attempt to hide his salacious gaze.

"Whatever it takes to bring you down."

He laid his gloves aside and climbed down the ladder. With his arm around her waist, they walked toward the house.

"What're you up to?" he asked.

"I was lonesome."

She appeared relaxed, apparently less fearful about her ex-husband since his visit to the hospital. They sat on the edge of the porch and dangled their feet.

"How's Jesse?"

"He's fine today; he's at school."

"Good."

"The sheds look so nice, and the house, like they were new buildings. I can't believe how much you've changed this place."

"Well, I won't get much done if you come around looking like this."

"I have to do something to get your attention. You go night and day; you never come over anymore."

He guessed she was fresh from a shower; a splash of Jean Nate' invited him. Hannah crossed his mind.

"You sure you want to fool around with this footloose no-account?" She stood. "Come on."

By the hand she guided him into the house. After shutting the door and sliding the deadbolt into place, Sally led him to his bedroom without a word and embraced him beside the bed.

"I want you so badly," she said.

"But we're *not going to get serious,*" they chimed in together. They laughed.

Then, tinder too close to the heat, they caught fire. They bred in a frenzy, as if they both suspected, like the Salmon, that soon after they finished they would die. Finally, he fell beside her, totally spent, and they snuggled under the sheets. Awaking with her movement, he'd slept peacefully, dreamlessly, for a time.

"I have to go," she said.

She kissed his bald head and snuggled close.

"You ever wonder who you are?" she said.

"Twenty-four hours a day."

"I mean I'm forty-two, I'll be without *both* of my children soon." She paused, as though swallowing the sorrow. "And I'll be working at Coast to Coast in Belgrade, Montana. I've started wondering what options are left for me, you know?"

"I know."

He pulled her close to him, his face pressed against her neck.

"What happened with your marriage?" she said.

"I'm not cut out for it, pure and simple."

"You're a gentle man."

"And you're a woman who knows how to love a man in the sack."

She kissed him on the mouth, on the chest, on the stomach. Then she swung her legs out of bed, sat up, and sorted her bra from the tangled clothing on the floor.

"You've got more muscles every time I undress you. Shingling do that for you?"

She laughed and squeezed his biceps.

"No, terror."

He turned on his side and watched her dress.

"Do you think Hannah is attractive?" she said.

"Hannah? Ah . . . oh, well . . . yeah, she's a pretty girl."

How the hell did Hannah get into bed with them?

"I worry about her." She pulled on her jeans. "I'm afraid she's gun-shy after Steve. It's been brutal for her, too; her bruises are inside. I hope he hasn't ruined her feelings for marriage."

She was dressed.

"She'll be all right. She's just a little ahead of the boys around here, thinks they're somewhat immature. There's no hurry."

"I hope you're right." Sally slipped into her shoes.

"You sure know how to kick the hell out of a shingling job."

"I've been trying for weeks. See you later."

She bent and kissed him on the mouth and she was gone. With his eyes closed, he stretched naked in the tangled sheets and wondered how much of her personal life she shared with her daughter. Nothing, he hoped.

On August thirty-first Hannah was twenty-two years old. Sonny stopped around supper time for the celebration and gave her a pair of riding boots, two books on whales, and four record albums. He'd bought twice as much, but at the last minute realized he was overdoing it. Butch was there with a gift of expensive binoculars, and they all had a piece of cake. Hannah's date picked her up, and they watched her go away with the college boy in a yellow VW convertible. The little party went on without her, but a pang in his chest told him that nothing in his life would go on without her.

Outside, Butch caught up with Sonny.

"Frank, could I ask you a question?"

Sonny stopped beside the pickup.

"Sure, fire away."

"Well, it's about Hannah." Butch looked down and kicked at the gravel.

"What about Hannah?"

"Well . . . we're friends, you know, and we hang out together and all. . . ."

"Yeah, so what's the question?"

"I want to ask her out on a date, just her and me."

"So, call her up and ask her," Sonny said.

"I'm afraid to, I'm afraid she'll laugh or something. I've wanted to ask her out for years, but I know she just thinks of me as a friend, one of the gang, and . . . darn it, Frank, I love her. I've always loved her since the first day we met and to her I'm just a pudgy kid she does stuff with."

Sonny saw the hopelessness in Butch's face. Who would have guessed they were fellow travelers, yoked to an impossible love for the same girl? Sonny felt Butch's pain, it was Sonny's as well.

"Just call her and take a shot at it," Sonny said. "You never know until you try."

As he drove away, Sonny wondered why he didn't take his own advice.

Chapter 40

WITH JESSE ASLEEP and Hannah in the shower, Sally halfheartedly watched TV, unwinding from a tiring week, thankful for the Labor Day weekend. Jesse had started school the first week but missed two days, and the teacher sent home his books and assignments as if he had the flu or something and would soon be back playing kickball at recess. It was nearly ten o'clock when Sally heard a knock at the door. She opened it with a smile, expecting Frank. What she got was Steve, smelling drunk and looking mean. He shoved his way inside and shut the door.

"You just waiting up for me, honey?"

He surveyed the trailer and smiled. Sally was in her terry cloth robe and the kids were all off to bed.

"Get out of here, Steve, right now!"

She looked him in the eye, attempting a firm stance.

"You all dainty for your bald-headed cowboy?"

He pressed toward her and she backed into the living room.

"You been whoring again, wife?"

His backhanded slap in the face snapped her head forcefully.

"No, Steve, please don't, please—"

"Been flaunting that pussy all over the country?"

The next blow brought blood instantly from both nostrils, and when she tried to protect her face with her free arm, he punched her in the stomach. Her world turned into a vacuum. She slumped to the carpet, searching the dimly-lit room for air. All oxygen had been sucked from her body; piercing lights flashed in her skull. While she clawed for a breath, he tore open her robe, rolled her on her back, and sat heavily across her naked hips.

"You just can't go off with every stallion that comes sniffing around, you goddamn slut."

A blow to the side of the head left a ringing in her skull like a tuning fork, but she no longer cared; she could breathe again, just when she thought she'd die. Holding her hands spread on the floor behind her head, he bent close, kissing her mouth, mixing blood with saliva, slobbering over her exposed breasts. The stench from his alcoholic breath engulfed her while he whispered obscenities, seemingly uncertain if he should rape her or beat her, his own filthy words igniting his already inflamed lust and anger. She tasted blood.

Hannah wandered lackadaisically out of the bathroom wearing only a long thin T-shirt for pajamas. Music and dialogue from the TV filled the front of the trailer home, and it took her several seconds to translate what was taking place on the living room floor into understanding.

"Stop it, I'll call the police!" She hurled a metal bowl half-filled with corn chips, narrowly missing his head. "Stop it, damn you!" She threw a can of Campbell's Soup, grazing his back.

"I'll get to you in a minute, you little bitch!"

He swayed atop Sally's body and almost fell off. At that instant Sally heaved with all her strength, propelling him into the coffee table. She scrambled up, but he caught the hem of her robe and hung on. She slipped out of one arm and was almost out of the other when he grabbed her ankle. With adrenalin-fueled strength she dragged him halfway into the kitchen before he swooped out his free arm and caught her other leg, sending her sprawling to the floor. He was about to drag her back into the living room when he looked at Hannah for the first time.

She stood just out of reach, threatening him with an iron skillet she held with one cocked arm. Sally could see that in her rage Hannah was unaware of her nakedness. He ignored the weapon and with his first staggering steps toward her, she fled down the narrow hallway into her room. Sally, realizing his intent, desperately clutched his shirt tail, holding him back, her legs braced against the kitchen counter. He turned and punched her in the head. She lost her grip; pain screamed behind her eyeballs.

Steve careened down the hall but stopped dead in his tracks short of her door. Guardian, from the doorway at the end of the hall, stalked forward slowly, his huge head held lower than his shoulders, the hair on his neck bristling, a low, menacing growl in his bared teeth. Even in his alcoholic bliss the teamster recognized pain on the hoof, and he slowly retreated.

"Here, poochie, nice dog," he said, patting his leg.

The ridgeback seemed to pick up the scent of fear and violence in the household and he wouldn't be had. With lips curled away from his large white fangs, he backed Ramsey into the kitchen. Like a lion trainer, he picked up a kitchen chair and started down the hall, jabbing its legs into Guardian's teeth.

"Get him!" Sally shouted, "sic him!"

The ridgeback snapped at the thrusting weapon, but slowly retreated as the metal legs repeatedly hit him in the head. At Hannah's room, Ramsey held the dog at bay with the chair and battered the door with his solid frame, shattering the cheap hollow plywood. Sally shouted.

"You leave her alone, damn you, don't you dare *touch* her!"

She tried to stand but nearly fainted, unable to find her balance. Ramsey noticed Jesse standing at the end of the hall behind the ridgeback, the boy watching him from hollow eyes, too sick to do more than stand. For a moment the bully abandoned his assault on the caving door and glanced back at the boy, wilting in his haunted gaze.

"Get him, boy," Jesse said softly.

Guardian snapped viciously at the chair and broke the spell. Ramsey held the dog off and shoved his way into Hannah's room.

Sally collected her wits, crawled to the phone, and dialed.

The newscaster on the TV gave baseball scores and expressed his personal remorse that Boston looked like it was folding. In only his Levis and sweatshirt, Sonny half-dozed in the stuffed chair and the ring of the phone blended with the television noise. When he finally sorted one from the other and picked up the phone, it took him several seconds to translate Sally's hysterical words into the scene that was raging only a mile down the road. Then he dashed out of the house barefooted, almost knocking the screen door off its hinges. He leaped into the pickup and Sally's words, thundering in his skull, transformed him into a madman.

"He's in Hannah's room!"

Chapter 41

HANNAH WAS FRANTICALLY struggling to wedge herself through the high, narrow window when he broke in, but it was too small, and he had her waist in his iron grip. In her stark terror she'd had the presence of mind to pull on panty hose, Levis, and as many shirts and sweaters as time allowed. He yanked her back into the room and flung her on the bed like a rag doll. Overmatched by his strength and weight, she struggled to kick with her legs, punch with her fists, but when her sweating step-father had managed to rip the clothing from the lower half of her body, he finally held her helpless in a penetrable position on the bed.

"Now I'm going to make a woman out of you, you feisty little bitch."

"You wanna bet!" Sonny shouted.

A startled expression crossed Ramsey's face the instant Sonny's sidewinder uppercut thudded into his jaw, catapulting him against the wall and setting Hannah free. The trucker slammed his arms out to the side against the wood paneling, trying to bring himself back up to a standing position like a bird flapping its wings, ripping pictures of whales off the wall.

Sonny drove his fist into Ramsey's exposed ribcage with crushing force and the rapist dropped to his knees, gasping. Hannah, unable to cross the small room because of the violence, crawled into the doorless closet. Like a wounded cat, Ramsey lunged forward and drove Sonny back into a mirror and stereo table, cracking Sonny's head amidst showering glass and plastic. Sally peered through the splintered door with Jesse and screamed hysterically.

Ramsey swung his arm blindly and caught Sonny in the face with his case-hardened fist. Shooting stars went off in his head. Dazed and staggered, Sonny grabbed the man from behind and locked his arms around him, buying time until the blur cleared. In the tiny closet Hannah screamed and pulled on every bit of clothing possible, the outcome still in doubt.

Ramsey strained to break the hold and with bulging faces they grappled, their heads side by side, mingling sweat, two madmen laboring to overpower each other. Two hominoids fighting over a woman in earth's oldest battle. The trailer rocked as they slammed from wall to wall, punched through plasterboard and paneling, scattered and pulverized everything in the room like a schizophrenic wrecking crew.

"Stop it, stop it!" Sally screamed.

Sonny's head was clearing. He released his bear hug and shoved Ramsey face first into the wall, then followed swiftly with repeated punches to the kidneys, hard, thudding blows. The man's knees buckled and he crashed onto the debris-strewn floor, rolling onto his back. Sonny pounced on him, kneeled across his stomach, and punched his head and face again and again with a long pent-up rage.

Hannah grabbed his arm, screaming.

"No, Frank, don't, you'll kill him, you'll go to jail!"

Sonny gave in and sat back, his breathing rapid, his nostrils flaring, his bloody fists slowly unclenched. The wife beater was barely conscious. Sonny stood abruptly, cleared the wreckage from in front of the splintered door, and dragged his battered foe out of the trailer by the ankles, banging his head on each step to the ground. He wrestled him into his car and slapped him into some state of consciousness. Sonny started the engine.

"Listen carefully, you possum-brained tub a guts. If I ever see you in this country again, I'll bury you in the manure pile for the maggots, you savvy?"

Ramsey nodded and Sonny slammed the door. The car slowly rolled away, weaving off into the darkness. When he turned and looked at the trailer, three heads and a dog watched from the doorway. Man oh man, it was just like one of his lousy movies, he was a hero!

But his winching body told him this really happened, his racing heart told him. Hannah ran to him through the darkness and lifted herself off the ground with her arms around his neck, nestled her head against his, the scent of her hair in his nostrils. Entangled in that scent, and emotionally and physically drained, he let himself go.

He wrapped his arms around her and held her with hands that felt broken, held her for all the times he'd never hold her, cuddling her softly, tenderly, in the summer night. Then he put her down, and without a word they walked to the trailer. He'd saved his unsullied girl from ravishment, and he swelled with a clean, self-satisfying pride, though he knew he'd saved her for someone else.

The trailer was a shambles. Except for a brief period of euphoria, it was an NFL locker room after a long and hard-fought victory. They all jabbered excitedly around the kitchen table, delivered for the moment from violence and terror.

"I knew you could whip him, Frank," Jesse kept proclaiming in exhilarated praise, "I knew it."

But Sonny knew it might have turned out differently if he hadn't had the advantage of catching the man half drunk, though he was surprised at, and somewhat proud of, his hard-earned strength.

"Your dog gave Frank the time to get here," Hannah told Jess while she rubbed the happy head of the ridgeback.

Hannah dabbed at a gash on Sonny's skull with a washcloth, and Sally cleaned the blood from his swollen hand.

"Gosh, you were mad," Hannah said. "I never saw anyone hit anything so hard." She laughed. "I think you're sprouting a little hair, you got so mad you started growing hair again."

He stood abruptly and diverted her attention to his other hand.

"It's a whole new ball game now," he said. "He attacked Hannah, that's not some marital dispute. I don't know what attempted rape is in this state, but it isn't just thirty days in the county jail. They'll put him away, hard time, maybe five years or more, but you've got to go to the police."

"I will," Sally said. "I can't take any more. I'm so sorry I dragged you into this, Frank, you know, he could've killed you. I'll lock him up, and if he comes back and does his worst when he's out, maybe five years of peace would be worth it."

She tried to smile, but as if her heart had too much agony, it came out in a woeful frown. She touched her puffed lip with a finger and her spirits seemed to sag. The left side of her face was turning color. Sonny, too, was coming back to earth in tune with his wounded body. This wasn't at all like the movies. A swollen shin, several cuts on his head and hands, his lip gashed, and worst of all, he was sure his right hand was broken, swelling so that the knuckles were no longer visible.

Sally started a pot of coffee and lost her resolve, said they'd have to move after all, disappear, start over somewhere else. Unable to bear the thought of Hannah going away, Sonny knew he'd have to deal with Ramsey once and for all. He would make an honest effort to buy Ramsey off; the man must surely want money. If that didn't work he'd find other means.

On Tuesday they found some relief from the small item on page two of the *Bozeman Daily Chronicle:*

> Also arrested Saturday at 11:08 pm, Steve Ramsey of Belgrade for drunken driving and resisting arrest. Ramsey was fined three hundred dollars, given thirty days in the Gallatin County Jail, and had his driver's license revoked for six months.

Steve Ramsey would not be trucking for six months, which only led Sonny to wonder what the malicious driver *would* be doing. At least that gave Sonny thirty days to contemplate what he'd do about this malignancy in their lives.

Chapter 42

WITH AN IMPATIENT FLAIR to their feeding, the swallows swooped through the barnyard as dusk whispered in. Soon gone—the approaching cold ending the season of the insect—Sonny sensed they were trying to tell him something. Bilbo and Fluff and Pebble and Feather, about to make their long journey to South America. Marking the days that Steve Ramsey was in jail, Sonny had looked back into the face of that night of violence and tasted its revulsion, and the cast on his right hand wouldn't let him forget. He lingered in the barnyard, reluctant to face what awaited him in the empty house. But it was time.

Nervously he locked the doors, left the lights out as darkness sifted down on the valley, and turned on the TV. His hand shook. Like an expectant father who feared a stillbirth, he had agonized all day. When it flared onto the screen, he slumped back in the stuffed chair, and the big Fall Special, *A Tribute to Sonny*, burst in upon him. No matter how well he thought he had prepared himself for the ordeal, he was utterly overwhelmed by the emotional trauma.

Johnny Carson hosted the event. Hundreds of top performers from music and screen and television were there, folk, rock, country, western, promoters, producers, and good old Corkey, right in the thick of it. With a choked voice, Corkey spoke of the wonderful years he traveled with Sonny to the top, and never one to sweep anything under the rug, even mentioned the hard times at the end. They sang his songs, showed tapes and films of his better performances, stills of his early life, his mother, his father, ironically on the tractor that killed him, and did a *This is Your Life* for the singer who had died tragically in a flaming highway accident.

When showing film clips of his movies—some that mortified him—they were described as Never an attempt at profound statements, but easy-going light entertainment. The celebrities came to the podium in between the visual history and expounded on what

Sonny had contributed to the world of music and entertainment, trying to outdo each other with praise, as though the departed might be looking down with some new power to bless.

He wept through most of the two hour show, mournfully huddled in the chair, the flickering light from the television dancing on the walls and ceiling. He wanted to believe all that they were saying about him but couldn't. It was crushing him, discovering how much he had moved people. Corkey had been right. When you die, everybody loves you. But Sonny couldn't deny that none of this would be happening if he hadn't touched people with some rare note, some seldom felt stroke to the aching place of their hearts.

When the show was about over, an unknown singer, dressed in Sonny's trademark red sequined shirt, stood alone on the stage and sang "Carefree Highway."

Wait a minute! Wait a minute!

The jerk wasn't just singing the song, he was *impersonating* Sonny! The mannerisms, the movements of his body, even the voice and the way he pronounced the words, obviously memorized from Sonny's recording. He came up out of the chair and paced the room like a madman in a cell. He couldn't believe it! The fraud was terrible. He wanted to turn it off but couldn't. To his astonishment the throng applauded, coming to their feet, whistling, shouting. Sonny was tormented, confused. Were they doing it for him, his memory, or for that turkey in a Halloween costume?

The commercial break cut off the applause, and he flopped into the chair, his stomach in a painful spasm from the long, memory-wrenching tribute. Thankfully they overlooked his lost years as though absolving him from the stench and he knew his mother would be watching. What would his father have made of all this, but of course, if his dad were alive to see it, Sonny would never have been the subject for a TV Special.

The commercials finished, they returned, live, to the stage where all the participants had formed a long line, holding hands and swaying together to the music, singing, celebrating, and right in the middle of the line was the impostor, trying to look like Sonny. And, as if that wasn't enough, next to the phony, swaying with the music, was Corkey Sullivan holding that turkey's hand!

With the music in crescendo and the celebrities waving to the packed theater and TV audience, the spotlight narrowed to the impersonator in Sonny's clothing. Sonny sprang from the chair, stomped into the bedroom, and from the doorway, fired the .44 with his left hand, turning the TV screen into an exploding mass of glass and smoke. The noise slammed around inside the house until it worked its way out through the cracks and chinks, leaving Sonny standing in the darkened, sooty room. He threw the heavy handgun back onto his bed and kicked over anything within range.

He had broken two bones in his hand on Steve's wrought-iron skull, but now something was breaking inside of him. All those people celebrating Sonny Hollister's life, and here he was, trapped in the isolation of Montana, dead and gone! Blindly, he kicked and stomped around the house in the dark, until he fetched his stethoscope, put a record on the stereo, and curled into the soft worn sofa.

Only moonlight from the window shadowed the room. The song began, the humpbacks sang from the salty depths, and he thought it appropriate that the tears washing his face were salt water. The voices of the whales echoed down through the eons of time, and he thought about the life he once had, an extraordinary chance to touch people with his song. With a shredding agony he realized that he never would again.

The eerie sounds of the whales became his blanket and at once he understood what they were saying, as though he always had. They were mourning because they only had their past, their future laid waste by butchering human beings, and though they still lived to sing at this moment, they knew they were the last, the living dead, without enough of them left to survive natural attrition.

He clung to the sofa and tried to ride out the storm, only the humpback with him in the night, but he feared that if he made it to dawn, when the sun's light would wipe out the darkness, the darkness would still be within him.

Chapter 43

IN THE EARLY LIGHT of dawn, they readied the impatient horses with creaking leather and cold bits, murky figures breathing steam into the frosty air. They mounted and left the barnyard, the horses hooves silent in the soft earth. The swallows had departed without notice; one morning they were gone. Sonny wished he could have bid them farewell for their long journey. The first fall storm had come and gone, leaving the high mountains plumed with fresh snow while the valley grasses were browning, the aspens quaked in reflective yellows, and the harvested fields shimmered a golden stubble.

Fallen Rock had emerged from the barn shortly after Hannah drove in and honked. Sonny had no idea when the young Indian had stolen into the barn or how long he'd been there, but Fallen Rock remembered he was going to throw in with the Linesinger roundup today. He rode the black mare, and Sonny thought it paradoxical that the original American was not at ease on a horse.

After the several times Sonny had cowboyed in the make-believe celluloid West, he was eager to participate in an authentic roundup. His hand had been out of the cast for two weeks and felt strong. When he had visited Ramsey in the county jail and offered him thirty thousand dollars for every year he stayed out of Montana, Sonny realized it sounded far-fetched. The prisoner smiled politely, nodded at everything Sonny suggested, and left Sonny with the feeling he was being hustled. When Ramsey was released, Sonny left a note for him on the message board at the Truck Stop but got no response.

They crossed onto Linesinger land, prodding their horses into a canter across the hay field where they had worked together in summer's light, and Sonny worried about Fallen Rock, recognizing the anesthetic affects of alcohol in the young man's eyes and manner. He flopped from side to side as if he were about to be catapulted from the saddle at any moment.

Hezekiah was waiting with a neighbor, Roy Penwell, their horses saddled, and they swung onto them as the three riders reigned up. Hezekiah squinted at them.

"Ya ready ta ride?"

"We're as ready as we'll ever be," Sonny said.

"Too early fer the little shaver?" Hezekiah asked.

"Too late," Sonny answered quickly.

"Let's git after 'em."

Hezekiah turned his roan, and the crew set out to round up the wild and woolly cows that had run free in the foothills all summer. Single file they followed Hezekiah out west of the buildings, down through the creek bottom, and north across the upper hay meadow. Sonny caught Hannah gazing at the spot where they had buried the black-footed ferrets. Through a four-wire gate, they started up into the breaks and hills, working their way through the sagebrush and juniper, the native grass, prickly pear and the last of the wild flowers.

The sun owned the crackling blue sky, and as they gained elevation they could see the mountain ranges ringing the valley in a jagged, stark outline, their cape of snow shimmering like a new winter garment. The horses' heads jerked up and down rhythmically as the climb grew steep, and the fat mare, out of condition, sweat more profusely than the other horses. They went single file into that bright day and memories, like arrows, came hurtling at Sonny; with the smell of sun-warmed horse hide and leather, with the swishing tail, the way he rocked with Keemosabee's gait. He remembered how it was for an eight-year-old boy riding a big black swaybacked gelding named Tramp across the fields of Minnesota.

The neighbor boy, Leroy, had a pony, and they would play cowboys and Indians along the marsh where the slough grass and cattails grew higher than the horse. He could feel the muggy heat, hear the blackbirds scolding, the insects buzzing, and he remembered Leroy's frantic cry for help when his pony was drowning in the swamp.

Leroy took his pony into the slough among the reeds to hide on Sonny and surprise him when he rode by. It never occurred to Leroy that his weight, plus that of the pony, was driving the animal's legs down into the soft bottom like fence posts. Sonny rode by, hunting for Leroy and Leroy spurred his pony to attack. The pony and rider stood there like statures mortared in concrete. When Leroy realized what had happened, he leaped into the bog and yelled for Sonny.

At first the two of them enjoyed the small emergency that gave them an excuse to wallow in the cool muck on that muggy summer day. They tried to pull the pony out by hand, shoving from behind, tugging on his neck. When that got them nowhere, they fetched a rope and attempted to yank him out with Tramp's horsepower, almost tearing the pony's head off. The pony remained calm, obviously enjoying the cool mud bath. But suddenly it began to panic, struggling frantically to free itself, and the more it struggled, the more deeply it became mired.

Leroy was the first to mention quicksand, and both boys were immediately struck with an awful dread. The pony worked itself deeper and deeper into the quagmire, its eyes bulged with fear and its chilling screams of terror scared the wits out of them. Leroy held the pony around the neck and tried to calm it, strained to keep its head still, sure that his pony would drown.

Sonny couldn't remember if the idea came to him before he left the marsh or if it took root in his mind as he galloped Tramp toward the farm, but once inside his father's workshop, he knew what he was looking for. Tramp's huge hooves thundered back across the pasture while Sonny clung to his mane with one hand and to the air pump and tractor inner tube with the other.

They dug muck from under the pony—submerged to the point that Sonny had to stick his head under the murky water to reach far enough—and worked the deflated inner tube under the pony's belly so that Leroy could pull it part way out on the other side. Leroy tried to steady the terrified animal that struggled frantically and shrieked.

"It'll never work," Leroy shouted through tears, "it'll never work!"

Sonny had to connect the short hose of the air pump to the valve on the inner tube and every time he about had it, the pony would lurch and flounder, dragging the valve away into the morass. When he finally got them hooked together, he could barely keep the air intake valve on the hand pump above the water, knowing if it became plugged the pony would go under.

Drained of all strength, the pony seemed to give up and attempted to lay his head down into the bog. Leroy cried while he supported the pony's head above the green slime, stumbled and wallowed himself, urging Sonny to pump. Sonny pumped until he thought his arms would shatter, struggled to keep the pump above the water when he couldn't find solid footing himself.

Slowly the inner tube began to fill, first steadying the animal and then gradually lifting him from the sucking slough. The boys cheered through tear-streaked faces, looking like coal miners, covered with the rich, black bog mud and bright green slime. The bulging rubber lifted the pony free, and they quickly shoved the floundering animal to the solid ground at the edge. The tube was wedged against all four legs, the pony's belly hanging inside, and they had to let the air out before the pony could jump free onto dry land. When it touched ground, it grunted strangely and ran until it was out of sight.

Sonny and Leroy hugged each other and twirled and wrestled in the slough grass, celebrated their victory over the dark bottomless swamp that had tried to suck down the pony. They had to sneak into the cattle tank on Leroy's farm and wash the inner tube as well as themselves with clothes intact. They found the pony hiding in a dark corner of the barn.

Sonny couldn't remember if he told his mother about that day, but he remembered how he felt. They had won that day, on their own, two small boys against a hidden darkness that even stalked them in the green summer days of their youth.

After almost two hours, Hezekiah turned west and followed a broad curved ridge, looking down into a wide, sloping basin. There to the west, the herd grazed, a quarter of a mile below them.

"They look bunched, must be gittin' homesick." The old cattleman snickered. "You two wait over there," he said, nodding at Sonny and Hannah. "We'll go around behind them. When we gits 'em movin', you come down this side. Watch fer strays."

The three of them rode off around the ridge and shrunk in size as the expansive land swallowed their forms, giving Sonny and Hannah time to get off and stretch their legs. They walked to the edge of the basin and watched the cattle feeding far below while their horses greedily sought what remnants the cattle and deer had missed.

"Do you think I'm awfully young?" she said softly.

"Young for what?"

"For anything, for life, for . . . oh, I don't know. This will sound dumb and stupid. . . ."

She bit her bottom lip for a moment, glancing into his eyes and then quickly away.

"I know you like Mom, a lot, and she, well, I think she loves you. You've been so good to us . . . to me. I like being with you, working with you, like today, but I know you think I'm just a kid, maybe even like your daughter."

She hesitated, searching for the right words, and then she broke down, losing control.

"Oh, what's the use. . . ."

She began to cry. He stood awkwardly beside her for a moment and then reached out and touched her shoulder. All the invitation she needed, Hannah came to his arms.

"It's not fair, I loved you before she did, I love you, Frank, and so does my mother. She tells me how much you mean to her, and I want to shout! I want to tell her I love you a thousand times more than that, but I can't hurt her, I can't."

She buried her sobbing face in his chest. He hunted for words and wondered how in the world he ever got into this.

"Listen, it'll be all right. In a year or so you may—"

"You're always saying we have to make the moments count with Jesse. Well, how about *us?* How many moments do we have?"

He had no response and he was forming the words to tell her how desperately he loved her when Hezekiah saved him. They had circled behind the herd and were whistling and shouting, prodding the cows and calves down the basin.

He grabbed her and kissed her with the urgency of parting lovers, those who know they might never see each other again. It would only muddle things further but he was unable to restrain himself with her standing there so lovely, so alluring, tears rolling down her cheeks, fearing his laughter and rejection yet brave enough to admit her love for him when he wasn't brave enough to admit his love for her. Startled by her voracious response, it was Natalie Jones come back to him again, multiplied by fire! He kissed her tears from her cheeks and held her head in his hands for a moment.

"They're looking for us," he said.

She smiled as though he'd told her everything she wanted to know, her face aglow. They swung onto their horses and started working down toward the cattle and he kept telling himself he was too old for this nonsense, this sweet, sweet nonsense.

Hannah took the left flank, he swung toward the back of the herd and savored the taste of her in his mind. Lordy, lordy, what had he just done! Penwell covered the right flank and Hezekiah, with Fallen Rock, drove cows at the back. From a distance Hezekiah appeared like a pony express rider who set out a hundred years ago to deliver the mail and never found its destination. In smooth-worn chaps, tarnished spurs, and unwashed bandanna, he pushed his cows for another year, his wide-brimmed hat protecting him from everything but his own tobacco juice. Between them rode Fallen Rock, and as Sonny watched him he was struck with sorrow, seeing this American Indian as a symbol of his race in the West: working for the white man, riding a borrowed horse he sat without skill over land that was no longer his, and as a final irony, he rode the black mare in shabby Adidas.

The cows were half-tame and seemed to know where they were heading, but their calves were wild, having spent most of their young lives running free in the foothills. They would break out of the bunch and run for the brush, and Sonny would charge after them, yelling and laughing at the handsome white-faced Herefords, admiring their pluck and swiftness of foot.

Quick to understand that the horse knew better what the two of them were doing, Sonny gave the horse his head as they chased the fleet-footed mavericks over rough terrain. More fun than he could remember in years, he kept his portion of the herd in line and wished they had to drive them to Belle Fouche or Wichita back when Fallen Rock's great grandfather was a boy on horseback.

They pushed and chased the sixty pair out of the hills and back onto Linesinger land after almost eight hours of riding. As they drove them through the creek bottom and approached the corral, the cows seemed eager to cooperate.

On his old roan mare, Hezekiah stayed mounted in the large pen, barked instructions to the foot soldiers, Rock and Sonny and Penwell, while Hannah worked the gate into the calf-pen. They cut out the calves, shouting and waving their arms and sliding in the dust and fresh manure, trying to prevent the darting young Herefords from circling back to the herd. When Hannah closed the gate on the last two, Hezekiah made his count and was satisfied.

Already bawling for their mothers, the penned-up kids increased their bellowing tenfold when the trail crew mounted up and drove the cows out of sight to the west hay field.

"You'll hear 'em all night as far as yer place," Hezekiah said to

Sonny as they trailed the herd. "Guess we all cried some when they took us from our mama's tit."

Hannah hooted at the unpretentious rancher, and neither she nor Sonny mentioned what had happened on the ridge that morning. They filled the normal spaces with small talk as the three of them cared for their weary horses and hung up the gear. Fallen Rock went home with Hannah for supper, and everything seemed normal as grade school.

Twilight gently dissolved and Sonny basked in the afterglow of this raw-edged day. He recalled his utter delight when he heard those startling words; he never imagined for a second that the enchanting young woman he loved felt the same way about him.

Sore and stiff, he walked to the corral to bid the horses a good night, calling to mind her kiss and wondering when he might sip from her well again. From the corner of his eye, he caught a glimpse of a figure moving stealthily toward him from behind the tool shed.

Chapter 44

WITHOUT PAUSING, Sonny ducked past the horses and fled into the barn, expecting the thunder of a gun blast in his skull. Once inside, he realized he was trapped, with no way out the other end. He scrambled to the stacked hay, pushed in the bale, and slid through to the milk room. With his heart pounding, he shoved the bale in place and waited, afraid to make another move, crouched on the cool concrete floor of the weight room.

From time to time he thought he heard footsteps, creaking boards in other parts of the building, vaguely, above him, on the ladder, a squeaking hinge. It soon became pitch black and he attempted to hush his own breathing, which seemed to echo off the bare walls and floor like a blast furnace, the thunder of blood in his ears. He couldn't rely on Corkey looking for him because he'd often go off for hours without Corkey paying any attention. Fear spread wildly within him and he was tempted to face what awaited him in the musty darkness, but he could visualize the trucker standing on the other side of the hay with a gun in his hand, and he held fast. It was almost funny: Costello would owe the trucker hit money for the contract.

After what must've been an hour, unable to stand it any longer, he cautiously pulled out the bale and stuck his head into the blackness of the barn. For a minute he couldn't differentiate the features of the building, but as his eyes became accustomed to the shadows, he saw someone silhouetted in the large doorway against the bleak night sky. Sonny held his breath. The figure was urinating, raising a little cloud of steam in the chilly night air.

A hell of a way to stalk someone you plan to kill.

Whoever it was finished and paused for a moment, looking out into the night. Then he turned and walked toward Sonny. Halfway across the barn the figure veered off into the blackness but not before Sonny recognized his angular physique. Fallen Rock.

The ladder creaked and the young man climbed into the loft.

Sonny slid out of his fraudulent haystack and replaced the bale. He waited a moment and listened. Then he went to the ladder and called softly,

"Rock, Rock, is that you?"

There was no response from the loft, and Sonny froze in place. Had he made a fatal mistake? When he'd made up his mind to bolt for the open doorway, he heard someone coming to the ladder.

"Hello, it's me, Rock."

Sonny climbed to the loft, snapped on the lights—three insect speckled bare light bulbs—and followed Fallen Rock to the far end. Come to find out, he'd been sleeping in the barn, off and on, arriving after dark, with a blanket roll stashed under the old hay. Sonny was out-and-out confused. Had it been Fallen Rock he saw in the peripheral dusk? Rock told him that after eating with Hannah's family, he'd come from behind the buildings at twilight. He'd been moving around some in the barn, thinking he heard someone else. Sonny tried to recapture the image at the corner of his eye, and he had the gut feeling it was Steve Ramsey. But now he was sure of nothing.

"Don't you have a place to stay, any family?" Sonny said.

"My people live near Havre."

"Why'd you leave?"

"Nothing there for me," Rock said quietly.

"Did you sleep in the barn last winter?"

"Some. Hope you don't mind?"

"No . . . no," Sonny said. "Can't you afford a place?"

"It isn't that . . . I like it alone."

"Away from those idiots in Bozeman?"

Fallen Rock glanced at Sonny. "Maybe."

"That why you drink?"

"I don't know . . . it makes things better for a while."

"Why the hell don't you screw those morons, spit in their eye and show them the best goddamn man who ever walked down their lousy streets. I know a little bit about being looked down on. I spit in their eye! But you know something. After a while you no longer want to do it just to show them, you want to do it to be your best, for yourself, because it's in you."

Fallen Rock did not respond, and Sonny felt he was walking where he hadn't been invited. He wished like crazy he could tell him who he was.

"How old are you?"

"Twenty-four . . . I think."

Fallen Rock squatted on his haunches and Sonny followed suit.

"What does your name mean; is it from something that happened in your life?" Sonny asked.

"No . . . my mother worries a lot."

"Jeez, your name sounds like you got clonked on the head when you were a kid."

"My mother is a spiritual woman. She thought it would be like a non-stop prayer, all over the country, repeated day and night as travelers read the road signs. WATCH OUT FOR FALLEN ROCK."

"No kidding, that's it, the road signs?" Sonny laughed.

A smile appeared at the corner of Fallen Rock's mouth.

"Your mother's a wise woman, very wise," Sonny said. "Reminds me of my mother. She'd always say 'Keep me in mind.'"

"My mother figured the signs would be like that, people keeping me in mind."

"Do you have any brothers or sisters?

"One brother."

"What did your mother—"

"Ice On Bridge."

Sonny roared, slapping Fallen Rock on the shoulder and rolling over backwards into the hay. He lay there a moment thinking. Then he pushed up on his knees.

"If we'd have been Indian, I'd want to be named Pulls His Own Weight."

The Indian boy nodded his approval.

"My grandmother saved me before I was born," Fallen Rock said. "I never saw her."

"How could that be?"

"When my father was boy he broke through the river ice and got sucked under. His mother, my grandmother, ran along as the current carried him down stream. She could see him. When she caught up to him she jumped and crashed through the ice. She grabbed him and shoved him onto solid ice. She tried to get out but the current took her. They never found her. Her people call her Saves Many. They believe if you save a child from death, you save thousands of others, his children, his children's children, down the generations. When I was very young they told me how she saved me when she saved my father. Otherwise my being would have died in that river long before I was born."

"She must have been a hell of a woman," Sonny said. Fallen Rock didn't respond. Sonny stood, deeply touched by the story.

"You can sleep here anytime you want and you don't have to sneak in, but wouldn't you rather be in the house?"

"No, I like the barn."

"Thanks for the help today. Good night."

Sonny moved toward the hay chute and ladder.

"Where do you go in the morning?" Rock said.

"What do you mean?" Sonny paused at the ladder.

"In the morning I hear you come into the barn. Then you disappear."

"Oh." Sonny laughed. "I'll show you some day in the light."

He wanted to tell him that his barn trick was nothing, that he had such strong medicine he'd been able to disappear from the face of the earth. He walked through the darkness to the house. He had a black-footed ferret sleeping in the barn, or a bowhead whale, vanishing from the face of the earth right before his eyes.

Sonny snapped on their new RCA television, jarring Corkey out of a nap.

"Where you been?" Corkey said.

"I thought I saw that damn trucker in the yard; I've been hiding in the barn like a stinking fugitive."

"Was it him?"

"I don't know," Sonny said and sat in the sofa.

"Judas Priest! I'll call the sheriff."

"No, it might have been Rock. He sleeps in the barn."

"Sleeps in the barn?"

"Yeah, he likes it out there."

"We're running a zoo around here."

They sat waiting for the evening news, and Sonny hoped there would be no more publicity for the latest impersonator, some moron in Chicago who was dressing like him, imitating his singing style, singing his songs. They were cropping up all over the country, trying to climb aboard the gravy train that was fueled by his memory. Sonny had grumbled when they heard of this most recent fraud.

"No one goes around impersonating Gable or Dean or Hendricks. Why the hell is everyone screwing up my act. Lousy bloodsuckers!"

"It's something about you, something no one can explain."

Sonny picked up his stethoscope and listened to his heart. After a few minutes he looked over at Corkey.

"Hey, Cork, want to listen to your heart?"

"Hell no."

"Are you afraid?"

"Hell no."

"You ought to listen to it, it will talk to you, tell you things," Sonny said.

"Jeez, I never think about it until I'm around you. You get a guy worrying with your loony stethoscope all the time. Judas Priest, you give me the willies."

"I don't want to die yet," Sonny said with a note of desperation.

"I don't blame you, I know what you mean."

No, not 'cause I'm scared. 'Cause I haven't found out why I'm here."

"Whatta ya mean, Why you're here? Who in the Sam Hill knows that?"

"I don't know who the hell I am, Cork."

"Whatta ya mean, you're Sonny Hollister."

"Who's Sonny Hollister?"

"What are you, a little nutty? Sonny Hollister is Sonny Hollister."

They gave in to the TV where an evangelist with a southern drawl was finishing his appeal. They watched him for several minutes as he stretched his words with oily sanctity, emotionally pleaded with them to give their lives to Jesus and their money to him.

"You believe any of that?" Sonny asked.

"No more than I believe you're dead."

Corkey yawned. A singing group wound it up with the address for donations superimposed over their scrubbed smiling faces.

"Christ would throw up watching that guy," Sonny said. "People watch this actor and think that's what it's all about. No wonder they don't believe, and God help those who do. Jeez!"

Sonny slammed his fist on the end table.

"What on earth is eating you?" Corkey said.

"I think it's Jesse. That game little kid has no doubt that when he dies he'll have a much better life with God, and I can't help thinking

What if he's wrong? And then this jackass counterfeit goes on TV and plays with it, uses it to make himself a wealthy man. I'd like to blow him off the air!"

Corkey sighed an obvious thanksgiving when the ten o'clock news broke onto the screen. They watched for any word about the impostors, but nothing was said. The news, weather, and sports went off without a hitch, but as Corkey was about to click it off, they previewed the special feature to follow, two men in different parts of the country who had cosmetic surgery to look like Sonny Hollister!

What followed nearly tore away Sonny's sanity. They documented the experience of the two men through the steps of surgery to reshape their faces, showing before and after comparisons. Bert Coates and a Henry Rawlins, guitar playing folk singers who planned to imitate Sonny around the country for his fans. And worst of all, they *did* look like Sonny, though they were fatter than Sonny now. He sat as silent as stone, devastated. When it was over, they went quietly to their rooms.

With the stethoscope and pistol within reach, he tied the rope around his waist and chased sleep, rode the crest of his raw emotion. They were impersonating Jesus on television and Sonny Hollister in the nightclubs. Jeez, maybe *he* was the impersonator, and had been all his life. He just never knew who he was imitating. He laughed. *They* were impersonating Sonny Hollister and *Sonny Hollister* was impersonating Frank Anderson. Then, like a newborn calf hitting the ground, it dropped on him.

His heart pounded, his breathing was forced, his prayer had been answered! He sat erect in the darkness, very still, and allowed it to immerse him in its sweet redeeming grace.

He could go back and sing for the people.

Frank Anderson would impersonate Sonny Hollister!

Chapter 45

ALONG THE WEST SIDE of the barn a row of towering cottonwoods
thrived, nurtured by the irrigation ditch they bordered. Sonny found
Jesse settled under one of the enduring trees on a bed of recently
fallen leaves, one arm around his convivial hound. When the boy
gathered the strength, Sally would bring him over for short stretch-
es, and he found great pleasure in hanging around his familiar
stamping ground. Sonny would fabricate some busyness nearby to
give Jesse free reign and still be able to keep a watchful eye on him.
He had lost track of where the two of them had wandered, and he
pulled up short when he ran across them as he came around the
corner of the barn.

"Are you finished?" Jesse asked.

"No . . . just taking a breather."

Sonny was hauling hay from the stack to the feed bunk.

"I wish I could help."

"I wish you could too, Jess."

Sonny squatted in the leaves along the ditch and immediately felt
ill at ease, realizing he'd intruded on the boy's solitude. They hung
out together under the burden of that solitude for some time, and
Sonny stifled his reoccurring inclination to chatter.

"I won't be here when the swallows come back," Jesse said matter-of-factly. "I'm going on a journey like they do, only I'm going
much farther, way past Venus and Mercury, even past the sun."

The boy spoke with animation and happiness, as though he were
embarking on a marvelous adventure. Sonny struggled to acknowledge his own desperate hope that it were true.

"Would you like to wear the helmet?"

"That would be cool, Frank," Jesse said, but after a moment's
thought added, "won't you need it?"

"No, no more racing for me."

A late-falling leaf dropped silently into the gurgling water and
bobbed down the ditch on the gentle current. They both watched
its passing.

"Do you know about angels?" Jesse asked.

"No."

"They're all around us, all over the place, you just can't see them."

"What do they do?"

"Nobody knows for sure," Jesse said. "They do good things, they help us, they watch over us."

They were quiet for a while, then talked about common things: horses and guitar playing, until Guardian sprang to his feet and raced after a gopher that scurried across the pasture. Sonny used the dog's charge as an easy out. He stood and told the boy he had to get back to work. Jesse stopped him with his words.

"Will you welcome the swallows for me, when they come back?"

"Yes . . . I will."

Sonny had to turn quickly and walk away.

It was early, just coming light, when they chugged out the field road for the west pasture. The half-loaded hay wagon left a solitary track in the fresh snow and Hezekiah turned the old John Deere toward the northwest corner along the creek bottom where the cattle took advantage of the brush and trees for protection from the wind. The cows started bellowing, appearing out of the frosty willows like lost souls on an ice flow in the Arctic Sea. Sonny cut the twine on a bale and let the compressed summer-green alfalfa tumble onto the snowy ground in a steady flow as they chugged by the herd. Hezekiah swung in a wide circle that was soon crowded with the milling white-faced cows, and Sonny hustled to keep the hay flowing, pre-occupied with his thoughts.

He had learned from the unanticipated and painful consequences of tinkering with fate and he decided to thoroughly think through this latest plan before mentioning it to Corkey or giving his heart to it. It riled his stomach and shortened his breath just thinking about it, and he felt a new exuberance and gladness quite difficult to contain.

Hannah and he acted normal when they met, always with other people around. She never gave any indication of a willingness to rendezvous with him, working more hours in Bozeman with a second job, waiting tables at the Black Angus supper club. With Jesse steadily sliding downhill, Sally was constantly on the go between the trailer and her job, taking more and more time off. They were all keeping busy, to get through the day, to stay one step ahead of the inevitable.

When the load was spread on the blanket of snow, Hezekiah walked among the feeding Herefords, eyeballed each animal, noticed things that escaped Sonny. After scrutinizing the full circle, he came back toward the wagon, called his dog, and bit off a fresh chew of tobacco. He leaned against the wagon next to Sonny.

"When ya gittin' yer own herd?"

"I think I'd like that," Sonny said.

"We can share bulls."

The sky was overcast but the day had brightened into a world of white; the cattle fed contently around them.

"I'd like ta know the herd'd keep agoin' on Linesinger land."

The old cowman looked over his cherished cattle.

"You ever have a family of your own?" Sonny asked.

"Nope, jes' Sarah. She was my woman fer more'n six years. Good woman, she was, hard working, good cook, bake an'athing on that ir'n stove. Was a Quaker girl, her folks didn't want her tie'n in with me, but she upped and left 'em and come out ta the ranch. The fool girl loved me. Ya know, she'd never let me go out an' start a day workin' without prayin' fer me and makin' me wear a clean shirt. Hell, the rest a me could be worn and dirty, but I had ta have a clean shirt. Heh, heh."

"Did you have any kids?"

"Never did, never did." Hezekiah spit. "We tried like hell. Guess one of us jes' warn't fertile."

"Did you love her?"

"Yep . . . I loved her, much as a body can I reckon."

The old man looked out over his cattle.

"I had a helluva quarter horse then. It kicked her and killed her jes' like that." Hezekiah snapped his head slightly, blinking his narrow eyes. "I shot the horse. Alwa's felt sorry, I shot it. I know'd it was kickin' at Quinine, our burro. Sarah jes' got between 'em. Horse never meant ta kick her. I alwa's wish'd I hadn't shot him." Hezekiah fell silent.

"No other woman ever catch your fancy?"

"Whal, Sara got kicked in the '30s. Things was purdee tough then. I fig'rd I'd wait till things got better 'fore I'd think about another woman. By the time things got better, I wasn't thinkin' about it no more. Heh, heh."

The craggy cattleman laughed at his loneliness and spit it on the ground. The land and the cattle were his lover, his family, his life, and Sonny guessed Hezekiah had never prayed or worn a clean shirt since.

Chapter 46

IT WAS PAST NINE in the evening when Sonny heard the soft rapping at the back door. He laid the guitar aside and crept into the dark kitchen, expecting Fallen Rock. Even with the colder weather, Rock occupied the barn off and on like a spirit. When Sonny peeked from the kitchen window, he was overcome with a rush of warmth and happiness. Hannah. He flung open the door.

"Hi, I saw the light, just stopped to say hello to Gusty and—"

"Come in, come in, gosh it's good to see you."

She stepped into the kitchen tentatively.

"Were you doing anything?"

"No, not really, just making noise on the guitar."

She slipped off the fleece-lined Levi jacket she wore over her waitress uniform.

"Can I stay awhile?"

"As long as you want."

His throat went dry, and he backed, almost stumbled, into the living room. She followed.

"Oh, you have a fire." She seemed pleased.

"Yeah. It takes the chill off."

She walked to him and put her arms around his waist. Her liquid eyes invited him to share her desire and he felt a rush of excitement at the thought of being with her. He leaned to her slowly and kissed her bee-stung lips, tasted a trace of lipstick and the rainbow.

"I'll throw a log on the fire," he whispered, and as he did, she turned off the lamp and curled up on the sofa.

"I thought you'd never come," he said.

He settled beside her and took her in his arms.

"I did my best, but I couldn't stand it another minute."

They flew off together into a stormy passion that threatened to overwhelm them, and though he knew he could have her for the taking, he knew he would not. They caressed and cuddled and kissed until the log had turned to ashes.

"I should go," she said.

"You'll always be my girl," he said as he released her.

He reached over and turned on the light. While she used the bathroom to straighten her hair, he watched from the hallway and wondered what insanity had invaded his life, knowing he could take her to his bed and become lost in her sweet, fertile blossoms. He helped her with her coat and kissed her at the door.

"I shouldn't have come," she said, her face turning sad and serious. "I've driven by so many times. I just didn't make it past tonight."

"Oh God, I'm glad you did, kitten."

"I'm glad too."

"Are you all right?" he asked, holding her against him.

"Yes, now I am. But after I drive away. . . ."

She was out the door and gone. Suddenly he felt as though he'd never be with her again, that this had been fate's one gracious gift, and he'd turned it down.

Sleep evaded him as he tossed in the solitary bed, imagining her naked beside him. On occasion he still had the recurring nightmare. They were burying him in the cemetery at Boyd, but he was alive, lying in the deep grave. He could see the rough earthen sides, their faces peering down at him: his mother, his father, Jesse, Hannah, Sally, Corkey, Hezekiah. He tried to tell them he was still alive, but they kept weeping and throwing lumps of dirt in on him. He screamed, but no sound would come out of his mouth.

The alarm interrupted his sleep like a freight train and his thoughts came muddled as he prodded his body out of the warm bed and dressed, half awake. He zipped Ned's grandson's insulated coat and pulled on his gloves, but even in the dimness Hannah found her way into his mind.

A cold front had stormed out of Alberta and stomped out all pockets of resistance under its glacial hooves. Eight inches of snow covered the level ground and temperatures plunged below zero. Outside, he paused a minute in the pale dawn and let the polar air nip at his face, partially reviving him. Then he started the reluctant pickup and spurred it for the Linesinger ranch.

When Sonny arrived, Hezekiah was connecting the battery he kept warm in the house overnight, and a light bulb hung under the oil pan of the John Deere. The faded green tractor started after about ten seconds of cranking, and Hezekiah backed it out of the tottering shed over to the hay wagon. Sonny dropped the pin connecting the wagon tongue, and the old cowman climbed off the tractor, leaving it idling against the still morning air.

"Ya make her all right?" Hezekiah shouted.

"Yeah, see you later."

They'd been dividing the feeding lately; Hezekiah took care of the yearlings while he tended the cows. He shoved the tractor into third gear and pulled the wagon out the field road for the west pasture, exactly as he had for weeks now.

Another early riser had answered his alarm that morning, and Steve Ramsey arrived before dawn. With his hunting license and all the paraphernalia to make him qualify as a legitimate deer hunter, he lay in the snow behind willow brush and waited, his Marlin hunting rifle with a .30-06 cartridge in the chamber. Under him lay a bright orange hunting vest that he'd slip on when he finished. The wait seemed endless, and he worried that maybe the bald-headed cowboy had changed the pattern he'd observed for days. There! He could hear the old tractor chugging up the road toward the gate.

This time there'd be no slipups. Hunting deer on a Saturday morning, like hundreds of others in the valley, he'd see a deer, shoot at it and miss. The shot would carry out of the brush and kill some poor rancher who was feeding cattle in the early morning light. Another one of those tragic hunting accidents, but everyone knew they happened all the time. Just too many out hunting these days. No, he hadn't seen that the land was posted. They'd scold him and probably take away his hunting privileges for a few years, but he'd smoke that bastard who was laying his wife, and then he'd pay another visit to the trailer and that luscious little bitch Sally had raised. What's a step-father for if not for teaching his stepchildren the ways of the world!

The tractor and wagon came into view, chugging through the snow across the field and the cows bellowed their welcome. He could see that mother now, see the breath puffing from his mouth in little clouds of vapor, and the cattle blew their own wisps of steam as they moved out of the underbrush, excited to feed in the crisp morning air. He lowered his head as the tractor approached, and the Herefords came between him and his target. He'd wait for the perfect shot.

Frank Anderson threw the tractor in neutral and jumped back onto the wagon, cutting twine and throwing hay off both sides. Then he scrambled back onto the idling tractor and moved ahead several yards before repeating the process. The milling cattle shouldered and butted one another to get at the green alfalfa, and the bearded cowboy turned a wide circle as the bales dwindled and the white field became dappled with green. Gradually Anderson swung parallel with the creek, about sixty yards from the edge of the brush, and with most of the hay on the ground, the bastard sat on a bale that remained on the wagon and watched the cows.

Steve cautiously raised his head and squinted through the undergrowth. He had his cheatin' wife's goddamn boyfriend directly in front of him like a sitting duck. He lifted the rifle, carefully shook the glove from his right hand, and snapped off the safety. Though his feet were numb with the cold, his face was damp with perspiration. He tipped his cap back and sighted through the scope. There was that mother as though he were in Steve's lap, clearly magnified in the cross-haired circle, talking to himself, or *singing?* He couldn't hear him, but he could almost read his lips. It was over!

Sonny *was* singing as he observed the cows toss chunks of hay into the air to get at the tender leaves at the bottom and he took great pleasure from this work. It surprised him that he liked the cows, enjoyed their gentle, earthy dispositions, hilarious sometimes in their displays of territorial rights and their almost human tendency to be bossy. They were as stable and reliable as gravity.

To get his feet wet and find his bearings, he planned to drive down into Wyoming—sparse, forsaken, uninhabited land, far from any vestige of media coverage—and sing in the small town taverns for whoever would listen.

A bunch of black-capped chickadees fluttered among the cows and scrambled to get their share of alfalfa seeds. Sonny noticed it was perfectly still, not a breath of wind, and he realized how much Hannah had become a part of his life, not only teaching him to recognize this robust little bird, but that they would never venture far from cover if there was wind, highly susceptible to its chill. Thinking about her and watching the delicate chickadees flitter around the steadfast cattle filled him with an unfamiliar serenity. Large drifting flakes began to fall from the wide white sky and the world turned into make-believe. He'd fallen in love with Hannah, he was falling in love with the world.

The shot exploded in the brittle morning air, so clear and tangible you could reach out and touch the sound of it. The cattle stopped chewing for an instant, jerked their faces out of the hay, as if trying to identify the discordant note resounding over the valley and echoing from the creek bottom. Several magpies flushed from the leafless willows, and Sonny rolled off the wagon and lay motionless in the snow.

Chapter 47

THE TRACTOR IDLED monotonously, indifferent to the blood ooz-ing into the splattered snow, a cow butted another away from its hay, and the chickadees returned to their feeding. Sonny lifted his head slightly and peered from behind the wheel of the wagon. Someone moved in the brush. He cursed his lack of caution, leaving the .44 in the pickup. Now there was no escape, only level open field for a quarter of a mile. Running in the snow he'd be an easy target. He felt his body to see if he'd been hit while he gazed from behind the wheel. A cow stood on the other side of the wagon and he peered between its legs. The figure just stood there, in the willows, looking down. That hat. God almighty! it was Hezekiah!

Sonny rose to a crouch behind the wagon to get a better look. No mistake, it was Hezekiah with a rifle slung under his arm. Sonny ran through the snow to the creek bottom.

"What in hell is going on?" he called.

Hezekiah looked up and spit. When Sonny arrived next to him, puffing, he found Steve Ramsey lying in the crimson snow, a mas-sive hole in the side of his head, his cap twenty feet west, caught in the brush where the impact had blown it. Poised to shoot, his finger was curled around the trigger, the muzzle of his rifle tipped into the snow. Sonny caught his breath and realized he'd been a heartbeat from gone! He found it hard to breathe; he felt faint.

"Oh, God, how did you know, how did you find him?"

"Crossed his track on the way ta the calves. Don't let no one hunt in here, so I figur'd I better see who's sneakin' around. I took the Winchester jes' in case. Didn't have time ta be polite. The polecat was about ta squeeze one off."

The old model 73 had taken out half his brain with the .45-70 slug. When he looked at Steve, motionless in the snow, Sonny went down on one knee, trembling. Snow flakes slowly covered the cool-ing blood. It was over! Neither he nor the psycho had finished it after all. It was Hezekiah who put a sudden and final end to it.

"What'll you do?" Sonny said. "Now you're in it, they'll put you away."

Sonny's revulsion turned to alarm over Hezekiah's plight.

"I's jes' hunting deer on ma place like al'ays. I seen this critter move an I know's it's a deer 'cause no body's allowed in here. Jes' one a them hunting accidents. Happens all the time."

Hezekiah calmly pulled the orange vest from under Steve's body.

"I'll git rida this. He's sposed ta be wearin' it. If'n he'd had one on, I'da never mistook him fer a critter, the bushwhacking skunk. He ain't gonna do no more back shootin.'"

"What are we going to do?" Sonny said.

"You haul ass outta here. I'll git Penwell, tell him about the accident. We'll load 'em on the wagon and haul 'em to the house. By the time the sheriff shows up the snow'll cover the tracks."

After snapping on the safety, Hezekiah pulled the rifle from the stalker's freezing grip. Sonny grabbed the right hand and dragged the body through the snow, out of the brush and onto the open field. Hezekiah followed with the orange vest, rifle and cap.

"What about the chunks of brain?" Sonny said.

"Oh, hell, a weasel'll eat 'em 'fore dark," the old rancher chuckled, appearing unperturbed by the grisly sight.

Or maybe a black-footed ferret, surviving another day on protein from the rapist's brain.

"You sure you can do it?" Sonny said.

"Yep. No use you gittin' mixed in it. They might find out he was layin' fer ya."

The large flakes settled silently on the wide brim of his hat, and with his rock-like assurance, he restored Sonny's confidence. In spite of that, Sonny hated leaving him, as though he were running out, but he knew what the consequences could be if they tied him in with it.

"Thanks. I owe you."

He drove out the road, shivering uncontrollably, unable to comprehend the horrible events of the early morning and clearly understanding that it could be him lying in the snow, unnoticed by the feeding cattle. What if Hezekiah hadn't seen the tracks, or arrived a few seconds later? That old buzzard. He could shoot the ass off a gopher halfway across the pasture with his aged rifle. Somehow he knew that the old cowman would pull it off. It was a very good story. There was no connection, no motive between the trucker and Hezekiah.

At the ranch he wanted to charge down the road and proclaim to Sally and Hannah that their warfare had ended, their nightmare was over, but he knew he had to play dumb until the six-o'clock news reported the neighborhood accident. He walked to the house and wondered how they'd tell Jesse that his father had been killed in the creek bottom where the boy loved to play. They hadn't told him about the black-footed ferrets. Maybe they need not tell him this.

He hung his coat with the accumulated clothes and boots in the entry and went to the kitchen table. He rotated the cylinder of the big handgun and dropped the shells onto the oak table one at a time. Click, thunk. Click, thunk. The deadly gun was empty, and he felt an overpowering relief. He wanted to tell his bow-legged friend who he was, that thousands of people would acclaim him for saving Sonny Hollister's life.

The sheriff's car sped past on the gravel and Sonny watched from the window, the dry fluffy snow billowing and obscuring his passing as if he had disappeared into thin air. He couldn't keep the worry from the outposts of his mind, yet he felt certain that his good neighbor would fare well. If not, he would bring in the best legal team money could buy. To protect Hezekiah, he could never tell anyone how it happened, not even Hannah or Sally or Corkey, though he knew they would probably figure it out. It didn't matter. Like Roy and Toro, Hezekiah had saved him.

He waited by the television at six o'clock and languished through news, weather, and sports, but not a word about the shooting. He'd have to sweat through four more hours before the ten o'clock version came on. The phone didn't ring, he knew they hadn't heard. He tried to sing, watched part of a movie, went out and fed the horses.

At ten he held his breath until the news finally lit up the television. The shooting was reported second behind national updates. A long-time rancher in the valley, Hezekiah Linesinger, who answered a reporter's questions with a twinkle in his eye, told how he mistook an intruder for a deer and shot him. Sonny pulled on his jacket and fled the house, taking only minutes to be at Sally's door.

Hannah let him into the kitchen where Sally sat on a stool with a dishtowel around her shoulders and Hannah, in an apron, was giving her a permanent. The trailer stunk.

"Did you have the TV on, did you hear the news? Steve Ramsey is dead. A deer hunting accident. Hezekiah shot him!"

"Oh! Oh!" Sally said and pulled off the dishtowel and held her head in her hands.

"Good for Hezekiah," Hannah said and she clapped her hands.

Sally stood looking out the window and she wept. Sonny didn't ask if it was relief or sorrow. Maybe both.

Hannah hugged Sally and the two women cried and then they smiled and then they were bouncing and then they were laughing. Sonny smacked his hands and laughed with them and they included him in their group hug.

"I can't believe it, I just can't believe it," Sally said.

"He'll never hurt you again," Sonny said.

"That's so hard to believe," Sally said.

"What about Jesse?" Hannah said.

"Oh . . . I don't know . . . his father," Sally said.

"Don't tell him," Sonny said.

"He's sleeping," Sally said. "He doesn't need to know."

They talked until midnight. Their feelings kept colliding, guilt over their thanks that he would no longer haunt them. Guilt over their joy. Sorrow for the sad sad life Steve Ramsey led. Sonny knew that Steve had destroyed himself in his passion to escape his loneliness.

Chapter 48

IT WAS STILL DARK when Sonny fired up the kerosene heater in the milk room before his run. At times the ice and snow made it too treacherous to run on the property, but the plowed gravel was passable. He ran into the murky dawn and rehearsed how he'd tell Corkey he was going back to singing, that out of his heart-stopping brush with death had come the resolve. He grew cowardly anticipating Corkey's explosive reaction. Over the phone he had excitedly narrated the deadly incident in the creek bottom to him. "Good riddance!" Corkey said and was elated that this final hurdle had been cleared. Now Sonny was about to announce that he had nailed together one more hurdle. He turned and headed back to the ranch.

Fallen Rock was coming down the ladder from the hayloft when Sonny jogged into the barn.

"Hey, aren't you freezing out here?" Sonny said.

"No. I'm fine."

"You getting anything to eat?"

"Plenty. Are you going to disappear now?" he asked, expectantly, as if he were about to witness witchcraft.

"Ha! Come on." Sonny headed for the hollow haystack at the other end of the barn.

He pushed the bale in, slid through, and replaced the bale. Then, laughing, he pulled in the bale and invited the barn-dreamer to follow him. Fallen Rock slid through, his face alert, scrutinizing the contents of the secret chamber. Sonny explained the weight room and asked him to keep it between the two of them, that it was simply a part of his life he wanted private. Fallen Rock nodded. Sonny demonstrated how the apparatus worked, and with great seriousness, the young Indian man experimented briefly with the weights. Sonny removed his jacket and prepared to run himself through an extensive workout.

"Does this really work?" Fallen Rock asked.

"I do it to stay healthy, it makes me feel good, but I'll tell you this for sure, I'm one helluva lot stronger than I ever was before."

Corkey arrived a week later and plopped himself down at the kitchen table. Sonny paced around the kitchen and brought him up to date on all the implications of the trucker's death and their good fortune in the face of that tragedy. He saved the obituary for Corkey. Ramsey had distant family who had him cremated and returned to Texas. Hezekiah had been summoned to an inquest by the county attorney at which the facts were reviewed and a decision reached. Steve Ramsey was trespassing on posted land; Hezekiah made a reasonable assumption, therefore, that no one was in the brush. Mr. Ramsey had no hunter's orange on his clothing as required by law. The decision was accidental manslaughter.

They also noted that Hezekiah was hunting without a license and revoked his right to hunt, forever, stating that he was too old, his eyesight failing. He had fired his Winchester from seventy yards, with brush and limbs crisscrossing his line of sight, and hit Ramsey just above the ear, within an inch of where he intended. His eyes were bad? Hezekiah made no comment at the hearing, and most of them knew he'd take a deer from his place any time he had a mind to.

With that out of the way, Corkey revealed his own press release. Though the word wasn't out yet, 20th Century Fox was going to produce a two-hour movie of Sonny's life; they were searching all over the country for someone new to play the part. Roger Least, who had finished *Shooting Down the Moon,* Sonny's biography, was collaborating on the screenplay. It would mean more money in the coffers. Sonny could restrain himself no longer.

"Can you get me a screen test?"

"A screen test! What in the hell have you been drinking?"

Corkey laughed.

"You know what's been going on out there. Men are cutting up the faces their mothers and fathers gave them so they can look like me. Well, I'm going to be one of them."

Sonny braced himself for the response.

"You're not serious. Tell me, dear God, that you're not serious. Tell me, please, that you're not serious."

Corkey was only mildly upset, as though assuming that Sonny was baiting him.

"I'm dead serious. If I don't do it, I'm just dead, forever and ever, amen, and I "

Corkey bolted up with alarm; Sonny wasn't kidding.

"Holy mother of God, you're outta your skull. If you think—"

"Listen to me, listen. I don't know how I got into this; maybe it was supposed to happen; maybe Roy Rogers was sent by someone, but what I never thought "

Corkey waved a hand at him. "I don't want to hear—"

"What I never thought of was a way out. That's what was wrong with it, there was no way out, ever. But with *this* there's always a way out."

"Yeah, a cell in the penitentiary," Corkey said.

"No, listen, if it doesn't work, I just come back here. Who in the universe ever heard of Frank Anderson, and who could care less. Don't you see, I can take this one a step at a time. If it works, I'm only a very good impersonator of the late Sonny Hollister. But blast it, Corkey, I'll be back, alive, singing again."

Corkey slumped into a kitchen chair and flopped his arms on the table.

"You've been up here in Montana too long, you're stark raving crazy."

"I'll be just another guy who had his face changed. Who on earth can look more like me than me?"

Corkey got up and paced rapidly between the living room and kitchen.

"They'll find out you didn't have any surgery."

"I'll have it, a few tucks, some sagging skin tightened, get all bandaged up and give the doctor credit for a hell of a job."

"And what if they recognize you, really recognize you?"

"Who? Look at me."

Sonny jerked off his shirt and flexed his torso and arms.

"This is the body of another man. I never looked like this in my entire life, not even when I was twenty-two years old. I was soft, and then I was cottage-cheese fat. You show me one person on God's earth who'd believe this was Sonny Hollister."

Corkey took stock of the hard, solid body displayed before him and nodded.

"No one."

He paced into the living room and came steaming back with another salvo.

"How about Sally and Jesse and Hannah and these people here?" Corkey shouted. "You sure as hell can't fool them. They'll figure it all out."

"I've thought of that. If by some outside chance I do the movie, I'll worry about them then. Otherwise, they'll never know I tried. They think I'm out land speculating in Montana and Wyoming. They've never seen me without a beard. You know how different you look after you remove a beard. I'll keep on shaving my head, for insurance. I'll use a wig. That way, the bald head, the body, the glasses, will give me a totally different profile. I can do it Cork, I have to do it!"

"I'm getting out of here."

With that the promoter grabbed his coat and drove off the ranch.

It was past midnight when Corkey returned, and Sonny couldn't figure out if he'd been drinking. In the living room, Sonny laid his guitar aside while Corkey stomped the snow off his good foot in the kitchen. Then he stepped to the doorway of the living room.

"You're a tough cookie," Corkey said. "By God, you're strong. After what you've faced this past year, to be able to stand up and keep coming shows me what you're really made of, ya know what I mean. I think your idea is completely nuts, I think you're off your rocker, bananas. I thought that about the first fandango, but I went along with it because I figured I owed you. But if you're crazy enough to want to try this, I won't try to stop you. Want to know why?"

"Yeah."

"I won't try to stop you because my foolhardy friend, you haven't got a prayer in hell."

Corkey glanced into Sonny's eyes.

"I only hope that you realize the possible mental anguish you're letting yourself in for. You won't be *numero uno* out there, you know. You'll be just another pissant imitator. Do you realize what you're exposing yourself to by climbing back up on that stage? Remember what Bogart said about James Dean, that if Dean lived, he'd never be able to live up to his publicity. Judas Priest, kid, think about it, because what I want to tell you is that either way, I'm out of it. I won't be here to pick up the pieces. I'm moving down to the house on Casey Key. You'll be on your own."

Sonny smiled, almost wishing Corkey had put up more of a fight, knowing he may be right, that the ground that looked so inviting out there was no more solid than the dark, black slough bottom that tried to kill Leroy's pony.

"I want to try out for the part in the movie!"

Sonny sprang up and slid past Corkey into the kitchen on emotional electricity, striding around the table on the balls of his feet.

"Who could act more like me than me? Just let your mind wander a minute; a dead man plays himself in the movie about his life. They'll have the most fantastic film ever made and they *won't even know it!* I'd have to win the Academy Award, I can play myself perfectly."

Sonny hooted and smacked his hands together.

"You'll never get a chance to try out. Remember, you're just run-of-the-mill now. How do you think a hick from Belgrade, Montana, could ever get a screen test?"

"By having a powerful friend in the entertainment business."

Leaning against the sink, Sonny looked at him expectantly.

"Oh no, oh no!" Corkey held up his hand.

"You could say you heard a guy up here—"

"No, no, no—"

"—that you think would be terrific for the part."

Corkey shook his head. "I can't do it, not anymore."

"The hell you can't; people owe you, I know."

Corkey slid onto a kitchen chair and gripped the seat with both hands as if he were on a roller-coaster. He didn't respond for several minutes, gazing down at his misshaped foot. Then slowly he looked up at Sonny.

"Holy cats, I didn't want to die in bed anyway. But remember this and remember it well. If they ever find out what you've done. they'll spit on your memory, they'll piss on your grave, you'd have jerked them off, mocked their grief, belittled their sorrow, profited on their love for you. The mention of your name will make them puke!"

The two warriors regarded each other across the homespun kitchen, digesting Corkey's words. They paused, then slowly they smiled. Then they laughed in the face of the danger and fear and that which conjured up their nightmares. Sonny rushed around the table and embraced his loyal ally. Corkey accepted the show of affection stiffly.

"Holy Mary mother of God, here we go again," Corkey said. "I'm beginning to *feel* like God. First I bury you, and then I resurrect you."

Chapter 49

SONNY GRABBED the motorcycle helmet on his way out. The rend in Sally's voice had driven a stake into his chest. He hurtled the rattling pickup over the county blacktop and passed the slower-moving vehicles without caution, but he couldn't outrun the vision of Jesse singing "Wildfire" on Thanksgiving.

Though his body appeared depleted, Jesse was stronger, and with his small soprano voice and his thin arms wrapped around the guitar, he sang the ballad he loved, enchanting all of them. They clapped and cheered to hide their tears and disguise the catch in their throats.

Sally organized the day in one last fling at happiness, hauling a huge stuffed turkey to Corkey's oven at six in the morning. She tiptoed into Sonny's bedroom and kissed him gently as he awoke. The menace of the trucker's presence had been erased from her life, and day by day the acceptance of that freedom brought a visible slackening to the tension in her face, but the weight of Jesse's withering illness kept its thumb on her spirit.

Butch and Hezekiah had come at Sally's invitation, and Hannah invited Allen, her current boyfriend. Fallen Rock never did show up, to no one's surprise. They filled the old oak table with an abundance of food and drink, and the cozy kitchen with the noise of happy nomads sheltered from the storm.

Sally had appeared happy, touched Sonny affectionately on occasion in front of the assembled host and everyone laughed at her frolicking. Sonny participated in the horseplay and, as best he could, contributed to the fragile gaiety of the day. Now, as he floorboarded the Dodge pickup along Interstate 90, the memory haunted him. This was the second time Jesse had been in the hospital since Thanksgiving.

Sprinting the three flights of stairs with the helmet in hand, he searched out Sally and Hannah and found them hovering at the bedside like old women at a wake. Sally rose to meet him, and the expression on her face said it all: no longer any relic of hope there, only an ironclad resignation to the unbearable inevitability. He embraced her and somehow knew he was embracing his mother with her raw and bloody hands.

They left it all unsaid, or recognized that it had all been said. The boy was comatose, loaded with pain-killing drugs. Sonny glanced into Hannah's reddened eyes for a moment, touched the pulse of her suffering, and turned away.

"He asked for you," Sally said. "I think he might come out of it if he heard your voice."

"I came as fast as I could."

They held on to each other, watching the little chalk boy dissolving before their eyes. Hannah took a hold of Sonny's arm.

"Frank?"

A wisp of a voice rode from that colorless face on a smile, nearly shattering Sonny where he stood. Sonny bent close.

"How are you doing, partner?" His voice broke.

"I'm not going home this time, Frank."

"You want the helmet?"

Jesse nodded, and Sonny slipped it gently on his head.

"We're going to miss you so much," he said. He knew there was no time to play the usual games, to try to duck it. The words had been there all along, but he always found them impossible to wrench from his throat. Now there was no more time.

"I love you, Jess, I love you like my own boy."

The words ripped away the pilings he'd so painstakingly driven into place and all of his agony and sorrow poured out onto the bedding. He crouched beside the bed and sobbed, laid his head on the pillow by the boy.

"If I can, I want to be your guardian angel," Jesse said. "I want to watch over you."

Sonny regarded Jesse with blurring eyes and swallowed his sobs the best he could. Hannah broke down.

"I sure could use some watching over."

"Don't feel bad, please," Jesse said, "I'll be all right."

"Sure you will, amigo." Sonny wiped his smeared face with his sleeve. "Is there anything you want me to do for you?"

"I'd like to see Guardian," Jesse whispered.

"They won't allow dogs in the hospital," Sally said.

"The hell you say." Sonny bolted up, sensing there was little time. "Where is he?"

"In the truck, I'll show you," Hannah said, dashing with him down the stairs and out across the street.

Sonny opened the door and called the dog, and the ridgeback seemed to know instantly where he was going. Bounding up the back stairway, an orderly stopped them on the second-floor landing, protesting the dog's presence. Sonny handed him the roll of bills from his pocket and told him to go away. He did. With Hannah out front scouting for nurses, they whisked the dog into the room and shut the door.

Guardian went directly to the bed and gently placed his front paws up on the sheets by Jesse's face. Somehow aware that his canine sidekick stood by, Jesse fought his way back to consciousness. No one could ever convince Sonny that the dog didn't know exactly what was happening. The full-grown ridgeback licked Jesse's face as though it were a fragile chick, his tail wagging weakly. It was as if the great hound understood that he could not live up to his reputation, could not save his dying mate from the currents of this river.

As softly as a cat, the large dog crawled up on the bed and lay beside the boy, grieving with a hushed whine. Jesse lifted his arm and draped it around Guardian's neck, and the bond they had cemented with their common venture in life drew them together in a silent private flight.

A nurse swished into the room and found the gravely-ill boy with a helmet on his head and a huge dog beside him in the bed.

"What's going on in here! You can't—"

Sonny turned and glared at her. "Go!"

"But I can't—"

"Go!" He pointed at the door.

She stopped in her tracks, closed her protesting mouth, and fled. Sally grabbed Sonny's arm and squeezed. He turned back to the bed too late. Jesse had flown away. In the moment the nurse had distracted him, the boy had flown through the roof and out to the stars and planets.

"Oh, God." Sally sobbed. "He's gone, Frank, he's gone."

She pressed her face against his chest and cried openly; he put an arm around her and tried to hold back his silent sobs. He glanced at Hannah. She met his eyes and broke down, her body shook, she covered her face with her hands. With his other arm he pulled her to him and held her tightly.

After a time, when he could no longer tell who was holding up whom, Sally slipped from his embrace and went for the nurse. The unnerved woman wanted to know why the boy had that helmet on.

"It's for his journey," Sonny said quietly.

No command, no amount of coaxing or bribery would move Guardian from Jesse's side. Sonny hoisted him under the shoulders, Hannah lifted his hind quarters, and together they transported the ridgeback down the back stairwell, startling several hospital visitors.

"What'sa matter with a doggie?" a small girl asked as they reached the street level.

"He has a broken heart," Sonny said.

They pushed out the door and lugged the dog to the truck, knowing Guardian felt he had failed.

Chapter 50

Sonny ducked out of the crowded trailer house, relieved to be in the fresh air and alone. The preacher and family friends had accumulated as the message of woe spattered the bleak winter landscape. He walked to the truck and realized something strange was happening. Somewhat startled, he stood in the gravelly yard and observed. Surely Jesse's death could have no bearing on the natural world!

Minutes ago it had been sunny and very cold. Now the cottonwoods and willows off behind the trailer hummed and moaned, bending and lashing with leafless limbs; the sky rapidly turned dark, heavy gray clouds slid overhead as if weeping, the sun would no longer show its face for sorrow, and the wind, howling and whistling out of the southwest, groaned a mournful song, its breath warm and tempestuous, hurling back winter's grip with a fury. Snow melted instantly, as if by command; puddles broke out over the ice on the road. He pulled off his insulated jacket and turned his face into the gusts. The wind was warm. Only around zero that morning, the temperature had to be well into the fifty-degree range where he stood. Impossible!

He drove to the ranch slowly, preoccupied with this convulsive change in the weather, almost expecting an earthquake next. He glanced north across the pasture and there, as if he were ridden, Wildfire ran with the wind. Sonny stopped the truck in the middle of the road and watched, overwhelmed by this baffling world around him. The other horses stood passively far to the east by the barnyard gate, unaffected by whatever prodded the sorrel gelding to fly. Darkness was taking the land in giant steps, and the horse was a vision cutting that darkness, its mane and tail flowing behind like a painted horse on the carousel. Sonny peered into the darkness until he could no longer make out images in the lightless field. The last one he saw was the solitary horse, propelled by rippled muscle, running with great speed.

He later had one of the phenomenon explained. That strong, sudden, snow-eating wind was not an uncommon winter occurrence, sometimes raising the temperature as much as sixty or seventy degrees in a few hours. Hezekiah called it a chinook and claimed it had saved his bacon more than once when he was short of hay. For the running horse Sonny found no explanation, and he never mentioned it to anyone, though he'd come to suspect that all of life was mystery.

After putting it off for an hour, he called Corkey in Florida. There was a long pause at the other end. Then the choking words:

"I guess I won't get to take him to Las Vegas."

Two days later the temperature dropped, bringing back winter's wind chill. Corkey used distance to duck out of the funeral, and Sonny didn't argue with his case-hardened manager who couldn't face the desolating ceremony with the undersized casket. Sonny would have avoided it at all costs if it weren't for Sally and Hannah.

The number of people at the funeral surprised him, friends and neighbors and schoolmates and teachers, all congregating in the little white church outside Belgrade. Corkey was not the only one missing. Hezekiah and Fallen Rock never made it either. Butch did, sitting up front with Sonny in the family pew.

While the simple service took place, Sonny thought back to his father's grave, the cold wind cutting at his watering eyes, and everyone thinking he was crying. Not crying, he was angry, but just now he couldn't recall why. Was it at the people for putting his dad in that awful hole in the ground, or at his father himself, for leaving him? He suspected he was really mad at God for taking his father away but didn't dare let on for fear God would stick him in the hole as well.

The preacher spoke briefly of Jesse's unwavering faith in the face of his terminal illness, and for once Sonny knew the eulogy was true. He'd seen that faith and wished that he possessed it. He sat woodenly in the mourner's bench, dreading the short journey out to the open grave, but he went, supposedly to steady Sally and Hannah, who clung to him like refugees. The congregation gathered tentatively in the small cemetery behind the church, standing mutely around the earthen tomb. The pallbearers, Jesse's classmates, set the small casket on nylon straps that held it suspended over the short trench while fresh-cut flowers blew away in the frigid wind. Sonny grit his teeth and had to look off to the mountains.

Except for isolated drifts, the ground was snowless in the valley, following the enigmatic chinook, but the temperature fell steadily now; the wind had swung around from the north and it made it difficult to catch the minister's words. During the brief ceremony, Sonny gazed at the casket and wondered if Jesse was already long gone on his voyage, or if, after the gravediggers lowered him into that hole and wedded him to the earth like a fossil, his only immortality would be his integration back into the atomic structure of this planet which would never acknowledge that he had been here, never recall the echo of his fine sweet voice. The Atlantic grey.

The service ended, and Sonny understood that his moments were also flying away in the winter wind, urging him to forfeit every delay on his pilgrimage back to the hurting with his song. His life was impoverished by Jesse's death, his heart ached, but Jesse was gone. With a renewed urgency, he vowed to make the moments count.

They stood for several minutes as the congregation drifted away over the brown winter grass. He shivered. The bitter wind blew a bouquet into the grave, and Hannah broke down. Sally sobbed uncontrollably. With an arm around each of them, he turned them from the desolate little coffin.

A heavyset woman lingered at the edge of the cemetery, waiting to offer her words of comfort.

"It's God's will," she said. "Take comfort from that, Sally, it's God's will."

"If that's true, ma'am," Sonny said softly, "then God is a homicidal maniac."

The woman stood frozen with her hand over her mouth. Sonny led them to the truck.

They regathered at the trailer, now jammed with people who acted as if they were attempting to crowd out memory and pain, to remain immune to their own death, bringing food enough for the town of Belgrade. He didn't think it proper to eat, turned down continuous offers of food, and retreated to Jesse's room where he spoke aloud to Jesse just in case the boy was right, that he'd be watching over Sonny, a guardian angel. It made him feel better.

Fallen Rock showed up around supper time, and the people began to thin out with the food. The last group rushed out as if someone had pulled the plug in the bathtub, as if none of them wanted to be the last one facing the haunting memory of Sally's boy without knowing what to say to her bleeding emptiness. Then they were alone. Hannah would give Rock a ride to Bozeman, but before she left she cornered Sonny in the living room.

"She needs you," she said with a woman's wisdom.

"I'll do what I can," he whispered.

At that moment he needed Hannah more than he ever had. She hugged Sally and fled from the trailer, leaving an unbearable ache in his chest. He flopped on the sofa and allowed Sally time to putter until he could no longer hear her. He found her on her knees in Jesse's room, filling a cardboard box.

"Look at all this. Bird feathers, nests, rocks, snake skins, animal claws. . . ."

"C'mon, you don't have to deal with this now."

They settled on her sofa, Sonny held her close. She trembled.

"It was devastating," she said. "I knew I wouldn't see him again, there were so many things I wanted to say, how proud I was of him, how brave I thought he was, how glad I was that he was my boy, but I couldn't get the words out. It was so stupid! We both talked about meaningless little things when we wanted to say goodbye and neither of us could."

"Maybe he knew the words you wanted to give him," Sonny said.

When she was all talked out, he tucked her in with a blanket and pillow on the sofa and he sat in the recliner beside her all through the night, a soldier guarding the wounded body of a fallen comrade. He had attempted to shield them from the winter's blast, but it didn't work. The winter's blast was in his heart.

Chapter 51

THE WYOMING LANDSCAPE flaunted an easy openness that drew Sonny in and disarmed him, enticed him to believe she was his for the taking. He anticipated that first public appearance, rudimentary as it might be, in some pedestrian tavern, in some obscure, out-of-the-way town, and he knew it would be so unlike the first time when he went unsuspectingly into that other world. He could visualize where it might take him this time, and he felt more tightly strung than his guitar. The country was arid, ranches scattered at great distances among the breaks, draws and small buttes against an endless horizon. Down here he'd be singing to oil roustabouts, coal miners, and the trailer salesmen who furnish them with boom-town housing.

The season had remembered its name and an Alberta clipper ran off the mild weather—colder than a witch's tit in Hezekiah's vernacular. On the flatlands between mountain ranges, the snow had blown and piled in the arroyos and washes leaving the ground bare and bleak. The Beartooth range stood brooding to the west and the Bighorns dauntless to the east with their muscled shoulders burdened in winter's tonnage. He traveled south and passed through several small communities that held little promise, but as night slid quickly over the Bighorns, he picked Powell as the place he'd unsheathe his guitar like some old U.S. Marshal unholstering his rusty six-shooter. Ignited with a spine-tingling sensation, he drove slowly through the windy town at dusk and considered the audacity of what he was about to do here.

At the second bar he tried, the Stockman, the proprietor was happy to have him, though the large, rounded man named Winesap admitted readily that he'd never heard of him. Sonny auditioned in the lardacious kitchen while an oriental cook chopped vegetables, and after listening deferentially to most of one song, Winesap slapped Sonny on the back and told him he could sing as much as he wanted that night, sick to hell of the jukebox and its tedious menu of western whining. With a makeshift sound system consisting of one dented microphone and a single speaker over the mirror of the ornate bar, Sonny squirmed on a stool in a corner of the dingy room, nervously tuning his guitar one last time just before nine. He said hello into the battered mike, and then sang a song he had picked for the irony. "Let's Go Out In A Blaze Of Glory."

Nervous tension drained from him with the lyrics, and he felt natural, something coming back to him faithfully. He joked with the people, sang a variety of songs, and accepted a beer from a young bearded man at the bar. He was singing to eleven people, not counting the help, in Powell, Wyoming, on a night when a winter storm kept people home. Those who'd ventured out that night casually drank their beer, conversed and laughed and rested from their day's work, occasionally applauding Frank Anderson as though he were a moonlighting cowboy trying his hand at singing.

While he sang he gazed into their faces and the incredible unreality of it led him to overdo. He sang three nights until the last dog died, and the jovial owner offered him sixty dollars. Reminding the huge apple of a man that he was looking for experience, he thanked him and turned down the cash. Winesap told him to stop again if he was passing through, and Sonny made a mental note that when he hit it big as an impersonator, he'd come and sing at the grimy Stockman and make some big money for the kind innkeeper who had taken him in.

He sang in Cody, Greybull, Worland, Thermopolis, Riverton, and Lander, using the performance in the last town as his reference for the next. He sang for good ol' boys and for drunks, for young bucks who had life by the tail and some who didn't expect to see spring, for women with hope in their eyes and men hunting by instinct. He sang for the obese and the healthy, the attractive and the ill-favored, big spenders and moochers, wranglers, truckers, hired hands and land owners.

Sonny loved it like never before, tried to cheer them on their journey, saw in them the face of humankind, enduring day after day, carrying on in spite of their crippling scars and shattering wounds. He wanted nothing in return, if only he could comfort them for a time, shore them up, nourish, even inspire them, affirm life to those who had given up.

One night in Greybull, he did his first impersonation of Sonny

Hollister by singing "Carefree Highway." When his instincts prodded him, he gave himself no time to procrastinate, announced it to a fairly good Friday-night crowd, and did it by rote. The Greybull response was boisterous and later, a middle-aged salesman who struck up a conversation with him at the bar said, "You really sounded like him, by god, you really did."

Thus encouraged, he did at least one impersonation each night, and in Riverton did a lengthy medley. When he imitated himself, his mind was in a constant upheaval as to what in the hell was going on. He was astonished that no one stood up amid the cigarette haze and beer breath and hollered, Oh my god, it's *HIM!*

Even when it's offered for free, lining up gigs can be difficult, and he didn't always find a place to sing. He respected Corkey's admonition about keeping a low profile; he was traveling in the Dodge pickup, knowing he could slide into his first Cadillac when he was a recognized impersonator, though the Cadillac seemed unimportant now.

He had hired Fallen Rock as caretaker of the ranch, to tend the horses, to live in the house and watch over the place. He gambled that it would give Rock some importance in his own eyes, hoped it would reduce his need to drink. Hannah was delighted about it and assured him that she'd keep tabs on her vagrant friend.

Sonny had pulled all the stops at Christmas, attempting to shunt the sorrow of Jesse's death. He and Corkey hosted a shindig at the ranch including everyone they knew in Gallatin County and a few they didn't. During the celebration, in which several grand meals were served and dozens of gifts given, Corkey surprised Sonny by presenting him with the deed to the ranch, playing down the magnitude of the gesture in the eyes of the guests by announcing his move to the balmy beaches of Casey Key, Florida. In a fleeting second, Sonny's eyes caught Hannah's among the frolicking celebrants, and the temptation to settle on that land with her struck him with unexpected force.

Not to forget Hezekiah, Sonny had a new John Deere 4240 tractor with cab and all accessories hidden in the barn. When Sonny drove it out into the yard, Hezekiah was flabbergasted along with everyone else. Sonny couldn't help but think, as the bewildered old rancher drove the bright green machine through the barnyard with all lights flashing, how he'd have loved to give his father such a gift.

With the roll-bar cab, it wouldn't have crushed out his life when it turned on him.

It was one helluva Christmas, though he knew it wouldn't work; that no material splurge could heal their weeping hearts, but he did notice astonishment on Sally's face during some of the extravagant displays, as if wondering whose company she was keeping, giving tractors and ranches away like they were a Christmas tie or a pair of socks. When Sally drove home with the seat laden with gifts, he knew she still had to deal with the empty room at the end of the hall.

Hezekiah had come in after playing with the tractor for almost an hour, his tracks crisscrossing the snow all around the barnyard and beyond. He was fascinated with the Sound-Guard cab with heater, air-conditioner, radio, CB, several sets of lights for all occasions, and the hydraulic loader which he had raised high into the night to measure the height of the stacks of hay he could build with it.

"You'll hafta stay an' help me wear out that fancy tractor, Frank," Hezekiah said. "Can't do it with jes' my place."

Sonny figured Hezekiah'd had little given to him in his lifetime, and the old rancher was caught out on uncharted ground. With his three-fingered hand he reached out and shook Sonny's firmly, glanced into Sonny's eyes. He gave his head a quick nod and turned away, but not before Sonny detected a tear working its way down the sun-hardened creases on his cheek.

Chapter 52

THOUGH IT WAS DIFFICULT in most towns, Sonny attempted to continue his workouts while he was on the road. He found few iron-pumping enthusiasts in the high plains of Wyoming, and then usually in a converted storefront or filling station. Running when the temperature moderated, he'd do what he could in some scruffy health club and return to his motel to shower and rest. Where he found nothing, it was back to the tedium of push-ups and sit-ups on the grimy shag-rug floors of his motel room, doing several hundred of both while watching soaps or game shows on the TV. He missed Hannah most when he returned to the empty room at one thirty or two in the morning. Still tying himself to the bed, he used the stethoscope out of habit.

Sometimes he would lay on his stomach in bed with the stethoscope under him, pressed against his sternum and fall asleep listening to the rhythmic thump of his heart as though he were recalling the utter peace he knew in his mother's womb.

One night while waiting to sing in a working man's saloon, an abrasive, mean-looking character started up on a brown-skinned man, part Indian or Mexican. The foul-mouthed local was baiting the ill-clothed breed without any response; to which a few of his drinking buddies applauded and laughed. The dark-skinned man, his face ravaged with pock marks, held his drink with both hands and looked into it stoically. With his insults ignored, the bully became more enraged, and the tension was clearly leading to confrontation. The other patrons looked on as mutely as the animal heads hung around the saloon, the human eyes as passive as the smoke-glazed glass in each trophy. Have another beer and watch another ethnic get his ass kicked just for the hell of it.

The surly honcho of the bad-tempered pack shoved his chair aside with a move John Wayne would have envied and strode up to the bar, a few feet from the solitary drinker. Measuring the home-town intimidator, Sonny felt confident in his rejuvenated body against the soft sloth who had been sitting in too many bars for far too long. Under Sonny's western cut shirt and jeans was the obvious silhouette of a hard body that could quickly be turned into an instrument of pain, and instead of only bluffing this idiot, Sonny was contemplating punching him in the face, even if it meant blowing the night's gig. But he also knew he couldn't afford another broken hand at this point in his schedule or a conversation with some sheriff. He stepped between them and looked sideways at the tough, still unsure of what he would do or say.

"Hey, bro, none of us should be fighting in here. Hell, we ought to be propping each other up. Outside that door," he nodded at the scarred wooden door, "is where the fight is, waiting for us to come out."

"What're you talking about?" the ornery man asked. "What fight?"

"The *real* fight—leukemia, cancer, accidents, loneliness, having the one you love walk out on you, losing a job, old age, hell, freezing to death. That's the stinking fight."

"What the hell business is it of yours?"

"I just hate to see people fighting the wrong fight."

"You a preacher or something?" the bully asked.

"No," Sonny said, glancing into his angry face. "I just buried my nine-year-old boy!"

The bigot looked at him intently for almost a minute and the loathing seemed to drain from his face.

"Your boy?"

"Yeah . . . in a cold hole in the ground."

The man gazed at his rough working hands.

"What the hell." He slid back to his table and let it go.

"Buy you a drink?" Sonny asked the guy at the bar.

"No."

The man finished his drink with one swig and slipped out the door like a shadow.

Before Sonny left for Wyoming, Corkey had made a final attempt to persuade him to give up this insanity, more fraught with the chance of miscarriage than the first.

"This is it, Cork, this is the last chance I'll have to count for something."

"Don't you think you already have? Don't you think you count for something here, with these people, with this life?"

"I want to make people forget, make them happy."

"You want to make yourself forget, you mean. This won't bring the kid back."

"Okay, so what's new? The average guy works his life away, supports a family, tries to pay the mortgage on time and slowly trades in his life. But he still wants to be a hero! He just doesn't know how anymore. I could work the land and love a woman and be content. I look out at the horses and the fields and I'm already feeling lonesome for this place. But if I don't do this now, I'll always wish I had. It's different for me this time. I want to sing for the people who know they're going to die."

When Sonny had convinced Corkey that he was committed, the manager's pragmatic mind turned to legal matters. He explained the financial arrangements he'd worked out for the future, giving Sonny the name and numbers of the financial brokers in L.A. who were handling the distribution of the money. He revealed to Sonny that he was leaving his wealth to a children's hospital in St. Louis. Corkey, notorious for salting away his fortune, unknown to anyone, was building a wing on the Carleton Julian Crippled Children's Hospital under an anonymous name.

"You son of a gun, hiding behind that tough old ass." Sonny laughed.

"Yeah, well it's a hospital where they fix little boys with cleft palates and clubfeet and curved spines so little girls will love them."

"You wouldn't want Molly if she'd leave you just because of your foot."

"That so? I'd want Molly any way I could have her. There is no pure love out there. You're goddamn right I'd want her if I could have a new foot. I'd go to sleep every night, thankful she was cuddled beside me, and pray like hell my foot wouldn't go bad on me while I slept."

"Why didn't you ever have surgery? There must have been something they could do."

"By then I wanted to show them a clubfoot could cut it and let them see what they missed out on."

Corkey laughed and held the deformed foot slightly forward. Sonny suspected it wasn't women in general Corkey wanted to show, but Molly, that his foot had become his bodyguard, his excuse for not taking a chance on love again. No one expects a clubfooted man to have a woman.

"When I was a kid I was a target for every bully in town," Corkey said. "I learned how to fight, by god, I bloodied a few noses. I was a loner, never accepted by the other kids, but I loved to play basketball, Jeez, I could shoot the ball from anywhere, ya know what I mean, but hell, I couldn't run. So I started promoting kids who could. I became the goddamn manager of the basketball team, bat boy for several baseball teams, a mascot, a freak."

Sonny understood, finally, why Corkey did such an excellent job of staying out of the limelight when they hit it big. An invisible manager, keeping his clubfooted self-image backstage, coaching from the wings, a young boy with his fists clenched and an ache in his heart, watching the other kids play.

Corkey explained again what Sonny should do if Corkey dropped dead, who to call, who was taking care of everything. "I always overpay my taxes. I've told them to keep doing the same for you. No investigations, no audits. You'll have more money than you can spend."

Out of his sojourn through the windswept hinterlands of Wyoming came the realization that he could mingle with people and sing his head off without ever being recognized. He had become Frank Anderson. In more than one tavern a woman had become friendly, but one night in Lander, a high-class woman in western garb and expensive jewelry caught him on his way to the lavatory during a break.

"Hello. You sing very well."

This was no barfly: a knock-out in high-heeled boots, jeans over long, lean legs, and a tight ruffled blouse beautifully orbicular above a slim waist.

"Thanks, I enjoy singing."

"I can tell, and when you did that Sonny thing I was impressed; you sounded just like him."

She stepped closer, crowding him back against the bar.

"Do you like western art?" she said with a smile dancing across her lips.

"Ah . . . yeah, I do, though I don't have any."

"Why don't you come out to my ranch when you're done. I've got some wonderful things I think you'd enjoy."

"I won't be done until midnight or more and—"

"That's all right, my place is only forty-three miles out."

She laughed. He swallowed.

"Look, I appreciate your invitation, but I'm in love, madly in love, and I think I'd better pass."

She looked straight into his eyes and a shadow of loneliness stole across her face.

"The real Sonny would have come to see my art," she said.

"You mean the old Sonny."

She moved back a step. "Thanks for being honest. All you good ones are taken."

"Hey, I'd bet men would cut their own throats to spend some time with you."

"Thanks for the compliment, but with the men we have around here, *I'll* probably end up cutting my throat. If you change your mind. . . ."

She turned quickly and went back to her table. He hurried for the men's room, thanking God for Hannah.

He talked to Corkey in Florida and assured him that his worry was for nought, that he'd become one of a multitude of itinerant balladeers on the back roads of the world, and no one was paying any attention. Corkey sounded relaxed, more than he had since he began this strange complicity, as though distance could protect him from the disaster of discovery.

Though Sonny felt he should stick with it for another week or more, he turned for Montana one morning after singing a two-night stand in Casper. It had been almost a month. He longed to see Hannah and had a gnawing anxiety that she would no longer love him. He'd called the ranch many times and only once roused Fallen Rock. In his indirect way, he indicated that all was well on the home range and that Hannah was at least still seen around there from time to time.

They were observing the anniversary of his death on the radio as he headed north, a steady stream of his golden hits. Outside of Buffalo, he picked up a hitch-hiker who was going home to a friend's wedding, a clean-cut college student with a serious smile. They visited and shared the driving all the way to Billings. The kid was coming from Denver, and after getting acquainted, he wanted to know if Sonny had been born again. Sonny assured him that he had.

Praise the Lord!

Chapter 53

FALLEN ROCK was nowhere to be found when Sonny arrived at the ranch. A foot of snow covered the ground and the desolation of Jesse's absence struck him without warning. While trying to hold off the sorrow, he entered the house and found it warm inside, food on the table, Rock couldn't be far. At this point, everyone but Corkey thought Sonny was out land speculating in Wyoming.

After he checked the horses and found them in fine fettle for midwinter, he spotted the caretaker and the great Rhodesian ridgeback coming out of the barn together and Guardian loped to greet Sonny. Fallen Rock was sweating profusely and seemed to stagger slightly as he walked. Something was wrong, the young man was terribly ill, or using.

"Hey, what's wrong?" Sonny said, "are you all right?"

"Oh, you're back," he said, glancing sheepishly out of one of Sonny's sweatshirts. "Yeah, I'm okay."

"You have a fever? You're sweating like crazy."

"No," Rock said, averting his eyes, "I've been working out."

It turned out the answer was simple. From the day Sonny showed him the milk room, he had followed Sonny's role model and become an iron-pumping maniac, spending hours at a time building muscle.

In the late afternoon, Rock took the pickup to town and Hannah stopped on her way home from work. Sonny spotted her from the window, flung open the door, and took her in his arms, kissing her face and lips and neck, refusing to put her down. She was more than he remembered.

"I love you, Hannah, I love you like crazy."

She consented to his rush of passion for a time and added her own fire to their long-deferred embrace. Then she broke away, moved across the kitchen, and turned to face him.

"First my father was killed. I think they were happy together, really happy. My mom recovered from that the best she could, and she ends up with Steve. For years she lived in that nightmare, always afraid, trying not to do anything that would upset him, tiptoeing around him like he was God himself. When she got up the nerve to divorce him, it was better for a while, until he started coming back and threatening her and beating her up; you know about that. Then, all those months she had to watch Jesse slowly die, and she's still standing. I think she loves you—"

"But I don't love—"

"Even if she wasn't my mother, I admire that woman so much I could never be the one to hurt her. No matter how much I love you, I can't do that to her, I can't. What would we have between us if it was at her expense?"

"She doesn't love me, she just kind of relies on me. We agreed from day one that we didn't want to get serious, just have some fun together."

"Well, the heart is a funny little muscle, sometimes it goes off on its own and falls in love."

There was nothing he could say. They held each other quietly for some time, and then she went home. Though he stopped to see Sally, had dinner at the trailer once, he ducked out most of the time with prefabricated excuses and didn't answer the phone, attempting to give the impression that he was knee-deep in business transactions, even at night. Somehow he hoped she'd realize, gradually and without much pain, that he didn't love her.

After making arrangements for cosmetic surgery in Minneapolis, his anticipation accelerated, and he never doubted that Corkey had the clout to get him a screen test. He forced himself into a new routine: help Hezekiah feed the cattle, visit the milk room for two hours, record his singing on a reel-to-reel recorder with what time remained, and duck Sally's company as kindly and cleverly as he could manage. Fallen Rock became his roommate, so to speak, though he was frequently absent with Sonny there to watch the place. Sonny said he would need him on a regular basis while he was on the road selling real estate and paid him a month in advance.

With two microphones hanging from the ceiling, he was working hard one afternoon when the weather was cold, the snow drifting. After singing, he would play it back, listen, and then do it again. Improvising without accompaniment, he tried some new things, but basically attempted to recapture his old sound exactly, though his voice had changed with age. When he finished "Look What They've Done To My Song" for the fifth time, he startled at the movement he caught out of the corner of his eye.

"I'm sorry," Hannah said, "I knocked and—"

"Jeez, you scared the jelly beans out of me!"

He stood and snapped off the recorder.

"I'm practicing."

"It sounded good."

"Aren't you supposed to be at work?"

"Aren't you supposed to be dead?"

Her words exploded like an errant hand grenade, ripped away all artificial pretense and niceties and left them standing defenseless, staring at each other in disbelief as if their bodies had turned to stone. He shouted orders to his body from some distant place, *Speak! Laugh! Move,* desperately hoped she'd only tripped upon those words without any inkling of their meaning.

"My singing that bad, huh?"

"I *know* who you are."

She stood, impaled on her own bayoneting words.

"Well that's good, because sometimes I sure don't."

"I know, *Sonny.* I have for a while."

"Oh God, oh God. . . ."

The room tipped, his balance left him, his knees buckled, and he slumped onto the sofa as if shot. She broke from her paralysis and rushed to his side and embraced him.

"Oh don't, don't, please, I'll never tell anyone as long as I live. Please, Sonny, don't be afraid. I love you."

With some force she turned his head with her hands and gazed into his face. Overcome with relief, he lost it. Waves of long-repressed sobs washed over the loneliness and shame he'd guarded secretly for so long. She held him in her arms, and he wept without restraint. Finally he broke free and went to the sink to wash his face. She followed him into the kitchen.

"How did you know?"

He wiped his face with a towel.

"I don't know. When I first got to know you, I felt something, I can't explain it, like you were hiding yourself from me. I knew you didn't need glasses, your head isn't really bald, and—"

"How do you know that?"

"The stubble I've felt. Then Rock showed me the milk room. Why would anyone go to so much trouble to hide body-building equipment? That was the one thing that kept me fooled, your body. After looking at pictures of Sonny from the past, I couldn't believe it could be you, I couldn't . . . until I saw your secret room."

"Rock shouldn't have—"

"When I heard you sing in the hospital something clicked. You showing up here with Corkey, Sonny Hollister's former manager, the money, it all kept stirring at the back of my mind. I don't think I'd have paid that much attention if I hadn't fallen in love with you. The funny thing is, Mom loves you and she hasn't the foggiest idea who you are."

She pulled off her jacket and laid it on the counter. Like someone who had just confessed there was no hope for her life, she sat at the table across from where Sonny stood.

"I came by yesterday and listened to you, and I knew for sure, but I was afraid. I closed the door quietly and left, I couldn't believe it, I mean, *Sonny Hollister alive!* It was scary. I decided last night to tell you, I love you, and I couldn't let this be between us on top of everything else."

"And what do you think of me, for what I did?"

"I don't know, you had your reasons, who was in the car?"

"A desert rat named Roy who stole everything I had."

"I thought it had to be something like that." She paused and glanced at him shyly. "Why didn't you   "

"I only had a few hours to think about it; there was a contract out on me, I was running for my life, running from my life, and then, just like that I was offered a second chance."

Sonny slid into a chair across the table from her. He glanced into her eyes and looked away.

"I never imagined anything would come of it; shoot, I thought people would write me off, good riddance! I've felt ashamed ever since, and the damnedest part now is I can't do a thing about it."

"That must be horrible for you. Why'd they want to kill you?"

"I accidentally heard things that would put a powerful man in jail. It was crazy. *They* were afraid of *me.* They only felt safe with me dead."

"And now they think you're dead."

"Now they think I'm dead. It's so weird; I was alive and broke, now I'm dead and wealthy; my fans were ashamed of me, now they worship me; I was a drunk, now I'm sober; I was a mannequin, now I'm a human being."

"I love you."

She reached across the table and touched his hand.

"Maybe now that you know who I am you can get over your school-girl crush and get on with your life."

He didn't look at her.

"Oh, oh . . . so that's what you think." She withdrew her hand. "Well, you're not talking to Little Bo Peep. I love you, not for what you've been, but for *who* you are, and I want the same from you."

Hannah spoke with a fierceness in her voice.

"Rock and I were in love awhile back, at least I thought it was love, but I think now I wanted to show the jerks in Bozeman that he was good and lovable."

"You and Rock!"

"Yes . . . it was exciting at first; he was awfully lonely—"

"I never would have guessed you and—"

"Yeah, well after a while I realized what a terrible bind I'd gotten into. He needed me, the one person who regarded him as worth a damn, and when I realized I didn't love him that way, I knew it would be the cruelest rejection of all, exactly what I was trying to protect him from."

She glanced at him shyly as though to monitor his reactions.

"I was terrified that he couldn't handle that, that he'd drown himself in a whiskey bottle or even commit suicide, so I stayed his lover for a time and tried to turn our relationship back to friendship. God, I don't know . . . it was really hard. Sometimes it was almost laughable; I'm trying to talk about his future while he's trying to remove my blouse; I'm trying to interest him in school while he's trying to get into my pants."

Sonny winced somewhere inside, and she went on as though she wanted to cleanse something old and rotting.

"I was easing him down, spending time with him, showing him how much I like him and respect him—he's an incredibly kind and sensitive man. Then, somehow, I got pregnant. I was using the pill."

She sighed and shook her head slightly.

"He wanted the baby, for us to stick together and raise it. I didn't know what to do, God, I was so confused, but I felt trapped and I panicked, I'd seen how that could turn out with my mother and step-father. I went to Spokane for an abortion, though I detested the idea. I was six to seven weeks along, microscopic. Now I think about that child every day of my life."

He wanted to comfort her, stunned with the portraits of pain spilling out on the worn oak table.

"While I was in Spokane, Rock got jumped by four local cowboys. Already with a load on, they forced him to drink hard alcohol until he passed out. When he woke up the next morning in a ditch five miles south of Bozeman, he'd been castrated, skillfully and cleanly—"

"Oh, God—"

"—his scrotum prepped with disinfectant and the incisions sewed up neat as could be."

"Son of a—"

"I had the end of his line sucked out of me and dumped in the garbage!"

"Oh, God, Hannah, did they catch the bastards?"

"Haw! Catch them; they'd give 'em medals."

She cupped her hands and looked into them.

"I don't know if the cowboys knew about Rock and me, but just before he passed out, he thought one of them said the filthy redskin wouldn't be knocking up anymore white girls. A girlfriend who goes to MSU got me the information about the abortion, but she swore she never told a soul."

He felt his stomach knot. "Those gutless bastards."

"Rock didn't want to be around me after that for a while, I'd have to go hunt him up in Bozeman. He knew our romance was over but I tried so hard to prove I was a friend. After all my good intentions, I'd smacked him with the worst possible rejection; I'd flushed his only child down the toilet."

She looked into his eyes.

"Now that you know who *I* am, a heartless, murdering bitch, you can get over your fantasy of a sweet young virgin and get on with your life!"

Her pitiful expression sought some sign from him, shattered his every defense.

"Oh, sweet sweet Hannah, don't you get it? I love you, right now, no matter what. None of that changes how I feel about you, nothing could."

She looked into his eyes and her tears ran freely. Without another thought he leaped up, scrambled around the table, and lifted her from the chair. With nothing hidden, he embraced her passionately and kissed her. It was Sonny Hollister kissing her instead of some fictitious Frank Anderson.

"O God, I'm glad you know," he half shouted, "so awfully glad!"

He swung her around the kitchen, laughing, blasting away the sadness and gloom that had descended upon them. "My god, I don't believe this!"

"*You* don't! How about *me?*" She squealed.

Both in a state of shock, they held each other without speaking, as if they suspected their time together was short. He told her he was planning on impersonating himself, and the only way she could express her reaction was that it gave her goose bumps to think about it. Fallen Rock came up the steps and into the house, postponing any further discussion, and Hannah small-talked her way out the door.

When he was alone, Sonny stood at the window and watched the young Indian fill the bunkers with fresh hay. Guardian was always close at his side; they had taken to each other as if they understood they both had lost the one they had loved the most. Sonny was swept up in the new sensation washing over him, the wonder that someone knew he was here! Finally, *someone knew that he was alive*, and it was the most important person in the world to him.

But as he watched Fallen Rock do the chores a freighted sorrow crept into his wonder, prevented him from going out there. The knowledge of what those redneck bastards had done stirred an untapped rage in him. He understood in part what that young man had lost. Not only the traumatic damage to his sexuality and his chance to be a father, as tragic as that was, but the sadness became acute, knowing what it would mean for Fallen Rock to have tasted Hannah's sweet love for a time and then to know he would never again for as long as he lived.

Fallen Rock's grandmother, Saves Many, would save no more from his line.

Chapter 54

ANOTHER BITTER COLD front slid down from Canada. "The cow shit's hard 'fore it hits the ground," Hezekiah bitched, and the kerosene heater could barely bring the milk room up to 48 degrees.

The book, *Shooting Down The Moon*, came out with fanfare and national publicity. The title had been taken from his youth when his mother always told him to "shoot for the moon." He'd been an obedient son. The book was instantly on the *New York Times* Best Seller list, picked for a main selection of The Book-of-The-Month Club, and paperback rights were being negotiated.

Hannah had been stronger than he could've been, for the most part staying out of sight, maybe understanding that neither of them could bear being close to the other. It was time to fly to Minneapolis and go through the minimal surgery in case anyone investigated after he made it big. He left Rock in charge of the ranch again. Watch out for Fallen Rock. Zip. Genocide. The road signs, his mother's hope, his grandmother's bravery, had not been enough.

When Sonny landed at Minneapolis International, he picked up a Hertz Ford LTD and checked in at a Sheraton across the freeway from the airport. After consulting with the doctor and confirming the date for his surgery, he poked around Minneapolis/St. Paul for a few hours, but like a sphere on an inclined plane, the past pulled at him with ever-increasing force, until he found himself driving west on old highway seven. Boyd was about one hundred fifty miles according to the map, but in his mind it was more than a light year.

He drove slowly through the business district of Montevideo, the closest large town to Boyd, and a certain recognition stabbed his memory. The Hollywood Theater reminded him of the times he cuddled there with Natalie, and he recalled how she willingly snuggled up to him for the first time during the movie *Shane* where Alan Ladd had ridden off at the end of the film, heroic, leaving behind the woman he loved but could never have. Had it been Shane he was imitating when he rode out of Boyd, alone?

With the countryside astonishingly familiar, farms and barns and silos, oak and maple groves, he couldn't escape the permanence of this scene against the brevity of his life, and the recurring notion that when he was racing over the clumps of plowing to save his father, that white barn stood right there; that windmill on the horizon turned under the stars when someone yelled insults about his mother while he walked Natalie Jones to the town cafe. The small towns he passed, with their grain elevators and water towers piercing the prairie skyline, stood as immutable as they had when he lived his unassuming school days in Boyd and learned to play the guitar the traveling salesman had given him.

He found the retirement home in Clarkfield, only eight miles from Boyd. He'd rehearsed his lines and no one at the home paid much attention. He went in the front door of the single-story building and no one in the office area said boo. It wasn't until he was far down one of the long halls off the central day room that an elderly woman in a nurse's uniform asked if she could help.

"Yes, thank you," Sonny said. "I'm looking for Betsy Hollister."

"Oh, how nice." The woman dropped her smile and scowled at him. "You're not one of those Sonny fans trying to get an autograph are you?"

"No, no, I'm Frank Anderson, my mother and Betsy were good friends back in Boyd. I try to stop when I'm in the country."

"Well, that's nice. Her room is the third one down on the left. She has a wreath on the door."

The woman went about her business and Sonny hurried to the room. He knocked lightly on the open door and walked in. Betsy sat in an upholstered chair, watching television.

"Hello, Mom." Sonny stood still as she glanced up at him.

"Hello. Would you like an autograph?"

"No, Mom, it's me, Sonny."

He bent down to her and gave her a long hug.

"Oh, my, oh, my, isn't that nice."

Sitting on the edge of the bed, he took hold of her hand.

"I know this is a shock for you, Mom, but I'm Sonny. I'm not dead like everyone thinks. I'm right here with you."

Betsy squinted slightly at him and studied his face.

"My boy died in a car accident. Who are you?"

"I'm Sonny, Mom."

He spent the next half hour reminding her of all the things they'd shared in common. Betsy listened intently and smiled at many of the things they'd done.

"You know so much about us. Did you read that new book?" She reached over and picked up a copy of *Shooting Down The Moon.* "I can't read much, my eyes going bad. But they tell me it's good."

"Mom, it's me. I'm alive. I can come and see you now, often, and we can remember all those good times together."

"Would you like an autograph?"

"No, Mom. Not today. I'll be back soon. You try and remember."

He leaned over and kissed her on the cheek.

"I love you, Mom."

"You're such a nice young man. Who should I tell my friends came to visit me?"

"Tell them your boy, Sonny, came to visit you."

"Oh, they'll be thrilled."

He took her hand, looking for the scars, but her wrinkled skin and skeletal fingers hid the past. He stood. "You tell all your friends that Sonny came to visit you."

"Oh, I will. Please come back again."

"I will, Mom, I'll see you soon, and if you want you can come to Montana with me and live on the ranch."

He hurried from the building. When things settled down, he'd bring her back to the ranch.

He turned west out of Clarkfield and in a few minutes saw the large sign near the turnoff brandishing Boyd's one claim of glory.

Visit The Home Of
SONNY HOLLISTER
Boyd, Minnesota
4 Miles.

Anticipation quickened his heartbeat. Though the trees were still leafless and the brown grass and weeds had only hints of green poking through, the day was bright and warm, almost still, and some farmers rode tractors working their fields. He approached from the south and only the grain elevator and the church steeple betrayed the presence of a town slumbering among the trees on the horizon.

Other than another billboard-size landmark that proclaimed you were in the hometown of the legendary singer, very little had changed. The eyes of a few residents on the street followed his course the length of the one block of stores, bars, and post office, a stranger in town. Knutson's hardware stood exactly as it had, and he guessed that some of the sparse inventory in the unwashed windows might be the same he saw as a boy.

At the north end of Main, across from the deteriorating town hall, a large tarnished metal building stood on the corner with a hand-painted sign hanging slightly cockeyed: SWINGLEY AUTO BODY & SALVAGE. The building itself could have been the salvage, surrounded in back and side by wrecked vehicles and parts. Several cars crowded inside where two solitary light bulbs pierced the oily atmosphere and the flash of arc welding lit up the garage for a few seconds as he passed. With his thumping heart trying to leap from his throat, he made a U-turn at the end of the main drag and rolled slowly back in front of Zeke Zwingley's enterprise.

As matter-of-fact as the town itself, she came from the gloomy garage in a bright flowered dress and turned the corner, still with her willowy body and graceful gait. He followed at a distance and watched her walk through her life as though he were watching someone out of a book. It seemed he'd been whisked here by a time machine, the whole town a throwback, changeless since the day he walked away.

He could recall the first time he kissed her, how she tasted, the scent of her skin. She waved at a stooped old man making his way toward town on the opposite side of the street and then she turned abruptly and disappeared into one of the provincial white houses that had hunkered down since the turn of the century against the prairie wind and blizzards.

He continued past, uncertain what to venture, then abruptly swung the car around and pulled up in front of her house, following an impulse that left him breathless. When he stepped onto the porch and knocked, he expected old man Jones to appear.

Natalie came to the door, little Natalie, only she was not so little. Far from a clone of her mother, she had certain features of face and figure that rang bells all over his nervous system.

"Hi, can I help you?"

The girl was somewhere close to the age Natalie was when he first noticed her.

"Ah, yes, is your mother home?"

He knew the girl could have answered his fabricated inquiry and hoped in the mundane exchange between mother and daughter neither would notice. Politely, and with a rural timidity toward strangers, she called her mother and disappeared into the house. His stomach tightened; his mouth went dry. Natalie appeared behind the screen door.

"Hello," she said.

She had already washed her hair and wrapped it in a towel.

"Watch those cookies," she called back into the house.

"Sorry to bother you, ma'am, but I wanted to see the home of Sonny Hollister. I thought the sign pointed up this street."

"It's just over a block. You can't miss it," she said, smiling. Her face had aged some, filled out a little, and it seemed the light had gone out of her eyes. The dress she wore was styled for a much older woman and it had seen its day.

"Was that your daughter?"

"Oh, yes, she's giving a 4-H demonstration at Ladies Aid this afternoon, supposed to show how to bake some fancy cookies. Guess who's baking them?"

"She looks like you."

"You think so? Funny, most don't see much of me in her."

He had the sensation that he no longer had legs, and he desperately wanted to prolong this moment.

"It must have been something to have him living here once."

"Yes, it was." She looked through the screen toward Sonny's house. "Though no one thought much of it at the time."

She said no more, and after hesitating until it was uncomfortable, he backed down the steps, his heart aching to make itself known.

"Thanks for the help."

"Are you from around here?" she said.

"No . . . Montana."

"Oh, you seemed familiar."

He moved toward the car feeling that his disguises were deserting him. She called after him, stepping part way out from behind the screen door.

"I used to know him, you know."

He turned and took a few steps back.

"What was he like?" he asked, risking an emotional battering.

"A nice, decent boy, as normal as any of us, liked to kick up his heels and have fun, but he was quiet and sensitive, too. We were all surprised when he became so rich and famous, like it wasn't the same person at all. He's buried out there now."

She threw a hand toward the southwest. He hesitated, thanked her again, and turned for the car, about to lose control. With the door open and almost a clean getaway, she called to him.

"I was his girlfriend for more than two years."

"Really." His throat filled, his eyes blurred, and he sensed she had not revealed that fact to many strangers.

"Yes. He was always nice to me," she said, and stepped out onto the porch, allowing the screen door to close softly. "One night we stopped and caught fireflies, put them in a jar and watched them light up the dark. He said they do that so they can find each other in the night, and that we were like the fireflies, our love the glow that helped us find each other. I always remembered that, I thought it was so romantic. Every time I see the fireflies I think of him."

Almost in a trance, she spoke as if she were alone.

"I go out to the grave sometimes."

She glanced over her shoulder as if to see if anyone in the house might overhear.

"After he went away I realized how much I loved him. I would have run away and joined him, but I never heard from him again."

"But. . . ."

"I don't blame him."

Oh, God, no. Don't lie, Natalie, please don't lie about that, not that.

She stood on the porch looking off with her arms folded over the flowered dress and the towel around her head, frozen in time.

"Thanks," he said and he slid into the car.

It felt as if the Oliver had overturned onto his chest and he gasped for breath. He gazed back at her standing on the porch as he slowly drove away. Overwhelming heartache told him he should have stayed away, whispered that he would never love anyone quite the way he loved Natalie Jones.

She and her daughter were about to go to Ladies' Aid and demonstrate how to make out-of-the-ordinary cookies out of their out-of-the-ordinary lives. Would she stir into the recipe an emptiness from her life? Would her daughter park tonight with her boyfriend in Walther's grove? Would any of them ever find the love their hearts were breaking for, fireflies blinking in the night?

Chapter 55

BY THE TIME Sonny drove the short distance to the house, he was in such a state of emotional wreckage he considered scrapping the whole idea. When he turned the corner, the enterprise startled him. Holy Jeez! A high wire fence surrounded the yard with a little gatehouse by the street and the Wilson house next door had been torn down for parking. The house was shingled and the stucco painted like new, the yard landscaped and manicured in a way he'd never seen.

A short, pot-bellied man sold him a five dollar admission ticket from the small gatehouse and told him apologetically it was mostly for the upkeep. Sonny asked if this was a normal day, there being only three other cars in the lot, and the meek, gray-haired man told him it was like the weather, hard to predict, but when it rained it poured, and that sometimes they were standing in line for an hour.

"He used to come in and get mail from me, you know."

"You were the postmaster back then?"

Sonny studied him intently, trying to conjure up his sad little face behind the post office window, but they had both changed too much.

"Until just a few years ago. After Sonny's father was killed, they moved in here across the street from us. I live right over there." He pointed at a white green-shuttered house. "He was my paper boy for a year or two, a good lad. Too bad he died so young."

A group of people passed through the gate on the way to their car, and Sonny used the opportunity to go into the house. He entered with caution, not to step on memories still lying on the floor, not to scatter faint images he might grasp before they faded forever.

The house was roped off so visitors could walk partially into each room and see the furniture, pictures and other memorabilia from his youth. Most of it was authentic as far as he could remember. When he moved his mother to California, she left everything, and the landlord rented the house furnished. Shortly after that, some of the progressive members of the town bought the house and preserved it as Sonny's fame skyrocketed.

The kitchen seemed most familiar, the icebox and wood-burning stove, the porcelain sink. Hundreds of trips from the shed with arm-loads of wood in all kinds of weather swept across the screen of his memory. The watchman inside the house had climbed the stairs to the second floor to keep an eye on those who were examining the bedrooms. Would they catch his mother and the salesman clinging to each other in her scandalous bed?

He held his head in his hands and stood very still while imprints from the past prodded him for recognition: the aroma of baked things, his mother's high voice, the radio playing, lying awake on muggy nights, the sound of popping corn in the iron skillet on winter nights, the quiet laugh of the traveling man, and playing his guitar in his room by the hour. Faintly he could hear those sweet voices, he could! Out of the walls and ceiling and floor, and he wanted desperately to hear what they were saying. He stood trans-fixed in the kitchen and failed to notice the gatekeeper who came in quietly behind him.

"Did you know the Hollisters?" he asked, startling Sonny.

"Oh, no. . . ." He turned. "I've read about him some. Is the old farm still there?"

"Yep, just like it always was," the conscientious man told him. "A fella by the name of Emil Gunderson owns it now. Used to be a sign, but Emil tore it down. Bothered too much by folks who wanted souvenirs from Sonny's past. Made him kinda surly."

The group from upstairs began clomping down the narrow wooden stairway, and the gatekeeper retreated to his post. Sonny wandered through the house with the watchman keeping him in view. From the window, he imagined his worn path to the shed under the sodded lawn, and he could distinctly hear his mother call-ing Son-ny! Son-ny! Others were coming in downstairs, chasing his mother's voice into the past.

"I remember when he went away," the gatekeeper picked up on their conversation as Sonny reached the gate. "Some folks around here thought poorly of him because his mother took up with a trav-eling man. Those days it was out-and-out sin. But I remember feel-ing sorry for the boy, and it tickled me pink when he became a big star. You should've heard those same people then. Why it was like he'd been their godchild to hear them tell it. I used to keep track of where he was by the letters. His mother wrote him every week or more, and he'd return one now and then. He sent a torrent of letters to his girlfriend at first, but her father picked up the family mail at the post office. I'd see him sort through the mail and tear up Sonny's letters and drop them in the wastepaper basket."

"He *did?*"

"Yep, every one of them."

Run away from here! Plug your ears and run!

"When I'd see that gal I had a mind to tell her, but I knew it wasn't my business. Now I wish I had." He looked up the street toward the post office. "Wish I had. After a while, the letters stopped coming."

"Did you ever tell that girl about the letters?"

"No, never did. Do you think I should?"

He asked with an openness that surprised Sonny.

"No, I don't think so, it would only cause pain now."

His words disaffirmed his emotions, and he admitted to himself that he wanted her to know, to know how he'd pleaded with her, that if she'd still be his girl, he'd come home, to know the anguish he felt when he'd rush into the post office in some strange town and ask if there was anything for him in general delivery, and when there was, almost come apart at the seams until he'd see it was only from his mother. He wanted Natalie to know that both of their lives would've been completely different if she'd picked up the family mail one day and found one of his letters, if she'd seen her father tear one up and retrieve the scraps from the public wastebasket, piece it together in the secret of her room as if stitching together his shredded heart.

"What happened to her father?"

"Poor man died awhile back. It's kinda funny. I've never gotten over the look on that man's face ever since we heard that Sonny was a millionaire. Her father was scratching out a living on some hard-scrabble ground east of here, and when he realized the thing he'd missed, his face froze into a permanent scowl. My missus told me she heard he'd tried to get the girl to contact Sonny after he made it big, but the girl refused. Probably ain't any truth to it. You know how these stories start up."

While the small man spoke, Sonny did remember him. He'd had dark hair and was much thinner back then.

"You been out to the grave?" he asked with some enthusiasm.

Sonny told him he intended to on his way out of town, and he wanted to tell him he should've taped his letters together and taken them to Natalie. Isn't that what the blasted mailman is supposed to do, see that the mail is delivered no matter what! But he said nothing and drove slowly to the cemetery.

There were more people there, coming and going. Sonny walked to the graves and read the etched granite tombstones. Corkey had done it up brown. Even replaced the simple little headstone his father had with a matching one like Sonny's. They were tasteful, not gaudy or overpowering, in this simple graveyard on a gentle hill where Sonny would honor his mother's request to be buried beside his father, never understanding why she'd want that after the way she'd been scorned here. As he contemplated the two graves he hoped there was nothing to the talk about any lasting importance placed on who we're buried with. When he died, there'd be no place for him beside his parents. Maybe in eternity they'd adopt the drifter Roy and Sonny would wander fatherless and motherless.

Several bunches of freshly cut flowers slowly wilted on his grave in the mild spring air while a watchman made himself inconspicuous, off a distance in a chair under a budding willow. Sonny wanted to speak aloud to his father, but there were always others standing at the chained-off graves. A woman who looked in her late forties, well-dressed, slightly heavy, stood quietly beside him. She glanced into his face for a moment with her tearful eyes, and he nodded his understanding.

"Wasn't he something," she said softly.

In that instant, the absurdity of his life struck him anew, and he couldn't respond. Holy Geez! He had the impulse to shout, to laugh, to leap over the chain and dance on his grave. Hey! Look! I'm not rotting under the sod. Touch me, look at me, I'm right here beside you.

She turned with a sigh and walked away with her sorrow, and he wanted to run after her and tell her. With his emotions churning and his mind in disarray, he fled to his car. Underneath it all he sensed an indomitable joy that he was alive.

Unsure if he would stop at the farm, he drove toward it, more by compulsion than reason, as though lured by spirits that he couldn't dismiss. He stopped close to the spot where it happened. The county road had been improved, the ditch widened some, but the field lay black and silent exactly as it had. No trace of the tractor's goring remained on the earth, no scars of the savage struggle. They were all within him now.

The slough where he'd been playing lay off to the southwest, and he could see the house where his mother had been working when the terrible silence brought her flying, the terrible silence that droned in the background of his life since that day, the terrible silence he feared he'd recognize with his last conscious thought. He stood on the spot and listened to the silence.

Apprehensively he drove south, scanning the yard and buildings as he approached, the climbing-tree dead but still standing, some of the wooden steps he'd nailed clinging cockeyed. A new metal building nestled among the old barn and other outbuildings, and the house looked much the same, in need of paint, though as a boy he couldn't remember noticing such things. The only difference was a high television antenna protruding from the roof.

At the drive he stopped momentarily and recalled the sounds of children laughing and shouting from the school bus, touching off dim images in his mind. Some of the apple trees were still standing, gnarled, old, uncared for in years, and instantly he recalled the aroma of apple wood from the kitchen stove. He yearned to drive in but he couldn't; a great weight grew in his chest with each memory. Some day he'd be able to come back, maybe buy the place and fix it up.

Little joys snuck through the shadows from his boyhood and delighted him momentarily, but the vale of sorrow won the day. He drove away slowly against the magnetic pull of the farm and looked back at the windmill and grove and buildings, all of them hurling memories like shafted arrows, until, with his last backward glance, he jammed on the brakes and skidded to an abrupt halt. The Oliver 90 tractor stood behind the old chicken coop among the trees. The Beast, free in the sunlight to brandish its ugliness and parade its victory despite its faded green and rusted parts. Whoever moved onto the farm must have been the high bidder for the tractor at that long-past auction.

It was obscene in his nostrils and the hatred and rage that became a young boy's blood brothers spewed forth from some deep boil in his soul. He spun the car around and whipped it toward the yard. Why hadn't someone hauled it away? Why hadn't someone melted it down for bullets so it could go on killing! Could there still be a thread of his father's clothing embedded in its frame? He'd finally deal with this demon from his childhood, once and for all!

Chapter 56

WITH FIRE GATHERING in his belly, he slammed the car door and charged toward the strangely-familiar house, across land that had once been his stamping ground. Two shaggy mongrels barked and intercepted him in the yard, but their tails were wagging, and he recognized them for good old farm hounds like the mutts he'd partnered with, sidekicks seeking adventure and surprises in a camaraderie of the earth.

"Whatta ya want?" a solid sour-faced woman asked from behind a torn screen door.

"I'm buying scrap-metal; I'll give you a hundred dollars cash for the old tractor."

The figureless woman stood staring for a moment as though the history of the human race were passing before her eyes. Then she called back into the house and the way she slurred the name he couldn't tell what it was. She held her post, scrutinizing him with some animosity and the callous developed warding off seed corn salesmen and Mormon missionaries.

A stocky man appeared and shoved past the woman in the doorway, suspicion as much his garment as the bib overalls and long underwear that appeared as though they hadn't seen the inside of a washing machine in recent times.

"Afternoon," the farmer said with a hoarse voice.

"I'm buying scrap metal, interested in that old tractor."

"You one of them damn souvenir hunters?"

"No, I'm on a committee for the county to beautify the landscape around here."

Sonny attempted to temper his anger which was seeping out of his pores like sweat.

"Never heard a no county committee fer that. Landscape looks fine to me."

The farmer shoved his thumbs into his bib overall suspenders and stood firm, upping the ante with a calculating expression on his weather-burned face.

"That's the tractor that killed Sonny Hollister's pappy I'm told," the man said.

"Who's Sonny Hollister?"

"Might be worth a whole bunch of money one of these days."

With his patience leaking onto the wooden step, he eyeballed the farmer and forced a reluctant smile.

"Well, how much is it worth today?"

"Oh . . . I'd take *two* hundred for it."

Sonny peeled two hundred-dollar bills from a fold of money and held them out. The man, whose veined cheeks sagged as though he already regretted he hadn't asked for three, opened the screen door and took the bills.

"Do you have a sledgehammer?" Sonny asked.

"Yep. Twelve pounder."

"I'll buy it."

Sonny handed him a fifty. The farmer accepted it and glanced at the woman with an expression that said they'd just found the biggest idiot in America.

"How fast can you get a backhoe in here?" Sonny asked.

"Got a neighbor with one; could be here right soon, if he ain't in the field."

"Get him here in a half hour and there'll be two hundred in it for him, two hundred more for you."

The man went past Sonny like his truck was on fire, and Sonny shouted after him.

"Where's the sledge?"

"Inside the metal shop!"

The farmer spun out of the barnyard with his two dogs barking excitedly from the muddied pickup bed.

Sonny found the sledgehammer amidst a tangle of greasy tools and marched out behind the buildings with the weapon in hand. There he paused, savoring the confrontation with the familiar iron brute, a moment he'd prayed for with a boy's terrible yearning for a lifetime. Like a boxer taking off his warmups he hung his jacket on a fence post and when he gripped the maul, the bitter anger and grief of a defenseless nine year old came surging through his adult body.

"I grew up, you murdering son of a bitch!"

With the first ferocious swing he bashed in the radiator, wiped the smile off that arrogant face and transformed it into a grimace of pain. The next caved in the hood. Grunting and roaring like a madman, he pounded and bashed the dragon that had slithered into his happy childhood with its filthy breath and devoured his father.

Time after time, with the leverage of hate, he smashed the maul into its vitals, hammered the engine, the fuel tank, the instruments, the steering wheel, the PTO levers. Unresolved rage flowed out of his back and shoulders, down forearms and oak handle into the twelve-pound maul turned fist that arced through space until it exploded against the iron carcass with multiplied foot-pounds of force per square inch. He shouted obscenities with every blow and allowed himself to go temporarily insane out behind the chicken coop. When he could no longer lift the twelve-pound weapon, he staggered, his chest heaved and he gasped for breath.

"C'mon, you stinking coward, you're not up against a boy anymore! Let's see that smirk on your face now."

He challenged it, taunted, but it had no voice, its tongue frozen in rust.

When the farmer returned and found Sonny sitting calmly beside the battered machine, his mouth went slack as he surveyed the destruction. He circled the demolished machine and regarded Sonny with a puzzled expression.

"You mad at someone?"

"Not any more."

Before his sweat cooled, the backhoe arrived, and they soon had an excavation in the layered soil that would do the job. Sonny allowed the operator to dig under the tractor until it was about to cave the ground beneath it and then Sonny waved him off. With his heels dug into the ground, he hunched his back against the Oliver and shoved with everything he had. Nothing happened.

"Want me to nudge her in?" the neighbor asked.

"No, this murdering butcher's mine!"

This time he'd move the Beast or die trying. For several minutes he strained against its mass, drove with his legs; his feet dug small pits in the ground. The farmers leaned with their bodies, itched to lend a hand, caught up in this unsuspected drama out beside the grove. Then, after another minute or two, hesitantly the battered tractor moved an inch. Sonny strained and the Beast began to slide, until finally, it went belly up into its grave. The two farmers cheered as if they understood in some small measure what weight Sonny had cast off his shoulders, purged from his heart.

While the backhoe operator was burying it, Sonny asked the befuddled farmer for a bill of sale, indicating that if he ever heard that the tractor was dug up, he'd have the law on him like dogs in heat. When the man returned from the house with the receipt, he asked Sonny who in the hell he was. Sonny told the two of them it was kind of a hobby with him, to spruce up the land, and that every time he came up with a little extra cash, he did something like this.

"I got an old manure spreader on the other side of the grove," the farmer said, "just rustin' away."

"There's a ugly old thrashing machine setting on my place," the neighbor said.

Sonny laughed. "I've kinda spent my wad for now, men."

When the hole was backfilled, the two men disappeared with their unexpected booty like kids headed for the county fair with cash in their overalls. Sonny lingered in the falling darkness and without warning long buried feelings swooped down, clogged his throat, teared his eyes. He slumped to his hands and knees in the soft black earth and tears came without restraint as the reservoir of shame and regret broke open and poured out onto the land. Like a rush of wind through his spirit, he felt vindicated in the eyes of his own youth.

I moved it, Dad. I pulled my own weight.

It was too early in the spring for fireflies, but he watched for them anyway. He had signaled in the night all his life for someone's love, and he suspected for the first time, as he knelt on the tractor's grave, it may not be the love of a woman. In the dark stillness of the grove, he sensed it was someone very near, someone who had always been there.

He drove back through the town and out the other side. What happened to those years as a boy? They seemed so remote. He was certain he'd been born at the age of eighteen with a Technicolor memory intact to account for those unaccountable times. Had he ever really known this strange boy who once lived here, who ran unseen through the tall corn, who rode the old work horse Tramp down to the slough, who left town alone with no one calling after him, Shane, come back, Shane? And where had the little boy gone when the world shaped and molded his shy, timid spirit into a superstar until he was obliterated, his soul effaced?

Maybe, with all the pretentious malarkey washed away, he was still that eighteen-year-old kid. He jammed his foot on the accelerator. He'd beaten the old Oliver and strutted on its grave, but he knew, deep inside, it was a shallow victory. It didn't bring his father one breath of air.

Chapter 57

At 4:30 in the morning he hacked and shaved away the beard that had hidden him in its underbrush for months. His heartbeat moved up into his throat. A stranger gazed back at him out of the steamed motel mirror and the transformation that took place under the beard over the past fourteen months stunned him. With fingertips he traced pale and tender skin; the bloated cheeks and fatstock jowls had melted away with the secretive months and the shaving cream. Only Hannah and Corkey knew that shaving would do more to make his face look like Sonny Hollister than any surgeon on earth.

Though Dr. Fitzpatrick would have released him sooner, Sonny insisted on remaining hospitalized until the bandages were reduced to a few Band-Aids, with most of the swelling and redness gone, more concerned over what Hannah would think of his new face than how the public would regard it. In the glaring light of the operating room, while the surgeon skillfully sliced at his numbed face, Sonny wondered what signatures of pain the surgeon was removing, and if the fingerprints of agony were removed from his face, would they also be removed from his soul?

He rode the Boeing 727 with his naked and sensitive face and his spirit was outdistancing the jetliner. The tightness around his eyes and jaw felt strange, his chin clean shaven, but he kept his glasses on, his head bald. He would regrow the beard as quickly as possible until the elusive screen test became a reality. A surge of joy filled him when the plane cut back power and he could see the Gallatin valley coming into view below.

The green Dodge pickup stood faithfully in the parking lot, and he hoped he could slip back to the ranch unnoticed. Hiding the truck behind the shed would prevent Sally and Hannah from spotting it. He wanted to give his beard another week before seeing either of them inasmuch as he was supposedly speculating on real estate over in Wyoming.

In the kitchen, he found a vast assortment of body-building food supplements and vitamin bottles. Fallen Rock had found a cause! It seemed the solitary caretaker would retreat no more. If the rednecks ever came for other body parts, they'd find a different batting order.

Fallen Rock showed up late that afternoon. With a solemn expression he studied Sonny's face for a moment but made no comment, agreeing not to let on to anyone that Frank was back. After making a thick concoction in the blender and downing the entire mess straight from the bowl, Rock was out the door and gone. Sonny caught sight of him from the window, bareback on Wildfire, running across the hayfield with the Rhodesian ridgeback close behind.

It was almost four days before Hannah appeared one night, somehow aware that Fallen Rock was elsewhere. She knocked lightly, then slipped into the kitchen. He hesitated a moment in the poorly-lit living room and then rushed to pick her off the floor and kiss her. When he put her down, she seemed to look past his face into his eyes, jabbering about little things, the local news, chit-chat, a fragile restraint he recognized as futile.

"I'm worried about Rock," she said. "When the veterinarian came out to worm the horses, Rock recognized the man's assistant as one of those who had attacked him two years ago. He didn't think the guy remembered him. When they did their dirty work it was night, and anyway, all Indians look alike to those morons."

"What is he planning to do?" Sonny asked, never taking his eyes from her alluring face.

"That's what worries me. I don't know, nothing, he says."

They moved into the other's embrace with the inevitability of the laws of physics and without letting go they slow danced to the bedroom. In the tangle of their passion, they feverishly peeled every stitch of clothing, and she was more than he could have dreamed, a woman created perfect from the mind of God. The touch of her skin, the scent of her hair, inflamed his senses, children playing in the forbidden Garden of Eden.

Finally, she shattered his bliss.

"I have to go, Mom will be worried."

To his surprise, it had been nearly two hours.

"Don't ever go," he whispered.

He clung to her, unwilling to part, and he contemplated giving up everything to be with her. He filled the empty space in her belly the way she filled the empty space in his heart and the sweetness of her was beyond his wildest fantasy.

"Mom's dating a dentist from Bozeman," Hannah said softly in the darkness with some hope in her voice.

"Is he a good man?"

"I think so. She says she's not getting serious."

Sonny felt a rush of joy, hoping Sally would find a decent man to love her and wed her and that he hadn't hurt her in their kind and loving relationship.

Sally was a lovely woman, strong and vulnerable, shapely and courageous, a woman he would be fortunate to have as his wife. She appealed to the practical side of him, that which had mellowed, the part now willing to accept things as they were. He was forty-four years old, time to face reality, settle down. Sally would be a marvelous companion to share the winter years, to warm his days with affection, growing old together.

With Hannah, a part of him that was very much alive reached for his sweet, shattered dreams, the adventure, to do what he believed he should, to risk, to grow. She was young and brave, beckoning to his reckless spirit to run after life, to grab for the ring, to go see the whales. He knew that he had no real choice in the matter. He loved Hannah with the blood of his soul, he'd tasted her honey, and he couldn't turn back.

When Hannah was gone, he could taste and smell her. He clung to the pillow with her scent, with their aroma. Why should he be given so great a gift? Once, while they were catching their breath, he asked if he could listen to her heart. He pressed the stethoscope close to her breast, and he listened to the rhythm of her life, a different beat than his, faster, lighter, sustaining her with vigor and warmth, a young, strong throb, relaying the voice of God to him through this pure, clear perfection of his creation. She wanted to listen to his heart, and she did.

He lay in the residue of their sweet copulation, and he knew his heart was terribly exposed, its happiness dependent on the favor of a young, captivating girl who worried she was stabbing her mother in the back by loving him. Like Corkey, he prayed he would not grow clubfoot as he slept.

When he talked to Corkey in Florida, the screen test wasn't assured as yet. Sonny couldn't tell if Corkey had grown cold feet, terrified he might still be implicated in this duplicity, or if he was truly finding it difficult to reach the right people. Corkey promised to keep trying, and Sonny knew the little man still threw a tremendous amount of weight around the entertainment world.

He would try to sleep, knowing he'd never be the same without Hannah. She'd taught him to see life in everything around him, to notice the world with wonder, and she'd taught him that it was by far better to be with her than to be without her. So much so, that he was instantly afraid that he could no longer go on unless she was at his side. He recognized he'd allowed himself to become vulnerable again, knowing he'd be crushed if she left him. How had he come to that perilous gamble of the heart, that terrifying necessity. Corkey would say he was a fool; Corkey would say he was the luckiest man on earth!

When they were making love and she was beginning to soar with their excited frenzy, he pressed the stethoscope between her breasts, listening again to her heart and timing his thrusts in cadence with its beat, her pulse orchestrating a frenetic pace, so erotic for both of them that they simultaneously flew off into new galaxies on a shooting star.

> *O ye atheists, O ye technicians,*
> *Who observe this miracle with blinking eyes and*
> *Fresh new theories of why it beats, beats, beats, beats. . . .*
> *Tell me there is no God keeping me a breath away from death.*
> *Tell me about the electrical impulse from some unknown source!*

Chapter 58

HEZEKIAH WAS MENDING fence along the boundary between their ranches and he took no notice of Sonny's face except he said that he'd have taken the Winchester to him if he hadn't recognized the truck. Sonny lent a hand and they visited. Spring was inseminating the valley with hope and expectation, the gophers were making whoopee on the greening carpet that mantled the landscape, and all creatures basked under cloudless skies. Sonny gazed across the field to the creek bottom, over the graves of the black-footed ferrets, over the bloody spot in the willows were Steve Ramsey died instantly, up into the foothills where he first kissed Hannah.

"I'm going away, Hezekiah."

"What fer?"

Hezekiah pumped the handle on the fence-stretcher several clicks.

"I'm going to go and sing."

"Sing? Ya mean like in church?"

"No, like at dance halls and taverns and shows."

Hezekiah squinted into Sonny's face.

"Hell, ya can do that right here."

Hezekiah spliced the tightened wire.

"I'm going to try to make it big, like the guys on the radio and TV."

"Gonna take the .44?"

"No, it wouldn't do any good in this business."

Sonny stapled the tightened wire to a gnarled post.

"What ya gonna do that fer? Ya don't need money."

"I want to make people happy; it's something I can do, make them stand and cheer. Does that sound crazy?"

Sonny peered under the black wide-brimmed hat for Hezekiah's approval.

"I did once. Hot diddly damn, I sure did once."

Hezekiah squinted out over the years.

"You did?"

"Yep."

He sat on the ground and leaned against a fence post while Sonny settled on his haunches beside him.

"I was sposed ta be irrigatin'. Hitched a ride over ta Livingston, rodeo goin' there. I's about sixteen and I'd hid away five dollars fer goin', lied about ma age, and enters the bronc ridin'. Whal, I drawed the meanest horse they had an the cowboys felt sorry fer me, knowin' I's jes' a kid an all, but they's glad none a them drawed Hammerhead. That's the horse I got, Hammerhead. No one'd stayed fer time on him that year. I got on that ornery critter and they opened the gate."

Hezekiah twisted his worn leather gloves in his hands.

"Whal, I know'd how you's sposed ta ride 'em, but that sonofabitch come outta the pen sideways, twisted and bucked an jumped all at once. I didn't know where the ground is, hangin' on fer fear a death, my arm nearly jerked clean outta my shoulder. More'n once that critter had me throwed clear, airborne, and then jumped sideways right under me agin. I wanted ta dive fer the dirt and ta hell with the prize money, but I couldn't get my hand outta that damn rope. It seemed I's on that man-killer fer an hour. The whistle blew, I'd rode out the time, but the pickup man can't ketch up ta me. Hammerhead's going sideways, twistin', tryin' ta kill me."

The old cowboy chuckled and leaned sideways and spit.

"Jes' as I's got my hand free and I's about to leap off, that widow-maker throws me against the dad-blasted fence. He turned ta stomp me some, but the pickup man shags 'em away. I's all busted up, I know'd it, but I gets up and walks past the grandstand, never lettin' on. I don't think I's walkin' very straight. Then I hear'd that crowd, hollerin' and clappin', wavin' their hats. Everybody in the seats is standin' and cheerin', all the cowboys is shoutin' and hollerin'. I jes' stood there. God almighty, it jes' took away all the pain and misery. I can still hear 'em and see 'em. Never had anything like it again. Never did, by golly."

Hezekiah spit at a gopher sticking its head out of a hole down the fence line as though it were eavesdropping.

"How bad were you hurt?"

"Busted arm, collar bone, some busted ribs, leg tore up, but the doc said it weren't broke. Made twenty dollars fer that ride and used it all up on doctorin'. My pappy's so mad when I gets home he makes me go right out and irrigate. Haw! I was a one-armed irrigator fer a spell."

Hezekiah slowly shoved himself upright and took hold of the fence.

"Ever rodeo again?" Sonny asked.

Nope . . . never did, never did, by golly. I's jest lucky."

He paused for a moment and squinted at Sonny from his ruddy face.

"You go, Frank. Make 'em get ta their feet and cheer. It jest might be the only time ya can."

Sonny stood and turned aside with the tears in his eyes betraying him. Sure that the old timer would think him loco to follow his quest, Hezekiah was urging him on.

"Ya takin' the gal with ya?"

"Sally?" He caught Sonny off guard.

"No, the young un."

"No, she's too young for me."

"Not if she's hankerin' fer ya. I seen you two. Hell, Sarah was sixteen when she come ta live with me. When they's that old, they know how ta love ya. That's fer sure, that's fer dang sure."

"I'm going alone."

"Ya comin' back?"

"Yes. I'm coming back. Rock will take care of the ranch while I'm away."

"He's a strange duck."

"He's a good friend."

Hezekiah regarded him with a quizzical expression.

"Ya sure got a bunch a funny friends."

"You're one of them," Sonny said.

"Thas what I *mean.*"

They worked for another hour. It was as if they knew they wouldn't see each other again but had silently agreed to act it out like all temporary partings. Sonny looked north to the creek bottom and remembered it was Hezekiah, on that cold November morning, who gave him his life again. When they said goodbye, Sonny broke across that invisible barrier and bear-hugged the little man, surprised at how small he was under his rough clothing and bluster. He didn't know how to thank him for his life, but as Hezekiah was pulling away in the relic Jeep, Sonny shouted.

"Remember, if I don't see you before, you aren't supposed to hunt this fall!"

Hezekiah grinned and tossed a wave. In a disheartened mood, Sonny drove to the ranch, feeling the sorrow of good-byes. As he pulled into the barnyard, suddenly the swallows overwhelmed him with rapture. They had *come back!*

They whisked and darted around the buildings and trees, flashed and swirled in and out of the barn, sprinkling the ranch with their bright joy and splendor. He ran from the pickup and stood between the corral and barn, where Jesse had stood. He shouted to the transcontinental spirits.

"Hello, Fluff, how are you? Hey, Pebble, good to see you! Yo, Feather, you son of a gun! Bilbo and Turnip, how in the world did you suckers make it back here again. Yah-hoo! Welcome back, you buggers, welcome back!"

He twirled around and waved his arms and laughed and danced until he was winded. With the birds winging above him, he fell to the ground and lay on his back and watched their gyrations in the sky. They were telling him something with their soaring and flurry, and he lay listening to them for a long time. Finally he whispered.

"Jesse, are you here? Are you here, Jess."

It startled him when he realized he'd remembered their names. How had he done that? Of course he didn't recognize one from the other, but he remembered their names. Fallen Rock was watching from the porch. He wanted to know how Sonny knew their names.

Corkey called with the good news. He'd pulled a screen test for Sonny out of his magician's hat and though Corkey wouldn't say what it cost him, he indicated that most of the IOUs he held were called in. Sonny felt fear and excitement mainlining along his spine and into his brain cells. It would be like Teddy Roosevelt trying out for the part of Teddy Roosevelt.

Hannah and he had managed to get away into the foothills several times on the horses and bed down in hidden ravines on the horse blankets. The sun warmed their naked bodies as they cherished one another in those stolen hours. They became more deeply attached and needed to be with each other with ever increasing intensity yet had to accomplish this in total secrecy, not daring to even let Fallen Rock suspect they were lovers. She did drive him to the airport.

With an eye out for anyone she might know, she held his hand tightly as they moved through the modest airport. He didn't look much her elder with his bronzed head, his newly grown beard, and a few crow's feet and such missing.

"I wake up nights wondering if this is really happening," she said, "catch myself forgetting for a moment and then suddenly remember *who* you are!"

They paused at the gift shop and she pointed out three magazines currently carrying his face on the cover.

"It's so incredible, all these people reading about you, remembering you, thinking you're dead, and here I'm standing with you, in love with you."

The Western flight was on time, and excitement and dread churned under his rib cage when they stopped in front of the metal detecting machine. You could see the 737 rolling slowly up to the telescoping ramp in front of the terminal. He took her in his arms and kissed her. People passed them without noticing; the metal detector beeped occasionally; the loudspeaker called the flight. Why was he leaving her, this girl he had looked for all his life?

"When you come back we'll go see the whales," she whispered into his ear, and they clung to each other.

He hurried through the security check and into a line of people who were disappearing into the boarding ramp. But just before he stepped in, he stopped and looked back. Her face was streaming with tears. Everyone went past him, and the gate attendant reminded him that he had to get on the plane. He startled the people at the gate with his bombastic farewell, booming over the din of the terminal.

"We'll go see the whales!"

"Yes!" Hannah waved, and he ducked into the ramp.

The Boeing lifted off the little strip and climbed quickly away, leaving the valley spreading below. He swallowed hard and looked north. He figured where the ranches lay, the road they drove to town, and he imagined Hezekiah out mending fence. Sally would be at the store as the town shrunk from view, and he could visualize Hannah, still standing in the airport, that sad little wave. He located the picturesque cemetery out behind the church where Jesse lay beneath the sod. Were these his people? Is this where he should stay and live his life? Was he forfeiting his destiny by leaving here, or rushing toward it with the thrust of the jet engines? He didn't know.

His anticipation for what lay ahead was overwhelmed by the pain he felt with his separation from Hannah. He'd come here to hide for a time, and without ever suspecting, they'd become his family.

The jet climbed away into some brilliant billowing clouds. He leaned back in his seat and closed his eyes. He could see Jesse and Guardian running across the pasture together, the dog's ears and Jesse's hair bouncing in the sunlight. And playing with them, leaping through the meadows of eternity, was the black-footed ferret. Somehow he knew they were not that far from him here in the glittering sky. He'd go and sing for a season, and then he'd come back. He'd fallen in love with Hannah, he'd fallen in love with the world. The thought that preoccupied his flight through the heavens was this: is it possible to fall in love with God?

Chapter 59

LOS ANGELES CAME into view over the right wing and sent such electrical charges though his nervous system it was difficult to stay in his seat. The terminal was awash with people who hurried and hugged and laughed and cried, and he caught himself searching for Hannah's face in the stark alienation of the jammed concourse. What he got was a pudgy-faced girl with a vacant stare, stabbing a flowered canister at his chest.

"Would you like to give something for the work of God?"

"I'd be glad to. Show him to me and I'll give him everything I have."

Standing in her long white dress and stringy hair she appeared stumped, and he wondered if she'd been kicked out or run away from home.

"It's for Christian youth work," she said, her ace in the hole.

"I'm sorry, girl, but I don't want to pay for the Kool-Aid. Why don't you try going back home."

In a rented Avis Pontiac he headed downtown, recalling how he never felt comfortable in Los Angeles—as though he didn't belong—but he was so super-charged that he relished mingling with the unsuspecting horde, sharing the sun-splashed rush and noise and traffic like the lyrics of life. He turned off the San Diego Freeway at Santa Monica Boulevard and drove into Beverly Hills. At the Beverly Hills Lincoln Mercury on Olympic, he hit the jackpot, a white '64 Cadillac Fleetwood Eldorado convertible with red leather uphol-stery in mint condition.

"I've been told that Sonny Hollister once owned it," the salesman said, admiring the spit-shined car.

"You think I look like him?" Sonny asked, still sporting a beard.

"Pardon me?"

Sonny removed his sun glasses.

"You think I look like Sonny?"

The impeccably dressed balding salesman looked at him for a

moment, as though unsure of his sincerity, then broke into a broad smile.

"I'll be damned if you don't, just need a little hair."

"I'll take it, especially if Sonny Hollister used to own it."

He paid for the convertible with cash, which raised no eyebrows in Beverly Hills, and after waiting impatiently for the paperwork and arrangements to have the Avis Pontiac returned, he drove out into the city, top down. First he picked up a script at 20th Century Fox Studios, then drove up Canon Drive to the Beverly Hills Hotel. Turning onto Sunset Boulevard, he tossed his bogus glasses on the seat and waved at two brash hookers on a street corner. He flowed with the traffic, with no destination in mind, almost in a panic to feel he belonged. He stopped for a steak sandwich at Musso and Frank's on Hollywood Boulevard but no matter what he did he couldn't stop the ache in his heart for Hannah. In this dance of the millions he felt utterly alone.

He beat the worst of the traffic by getting downtown just after three. Without a plan, he pulled up to the Los Angeles Bonaventure Hotel in the heart of the city, a building out of a Buck Rodgers world with five glass silos reflecting clouds and sunlight. A valet took the Cadillac, a bellhop his bags, and he entered the spacious lobby, a city unto itself with elevators plunging through the glass ceiling in tubes, monorails to heaven. Used to being escorted in the back way, up a delivery elevator to some exclusive suite, and never seeing anyone but hotel staff, he stood in line with other tourists to get a room. When his turn came, he was tempted to get the largest suite available, but he took a single, feeling more like the homeless boy from Boyd than royalty returning to claim a throne.

Forty-nine dollars a day, and he followed the bellhop to the color-coded tower to ride a magic capsule to his castle in the sky. From the twenty-fifth floor, he surveyed the city, spread out below, breezy and festive and starkly indifferent. Suddenly filled with panic, he took the elevator to the ground floor and ran the stairs twenty-five floors back to his room. Disoriented and exhausted, he curled up on the large bed, thinking of Hannah as he fell asleep.

When he awoke, twilight colored the expansive metropolis, and a roaring emptiness ambushed him. He showered and dressed and hurried to the streets, walking without direction in a forbidding land that was rapidly turning dark, unable to understand what was going on inside himself. He felt like an open wound, hyper-sensitive to each face he saw, to the suffering of strangers, to every human story. An old man carrying a plastic garbage bag searched along the gutter, a Hezekiah clone, and Sonny shoved a wad of bills into the man's suspicious hand.

With a quickened pace he hurried past the scattered people who shared the street at night like fugitives, glancing quickly, hurrying by, afraid of being hustled, afraid of being robbed, afraid of being killed. His heart ached, accustomed to seeing them smiling, celebrating, happy and friendly. Was it always like this! Had he been indifferent to all this in his other life? Two drivers swore at each other at an intersection, their voices filled with rage, and he felt a desperation to sing for them, to turn them from their fear and anger. He rounded a corner and spotted a young black boy inside a hotel lobby with a shoeshine box. He went for a shine.

"Aren't you up pretty late for a young fella?" Sonny asked.

"It's good business now."

His thin arms snapped the rag across Sonny's shoe. It could be Jesse. It could be Sonny, many years ago.

"You going to school?"

"You the law?" the boy said without looking up.

"No."

"Yeah, I go . . . sometimes."

"How would you like a horse?"

"Sure, man, I'll keep it under my bed." The boy smirked.

"His name is Wildfire."

"My name is Superman. That'll be three dollars."

The boy stood and held out his spindly hand.

"My name is Sonny Hollister. You see, I'm not really dead."

"Sure, man, whatever turns you on."

He kept his hand extended and Sonny put a fifty-dollar bill in it.

"Hey, man, I can't change this."

"Sonny Hollister never asks for change."

Sonny patted him on the head and ran for the Bonaventure, leaving the street-tough kid standing with his mouth hanging open. He sprinted past startled pedestrians who veered out of his path and crossed streets against the traffic lights. He had to chance calling Hannah; he was drowning in loneliness.

"Mom's asleep, I'm glad you called," Hannah said, sounding sleepy.

"I miss you like crazy," he said. "I feel lost."

They talked for more than an hour.

"I spoke with one of the top men in Greenpeace," she said. "He invited us to come and work with them when you get back, help fight for the whales. I told him you'd give a lot of money."

She laughed.

"We'll do it, kitten, just so we're together."

The city seemed to have found its spirit in the sunlight, and after finding a wig in North Hollywood, he drove over to Santa Monica. He left the wig in the Cadillac and took to the beach, walked for several hours, contemplated how Hannah would love the ocean: the gulls, the pounding surf, the sense of something eternal, and he was anxious to show it to her. When the sun arced for the Pacific horizon, he found a dinner club in Santa Monica, starving, but he felt too presumptuous with the wig and he went in bald.

Tempted to soothe his anxiety with the slight numbing effect of a few drinks, he settled for a tall orange juice. He tried to enjoy himself in the crowd, but a hollowness sat with him at his solitary table. While his meal was coming, he went to a phone and called the trailer, hoping Hannah would be home alone. No one answered. While he ate he noticed couples who nudged each other, looked sensually into each other's eyes, touched and danced and stole kisses in their booths. He fled, left the beach to the sun-kissed players, the night clubs to the lovers, the freeways to those with somewhere to go. It seemed, as he hurried down the freeway, that he'd always been alone, but now, with his second chance, he hoped that would change, that *this time* he could share his life with his blue-jeaned mountain girl.

". . . and I found a guitar," Sonny told Corkey on the phone, "a used Guild exactly like my old one, and I got fitted at Neudie's, ordered four—"

"You went to Neudie's!" Corkey barked with a froggy voice. "Please tell me you didn't go to Neudie's. Please, Mary mother of God, tell me you didn't go to Neudie's!"

"I'm tellin' ya, but don't worry about it, it was depressing. I'm standing beside one of my outfits they've displayed under glass, there's a huge photo on the wall of me and Neudie standing together like old buddies, and the tailor who fitted me didn't bat an eye, said I was the eighth or ninth impersonator he'd worked on, hinted that I was too solidly built to look like Sonny anyway."

"I told you it wouldn't be easy, ya know what I mean."

"But I found a great wig out at Wilshire Wigs and Toupees. The guy thought I looked just like Sonny; he couldn't get over it. I felt a lot better."

"I'm glad; you're a tough kid, but after this, call a little earlier, will ya. It's two o'clock in the morning here."

The tension mounted, he pondered the script, and the days minced by. With his confidence running out, his nerve all but gone, the night before the screen test he found a theater in the paper that was showing one of his old movies. He wanted to observe himself back in the late 60's, remember gestures, movements, any trademarks as if he'd forgotten how to be himself. His fright became almost humorous. Who in hell could imitate him better? All he had to do was walk in.

He drove to the theater in Santa Monica, and the frizzy-haired lady with a sad, saggy face paid him no heed when he bought a ticket and went in. It was a western with Rachel Newberry. He intended to study himself on the screen, but with the eerie feelings of one who had returned from the dead, he ended up more fascinated with the people in the theater.

A middle-aged couple to his left were engrossed in the film. Had they held hands the first time they saw it and gone out and made love? He couldn't tell the ages of the three women who sat in front of him, eating pop-corn and watching the legend who had passed on ahead of them. Did they remember what their lives were like when they cheered at his concerts, when they had hope, when they nurtured dreams? For all those he could observe in the semi-darkness, he imagined a scenario; how their lives had been touched by his, how their histories intertwined. He hardly noticed the movie, preoccupied with the audience, but he was embarrassed at how pasty and soft his body was even in his twenties.

It was the one movie in which he died in the end, maybe the reason it was showing. When it was over, he filed out with them, listened to their muted comments, and yearned to talk to them, standing alone in front of the theater until the last had taken to their cars and the deserted street turned silent under the darkened marquee.

Unable to erase those people from his mind, he drove back to the Bonaventure. They considered him a hero, but maybe life was all turned around. He'd never know if he could make it as a father, endure through the years with patience and kindness and understanding. Could he make it as a husband in an ongoing relationship with a woman? His failures were excused away with his stardom, but he knew that was a cop-out. Could he have made it as an ordinary man, work forty hours a week, pay off the mortgage, paint the house in the summer and take his two weeks vacation? These were the people who carried on throughout their lives without attention, the faces at a ball game who wave frantically into the TV camera's eye as though it were God's, shouting desperately to be noticed.

They were the ones who were brave and strong, the Hezekiahs and Sallys and Butches and Fallen Rocks who endured day after day, carried on in the face of failure, meaninglessness, and obscurity, often without love, without hope. They were the heroic. He would stand and cheer for them, for their courage, for their tenacity, and applaud them with his songs.

Chapter 60

THE SCREEN TEST was postponed twice; they were running behind and driving Sonny up the wall. When his time came, he drove the vintage Cadillac to the studio in a dither. Off Pico into 20th Century Fox Studios, he was stopped at a gatehouse by a security officer. Sonny smiled up at him from the white convertible.

"Sonny Hollister for a screen test."

The humorless man looked over a clip-board.

"You Frank Anderson?"

"Yep, Frank Anderson going in, Sonny Hollister coming out."

Without reaction the guard gave him directions to the right building. He hadn't worked on a movie lot for a decade or more, but he still knew his way around. With his glasses in place and his wig in a cosmetic bag, he stewed in a reception room for nearly an hour, like a dentist's office where you know you're going to have your gums removed or worse when the door opens. How do you get ready to be yourself? He thumbed through magazines and checked his guitar.

A no-nonsense executive-type man came through the inner door.

"You're Frank Anderson?"

"Yeah."

Sonny stood, feeling like a bit-part actor begging for a crumb at the door of his power.

"Follow me," he said, giving the air that this was some tedious favor he was doing just to say he had.

He deposited Sonny with a phlegmatic makeup man and disappeared down the narrow hall. The dainty mustached artist sat Sonny in a swivel chair in front of a brightly-lit mirror and helped him adjust the wig.

"The hairpiece isn't right," he said dryly.

"You wanna bet!"

The nimble cosmetologist snickered. "You think you have him in your pocket huh?"

"Let's just say I'm one helluva lot closer than you'll ever be!"

It was exactly what Sonny needed, some incompetent nincompoop to instruct him about Sonny Hollister, recycling his misgivings and insecurity into anger. When the flake was done dabbing at his face, Sonny took his guitar and shoved his way down the hall to the studio, all hesitancy and faintheartedness left in the make-up room mirror. He'd waited too long for this, and by God, he was ready— he'd knock them on their asses.

Several technicians and cameramen were scurrying about when he walked on the spacious set. Two of them stopped what they were doing and gazed at him.

"Frank Anderson?" one of the men asked, dressed informally in slacks, open shirt and heavy gold necklace. He extended a hand. "You sure as hell look like him."

Sonny shook his hand. "Yeah, my face was done by the best there is."

"I'm Howard Palms. Good to meet you. Have you got your script?"

"Yes."

Sonny set down his guitar case and took out the script. The movie-maker saw his stethoscope curled next to the Guild.

"What's that for?" he asked.

"I fine tune my guitar with it."

"Didn't—"

"Yeah, I read he used one some," Sonny said.

"You don't miss any details, do you?"

"No . . . I want them to think Sonny Hollister has risen from the grave."

"Okay, now, before we're ready for you in here, they want you upstairs."

"Upstairs? Who's they?"

"You'll read for the producer, director, the casting director, and the writer. You can leave your guitar here. Take the back stairs over there, it's the first door on the right in the upper hall." He glanced at his wristwatch. "You can go up now. Take your script."

Sonny turned for the narrow wooden stairway. His troops were retreating. His legs felt wobbly climbing the stairs and his throat parched. Then he found himself.

To hell with this noise! He'd go into that room on the first eight bars of "Don Quixote!"

An attractive authoritative woman in a blue pants suit stopped him in his tracks and briskly indicated what they wanted him to read. A woman with thick glasses would read the lines with him in the bleak Spartan room. Five men sat in upholstered leather chairs staring at him indifferently. Jeez, who in tarnation could he play to?

In the script he was talking to his mother, and he flew back in his memory to the way it was when this scene took place, called up her image in that smoky room, his brave and courageous mother. He took a deep breath and looked behind the stinking cigars and three-piece suits, into the souls of these powerful men who were trying desperately to be heroic by making great motion pictures or by making great piles of money. He recognized their weeping hearts, their desperate need to be wanted and loved, and he played to those hurting, boyish, unloved people, showing them what it had been like between his mother and he. Damn, it was easy, and he found it natural to laugh and weep.

When he finished, the cool, efficient woman thanked him and escorted him to the hall.

"You can go down to the set now."

She nodded at the stairway and made no comment about the reading. The five men had given no indication one way or the other, though none of them had been yawning. But he didn't need that; he knew how good it was. Years ago he rode into films on the locomotive of his immense popularity and he'd never been an actor, but the performance he'd just given would have won the role even if he wasn't Sonny Hollister!

On his way down to the screen test, one of the men who'd been in the room intercepted him in the hall.

"What's your connection with Corkey Sullivan?" he asked.

"No connection. He heard me sing in Montana and thought I was good, offered to get me a shot at this part."

"Where have you been up to now?" he said, his eyes penetrating.

"Nowhere special, just making a living."

"You under contract with anyone?"

"No . . . no one."

The man who wore authority like a garment turned and strode down the hall, leaving Sonny with another set of jitters. Was he Corkey's debtor, delivering on an old IOU? Had Sonny been too good in there, setting the wheels spinning in this man's mind?

Under the lights he worked with an actress named Lisa, a scene where she was his wife, Julia. She had done this part with dozens of Sonny hopefuls. After filming the scene, which went fairly well, they handed him the music for "If You Could Read My Mind" and asked him to interpret it. He asked them if they meant sing it, and they said yes. He had to do it cold, no accompaniment, no audience, but this time he had them by the ass.

While he waited for their cue, he flew away to the hundreds of stages and auditoriums he'd played, called up the cheering, swaying fans that none of the other pretenders had in their memory's portfolio, heard the thunderous tide of applause. The cameraman could see only the glaring lights and the empty set beyond, but he was empowered by the wellspring of experience that backed him up, the arsenal of love and triumph. He sang and moved around the stage as though surrounded by his fans, animated and alive as he'd ever been, imagined their faces beyond the floodlight glare. The lights changed, the cameras moved in and out, the professionals did their work, and no one applauded. It was their job, they wrapped it up.

He was soaking wet and never noticed until the lights shut down. The set quickly became deserted. He went to the make-up room, removed his wig, wiped himself dry, and met the head honcho of the set in the corridor.

"How was it?" Sonny asked.

"Terrific, perfect, we got good film, we'll have it ready for them next week sometime. Thanks for your work. I don't know if I'm getting punchy with all of this, but for a minute there. . . ."

Sonny skipped down the hall and out into the sunlight. At least one damn person was awake! He couldn't wait to talk to Hannah. Wait until the big boys see that film. They'll recognize instantly that their search is over. The numbskull film crew should've been dumbfounded at what they saw, the technicians up and cheering, but they were programmed against the impossible, the supernatural. When it takes place in their laps they don't recognize it. They live in a closed universe, everything tidy, in its place, everything explained. He gunned the big Cadillac out of the studio lot. How long would it take in the bureaucracy of the film industry to stumble onto a miracle. It was only a matter of time.

Chapter 61

IN THE PERILOUS GAME of nerve and audacity, the possibility of recognition haunted Sonny. He drove himself harder than ever to improve his greatest disguise. He rose early, walked up Sixth Street to MacArthur park, then ran around it for most of an hour. Back to the hotel, he checked if there was a call, ate breakfast, sang for an hour, then off to the hotel health spa for a hard workout with the weights. He hurried back to see if they had called, had a salad and natural foods for mid-afternoon lunch, then a nap. The nights were the worst as the anxiety mounted, although the strenuous exercise helped drain it away. Each night he sang for hours, took the elevator to ground level, and ran the stairs until he was exhausted. Then he'd flop on his bed until he regained enough energy to run them again.

Hannah answered the phone in the afternoon when Sally was at work.

"Hi, how did the screen test go?"

"Good, great, I think I left them speechless. I expect a call any day now. How are you?"

"Okay, but I miss you terribly."

"I'm sure I can get back there before they start shooting. God, it's so special knowing you're there for me."

"We never should have started." She sighed. "When I get horny for you, I do a lot of riding."

They visited for an hour and at more than one point he was ready to bag it and catch the next plane for Montana.

"I'm worried about Rock," she said. A guy was found early Wednesday morning tied to a road sign east of Bozeman. He was bare-assed and his genitals had been painted, prepped with methiolate."

"Crazy, but what's that got to do with Rock?"

"It was the vet's assistant, the one who had been with the bunch who castrated him. Don't you see, he counted coup, the Indian way of humiliating an enemy by showing what he could've done but didn't."

"What does Fallen Rock say?"

"He says he doesn't know anything about it, but he can't fool me. I'm afraid he'll go for the others, if he can find them, and things could get ugly."

"How do you know it was him?" Sonny asked.

"The road sign the guy was tied to was WATCH FOR FALLEN ROCK."

He gave her his number and asked her to call collect whenever she missed him. She called back three minutes later.

Sonny waited five days and then called Corkey, somewhat nervous at having him contact anyone after the movie mogul's loaded questions.

"I'll do what I can, but it'll do no good to crowd 'em. Give 'em time. If it went as well as you say, just relax," Corkey said. "I met a widow walking the beach, been seeing her some, ya know what I mean. Angeline. She has me hunting shells, if you can believe that. She never seemed to notice my foot."

"Maybe it's not your foot she's interested in."

Sonny couldn't help but laugh.

When he arrived back at the hotel from picking up his outfits at Neudie's, there was a message waiting. Corkey still had clout. He dialed the number with a trembling hand and talked to Douglas Smith, a faceless executive with a George Patton manner.

"Yeah, Frank the test was good, you did a helluva job, kid, but we're going with a younger man."

The words freeze-framed Sonny where he sat.

"Listen, sweetheart, you were terrific, but we're looking for an image, you know, authenticity. Your physical likeness was terrific, fascinating, but that's not our biggest problem. The charisma wasn't there. Hollister had a charisma that came across like gangbusters, you know. Sorry, kid, and thanks."

His body went numb. The dead line hummed indifferently for a howling stretch of time and then he gently put the phone in its cradle. He peered from the curving window at the city below and turned to stone, sand filled his lungs, and he felt an urgency to tell someone what a terrible mistake they were making. The reality of what was happening became almost impossible for him to grasp. He slumped onto the bed. He had to find a logical explanation for this nightmare or go mad.

It had all been decided before he took the screen test, that was it. They probably want some well-known, younger actor and never looked at Sonny's film. He, better than anyone, should know what it's like in this business. Someone put him through all that to pay Corkey back for a favor. The men with the money decided, and it had nothing to do with how good he'd been. If he didn't convince himself of that, he'd never make it out of that room.

In sweat suit and running shoes, he fell with the elevator through the glass tube to the ground and sprinted out into the sun and the teeming populace of the streets.

Run, run for your life!

Morons! Idiots! Don't recognize a miracle in their pocket! Mechanical puppets, always looking for the spectacular, something utterly unique, always trying for the incredible, and they have eyes of marble. He'd go to the people themselves, where he could touch them with his voice and his presence, where no shrivel-assed executive who wouldn't know authenticity if it punched him in the face could cut him off like God himself. He had to get a grip on himself, knew he was close to the edge. Good God, if the world was deaf and sightless, he'd go back to Montana and Hannah. What should he care?

Run and shout! Under the freeway, run!

The sweat flowed. He dodged traffic and pedestrians, and with his chest heaving, collapsed on the grass in MacArthur park.

He sang his song for them to record and film, and they threw it out with the day's garbage, flushed it with the morning's shit. He wanted to tell people around him: Go to the garbage dumpster and salvage the most phenomenal film ever shot. Someone in the city had to know what they had done to him on the cutting floor, what they all had lost in the twinkling of an eye.

Late that night, rising from his sleepless bed, he pulled open the drape and viewed the panoramic lights of the city from his lofty perch. The startling revelation broke in on him high above Los Angeles in the early hours of the morning.

Many people would be terribly disappointed if he turned up alive! It would ruin their business, put people out of work, smash mounting profits, rout the impersonators, stop the stupendous album sales, cancel his old movie bookings, halt the production of the movie about his life, bankrupt the investors in their merchandising promotions, ruin the advent of his biography *Shooting Down The Moon,* and disappoint the hell out of all the people who were deriving pleasure from their sad memories of him and the good old days.

They didn't want him back alive!

They were in love with his *memory,* and they didn't want anyone trifling with their illusion, not even Sonny Hollister himself! Unconsciously, like the Romans, they stationed guards at the tomb, to let no one trifle with the body.

Chapter 62

HE ALWAYS KNEW he should never have messed with movies, he was a singer, one who met people face to face and spontaneously responded to their vibrations and mood. With the convertible laden with all that he'd need in Las Vegas, he squealed the tires pulling away from the hotel into the traffic on Flower, a gesture of shaking the dust of Los Angeles from his feet as a judgment on the city. The light stopped traffic at Fifth.

"Hey, man! Sonny Hollister!" a voice shouted from the crowded sidewalk.

He searched the sea of faces for some recognition until a bright-eyed black boy with an armload of newspapers ran to the side of the convertible in the waiting line of traffic.

"Hello," Sonny said.

"I'll take that horse." The boy grinned ear to ear.

"Aha! A believer. What's your name?"

"Willis Jefferson Cooper."

"Well, you're a very astute boy, Willis Jefferson Cooper." Sonny laughed. The light changed and the horns behind him blared instantly.

"Right on, man, I know who you are. I told 'em I shined your shoes. They said I was crazy, but I keep telling 'em anyway."

Cursing rose from behind the Cadillac.

"Listen, Willis, this whole stinking city will be saved from the great earthquake because you believed. Be careful getting to the curb. Adios, amigo!"

When he pulled away and waved at the smiling boy, he felt a personal bond with him and promised himself to come back and find Willis Jefferson and make his life better. He kept pace with the traffic and shouted at the pedestrians.

"The city shall be spared, for one believer was found in your midst!"

Interstate 15 to Las Vegas was as familiar as that path to the wood-shed and, in some ways, he felt like he was going home. The irre-pressible manipulator, Corkey, had done it again, if reluctantly. There was a cancellation at the Hilton; Wayne Newton had to undergo sur-gery, and they were giving Frank Anderson a week impersonating Sonny Hollister completely on Corkey's word. At the end of the phone conversation, Corkey mentioned he'd moved in with Angeline temporarily, just to make things easier, meals, driving, and so on. Sonny laughed and told him they used to call it shacking up.

With the Hilton bombshell still reverberating in his skull, the fail-ure and frustration of Los Angeles had been somewhat tempered. By phone he had arranged to have three musicians waiting for him; a rhythm guitar, a base, and a drummer, all of whom had years of experience, much of it in the big time with heavy hitters. They only had three days to prepare, and he warned them that the pay would be fantastic but they'd be expected to work whatever hours it took right up to show time. There had been a complete turnover in man-agement at the Hilton since he starred there, but he thought it best if he stayed somewhere else until the day of the performance.

He registered at Caesar's Palace and the bellhop had no more than set his bags in his room before Sonny was roaming the casinos. He mingled with the people and enjoyed the tourists and gamblers in a way he'd never been able to before, locked away in a suite until he went on stage.

In his red sequined shirt and jeans, he drove to the appointment with the new manager of the Hilton. In spite of Corkey's reputation and influence, the man wanted to taste the wine before he served it to hundreds of guests. The receptionist blinked her long eye-lashes and embraced him with a sensuous smile. She kept him to herself until it was becoming uncomfortably obvious, informed him that she was single, and that she thought he looked magnificent. Her inter-com buzzed, and she ushered him into the manager, a dark, curly-haired man with watery blue eyes.

"If Corkey Sullivan says you're good, I know you're damn good. Just want to listen enough to see what we might do with sound, lights, you know."

Friendly and efficient, the manager led Sonny to the familiar showroom, where employees set tables, wiped down chairs, and vacuumed the carpet. The manager sat back a ways in one of the upholstered booths. Sonny strummed a few chords and searched for the right mood.

He sang "Fire and Rain," and despite the hollow showroom, he had no trouble getting into the song and breathing life into it. Some of the staff hesitated in their labor momentarily and listened, cocking their heads as if thinking, then went on with their tasks while he sang. When he finished, a few of the employees in the shadowy depths of the auditorium applauded, several lights on the dimly-lit stage went out, and the manager waved at Sonny, already heading back toward his offices.

"Wow, you've got him down pretty good, pretty damn good," he said as he hustled along the passageway, "the genuine article." Sonny kept abreast. "Corkey Sullivan knows what he's talking about, damn it. You'll be a big hit, a big hit. You been working on this long?"

"Yeah . . . most of my life."

"See my girl in the office; she'll give you a rehearsal schedule for the showroom."

He went on about the financial rewards for the engagement but Sonny couldn't concentrate on the conversation. There was too much oxygen in his bloodstream, too much joy in the world. After a quick See you later, Sonny bounced into the Cadillac, pumped. Son of a gun, think what it would be like when the showroom was jammed, when he could look at the audience and respond to their faces, to their loneliness! He would sell the place out for weeks, like he always did, forcing them to postpone whoever was scheduled next.

The sun christened the white convertible with shimmering halos as he drove up the Strip. He was flying, he was back, he had his second chance to sing!

With the three musicians he worked relentlessly to prepare himself, practiced hours, and they proved to be good, knew Sonny Hollister's music, and were willing to give it their best shot. On a deserted road just south of the strip he ran every morning and worked out later in the day at the spa in Caesar's Palace. The tension mounted, resurrection day moved closer, the advertising appeared all over the strip: SONNY HOLLISTER RETURNS TO THE HILTON featuring Frank Anderson.

Hannah's voice came like rare mountain air in this desert. He asked her to come down and be with him. She said she couldn't.

"I'm so sorry about the movie," Hannah said. "It's incredible!"

"I know, it's insane, but Friday night I open at the Hilton, and all that will end."

"The Hilton!"

"Yeah, Corkey strikes again. But doggone it, I wish you could be here. How are you, kitten?"

"I'm all right. No, I'm not, I miss you, I—"

"I know, me too. Do you know how much I love you?"

"Yes . . . I do."

"I think I'll be good, kitten, better than I've ever been, I just feel it. I'm so damn thankful for the chance. Think of it, a chance to do it over."

When they hung up, a demon of despair crept into his heart and bedded down.

So jittery he couldn't fasten his buttons when he dressed, Sonny's legs wobbled and his stomach feasted on itself. The stage manager, a skinny guy in a tux, bustled into the dressing room and shook him loose.

"Okay, you're on."

He led Sonny through the passageway that delivered him on stage. With the curtain closed, the musicians nodded at the ready, and he steadied himself in front of the microphone while the stage manager announced him with fanfare and emotion.

"The Hilton brings you Frank Anderson as S-o-n-n-y H-o-l-l-i-s-t-e-r!"

The curtains ran to the sides and left him exposed to the packed showroom. For an instant he looked into the darkness, barely able to distinguish people at their candle-lit tables. He'd stood here before in what seemed like another lifetime. Already sweating, he strummed a chord, his backup picked up the beat, and he sang like he had never been away.

"If you could read my mind, love,
what a tale my thoughts could tell . . ."

With emotion that had accrued for years, he poured out his energy, the guitar an extension of his spirit, and happiness came to him like sunshine. He had come all the way back from the despair and hopelessness of the grave to sing again, only this time he did it for them: his mother, Hezekiah and Hannah, for Corkey and Sally and Fallen Rock and Butch, and he did it for Jesse. He sang to make people smile and sway and forget their loss for a while—searched the darkness for their faces, identified with their struggles, their triumphs, their dreams.

"But heroes often fail,
And you won't read that book again
Because the ending's just too hard to take!"

He hit the final strum and lifted his arm high, stepping back from the microphone, bowing and smiling into the glaring lights. For a moment not a sound; he held his breath. Sweat rolled from his face, his heart pounded. Had he overdone it? Had they recognized him and now had to explain the miracle in their minds before they could shake themselves into some response?

He stood frozen before them in the breathless silence.

Chapter 63

OUT OF THE clinking-silverware silence came a scattering of applause, and when he expected a crescendo, it fell back into the leather-upholstered showroom as if swallowed in outer space. The stage floor seemed to tip under him; he fought for balance. People chit-chatted over their meals, laughed in muffled tones, and blew smoke in the air. A paralysis gripped him and held him powerless in the spotlights. His soul was draining out onto the stage.

"Thank you, thank you," he said, "and now one of Sonny's many favorites."

In the teeth of their stingy tribute, he forced himself into "Carefree Highway" while some great weight forced the breath from his chest.

What do you expect from one song?

He would warm them up.

Afraid to hesitate, he carried on, embarrassed that he was bleeding in front of them without their slightest regard. The show went on, and memories overwhelmed him with the lyrics of the song. Natalie's sad smile, his mother's bloody hands, Hannah riding the Appaloosa, Roy driving away and stranding him in the desert, Jesse's small head in the hospital sheets, Steve's body in the bloody snow, hitchhiking out of Boyd with his guitar, Sally's swollen face, Corkey asking if he had a manager, Guardian playing with Jess, the battered Oliver tipping into its grave.

He kept the lyrics coming in a constant stream lest he hear their disapproval, or worse, their scorn. He gave from the hurting center of his heart, and they chewed their steak and picked their teeth.

"See you at 12:30," the drummer said when the curtains had closed the first show.

Sonny sat in his dressing room; he knew it was only one performance, one lukewarm crowd who may never have liked his music in the first place. He wanted to call Hannah.

After the second show, where the audience showed slightly more enthusiasm, the Hilton manager told Sonny it would build. But the next night, and the next, the showroom didn't fill, tables sat empty. Sonny would stare into the dressing room mirror, adjust his wig, and go out and die. He struggled for understanding, some explanation for what was happening. He was Sonny Hollister, singing his old songs for them, and they had ears of stone.

One night, between shows, a woman about his age approached him in the casino. She'd been crying.

"I'm really worried about myself," she said, laughing through her frown. "I've got the feeling you're really Sonny. I saw him in person many times, and I always got a special feeling." She pressed a hand against her chest. "Tonight, when you were singing, I got that feeling . . . and yet I know you're really not him, that he's dead. Am I going crazy?"

Hamstrung, he wanted to embrace her and tell her it was all right, she wasn't crazy, her instincts were perfect.

"Thank you for that wonderful compliment," he said. "The best I've ever had."

He squeezed her arm and turned away quickly.

The greatest irony happened on his last night at the Hilton. Between acts, Tony Costello came back stage and slobbered all over Sonny. "I always loved the kid," Costello said, "and you were incredible. For a while I thought you . . . I thought you was him." He hugged Sonny and kissed him on the cheeks. "It was a terrible loss when he left us, a terrible loss. I really miss the guy."

Sonny couldn't help but smile. He had a terrible urge to show Costello who he was but this murdering outlaw, like the rest, wouldn't believe him.

In the Las Vegas reviews he was mentioned twice. One praised his performance as a true portrayal of Hollister, powerful, wonderful. The critic wondered why more of the audience did not respond to his excellent impersonation. The other mentioned Frank Anderson now performing at the Hilton.

> "He presented a striking likeness at times, with an excellent repertoire of the late singer's songs, done with perfect imitation of style, but Anderson lacks the energy, the earthy, vibrant power of the one and only Sonny Hollister."

"Corkey wrangled me a spot at the Silver Bird," Sonny told Hannah late one night on the phone, "between George Burns and Dean Martin. There wasn't much publicity, but I've made it through two nights. If I can just hang in there a while longer, I keep thinking maybe they'll start to hear me."

"I don't know how you do it, it's maddening. Come home."

The word "home" cut through it all and nearly sent him packing.

"I just grit my teeth, suck it up, and shove myself onto the stage. I know it isn't my singing; that's as good as it ever was."

"Don't do this to yourself any more, you've tried, you've done everything you could."

"You should hear what they say to me—You're too young, you're too well built, you're too old, you're not as electrifying, you're not as crazy, until I don't know what to do, what to try. I'm me, for God's sake."

"Give it up, come home."

"I will, I will, but not just yet. Doggone it, it's as if my reputation goes on without me, my mystique has its own life and I can never live up to it. One manager told me the people wanted a younger Sonny, the way he was in his prime."

When she hung up, he couldn't get to sleep so he woke Corkey in Florida, and after Corkey cleared the drowsiness from his head he sounded optimistic and happy.

"Remember, it takes time in the beginning," Corkey said, "it takes a little time, ya know what I mean. Remember when you were acting crazy and tossing away money like it was gumdrops and I would tell you you were nuts? You'd always say You don't come back for an encore in life. Well, Judas Priest, you did." Corkey laughed. *"You did!"*

"Yeah, you're right, but the audience has all gone home, it's an encore to an empty house."

He kept trying, working smaller and smaller places, some hotel lounges, able to make a good impression on the local managers, but unable to touch the people with his songs. There were some. They'd come up after a set and tell him he was unbelievable, perfect, that he reminded them of Sonny himself. He got the other side too. "Where do you get off trying to imitate Sonny Hollister? He was the best ever. You can't touch him."

One morning, driving back to the city after his desert run, he was feeling down. On the interstate he came upon a cattle truck chugging along in the slow lane. It was the same kind of rig he hitched a ride in what seemed so long ago. As he pulled alongside, he saw that one of the animals had stuck his nose as far as possible out one of the ventilation holes, drinking in as much of the last sweet air as he could on this ride to the slaughterhouse. And through the next ventilation hole, the eye, the large, warm eye pleading with Sonny. Toro! Sonny stayed even, glancing at that eye, that steer that knew it had been betrayed, abandoned. The idea came to him like a thunderbolt.

Sonny accelerated and pulled even with the driver. He motioned for him to pull over, honking and shouting and waving from the convertible. The truck slowed for a stretch and then crawled off the highway on a wide shoulder where it was safe to stop. The driver jumped out as Sonny pulled in behind. The man limped as he hurried back along the trailer, dressed in worn denim and a beat up cowboy hat that appeared as though it had grown on his head.

"What's the matter, I got a bad tire?" he said as he reached Sonny, a little out of breath.

"No, no, your tires are fine."

"Then what's all the whoopin' and hollerin'?"

"I'm after your cattle."

"My cattle?"

The short middle-aged man had the stub of an unlit cigar in the corner of his mouth and he squinted at Sonny out of a weathered face.

"I want to buy them," Sonny said.

The man looked over Sonny's bright red and white running outfit. "You want to buy my cattle? You're joshing me."

"No I'm not kidding."

"What would you want with a bunch of cattle?"

"They are for sale aren't they?"

"Yeah, sure, I'm on the way to the sale."

Sonny reached out with his hand. "I'm Frank."

"Yes, sir, I'm Floyd Tollefson, they call me Shorty."

He shook Sonny's hand with an iron grip.

Sonny grabbed the rope at the back of the trailer. "Well, Shorty, can I take a look?"

"Well, dang, I suppose but. . . ."

Sonny pulled the rope, lifting the narrow door in its track. He looked in at the doomed cattle. Steers. Herefords. The animals had found their balance and stood staring at Sonny, a few backing into the herd for cover. He thought about his ride with Toro.

"Hello, boys, you're goin' home!" Sonny shouted, smacking his hands together. "Whooeee, you're goin' home by God!"

One Hereford, staring at him with curiosity, reminded him of Toro. Like the others, he had a yellow plastic marker in his ear. He was number 108.

"See that one," Sonny said, pointing him out to Shorty, "number 108. That's Toro, that's Toro Two."

Sonny let the door down and turned to the driver.

"I want them all."

"I swear," Shorty said, slowly shaking his head. "Mister, if you don't mind, I got ta get down the road."

"How many you got in there?"

"Thirty-seven," the man said with a baffled look. "I don't want to offend you or nuthin' but are you some kind of a nut?" He forced a thin smile.

"How much you want for the lot of them?"

"Well, I don't rightly know right off. The price's been hemmin' and hawin' around seventy cents."

"Let's make this easy. You figure what you hoped to get for them at the stockyard. Go ahead."

He moved the cigar to the other side of his mouth without touching it and studied Sonny.

"You're plumb loco. I can't sell them out here in the middle of the desert, with no scale, no competition, even if you was serious."

"Oh I'm serious. You just tell me what they're worth. That shouldn't be too hard."

The driver limped to the cab and pulled out a metal clip board. Sonny went to the convertible and came back with several bundles of one-hundred-dollar bills, five thousand dollars a bundle. He held them behind his back with one hand and waited as the rancher tipped his hat back, licked the end of his pencil several times, and went to figuring. Like a calculator, his tongue was adding and multiplying lickety-split. In a couple of minutes he came up with the number.

"I figured I'd get twenty thousand, seven hundred and twenty dollars for 'em, more or less." Shorty held his breath.

Sonny regarded him with a poker face, as though he were considering the price. He noticed the rancher's wornout boots. Then he smiled.

"Would you take twenty-five thousand for 'em?"

Shorty bit down on the cigar stub and nearly swallowed it.

"You're loco. You're out here in the middle of the desert pullin' my leg and it ain't funny." He shut his clip board. "You pull me over to make fun of me? I gotta get goin.'"

Sonny held up five bundles of cash. "Twenty-five thousand. Is it a deal?"

With widening eyes, Shorty studied the bundles of cash and spit the cigar onto the ground.

"You can't get anywhere near that for 'em," Shorty said.

"I'm not going to sell 'em. Is it a deal?"

They shook hands vigorously.

"If you're crazy enough to give me all that money I'd be a fool to argue with you. It's a deal."

Sonny handed Shorty the neatly bound bills, and Shorty seemed a bit numb at that point. He stood there counting it with an expression of disbelief on his sun-beaten face. Finally, satisfied, he chuckled to himself and said, "I ain't never seen this much cash. You sure they ain't counterfeit?"

"They're as good as gold," Sonny said.

"Where do you want me to unload 'em?"

"In Montana."

"Montana!"

"Yep, up near Bozeman."

"Mister, I gotta tell you, you're loco, plumb loco."

"No, don't you see. That's the way it's supposed to happen, these animals had the knife at their throats, goners, their lives over, and Boom! like a bolt of lightning, they're on their way to a new life, a mountain valley where they'll die of old age."

The driver shook his head slowly. "I declare."

"Now, can you deliver them to Montana?"

"Yeah, I reckon so. Have ta call my wife, let her know."

"You call her, take her along. This is a happy trip. You'll have to stop overnight twice. I want you to unload the steers each night at a local stockyard, feed them, water them, and hose out the trailer good. Here's five thousand for the hauling and the trip."

Sonny gave him another bundle.

"There'll be another five thousand when you get them to the ranch. Hannah and Hezekiah will be waiting for you."

"I swear," Shorty said, getting into the spirit of things. "Where on God's earth did you come from?"

"A long time ago I came from a farm in Minnesota."

They did the paperwork including the bill of sale which listed Frank Anderson as the owner of the steers. Sonny drew a map to show him how to get to Hezekiah's ranch from Belgrade because Hezekiah had a loading shoot. When all details were taken care of, Sonny lifted the door at the back of the trailer and surveyed his new herd. He was a rancher.

"Pass the good word, boys!" he shouted, "you're going home. I'll see you in Montana!"

Sonny shut the door and Shorty regarded him with a sheepish grin.

"I feel kinda foolish tellin' you this, but I borned and raised these buggers and I'm kinda glad you ain't goin' to butcher 'em, I'm glad they's goin' ta die of old age."

They shook hands and Shorty climbed up into the rig. When the truck pulled out onto the highway, Sonny caught up with it. He honked and waved alongside his cattle on their happy trip home!

He didn't catch Hannah on the phone until evening, and she cheered and laughed when he told her their strange herd was on the way home. She'd get Rock and Hezekiah to help unload and drive the steers onto their north pasture for the time being. When Hezekiah saw the herd, he'd probably think Frank hadn't learned much about ranching.

Each day he struggled to stay above the deep water and Hannah, with the lifeline provided by AT&T, kept him afloat like his daddy's inner tube kept Leroy's pony from drowning in the dark sucking slough.

The cattle had arrived and were acting as though they knew what the deal was, running and bucking in the north pasture like kids at recess. Hannah was in the process of naming them: Einstein, Popeye, Leonardo, Clark, Galileo, and so on. And, yes, Hezekiah thought Frank had missed one of the fundamental principles of ranching that he said he would explain to Frank when he got home.

"Rock got cornered by several cowboys when he took the mare to the vets," Hannah said over the phone. "Four of them were backing him into a stock pen in broad daylight and no one would help him. When it looked like he was about to get the crap beat out of him, Hezekiah showed up with his Winchester and evened the sides."

She gave a little hoot. It made Sonny smile and wonder if that wasn't where he belonged.

He tried to stay in the public eye somewhere, in whatever nightclub or lounge he could line up. His week at the Hilton carried a residue of prestige in spite of the outcome and he found an opening at the Banjo Lounge and Nightclub off the strip in downtown Las Vegas. The scattered customers ate and drank at tables in the modest-sized showroom while Sonny entertained them. Hannah, in jeans and a western blouse, hid far back in the shadows of the bar and observed. She knew what he was feeling, saw people kid him, joke around, but not take him seriously.

Some low-life heckled him from time to time, and Sonny was polite and continued singing in spite of the blatant disrespect. When she couldn't bear it any longer, she wove through the tables and came from his left where Sonny wouldn't notice her. Up onto the small stage, she walked to him in the middle of a song. He turned and she threw her arms around him and kissed him, squelching his song in his throat. The raucous audience whistled and applauded while Sonny embraced her with his one free arm.

"What are you doing here?"

"I came to be with you."

"Watch out for rotten fruit; they don't think a helluva lot of my impersonation."

"So what, you're wonderful and I love you."

She put her mouth to the microphone and glared at the people.

"You're all blind and deaf and numb! A little glaucoma out there? A little astigmatism?"

The crowd clapped and cheered, and Sonny held her in his arms, overcome with a sense of well-being. Hannah jumped from the stage and settled at an empty table directly beneath the microphone. From then on he sang to her alone, and something happened to the crowd, to the uncouth loudmouth, and they listened. As boorish and ill-mannered as the clientele had acted, for a while they accepted the gift he was trying so desperately to give them. For a brief moment it seemed they heard, allowed a tear in their collective eye.

Hannah went with him to Caesar's Palace, and they made glorious love until dawn, from the tub to the bed to the plush carpeted floor. She was intrigued with the bizarre characters and life forms on the strip, and they wandered, Hannah taking in the strange casino scene like a kid at the zoo. They ate sumptuously, returned to their room to make love several times during the day, and slept in each other's arms with a contentment he could not remember. With some coaxing, she sang with him in the room as he played, and he was enchanted by her clear, strong voice, their natural harmony.

And then it was time for her to leave.

"How do you do it?" she said as she packed her few things. "I wouldn't put up with it, I'd walk right out the door."

"It's all changed. I don't want their approval or their money. I want to give them something, something they can use; I don't know what it is, hope, happiness, love? I want them to find the courage to face their losses, to get back on their feet and try."

At the airport he wanted to beg her to stay. When she flew away into a gray sky, he felt something slide into place in his heart that had never done so before.

Lou Pinnelli was eating supper at the Rodeo Tavern in Rodeo, New Mexico. He was on a story from Vietnam but couldn't find the soldier involved. Supposedly the guy was living somewhere in the Chiricahua Mountains. Lou had flirted with the attractive blonde waitress, Linda Jean, in her early forties he guessed and well able to handle the likes of him. He asked for whatever newspaper they had in that Godforsaken country and all she could come up with was a Phoenix paper that was shopworn and long outdated.

He worked on his chicken fried steak and browsed through the paper. When he turned to the entertainment section his eyes fell on the highlighted advertisement.

SONNY HOLLISTER RETURNS
TO THE LAS VEGAS HILTON
FEATURING FRANK ANDERSON.

He stared at the black print for most of a minute. He couldn't catch his breath, sweat beaded on his face. *Frank Anderson!* He was right! He'd been right all along! He felt faint. He checked the date of the paper. It was almost three weeks old. He wedged himself out of the booth, slammed a twenty-dollar bill on the table and thundered to the pay phone back near the kitchen.

After talking to three different employees at the Las Vegas Hilton, he found out that Frank Anderson left there about three weeks ago. One of them thought the Sonny Hollister impersonator had gone to the Silver Bird, but wasn't sure.

Lou figured if he drove all night, he could be in Las Vegas by mid-morning. Son of a bitch! It was the biggest story he'd ever broken and it was all his. He'd knock the country on its ass! He left Rodeo while the sun still hung in the west. He would find Sonny Hollister, very much alive, and shock the world.

In the middle of the morning he woke from a fitful, sweaty sleep and answered the phone. Corkey had lined up a spot for him in Reno. A heavy gig, a weekend start on a billing with Donna Summers and Bobby Goldsboro. His bad rap would not have reached Reno yet, and he could come to them fresh. He had that feeling, remembered how he had to persevere in the beginning until he hit.

He called Hannah and caught her at home, told her about Reno and his good feelings about it.

"But it won't matter anymore if they hear me or not. It's all right, I'll have given it my best shot, Jesse knows that. I have another life now, with you, there. I'm coming home, kitten, to Montana and you. Will you marry me?"

"Marry you! O-o-oh, YES, of course, I love you. Forget Reno, come home now. We can go see the whales."

"I'll give it one more try, there'll be some big audiences, maybe I'll make some of them sing and dance. Then, when we feel like it, we'll go and sing together in the small town taverns."

"That sounds nice."

"I'll call you after the first night. Keep me in mind."

The day went fast. He had his outfits dry cleaned, jogged out the desert road, and checked out of Caesar's a little after noon with hope and a sense of promise.

On the phone, in his car, on foot, Lou Pinnelli bowling-balled up and down the Strip, stalking Frank Anderson or any word about him. Each stage he located where Frank had performed Lou was a few days closer. A guy at the Banjo Lounge sent him to the Wedgewood Nightclub. There he caught the manager eating lunch in his small office, the fast food spread out on his desk.

"So he was here?" Lou said, standing breathless in front of the desk.

"Yep, just last night," the man said with a nervous manner.

"Is he coming back?"

"Nope, last night was it."

"Did he say where he was going?"

"He wasn't bad, either, not bad at all. He might make it big some day."

"Did he say where he was going?" Lou said, shifting from foot to foot with impatience.

"No . . . no, I don't remember anything."

The man swiveled in his chair and called into the next room.

"Trudy, did Frank Anderson say where he was playing next?"

"Yeah," a woman's voice called. "Said he had a gig in Reno for this weekend."

"Did he say where?" Lou called back to the unseen woman.

"Nope, just a gig in Reno."

"Thanks, thanks a lot."

Lou was halfway out the door when the manager called after him. "The guy wasn't bad."

Sonny's mind was muddled as he drove across the desert. Traffic was light and the landscapes seemed newly created just for him. He slowed down through Scotty's Junction, catching himself going over the limit. He was in no hurry. He sang to himself and knew the crucial moment was near. He wondered if other people knew when they came face to face with their fork in the road? When he reached the intersection at Tonopah around five he paused at the stop sign. Reno to the left up US Highway 95, Montana to the right on US 6. He took a deep breath, knowing he had made his decision, his scary, wonderful, terrifying decision. With a surge of joy he turned right. He had given what he could. It was time to move on. If he didn't stop to sleep he could be home late the next day. He'd get some coffee; his heart sang, finally free to live his life with Hannah. They would be inseparable.

Chapter 64

LOU PINNELLI was driving too fast, he knew it, but he was so close. He'd break the most incredible story the country had ever heard, the story of the year, the story of the decade. And only Lou Pinnelli had scratched and clawed until he found it while everyone else had missed it, asleep at the wheel. He couldn't imagine the money to be made, a multi-million-dollar story. He could hear his story going out over the networks, see it breaking over the television news, imagine his photo on the cover of magazines, with shots of Sonny Hollister, the renowned folk singer everyone thought was dead.

He flew through Scotty's Junction, praying no speed trap was lying in wait. He kept an eye on the rearview mirror and stepped on it. He realized he hadn't eaten or slept for nearly thirty-six hours, but so what. He'd catch up to Frank in Reno and then show the world that Sonny Hollister was still alive.

The sun was hurrying west when he reached the junction at Tonopah. He honked at some slowpoke in front of him and turned left for Reno. He was half way there and the adrenalin was pumping faster than ever. It would be dark by the time he arrived but he'd find him, he'd find out where he'd be doing his act. He couldn't wait to see the look on Frank Anderson's face when ol' Lou Pinnelli was sitting in the front row.

A serenity engulfed Sonny like never before as he drove north. He was going home to Hannah and Montana. Only by chance he noticed the gas gauge. He was about out! Sweating it out for the next twenty minutes, he spotted a scruffy station that could serve as a movie set from back in the forties. A large rusted sign creaked in the wind, the flying horse, Pegasus, Mobil. He thought of Wildfire and pulled up to the three pumps, thankful he'd made it to gas of any kind. One of the pumps had a scrawled OUT OF ORDER sign hanging on it. He expected sand to come out of the nozzle he used, but he filled the convertible's tank with what smelled like gas.

The station had a building attached that appeared to have been a restaurant at one time but now was being eroded by desert sun and wind. He paid the stout woman with a hawkish nose, exchanged the usual pleasantries, and she directed him to the restroom. As he came out of the restroom, he heard a strong young voice singing to the strum of a guitar. He turned into what was once the kitchen and came upon a young guy sitting on a stool and singing.

As though he'd been sneaking a beer, the thin kid with blond tousled hair stopped singing when he saw Sonny.

"Sounds good," Sonny said.

"Thanks," the boy said with a desert shyness. In jeans and a grimy white T shirt he appeared to be at home in the station.

"You like playing?"

"Yeah."

"You play a lot?"

"Yeah," the likeable-looking kid said.

"What's your name?"

"Matt."

"How old are you, Matt?"

"Seventeen."

"Your dad own this place?"

"My dad died."

Sonny paused, thinking a moment.

"Don't go away, I'll be right back."

Sonny went to the convertible, opened the trunk, and gathered up all of his performing outfits. He snatched his guitar from the back seat and hurried into the decrepit building. The boy stood and set his guitar down as Sonny laid the spangled costumes on a counter.

"You can make better use of this stuff than I can."

Sonny handed him his guitar and the boy's face lit up as if he comprehended the value of the Guild.

"Try this one," Sonny said.

Matt strummed several chords and runs.

"Wow."

"Sounds a little better, huh?" Sonny said.

The boy stood flabbergasted. Sonny picked up one of the outfits from Neudie's and held it up to the boy's shoulders. It was too big for now.

"You keep growing and playing and this'll fit you just perfect."

"You just givin' this to me?" the kid said.

"Yep."

"Why?"

"I'm playing a hunch."

"Gosh, thanks, mister, I don't know what to say."

"Say it with your singing. Keep me in mind."

Sonny turned and started out of the building.

"Hey, mister, what's your name?"

Sonny looked back at the kid and paused, thinking.

"Frank, my name's Frank."

Awhile down the road, Sonny glanced over and spotted his wig on the passenger seat. He picked it up and flung it to the wind. Frank Anderson was going home.

When Sonny rounded a long curve he could see an accident ahead and the deja vu hit him in the stomach with an iron fist. A few cars and pickups had been pulled over onto the shoulder and people were standing in small clusters a ways back from the crash. A huge tanker lay on its side with a station wagon beside it also on its side. Sonny pulled over on the shoulder and hurried to the scene where a man, he assumed must be the trucker, was restraining a petite woman who fought to get free. The driver, a big man with a huge pot belly, had oil all over his pants, one boot missing, and a bloody gash on his bald head.

"Get back!" he shouted as he held on to the woman's arm and waved at the spectators with his free hand. "All of you, get back. She's going to blow!"

"Please! Please!" the woman shouted. "Please!"

In worn denim jeans and jacket, she had a black ponytail sticking out the back of her cap and she fought fiercely.

"Those are my children in there!"

The driver, twice her size, dragged her inch by inch further from the wreckage. Fire danced along the pavement under the tractor. Sonny ran to the trucker.

"Are you all right?" Sonny shouted.

"Yeah, yeah, but these damn people are too close!"

"Anything I can do?"

"Oh, please!" the woman yelled. "Get my children, my boy and girl! They're in there! They're alive!"

"Just help get these damn people back," the trucker yelled at Sonny.

The woman caught Sonny's arm with her free hand.

"Help me, please! My children! They're alive!"

"Everyone get back!" the trucker shouted. "She's going to blow!"

He dragged the woman, foot by foot, and the small band of spectators reluctantly moved further from the wreck.

Sonny looked into the woman's dark eyes. It was his mother, pleading desperately for his father's life all over again. Against gravity, against weight, against time.

"Look! You can see his arm, its moving! He's still alive," the woman shrieked. "Please! Please save them."

"She's going to blow, get back, way back," the trucker shouted. The woman struggled furiously against his brawny grip, kicked at his legs, tried to bite his hand. The fire crept along the pavement under the tractor toward the tank trailer.

"I'll get them," Sonny said and he dashed to the wreck.

"No! Come back here!" the trucker shouted. "You'll never make it. It's going up any second!"

Sonny could see the boy's arm sticking out through the narrow space between the roof line of the station wagon and the pavement. Tipped on its side, the wagon's caved-in roof faced Sonny. The boy was waving his thin little arm and shouting. "I'm in here, Mom! Help! Help!" It was Jesse's arm; it was Sonny's arm, back on the Minnesota farm.

Sonny kneeled and shouted. "Listen, kid, I'm going to lift the car. When you have enough of a crack, you scramble out quick. Then pull your sister through and run like hell! You got that?"

"Yeah, mister, can you lift the car?"

Sonny didn't know. He spread his feet slightly and bent his legs as if he were going to do a squat with the barbell. He grabbed the wagon at the edge of the broken-out side window. He lifted.

Nothing.

Fire flared under the tractor. He could feel the heat. He could no longer hear the trucker, only the growing roar of the flames.

He took a deep breath.

"You ready, kid?"

"Yeah, mister, I'm ready."

Sonny spread his feet a few inches more, bent his legs into a squat. He got a new grip and he lifted. The wagon moved an inch. He looked down. It was his father's bursting face looking back at him. *Not again. Not this time, by God!*

With everything he had Sonny heaved. He could feel the veins in his head about to pop, the car frame cutting into his hands, something in his back giving way. He howled like an animal, driving his body upward.

The car moved, three inches, then five, then eight. His legs were just about straight when the kid slithered through. The boy quickly turned and pulled his little sister out.

"Go! Go!" Sonny shouted.

They ran toward their screaming mother. People cheered.

Sonny dropped the Ford and turned to run.

He dreams of what it would be like. They would be haying, Hezekiah on the haybuck, Jesse driving the Jeep while Guardian runs alongside . . . his father on the tractor, his mother bringing lunch out to them, he could see them, Natalie Jones and the traveling salesman and Julia and Tommy and Corkey and Oscar the postmaster and Sally and Fallen Rock . . . Hannah and Butch were waving from atop the stack and he runs across the hayfield toward her, toward all of them, calling . . . he has something he wants to tell them.

Chapter 65

IN HER ROBE, Sally had coffee going in the kitchen. Hannah was sleeping in. The phone rang. Sally glanced at the clock. Seven-twenty. She picked it up.

"Hello."

"Hello, ma'am," a man's voice. "Is there a Mrs. Frank Anderson there?"

"No." Were the telemarketers calling mornings now?

"Is there a Hannah Anderson there?"

"Who is this?" Sally was about to hang up.

"I'm sorry, ma'am, this is the sheriff's office in White Pine County, Nevada, and we're trying to locate the family of Frank Anderson."

"What's wrong? Is anything wrong? Is he okay?"

"Are you family?" His voice was soft and kind.

"Yes, yes, we're his family, what's wrong? Has he been hurt?"

"I'm sorry to inform you that a Frank Anderson was killed last night at a crash site on Highway 6 near Saulsbury Pass."

"Oh, god, oh no, there's some mistake, please, God, it's a mistake—"

"I'm sorry, ma'am, but a Frank Anderson was killed last night. We got this information from the glove box in his car. Is his address Route 1, Box 386, Belgrade, Montana—"

"Oh no, o-o-o-h, God. . . ."

"He was driving a 1965 Cadillac convertible, is that correct, ma'am?"

"Yes . . . I don't know, oh, God, Hannah would know."

"This office will call you later this morning to make arrangements for the body—"

"I can't do this. . . ." Sally dropped the phone. "Hannah! Hannah! Come quick!"

Hannah rushed into the kitchen in her flannel pajamas.

"What, Mom, what!"

Sally screamed as if she were dying. She handed Hannah the phone. Hannah put it to her ear, held her breath, and stood as if she were carved in stone. She nodded. She said "Yes." Her face washed with tears and still she stood. Finally, after several minutes, she hung up. Sally wrapped her arms around her daughter and they shrieked, howled with animallike sounds from the beginning of creation.

They collapsed on the sofa and clung to each other like survivors of an earthquake desperately hanging onto a rocky edge of the earth. Sally's mind whirled in flurries of memory. It couldn't be true. Frank couldn't be gone.

When they couldn't cry anymore, Hannah spoke softly, as if she were reading a book. "He was trying to save some people who were in the crash. The truck driver who saw it said that the man was blown to hell and gone. He wasn't even in the accident. He wasn't even in the accident."

Sally couldn't believe how Hannah took over. Making the phone calls, making the arrangements. Hannah called Corkey in Florida. She told Sally that Corkey couldn't speak for several minutes and told her he would have someone take care of the legal stuff.

Hannah insisted on flying to Nevada to bring Frank home, and though she dreaded it, Sally couldn't let her go alone. She had no idea that Frank was speculating in Nevada. They rode in a hearse with Sonny's body from Ely to Salt Lake City, and then flew Frank home to the Gallatin Valley. Scanning the mountains below them as they flew, Hannah repeated herself, over and over.

"He was coming home. He was on US 6, the highway to Montana. He wasn't going to Reno. He was coming home."

They had a simple service at the graveside, the high ground near the creek bottom next to the slab rock where they buried the black-footed ferrets. The preacher who buried Jesse did the words, and Hannah, Sally, Hezekiah, Butch, and Fallen Rock were present. Corkey said he couldn't bear it, that he'd come back in a week or so.

Hannah had a wrought-iron fence erected around the grave site to keep the cattle off. There was room for more than one grave in the plot. Hannah had a marble headstone engraved in Bozeman. The day it was finished she dug out a place and set it level with the ground. When she was done, she knelt by the grave for a long time and found herself singing the words he'd taught her.

"You won't read that book again,
because the ending's just too hard to take."

Fallen Rock said that Frank would be known as "He Saves Many" among his people. Hannah thought the name was good.

A week after Frank's death, a note came in the mail to Frank Anderson's family. Hannah had checked his mailbox every day and found nothing but advertisements and his monthly bank statement until this note arrived personally addressed. Hannah opened it sitting in the pickup. It was from Rosalee Sanchez, the woman whose children were trapped in the wreck. She thanked Frank's family profusely for what he had done and then she ended with one question.

"Why did he do it?"

Hannah slipped the note back into the envelop. One day she would write Rosalee and answer that question.

It was more than three weeks before Corkey flew in from Florida, and when he pulled into Hezekiah's yard, the old cowman walked him out to where Sonny was buried. Hezekiah hung back and allowed Corkey to go to the grave alone. Corkey stood outside the black iron fence and read the words on the headstone.

FRANK G. ANDERSON

BORN JANUARY 5, 1978

DIED AUGUST 7, 1980

"He pulled his own weight"

She *knew!* Hannah *knew!* Holy mother of God, Hannah knew! Corkey would talk about it with her some day, when he could bear the anguish. How long had she known? He prayed to God that she let Sonny know that she knew, that he had one other person in his life who knew he was alive. Sonny had gone to a lawyer and drawn up a will before he left as if he had a premonition. He sent Corkey a copy. Left the ranch to Hannah and more money than she'd ever need. Said she could raise horses and go see the whales. And when Hezekiah died, the ranches would be joined, the black-footed ferret protected. He gazed out across the land and spoke softly.

"Keep me in mind, Son, keep me in mind."

When he turned from the grave, Hezekiah was gone. He walked back to his car and drove into Belgrade. He wanted to tell someone that Sonny Hollister had gotten it right. He had an hour to burn and he wandered into the Hub bar. He settled at a table, ordered a beer, and watched the five o'clock news. Someone stood at his side.

"Mr. Sullivan?"

"Oh, Butch, how are you?"

"Okay."

"Sit down, can I buy you one, I'm just waiting for a plane."

"Yeah, sure," Butch said and sat next to him. "I'm waiting for the ABC national news. Hannah called yesterday and said she might be on. They were filming Greenpeace battling with the Russian whalers."

"Look!" Butch shouted and pointed.

Corkey turned to watch.

On the TV they showed a dinghy with an outboard motor dashing in front of a Russian whaling ship, trying to cut it off from a pod of whales.

"Look," Butch shouted excitedly, "it's Hannah."

All eyes in the bar turned to the television. Corkey squinted in time to see the raft, skipping across the ocean's swells, narrowly missing the steel bow of the whaling ship. The camera zoomed in on the four occupants of the Greenpeace dinghy and he saw Hannah, her hair rippling behind her in the wind, hanging on for dear life and looking out at the whales, placing herself between them and the harpoon cannon.

Then the TV cut to the newscaster.

"Did you see her?" Butch said as he stood staring into the television screen, "did you see her?"

Corkey had no voice. He nodded.

Butch sat down. "Hannah said she's coming back to live on the ranch, but she had to do this for a while."

"She's a brave kid," Corkey said. "A brave kid."

"Before she left, she went out to Frank's grave early one morning and she spotted something on the grave. She hid behind the fence line and it stood up, on the grave, and looked all around. It was a black-footed ferret. It stood there for a long time, and then it ran off. You won't tell anyone, will you Mr. Sullivan?"

"No, Butch, I won't tell a soul."

"Hannah said it was Frank's way of telling her he's all right."

Butch glanced into Corkey's eyes. "Do you believe that, Mr. Sullivan, that Frank could do that?"

"Yes. Right now I believe Frank could do that."

Corkey was losing it. He stood abruptly, laid ten dollars on the table, and placed a hand on the young man's shoulder.

"Good bye, Butch."

"Good bye, Mr. Sullivan. Will you be coming back?"

"No."

Corkey made his way through the bar and went out the door.

THE END

Afterword

Hezekiah died in his sleep a month later after he'd been baling alfalfa for his beloved herd and went to bed with the sun.

Lou Pinnelli spent three weeks trying to find Frank Anderson in the Reno area and finally drove to the ranch. He turned pale when Hannah told him Frank Anderson had been killed. He shared his secret with Hannah, who admitting nothing, only regarded him with a sad smile. What could he do? Who would believe him? Just another reporter trying to make the scandal sheets. What the hell. He would let it go with some sense of pride that he alone had found the truth.

The two ranches became one in Hannah's name. She had a large sign hung over the arch at the turn-in: HOLLISTER/LINESINGER RANCH. People, including Sally, wondered where the Hollister came from. Hannah just said she liked the sound of it. She spent half her time out in the world fighting for the earth's endangered species and half her time at the ranch.

Sally married the dentist and moved into a large home on Nob Hill in Bozeman. She kept busy helping her new husband raising his three boys. She brought them out to the ranch often where they could ride horses and chase steers and just roam, like Jesse.

Fallen Rock, with Hannah's financial help, took every course offered at Montana State University on alcoholism, addiction and counseling. He even took post-graduate courses before he returned to the Rocky Boy Reservation to work with Indian youth.

Butch became an excellent horseman and lost twenty pounds. He worked on the ranch much of the time and spent hours in the saddle. They used the Thirty-Seven to practice roping, but the steers got so tame with the repetition that when they'd be released out of the shoot, they'd only run a few steps and then stop dead in their tracks, watching the horse and rider go roaring by without a target. Hannah had two excellent stallions and more than twenty other horses at different stages of training. They spent a lot of time working their cutting horses.

Butch stayed at the ranch house when Hannah was gone. Sometimes he stayed at the house when Hannah was home.

Corkey and Angeline got married. They were living in Florida and trying to make up for lost time, if ya know what I mean. He never came back to Montana.

Sometimes, when Sally was at the ranch, she'd tell Hannah that she believed Frank was an angel who came to her as answered prayer and stood by her through the terror of Steve's brutality and the unbearable sorrow of watching Jesse die. Hannah would just nod.

She planned on telling Sally one day who Frank really was. She'd tell others, too. She didn't want them thinking Sonny Hollister was a failure who squandered away his life. She wanted them to know that when Sonny got his second chance at life, he got it right.

Toro Two lived fourteen years.

No one ever saw the black-footed ferret again.